FORCE NO ONE

STORM CELL THRILLER #1

Daniel Charles Ross

Non sibi sed patriae
Not for self but for country

FORCE POSEIDON

LIMA DETROIT SOUTH PADRE ISLAND

Force Poseidon is an imprint of Artisanal Publishers LLC
2981 Zurmehly Road, Lima Ohio 45806-1428
forceposeidon.com

Library of Congress Cataloging-in-Publication Data has been applied for.

Force Poseidon eBook edition
  September 2018 ISBN-13 978-0-57841-077-7

Force Poseidon trade paperback
  September 2018 ISBN-13 978-1-52173-795-8

Force Poseidon, by name and colophon, are trademarks of Artisanal Publishers LLC. This book was produced in Adobe InDesign CC 2020 using Crimson 11/16 for body copy and Urban Jungle licensed from kcfonts.com for headings and dropcaps.

Piracy is theft. For information about special discount bulk purchases of paper or ebooks, please contact Force Poseidon Direct Sales via email at reachout@forceposeidon.com, or write to Force Poseidon,
2981 Zurmehly Road, Lima Ohio 45806-1428

Manufactured in the United States of America.

 @genuineDCR - genuineDCR.com

To Jim Schefter (1940-2001)
who always believed in me more than I did myself.
Requiesce in pace, mi frater.

And to Donald Steinhoff, my journalism teacher
at East Detroit High School, who is the sole
reason why I am anything today.

FORCE NO ONE

STORM CELL THRILLER #1

Quis Custodiet Ipsos Custodes?

Who will guard the guards themselves?

CHAPTER ONE

If you know the enemy and know yourself,
you need not fear the results of a hundred battles.

Sun Tzu (Unknown-496 BC), Chinese philosopher

S o, Joe, my friend, you owe me. You owe me, and you have been *dodging* me." Xavier Cloud—Zave to his friends—had been looking for his friend for a long time, and he was often not a patient man.

The two men were isolated in an empty Detroit warehouse under the bright yellow cone provided by a shaded light. It hung from an industrial I-beam, a rafter thick with countless coats of institutional green paint. Translucent dust particles, random bits of asbestos, and traces of animal feces floated in the dirty beam.

In the distance, a summer storm birthed powerful rumbles as it drew closer.

"You were supposed to find me, weren't you? And yet it was I who had to find you. I understand you don't want to give me the briefcase. I understand the reasons why you have been a ghost for twelve years—all one hundred million of them. But your loyalties are divided, aren't they, Joe? They need a tune-up. That's why we're old friends, bro. And friends don't let friends screw up."

He paused for a moment, making an allowance for their shared history. There was a lot of it.

"Therefore ... *my friend* ... I am here to help you in the not screwing up part."

Without a breeze to relieve the dank conditions in the space, the two men had dissolved into their shirts. One, however, sweated more vigorously than the other.

With seven feet of what the men used to call green Army tape around Joe's mouth and head and another two rolls making him one, neck to ankles, with the chair he'd awakened in, Joe could hardly breathe. He had cause to sweat beyond the humidity.

Cloud sat in a creaky green metal office chair turned backwards, muscular arms crossed on the back of his perch. His sleeves were rolled up above the elbows to reveal a tattoo on his thick right forearm, a death's head skull with a stiletto plunged into the right eye socket. The socket leaked a single teardrop of blood and the red-lipped skull was Joker-grinning like it had escaped from a Batman movie, the best one, with Jack Nicholson. Blackish text fading to old green in an arc under the Joker's angular chin read *The Gutter Lilies.*

Joe sat immobile, one leg beginning to quiver, while Cloud regarded him. He chewed with an absent smile on the crust of a cheeseburger—mustard, no pickles—then pitched the burger fragment into the humid darkness. Unseen things scrabbled after the food and trailed high-pitched squeaks as they ran away with it, fighting viciously.

"Joe, Joe," Cloud said. He shook his head as if disappointed in a child, and rubbed his hands together to dislodge the greasy crumbs of his short dinner. Like you would do before going to work.

"Did you know I was a computer programmer at one time? Yeah, after *Desert Storm*, after I got out of the Army the first time, way before we knew each other." He didn't pause for an answer. "True story, systems analyst. Can you believe it? Jee-*zus*, I hated that job. I enjoy the order, though, the logic of programming. Still do some development for my own amusement."

Cloud smiled. He had Pentagon investigators chasing phantom Chinamen for months that time.

"But I just couldn't stomach the *epic* idiots I worked with."

He remembered how much wicked fun it was the day he finally quit. You jerk with the bull and you get the horns, dimmy. The building had been too damaged to reopen and the company quietly folded shortly thereafter.

Good times, man. Good times.

"I guess I wasn't cut out to deal with civilian assholes. Army ones? Sure, maybe. At least there is some commonality of purpose, some generally shared mindset. Commitment, y'know? Honor. Civilians, pure ones, no military experience, they don't have any of that. They chase after wealth without any sense of compassion. Crave power without accountability. Demand respect without earning it. And what the fuck is *gluten-free* all about, anyway? I believe you know these things."

As bound up as he was, Joe nodded in agreement. It was hard to do under all the green Army tape.

"Civilian life is overrated and, apparently, it's against the law to kill the assholes. I find that short-sighted. I was reenlisted by late '99. Then 9/11 happened, and I was back in the show with you and our team."

Cloud unconsciously rubbed his hand up and down his tattoo.

"Lost track of you when you got out, though. That wasn't supposed to happen, was it? Twelve years you've been missing, man. I'm looking forward to catching up with you when all *this*"—he waved his hands in circles, fingers spread—"is over."

Cloud paused.

"Maybe you saw my name in the news in recent years." Joe's eyes widened just a little. He had, and it frightened him.

"Yeah, well. Don't believe everything you hear, and none of what you read."

Cloud's face hardened. "Civilian life was okay, just not my sense, as my Japanese friends say. But even bad experiences usually produce some valuable take-away, Joe, y'know? Some lesson that is learned if your mind is right. And I learned a valuable life lesson from working with computers. There are only two answers to every question, Joe: Yes, or no."

Cloud heaved a reluctant sigh. The men had been friends a long time. Battle buddies. It shouldn't have to go like this, but it is what it is. Just business.

"Well, listen," he said, "can I getcha anything?" There was no reply. "Can I ask you one more time, please-*please* tell me where the case is? Then we'll get you spruced up, forget all this bullshit ever happened and get a few beers. No harm, no foul, huh? The Tigers' pennant game replay is on a big-screen down at the Hard Rock."

There was no immediate reply, but Joe wasn't born stupid and he did consider the last-ditch offer. This was an opportunity to avoid definite unpleasantness and restore an old friendship with the man, a friendship that would result in much hilarity, great food, many adult beverages and many adult females, among other consumables. You wanted the man to be your friend, because he was proven to be a damned good one. There were legendary reasons why you wanted him to be your friend much more than you wanted him to be your enemy.

Those had been proven, too.

But while it was apparent that Joe was in very serious trouble, he believed the equally sure consequences of surrendering information on the people who now possessed the silver Halliburton case with the combination lock were probably grimmer, even if he could give it up. That had been made clear to Joe when the Arabs tortured him to get the briefcase, weeks before.

Now his friend was doing the same thing his enemies had, for the same reason—but Joe really didn't know where the Arabs had gone with the case, which was unfortunate. But whatever happened tonight, Joe didn't believe his friend would kill him. Or what are friends for?

Joe finished his internal debate and presented a head tilt and shrug of his shoulders that telegraphed a negative reply.

"Okay then," Cloud said. "You always were a tough bastard, weren'tcha? Y'know what, though?" He brightened and sat up straight in the chair. "We've been in tougher spots than this before, right? You and me?"

He stood and raised an imaginary M4 special operations carbine to his left shoulder and silently shook it a few times, as if firing on full auto. Lowering the invisible weapon, he looked down at Joe and smiled warmly.

"We've helped each other through some close calls before. And we'll get through this one together, too."

Cloud raised his eyebrows and leaned slightly in, peering at his friend as if for affirmation. None was forthcoming. Cloud nodded his head once, businesslike, and began.

"There are only two things in life to worry about, Joe. See there? Ones and zeroes, yes or no. Either you are healthy, or you are sick. If you are healthy, there is nothing to worry about. But if you are sick, there are only two things to worry about: Either you get better, or you die."

On a table next to Cloud's chair was an old ice pick and a new five-pound hammer. The ice pick was a classic and he picked it up carefully, suspended between his thumb and two fingers.

Through an opening in the cinder block wall where a window used to be, peals of thunder and strobes of lightning crawled closer.

✪

Weathered, stained and rusty, the ice pick hadn't been used to pick ice since Cloud's father had driven a milk route in the 1960s. Cloud kept it as a warmhearted souvenir of those days when he jumped from his dad's boxy, slope-nosed Divco milk truck as a boy, and double-timed a wire rack of clanky glass milk bottles, or orange juice or butter, to an unpainted metal box lined with cork on a porch or to a built-in milk chute, like some of the houses had.

He'd swap the full containers for the empties and run back to the truck. Every single trip his father would say, "Good job, mister!" and smile warmly at his boy. Every single trip.

Their second-hand milk truck in those days wasn't refrigerated. The milk and other products were kept fresh with angular blocks of crystal-clear ice the size of beer kegs. It was the boy's job to use his ice pick to dismantle the blocks and distribute the fragments over the dairy products so that nothing spoiled or was delivered to a customer warm.

The boy knew taking care of people was what kept the milk route alive, even as big grocery chains built their soulless superstores on every other block, the bastards.

As golden sun streaked the heavens above Norman Rockwell streets, the faded creamy yellow-and-green milk truck would trundle back to the dairy. The cranky diesel engine, happy at last, purred its approval. The last of the ice dissolved to water and left drippy wet trails, like memories, on the road.

Xavier Cloud's father would reach out and clamp a giant's right hand on his boy's shoulder. He would give it a strong squeeze and say with honest sincerity, "Thank you, son. *Thank you* for helping me today."

The boy would beam with pride in himself, in his work, and with an abiding love for his father. On chilly mornings, they would sip pungent, unsweetened coffee poured into a dented aluminum Thermos-bottle cup and agree not to tell his mother, their little secret, fun and only for the boys.

"Good and black," his father would say with his big grin, hoisting the battered cup in their regular toast, "just as God and the U.S. Navy intended."

It was a glorious time, every precious moment. The worst day he'd ever had on that milk truck had been great. Those were the days, man, those were really the days. But those days were long gone.

The milk route finally died out in time. Soon after, the boy's father died along with it. Life was unfair, but death was a bitch. This was a life lesson Cloud had reinforced many times in life, though he often thought calling it a "life" lesson was a contradiction in terms.

✪

Unlike the ice pick, the hammer possessed no such golden glow. It was a spanking new Stanley Anti-Vibe 24 you could buy at Lowe's or Home Depot for a reasonable price. It was a durable tool, with a wide head, a robust steel shank and a grippy, rubber-clad handle.

Some wretched workmen in a smoky Taiwanese factory somewhere probably churned them out hundreds or even thousands per day, but so what? A nice tool was a nice tool. The hammer gleamed in the dim light in stark contrast to the rusty ice pick, but not all the dark red stains on the ice pick were rust.

"So, Joe, see, if you're sick and you get better," Cloud continued, "there is nothing to worry about. But if you die, there are two things to worry about: Either you go to Heaven, or you go to Hell."

Cloud slowly rolled the ice pick back and forth in his right hand and that wry smile creased his face one more time. How might have things gone differently in life, he thought once again, if his father had lived, if his lonely mother hadn't rebounded and married that abusive prick?

Well, that little love-nest deal hadn't ended very well for old step dad, had it?

Cloud picked up the hammer and positioned the ice pick just above Joe's left kneecap. He moved it around his friend's pressed and creased blue jeans until he found the location he was looking for, the quadriceps tendon at the top of the patella. From there it was a straight shot into the marrow of the tibia.

Joe's eyes got big and watery then. The lower half of his face was so wrapped in the green tape that he could scarcely get much air through his nose, let alone cry out. That was going to be a cast-iron bitch when it came off his beard. Joe was as scared as a helpless man can be, especially a big man used to being in complete control.

A man who would do this same thing to someone else.

In last-ditch panic, Joe sucked in a deep, watery breath through his runny nose and bore down with all his might, grunting and flexing his big upper body to try and break the tape holding him.

Cloud sat back a few inches and waited, picturing cartoon steam jets shooting out of Joe's ears to the sound of a *Loony Tunes* train whistle. But Joe's effort to break free, as they both knew it would be, was momentary. And futile.

A wet stain smelling strongly of ammonia, body-building supplements, and inevitability spread in the crotch of Joe's jeans. If Joe's sweat-soaked right sleeve had been rolled up, it would have revealed a death's head skull with a stiletto plunged into the right eye socket. The socket leaked a single teardrop of blood and the red-lipped skull was Joker-grinning like it had escaped from a Batman movie, the best one, with Jack Nicholson.

Blackish text fading to old green in an arc under the Joker's angular chin read *The Gutter Lilies*, but it was hard to discern under Joe's dark skin, so Joe'd had the letters scarred in. That effect raised them so well above the skin that even Stevie Wonder could read them.

Cloud held the hammer at about half-choke for accuracy. This was a soft spot in the flesh and required little real force, but he couldn't jab like he used to before the stinging carpal tunnel set in. He raised the hammer over the ice pick on his friend's kneecap until it was even with his black shark's eyes, fixing the sight picture just as he once did with a rifle aimed at bad guys.

"If you go to Heaven, Joe, there's nothing to worry about." He took a steadying breath, and exhaled.

Outside, the storm that had been threatening all evening let loose a monstrous thunderclap that shook dust from the building.

"But Joe, man, if you go to *Hell* ..."

CHAPTER TWO

*I choose my friends for their good looks, my acquaintances
for their good characters, and my enemies for their intellects.
A man cannot be too careful in the choice of his enemies.*

Oscar Wilde (1854-1900), Irish playwright and novelist

A yellow 2013 Corvette Z06 convertible rolled to a precise stop at the red traffic light. This Vette rumbled with low and spiteful intent, just a click more impatient than the factory intended when the car left its ancestral birthplace in Bowling Green, Kentucky.

The engine had been breathed on a little, and the seven hundred *right-now* horsepower the V-8 produced was invisible when just looking at the car on the street except for a slightly more aggressive exhaust tone. From the sidewalk, even a casual glance would confirm that the Chevy's nose matched the leading edge of the faded white line describing the crosswalk. Car control, like every other important thing else in life, required precision every moment.

The blonde driver drew admiring glances from passers-by, men and women alike. Amber "Corvette" Watson pulled 58 mm Ray-Ban aviators from her face and turned to her conspicuous redhead passenger, Tracey Lexcellent. They were talking about Amber's on again-off again long-distance romance with a much younger Michigan State Trooper boyfriend.

"It was great when he was still stationed in the Detroit post," Amber groaned, "but since his transfer he lives just about in the ass-crack of nowhere, outside Traverse City. Only it's a beautiful little town and smells a lot better than this place."

She gestured to the downtown cityscape that surrounded them, and put her sunglasses back on.

"But man, you can't get there from here, nearly. I can drive there faster than I can fly." She blipped the Corvette's throttle and the car rocked with an edgy growl. "And when I drive, I don't feel like I'm crammed in a crowded Greyhound bus with everything but chickens flyin' around the cabin."

Amber reached over with her left hand and squeezed the cross-draw leather holster on her right hip, a habitual move that reassured her the gun was still there. She often did the same check with her leather credentials wallet.

"And I also don't have to worry about getting my hardware through security with those TSA boneheads."

Tracey laughed.

"I know, right? Every one of those birds is absolutely sure he's gonna bust Osama bin Laden coming through on a tourist visa. I think most of them don't even know he's dead."

Amber smiled her secret smile, thought again about her muscular, youthful state trooper boyfriend and shook her head slowly. He did live way up north and, yes, they had to find time to be together and, yes, it was hardly ever convenient—but *yes*, the former active duty Recon Marine officer took pride in his physical appearance, and he was a very collectable specimen.

"I dunno if I'm going up there this weekend or not," she said. "We might have to work. We workin'?"

Tracey shrugged indecisively.

"But my boy makes me feel better, y'know?" She revved the car's growly V-8 a few hundred rpm and held it for emphasis, and the two women grinned.

"A *lot* better."

The traffic light changed. With only the smallest chirp of wheelspin, the Vette accelerated smartly away from the intersection under the green.

Stopped in a vehicle behind the Corvette, a man had been admiring the bright yellow sports car and its scenic occupants. He smiled at the classic white-on-blue Michigan license plate reading 2HOTT4U bolted in the Corvette's license plate receptacle as it receded from him. The man had an interest in personalized license plates, and the coincidence he enjoyed was remarkable even to him.

Michigan didn't require a front license plate, but if it had, Amber might have considered her rear-view mirror as she pulled away and wondered about the license plate on the black Dodge Magnum R/T station wagon that read IMHOT4U.

The man in the powerful car smiled. As he turned left off Woodward Avenue, he wondered idly whether he might ever see them again.

CHAPTER THREE

It ain't what they call you, it's what you answer to.
W.C. Fields (1880-1946), American actor and comedian

Tabithae Wilkins is a stout woman who supervises a Michigan Secretary of State office in downtown Detroit. This is the familiar state office for acquiring vehicle registrations and license plates, driver's licenses, and so on.

Her mother named her for Samantha Stevens' little white girl, Tabitha, in the old TV series *Bewitched*, but she wanted her daughter's name to be more distinctive, so she added the letter "e" at the end and pronounced it Tah-*BEE*-thay. With similar inspiration drawn through a four-inch length of glass crack pipe one day, her mother later named Tabithae's younger brother Lemonjello, and pronounced it La-*MOHN*-shello. That poor boy was ate up with the dumb-ass because of his mother's drug use during pregnancy, and he spent most of his time down at the Goodwill, sorting clothes.

Tabithae wasn't a bad person. She was a lonely, slightly heavy, never-married single woman, almost broke sometimes, who just got by on her salary, paycheck to paycheck. A woman her age had needs she couldn't satisfy with the money the State of Michigan paid her to renew driver's licenses and issue car tags and manage an office of mostly menopausal or high or angry women, as well as a few old men who did the same things the women did, just slower and with more bitching.

So, when special circumstances arose, or she was sent a friend of a friend, of a friend, she wouldn't do anything too terribly out of the ordinary, but she could help people out of some jams or get a registration squared away that sometimes didn't have all the most perfect paperwork on Earth. She also helped people get personalized vehicle license plates that wouldn't normally be available.

Like other states with vanity license plate programs, Michigan does not permit obvious profanities or expressions that might offend tender public sensibilities. Absent that, almost anything was fair game if it wasn't spoken for by someone else and could be spelled with a combination of seven or fewer letters, numbers, or a few symbols. What remained was a broad and creative range of possibilities.

Ambiguous plate requests, often turned down by one of the anxious old biddies at the customer counter, sometimes could get through with her approval, though. Like the time a friend of a friend, a shapely working girl who had a specific clientele with special desires, wanted ULICKME. That couldn't get through the computer even with Tabithae's help, but she convinced the customer that ULIKME would get through if she told the desk clerk it meant *you like me.*

Small victories were still victories, and she still got paid.

Under different circumstances—like a higher salary—Tabithae would never have entertained the unusual requests, because special treatment was strictly against the regulations. She was careful, though, didn't bend the rules too much, and she made a lot of friends in high places.

High friends in low places, really, is what she would bray at parties when drinking too much, laughing too loud, and being way too indiscreet, but what was the difference? These people all had money they wanted to spend and, at the end of the day, she was a public servant in the customer satisfaction business.

So, when the man phoned and said Bobby sent him, and could she help him with a licensing thing, Tabithae said yes, yes she could.

Eighteen minutes after closing time she let him in through the office back door. All the other good state employees had bolted about eighteen minutes prior, so there were no worries about anyone observing the curious work ahead.

The tall, handsome man was obviously in great shape, even under his expensive suit coat. He was very attractive in that slightly "older guy" way, though she saw the birth date on a strange federal police credential he displayed and he was fifteen or twenty years older than he looked, the blue-eyed devil.

If Tabithae wasn't a particularly law-abiding state employee, she was indeed a loyal American. She took immediate note of the man's Middle Eastern name on his business card, plus he was a cop of some kind, seemed like, and here he was making a side deal with Tabithae after closing time.

She worried for a moment about getting rolled up in some sting. Every person she had ever done a favor for—*that Bobby, one*—would give her up in a hot second if they thought it would keep their own asses out of a jam. The attractive man's money promise wasn't enough to make her go to jail.

All this rattled around in Tabithae's head until the olive-skinned man fixed those blue eyes and long eyelashes on her and smiled. That lit her up like the marquee of the Fox Theater on opening night. She forgot everything else. *If this gorgeous man is here to sting me,* Tabithae thought dreamily, *let's get to stingin'.*

The man wanted a certain combination of letters and numbers that spelled no profanity and made no off-color joke—in fact, she discovered the perfectly legal license combination had already been issued randomly to a motorist in her county of Wayne. That meant it was even easier to help the gentleman. She had done such things before.

Tabithae called the motorist from her office phone so that telephone Caller ID would indicate ST OF MICH. She informed him in her most sincere, bureaucratic manner that the plate had been flagged for an unspecified problem that she couldn't discuss.

No, she told the motorist, he wasn't in trouble—and wouldn't it just be easier for everyone if it stayed that way?

However, Tabithae said, the problem was such that, regrettably, the state was canceling the motorist's current registration and she was sending an officer to retrieve the plate right away.

The woman talked the motorist through the procedure of ordering a new license plate, which she was happy to execute right there on the phone while he waited. The motorist had a personalized plate option in mind and, bonus, it was available in the system. Tabithae told the obliging man that, in recognition of his cooperation, she wouldn't charge the extra fee the state demanded for a custom license plate.

In fact, the state computer didn't permit such generosity at taxpayer expense, but she would pay the fee from a debit card she maintained for certain personal purchases, some via the internet, that required more discretion. The balance on this account had run down nearly to the basement, but she had enough in there to pay the registration fee tonight and, *yesss baby*, by lunchtime tomorrow the account balance would be at an all-time high. *An all-time high*, do you hear me?

She promised the man on the phone that his new plate would arrive within ten to fourteen business days, she clucked sympathetically about how 9/11 had changed everything in America, *blah-blah*, she thanked him again, and the thing was done.

Before leaving to get the plate, the handsome man took Tabithae's limp, damp handshake and thanked her, all up close and in her personal space. He was so close that she was certain the back of his hand brushed a fat breast and she thought she might fall light-headed to the floor right in front of him.

When he smiled that smile at Tabithae, a bead of sweat ran straight and cool down her spine and she could taste that coppery, electric taste on her tongue. Then he was gone, leaving her slightly delirious and with a steadying hand on the counter.

✪

The attractive man drove up Jefferson to the motorist's flat on the north side of Beaconsfield, just down from the Detroit-Grosse Pointe Park border. He parked a solid black Chevy Tahoe SUV porcupined with extra roof antennas and shrouded in the blackest window glass in front of an older two-family house with a large covered porch and two opposing sets of steps.

At the lower-flat door to the motorist's home, the man pulled from a different pocket a second police ID wallet with the gold badge of a Michigan State Police lieutenant and matching photo credentials. He did his own curt *yeah-this-sucks* sympathy act, got the plate off the man's station wagon himself, and delivered the temporary registration for the new personalized plate the cooperative man had asked Tabithae to issue.

"Okay, Mr. Sal—Sala—*Saladin*, is it?" the man said. "We appreciate your cooperation. Here's the paperwork. Have a nice rest of your day."

When the paperwork exchange occurred, the motorist had to lean out of the door of his flat just a bit and into the fading light. When he did so, an American flag pin in the officer's lapel silently captured the motorist's crystal-clear digital image.

The paperwork said the motorist was getting a new vanity plate that read IMHOT4U. The agent shook his head as he drove away in the black Tahoe, thinking IMHOT4U is such a *stinking load of bullshit*.

The man returned to the licensing office and Tabithae. She concluded the transaction by re-registering the confiscated plate to information the attractive man provided from a black leather Levenger notebook. He didn't show any prior registration or insurance documents, like the state required for plate transfers, but he had all the correct insurance policy and vehicle identification numbers for a run-of-the-mill 1978 Chrysler Newport four-door. Mint green.

He had shown her that impressive federal gold badge, though, and a fine business card that said he was from some Homeland Security office or another, but he didn't let her keep the card or any of his notes. When she asked him why he didn't take care of this in his office, he just smiled and said nothing.

The state's computers cross-checked the data for accuracy and she approved it, processing the transaction.

The attractive man thanked Tabithae and complimented her on her efficiency and patriotism. He emphasized the need for discretion and con-firmed her agreement with that. She thought he might have been openly flirting with her a little bit now that the business segment of the program was concluded.

He held her departing handshake for additional seconds, and told her how much he personally appreciated a state office working so well with a federal office. While he couldn't tell her why this deal seemed so odd and hush-hush, he implied that grave national security issues were at stake, and then he paid her in bundles of brand-new hundred-dollar notes—a *lot* of them—pulled from one of those wide black briefcases she'd seen pilots carry onto airplanes.

Tabithae's breath quickened with every bundle dropping onto the countertop, plentiful as autumn leaves, and she thought that this was all she really needed to know.

As the attractive man drove away, Tabithae daydreamed about what having a class act like that in her life could mean. He was obviously a powerful man, physically and professionally, a person with connections, with class. She loved that he was so good looking—and he had money, *lord*.

He had given her enough cash in this one deal that she needed to borrow an office cash bag to carry it to her night deposit. The big one. Now she could buy a solid black Buick Lacrosse, the all-wheel-drive one, that was her modest dream car.

Honey, he just dripped status, too. He wore a two-piece dark-blue suit with a little faint stripe to it that whispered *powerrr* ever so faintly. She thought it was expensive and probably had a very recognizable label sewn into its lining. And he wore the most highly polished shoes she had ever seen, those fancy ones that businessmen wore with the swirls and holes punched in the toes and sides.

Most crazy of all was the expensive deal he'd made for a simple license plate that wasn't even personalized.

CHAPTER FOUR

Needing to have things perfect is the surest
way to immobilize yourself with frustration.
Wayne Dyer (1940-2015), American psychologist

Corvette Watson and Tracey Lexcellent accelerated hard down south-bound Woodward Avenue, but only covered four blocks when they were slowed to a crawl and then a dead stop next to Campus Martius Park in a sudden gridlocked traffic backup.

"Come on!" Tracey yelled to no one. "We have no freakin' time for this right now."

Tracey typically had two speeds, fast and faster. She unbuckled her seat belt, raised manicured hands to the convertible's windshield header, and pulled herself up into a standing position.

Behind the Vette and on both sides, the heads of three men and one woman swiveled up in unison and locked on her as if commanded by the same robotic programming. Their gazes lingered just a little long and then they looked away, afraid she would catch them staring in open admiration.

Tracey stood a wasp-waisted five feet, nine and one-half inches tall, with alabaster skin, large breasts, and an unruly mane of thick, red hair. Standing in the open-top sports car, Tracey, the men, and the woman all appreciated their points of view for entirely different reasons.

"Can you see what the hold-up is, Trace?" Amber asked. She took a fast habitual glance at her instrument panel to review the gauges and determine all was well with the car.

"No, *Christ*," she said in frustration, using the palm of her right hand to push a wind-blown tangle of red hair off her face. "But there are blue lights by the City-County Building and there is one dark ambulance on the sidewalk on the Woodward side. Uniforms are detouring the traffic away from Woodward at the Larned and Jefferson lights."

Tracey looked around and surveyed the scene in their immediate area. In the center of three lanes just north of Fort Street, the Chevy was locked in by unbroken southbound traffic in the left lane, and by a smoking rustbucket of prehistoric Plymouth Voyager minivan to the rear. The string of stopped traffic gummed up the southbound lane to their right—but there was still a little bit of space behind a hulking SUV next to the Corvette.

A chubby, middle-aged woman in a black Buick Lacrosse was thoughtfully stopped about a half a car length behind the SUV. The woman craned her head out of her window to see what was going on up ahead, though all she could see was a conga line of brake lights.

Tracey did a fast 360-degree look-around, lingering for just a moment on the hulking Ford truck stopped in the lane next to them.

"Hold on a sec," she said. "Pull forward a few inches. I have an idea."

Tracey removed her expensive left shoe, stepped on the top of the Corvette's door and planted a perfect right foot and metallic pink Jimmy Choo strappy sandal in the open window of the Ford Excursion SUV stuck next to them in traffic. The driver, preoccupied with a cellphone screwed into his left ear, looked up with a start and followed flawless pink toes down about six miles of clingy black tights to a huge shock of red hair and a dazzling smile.

Then with admirable muscle control and impossible flexibility, Tracey relaxed her leg and slowly, theatrically levered her body forward until the cute oval of her freckled face was dead level with the driver of the SUV.

"Honey," she breathed at the man, all puffy pink lips and exquisitely white teeth. "I have a problem only *you* can solve."

The man would later remember Tracey's breath as an intoxicating swirl of minted promise. His mouth hung open in surprise. The poor bastard in the truck had no chance at all. Resistance, had there been any, was futile.

But his cigar-and-black-coffee breath was *kicking.*

"Y'see mister, *lissen,*" she said, forcing a skillful little-Southern-girl accent into her voice, "we just *gotta* get out of this lane, and we can't do that unless you can, like, back your *huuuge* truck up a just few feet so we can get by you."

Tracey leaned forward a bit more until her sizable breast, already crushed against the rigid upraised leg, ballooned up a menacing additional inch or two.

"So," she said a little breathlessly, "do you think you can help us—at all?"

Mesmerized, the man slowly nodded in the affirmative.

Tracey's 126.4 pounds of experience, muscle, intellect and hair dropped back into the Corvette's leather-wrapped bucket seat.

"Back up a little and turn into the right lane." She grinned with enthusiasm at Amber and rocked a thumb back toward the SUV. "*This* guy is letting us around."

The women laughed and smiled at each other, shook their heads and thought the same thing: *If only we could harness the hormones of men for good, not evil.*

The Ford Excursion driver backed up as far as he could, then backed up a few more inches when the chubby woman in the Buick sedan behind him saw he was backing. Amber waved frantically and, edging to the right as best she could, backed up the nearly three feet or so she could wheedle out of the sweaty Middle Eastern driver of the Plymouth minivan behind her.

Amber changed gears from reverse to first and eyeball-calibrated the small gap in the lane next to her. She wasn't sure the nose of the Vette would quite clear the space opened by the SUV, but they were in a hurry and life was meant to be a crapshoot. This was just another one of those times. Cars in this line of work got pranged all the time, though never before by Amber. Never.

Her left foot pinned the clutch to the floor. She planted the pert toe of her right foot hard on the power brakes and rolled the ball of her foot onto the gas pedal, line-locking the sports car to the street and revving the modified 7-liter V-8 up to about 5,700 rpm.

When she sidestepped the clutch, the powerful front brakes held but the Corvette's potent 700-plus horsepower instantly and violently overwhelmed the rear brakes. Howling rear tires spun so energetically that billows of gray-white smoke clouded the small space where the Corvette was trapped in traffic.

Pirouetting on the slowly rolling front wheels cocked hard over to the right, the car rotated neatly in little more than its own length. With the nose pointed into the narrow gap in the right lane, Amber released pressure on the brakes and gas pedal at the same time and the car swung elegantly nose-first into the empty parking lane. She flicked the car left, turned right again, and with a scattering of dust and yellowed pages from the free *Metro Times* newspaper, the convertible emerged onto Fort Street.

No cars would be pranged today. Three slots behind the Vette's now unoccupied traffic hole, it appeared to other drivers like the convertible had disappeared in a puff of smoke.

Amber turned left off Fort onto parallel Griswold, dropped the hammer hard and surged forward for three long blocks, catching all the lights green and shifting only briefly into second gear. The modified Chevy V-8 bellowed powerful engine music off the downtown buildings, even through its factory exhaust tubes.

She hung a left onto Jefferson Avenue and another left back toward northbound Woodward, rolling up to a small crowd of spectators against a barrier of yellow and black plastic tape imprinted POLICE CRIME SCENE DO NOT CROSS. A large section of street had been taped off there, from the front of the City-County Building and the *Spirit of Detroit* statue over to the trolley-loop People Mover pillars at Larned Street. Within the closed area were a few Detroit police cars with their blue lights dark, and a city EMS ambulance, emergency lights also off signaling a lack of urgency. Both were parked up on the sidewalk in front of the *Spirit of Detroit.*

As the sports car peaceably approached the crowd, Amber pushed an unlabeled black button on the console and tapped the car's horn button twice. Instead of the GM-issued horn tones, an electronic siren in the Vette's nose bleeped a couple of sharp, official-sounding *whoop-whoops.* The crowd of people turned as one and parted like the Red Sea before Moses.

A man standing on the corner next to a hot dog cart waved at the

Vette and smiled, and Amber waved back.

Previously invisible in the convertible's windshield header, behind the dark-tinted top of the glass, was a high-intensity strip of unique LEDs now flashing as yellow arrows that began in the center and flowed outward toward each side of the car, ending in large arrowheads. Though this wasn't a standard police vehicle, the lights clearly commanded *Move out of our way, please.* Flashing blue and white mini-strobes alternated in the nose of the car. The LED strip could also operate in alternating blue and red emergency mode when necessary.

At only forty-nine inches tall, the Corvette had no trouble gliding under the crime scene tape, disturbing it only with an invisible, slow-motion bow wave of air that spilled over the top of the car. Amber pulled to the side of the street with the two right wheels up on the bricked sidewalk and shut the car down in first gear, set the hand brake, and grabbed a small purse. Tracey fooled around with her hair. Tracey always fooled around with her hair, and now she grabbed a piece of Juicy Fruit from a fresh pack of gum.

The women released their seat belts and were unfolding themselves from the convertible when a uniformed police sergeant trotted over. He took fleeting notice of the sports car as he slowed to a stroll. In plain view on the sidewalk behind and to the side of the Spirit of Detroit backdrop structure was a rubberized white sheet draped over a dead guy whose legs and feet extended from under the cracked fabric.

Amber noticed he was wearing a nice, dark-blue suit with a nearly invisible chalk stripe. She thought it looked expensive, but who knew? What really stuck out, literally and figuratively, were perfect black Wing Tip-style shoes burnished to a mirror-like shine.

It made her think of the leather shoes her boyfriend wore. As a Michigan State Police sergeant and a U.S. Marine Corps Reserve major, he refused to wear the poromeric Corfam plastic or even patent leather shoes. He polished his own all-leather shoes every day as part of his routine, like eating and working out and cleaning his weapon, *ooo-RAH.* So, the dead guy might have been former law enforcement, former military, or none of the above. Or maybe he was just wealthy and his valet polished the shoes for him. Maybe the valet was former military.

Whatever, Amber knew, Tracey would find out. She had the *quon* for this stuff.

Being attended to by the paramedics was a middle-aged white woman with disarranged clothes, smeared lipstick, and wild hair. Not good-wild, Tracey, an expert on good-wild, thought to herself.

Maggie Prynne—she called herself after Hester Prynne in *The Scarlet Letter*. No one knew why—lived on the economy. They recognized the homeless woman from her routine patrol of downtown trash bins around Hart Plaza, back across Jefferson, looking for returnable bottles and cans after the summer series of week-end festivals.

The disheveled woman didn't struggle with the medics, but rocked back and forth where she sat, lost in a vacant stare and focused on something seen in another dimension or space-time continuum. Maggie had seen something so bad that it had scared senseless a woman who, in her years on the street, had seen lots of ugly things before.

Tracey looked at Maggie and then back at the sheet-covered body. She thought she knew what the ugly thing was.

The women pulled beaded chains over their heads and badges settled onto their chests. The joint task force of FBI Special Agent Amber Watson and Detroit Police Homicide Detective Sergeant Tracey Lexcellent turned to DPD patrol supervisor Sergeant Flex Plexico, who had waited patiently while the two women emerged from the car like butterflies from a cocoon.

"So, what the heck's goin' on here, then?" Amber asked.

"This gonna be a JTF case?" Plexico asked. He gave the Corvette another admiring look. "Not your usual cup of gruel."

"Dunno, man." Tracey popped her gum. "Let us see what we shall see."

Maggie Prynne's grimy face was streaked white by tears. Her wide eyes, filled with whites and terror, swiveled with recognition in the direction of Tracey's voice, but she only rocked and repeated a single forlorn phrase, again and again.

"Force no one. Force no one. Force no one."

CHAPTER FIVE

Talent hits a target no one else can hit;
Genius hits a target no one else can see.
Arthur Schopenhauer (1788-1860), German philosopher

First responders and duty detectives had secured the crime scene well before Tracey and Amber rolled in. The scene had been processed, the medical examiner had pronounced the dead guy in-fact dead and called for the pick-up, and even the WDIV TV-4 remote truck was packing up to return to the station's downtown studios. All that remained was for Tracey's senior investigator's gaze to scan what remained of the scene with her brand of insight. It wasn't her case, but she had been asked by the duty detectives for a roll-by.

The three walked over to the prone figure.

"Well," Flex said, gesturing toward the man under the sheet, "this would be your Dee-troit dead guy *du jour.*"

The dead guy *du jour* lay under a well-worn rubberized sheet that covered him from above his head to just above his ankles. A large blood-stain spread across the concrete in a complicated Rorschach pattern at his head area. His feet were distinguished by perfect Wing Tip footwear, easily reflecting light from the sky.

Flex, Amber, and Tracey looked down as one. Tracey popped her chewing gum. After a few silent moments of reverie, Tracey spoke.

"Those are some nice shoes."

"Yeah, saw that. Nice clothes, too," the uniformed sergeant said. He looked up at Tracey. "The shoes look new but they show stress cracks in the folds where the leather is starting to dry out a bit, and the soles are old, so, well-maintained. The suit is a very nice Armani. He had his wallet in his right inside-front jacket pocket—probably makes him a left-hander—and it's full of credit cards and driver's licenses. He also had federal and state police credentials in two different pockets."

The women both looked up at that. Plexico nodded.

"Yep. Driver's licenses from Michigan, Illinois, and Ohio in our neck of the woods, plus Maryland, Virginia, DC, and California. He had a very disturbing wad of what looked to be hunner-dollar bills, non-sequential, but fresh from the vine, or Kinko's. I think they're genuine, though, so probably not a robbery. And he has that interesting ring on his left hand ..."

The sergeant pointed to the dead guy's left hand extending beyond the privacy of the rubber sheet.

"... along with a thin, gold-in-color, probable wedding band on the same finger."

Tracey bent over and looked closely at the dead guy's left hand without touching it. He wore a U.S. Navy ring that looked to be a high-end custom, well-crafted and with high gold content. This wasn't some piece-of-crap military ring the young enlisted guys bought mail-order when they were sprung from boot camp that soon turned their fingers black.

It was set with a smooth green stone embossed with the letters "USN" and a bright gold fouled anchor. A panel on one side had a familiar eagle and crest insignia and the numbers "1983." The panel on the ring's opposite side had oak leaves and the letters "USN" over another anchor.

Amber grinned at the ring's design. Her Marine Corps Reserve officer boyfriend told a story about being on a joint exercise during his two weeks of annual active duty training. A spanking-new Navy Reserve junior officer was impressed with himself on the beach where the team exercised one morning, and the kid imperiously asked a long-serving enlisted Senior Chief why he thought the Navy decided to use oak leaves as the insignia for lieutenant commanders and commanders.

Senior Chief was doing his sit-ups and didn't even slow down.

"Well sir [breath] in the Garden of Eden [breath] God Hisownself [breath] gave us leaves to [breath] cover our pricks with."

Amber suspected such a ring also had some inscription inside that would help tell the dead guy's backstory once the M.E. got it off.

"He had a credential wallet with his photo on a state police identification card, and a lieutenant's badge," Plexico said. "We checked, though, and it's bogus, but it woulda fooled me. He has Homeland Security creds, too, but we haven't called on them yet." He smiled at Tracey and Amber. "I mean, you guys gotta have something to do, right?"

Amber punched him playfully in the arm, and he continued.

"And, the piece of resist-*ahnce*, he had seven of these business cards in his shirt pocket. Six now, actually, since I executed the *habeas grabbus* on this one." He handed the card to Tracey. "We recorded that on the inventory. You're it now," Plexico said, playing evidence chain-of-custody tag.

A warm breeze had kicked up across the Detroit River from the Canadian side. The sun was behind the downtown office towers, but there was plenty enough light to read the raised lettering on the ivory card.

It said the dead guy's name might have been Mohammed al-Taja. It bore the elaborate embossed seal of the Department of Homeland Security. It said his title was Assistant Deputy Chief, Investigative and Enforcement Division. The backside of the card seemed to offer the same information. In Arabic.

Amber's full federal attention was now focused on the card, like she thought it might turn into a wisp of smoke and blow away. Investigative and Enforcement Division? As far as she knew, no such office of Homeland Security existed, and the presence of this crisp business card didn't create it. Passports were lots harder to fake than business cards, and she'd seen a metric ton of pretty great fake passports. But even as she formed these thoughts, she recognized that the operative phrase was *as far as she knew*.

Investigative? Sure, maybe. Plausible. But what in God's name was the Enforcement Division?

"Trace ..." Amber said slowly, "looks like we might partner up on this one after all."

"The duty M.E. has processed the gentleman, so you *gals*," Plexico joked, "can have your way with him until the pickup."

"When do you expect the wagon?" Tracey asked. She pulled latex sur-gical gloves from her tiny purse and was already deep-thinking about the dead guy, about his condition, his surroundings and a thousand other details invisible to mortal men.

Flex turned to her and produced a cartoonish shrug.

"Damned if I know. They got, how you say, 'staffing challenges' down there at Wayne County since they cut everybody's budgets again last year. Pretty soon, though." Flex nodded at his rookie who stood a respectful distance away listening to the conversation. The officer turned around and started talking into his radio for a wagon update.

"Any suggestion as to cause of death?" Amber asked. She balanced her weight on one leg. Flex couldn't help but notice how her leg muscles bloomed and became rigid under the tight fabric of her tailored pants leg. He was a cop, after all. He noticed things. Then he silently wondered some other stuff, but being her pal and a happily married guy, he refrained from any additional meditations.

"Well, I ain't the M.E.," Flex said. He pointed toward the top of the 318-foot Coleman A. Young Municipal Building that everyone still called the City-County Building. "But I'd say deceleration trauma."

Flex whipped the bloodstained rubberized sheet off the dead guy's head area with the toe of his matte-black work boot. By the sad form of the victim's shattered skull and the exploded star of the blood pool, he had obviously come from the top of the building and landed like a lawn dart head first on the concrete pad surrounding the *Spirit* statue instal-lation. *Hard.*

Tracey would later remark that the skull looked like it had been dis-assembled with a five-pound sledgehammer. They only knew the pile of flesh and bone fragments had been the man's skull because it still sat at the top of his shoulders. Mostly.

A man of this size and evident level of fitness normally doesn't fall accidentally, and he looked way too successful to have committed suicide. People with pockets full of cash sometimes do kill themselves. Not often. That could mean he was tossed from the building. Or chased. And what was he doing up there, anyway?

The women looked up from the dead man to Flex, and then all three heads angled up the unbroken façade of the building twenty floors above the sidewalk. A Detroit cop's head was just poking over the ledge to survey the scene and get wide documentary photographs with a Nikon D90 digital camera, the strobe capturing the three in the same photo as the dead guy.

"Yeah," Flex said, turning back to Tracey. He rubbed the purple flash blindness from his eyes. "My Dad used to say, it ain't the fall that kills ya. It's the sudden stop."

CHAPTER SIX

Our fatigue is often caused not by work,
but by worry, frustration and resentment.
Dale Carnegie (1888-1955), American writer

The task force that paired FBI Special Agent Watson and DPD Detective Sergeant Lexcellent hadn't provided them with much of a mission profile, just "work together, get along, and just don't screw up."

The Bureau and the DPD had suffered a run of bad interdepartmental relations. It happened now and then, depending on the caseloads of each office, the types of cases, and the personalities who worked them. After a bad jurisdictional storm the previous year over a case the FBI supervisor grabbed because he thought would enhance his career, the Detroit police chief called on the FBI boss for lunch. Four hours later the joint task force— the JTF—was born.

Foster Heath Benoit III was the FBI's Special Agent in Charge—the SAC—in the Detroit office. He was acknowledged far and wide as the biggest tool in the tri-county law enforcement shed. Benoit hated the idea of lowering himself to cooperating with locals only slightly less than he hated looking to his own superbosses in Washington like a tight-lipped, tight-assed, self-aggrandizing roadblock. It was a tough balancing act.

A JTF wasn't going to resolve much friction between the city and the feds, but this special agent in charge aspired beyond simple, pedestrian federal service. He needed to be seen in Washington as a get-it-done kind of office runner, even when he hardly ever got anything done himself. And his was a hot command.

With its Patrick V. McNamara Federal Building location only a few miles down Michigan Avenue from the Middle Eastern hotbed of suburban Dearborn, since 9/11 the Detroit office had become one of the most coveted commands in an FBI more sharply refocused on terrorism than at any time since World War II.

Benoit's entire career had been built on a foundation of good work done by his subordinates. His was a classic case of If my people are working well, my job is done. Some would say that was effort enough and Benoit's credit and impressive career had been earned nonetheless. Most others, however, just thought he was an effete, ass-kissing idiot child who appropriated the best work of his subordinates and used it to fuel his own advancement.

This actually was true. It did nothing to dispel the childhood axiom, "Cheaters never prosper."

It didn't help that he was a snobby, condescending native of posh Grosse Pointe, the best known of the wealthy conclave of suburban Detroit Grosse Pointes that boasted some of the richest families in America. Spectacular family wealth allowed him to live there in his old family compound, and commute downtown in his own high-performance S65 AMG-Mercedes sedan instead of a government-issued G-car. Most of his agents lived in more prosaic neighborhoods. They often drove high-mileage beaters bearing white U.S. Government license plates.

The Byzantine Detroit experience wasn't how most FBI offices ran. Before they were advanced to command, most special agents in charge had been hard-working, up-from-the-ranks men and women who had done plenty of grunt work they believed in, and well, before being selected to run a field office. But the Detroit office, and the offices in which Benoit had served before, were not such places.

Enter Special Agent Davis Allen Kennedy—an American by birthright, and a Texan by the grace of God.

In any law enforcement job where special agents are in charge, the SAC acronym is pronounced "the sack." Benoit's first posting as the SAC was in the old Houston office with Special Agent Kennedy, an equally notorious

FBI case agent. Mr. Kennedy was a former active-duty special agent from the U.S. Army's Criminal Investigation Division. Though a man who had spent his entire adult life enforcing laws, he carried a healthy disdain for most authority.

In the Houston office, it was commonplace for Mr. Kennedy, hearing Benoit referred to as the SAC, to remark in an aggravated Texan twang, "Sack? SACK? Sack 'a whut? Sack 'a *SHEE-IT?!*"

Mr. Kennedy had taken an immediate dislike to Benoit's habit of pulling himself, and his career, up by the bootstraps of his agents. Everyone else in that office was weary of it too, but Mr. Kennedy was a man of action when he took a notion.

After connecting socially with his boss's wife a few times, and hearing tale after tale of Benoit's additional failures at home, Mr. Kennedy connected with Mrs. Benoit in her own marital bed over most of his last year in that office. Mr. Kennedy's most trusted colleagues saw the photos.

But over time, Benoit was transferred to a succession of new posts to command and Mr. Kennedy's career took him elsewhere, too. But like a virus, Benoit and his legend preceded him. It spread with every passing month until pretty much every FBI agent of any longevity around the country now found an opportunity, one way or another, to poke his own supervisor in a mock Texan twang.

"Sack? SACK? Sack 'a whut? Sack 'a *SHEE-IT?!*"

Amber Watson never understood how men in positions of authority so often thought that entitled them to positions from the Kama Sutra, but Benoit, in all his creepy, bad-breath-having, extra-cologne-wearing Old Guy ways, was a lion of his breed.

The first time Benoit cornered Amber in a hallway and stuttered a nervous, breathy come-on, she thought it was some bizarre hazing ritual of the new girl since it was clearly out of bounds for her boss to hit on her. She laughed out loud and asked, "Has this sort of thing ever worked for you before?"

Amber had been drop-dead gorgeous her entire life. She wasn't even offended, most times, by the rude passes men sometimes had made at her over more than three decades of police work. She had badged up against walls more than one civilian senseless or drunk enough to press her too hard in a bar or a parking lot.

Cops or law enforcement types got a wry smile and a good-natured bird flipped in their direction. Because they were her brothers in arms, even the dipshits deserved some slack as they were declined. But while cops and law enforcement types were brothers in arms, they often had egos that couldn't contemplate the prospect of failing to attract this woman.

Rejection made such men gruff or lewd. They would rationalize failure by teasing her about being a lesbian, or any other reason that didn't lay the stinking carcass of *No thanks!* at their feet, like a cat returning a dead rat to its owner. It was too often the general fate of women who work in a male environment, when men mistake testosterone for charm.

✪

Suddenly, at the crime scene, Amber felt the need to be appreciated in authentic terms. There was going to be a boatload of work to do on this case, she knew, and it started now. She looked down to the dead guy again, scrubbed growing fatigue from her eyes and thought, *Who are you really, dude?*

"Trace, I'm going to go make a few calls. I'll be by the car."

Tracey didn't look up. "Okay, hon," she said absently. She punctuated the sentence by popping her gum and going to one knee, tenderly pulling the rest of the rubber sheet from the mysterious, dapper dead guy.

Amber walked away and in just a few steps was sitting in her car. She started it, then pushed a black button in the lower frame of the rear-view mirror.

"*OnStar ready,*" responded a well-modulated female voice.

"Call." Amber pulled the power window switches and the door glass rose in both doors between her, muting the street and the crime scene.

"*Nametag please.*"

"Super Trooper."

"Calling, Super Trooper ..."

Amber's mouth turned up at the corners in her secret smile. Yes, she thought, my boy makes me feel good. Tomorrow was Friday and had been looking a lot like a personal day off on her timesheet if she could have gotten it. This had been her last best chance to get out of town for a while. Not now, though. Personal time was always secondary to the demands of the job. This was the mission she signed up for, and she knew her Super Trooper would relate to that.

Then she was going to have to call Benoit about the well-dressed, short-haired dead guy *du jour* with the Arabic name, the fake credentials, and his very interesting official-looking business cards. Benoit's OnStar nametag was NTAC, pronounced *EN*-tac. It stood for No-Talent Ass-Clown.

Sure it was silly, but it made her grin.

CHAPTER SEVEN

When I am silent, I have thunder hidden inside.
Jelaluddin Rumi (1207-1273), 13th century Persian mystic poet

The Red Flag Chinese restaurant is on Michigan Avenue in Detroit's suburb of Dearborn. Xavier Cloud liked to eat there when he was in town because the food was good and plentiful, the prices were reasonable, and it somehow offered him an indefinable vibe that was at once familiar and strange. Today he introduced Joe to the inscrutable delights of its menu.

"I can't read a *got*-damn thing on this page," Joe complained.

All the large type was in Chinese Mandarin characters. The descriptive English subtitles were set in print so small that Joe couldn't read them in the half-light of a booth shrouded in heavy burgundy curtains pulled back and secured just so.

Truth be told, he would have had a hard time reading the menu in the noonday sun without his glasses, which, like today, he usually forgot to wear.

"I can order for you," Cloud said. "Still like seafood, right? You can't go wrong here with that."

Joe fussed over trying to read the menu for a moment longer, until Cloud reached across the table and pulled down on the top of the tall trifold so he could see Joe's frown.

"No worries, bro. I got you."

Joe lowered the menu, looking around at the nearly empty dining area. "This place so good, where the people at?" He rubbed his left knee.

"Best-kept secret, maybe. How is your knee coming along?" Cloud asked without looking up.

"It's a lot better, dickhead," Joe shot back. "It's stiffer'n shit, thanks to you, but the infection is under control. I'm workin' it out in the gym."

Cloud raised his eyes over the menu and smiled at Joe, sharing the secret as well as his friend's pain. Business was business, but dinner was dinner. And friends for life meant that exactly. He had no difficulty distinguishing the lines of demarcation among those seemingly inconsistent vectors.

A waiter materialized at Cloud's right elbow.

"Excellent to see you again tonight, Mr. Cloud," the young Chinese man said with a mild accent and a modest bow. He knew his tip from this table would be substantial. "How may we serve you today?"

His hands held an iPad and a rubber-tipped stylus. A subwaiter arrived carrying a hammered metal tray bearing two white ceramic teapots and two small cups, each filigreed with ornate, hand-painted baby blue dragons twisting and writhing in a seascape. Cloud needed neither the menu nor its English translations.

In perfect Mandarin, he ordered his usual, shrimp with snow peas. From previous experience, the kitchen knew to add a triple order of shrimp and a bit less sauce. He ordered shrimp with lobster sauce for Joe. Simple food, simply delicious, no distracting additions. No soup, no salad, no appetizers. Yes, just the green tea, please. Thank you.

The waiter tapped on the iPad screen with the stylus a few times and expressed once again his profound gratitude for the return visit, in Chinese this time. He bowed and backed away toward the brightly lit kitchen.

"I didn't know you rap that shit," Joe said. "When did you learn to talk like a Chinaman?"

"One leads a full life, as conditions permit. I picked it up in the prison library when I was in Leavenworth."

Joe blew air across the top of his steaming teacup and spilled the hot liquid on his thumb when he laughed out loud.

"In Leavenworth? Before you escaped? Damn son, you a quick study, ain'tcha?"

That remark made even Cloud chuckle. A man with a photographic memory could learn many things when all he could do was read books. "Yeah, I suppose I am."

"You was only in there, what? A few months, right?" Joe said. Cloud just grinned. "By my reckoning, that means you still owe Uncle Sugar about thirty-seven more years, to *life*." Joe picked up the tea again and blew on it. "Give or take."

"Give or take," Cloud repeated. His gaze narrowed. Joe got the hint to change the subject.

"Did you get to make those calls?" Joe asked.

"I did. Curious of them to give you a phone number to call if anyone asked you about the briefcase. I got voicemail each time, as we thought we would. But four calls in a row to voicemail tells them that I'm desperate to make this deal. You shouldn't have given them the case in the first place."

Indignation boiled out of Joe like a dark cloud of fierce bees. He leaned in to keep his voice low.

"I didn't know where the *hell* you was at for years, man, and then I seen you was in prison, right? I didn't know you was gonna bust out there like you could friggin' fly or some damn thing. What you expected me to do?"

Joe hadn't heard the details of Cloud's escape story, and wouldn't. He could be forgiven if he thought Cloud, sentenced for a gruesome war crime committed while on active Army duty as a Ranger, might be behind bars for some time.

"And listen, those Saudi fuckers tied me up good as you, man, but they wasn't nearly as courteous, you dig? So after about an hour of being poked at with sharp objects and jumper cables on a *got*-damn Diehard, well yeah—*fuck yeah!*—I told them little fuckers where they could find the damn case."

Joe took a sip of the unsweetened Chinese tea and made a tight disapproving face.

"How d'you drink this rat piss? So I give them the case, I surely did. They was gonna cut off my *dick*, man! Who the hell knew you'd ever be back? It was twelve years, man—twelve fuckin' years—I ain't heard *jack* from you. So I figured keepin' my junk was a better deal than keepin' some stupid-ass money map I was never gonna use again anyway, you dig? They can have the fuckin' money, they can find it. I'm keepin' my damn joint."

Passion dissipated, Joe chuckled. "I tell you what, doh, they cuttin' off my unit, they's gonna need a bigger knife."

Cloud smiled. "You're sure the coordinates are still in that case, though, yes?"

"Last time I saw it, yeah. If you'da seen them before we unassed the desert that last day, we wouldn't have to conversate about this at all. You'da remembered that shit."

Cloud nodded in the gloom of the booth. "Yes, I imagine I would remember the coordinates to one hundred million dollars."

Xavier Cloud possessed a photographic memory that was well documented and well exploited by his former military commanders. His Army lawyers had tried to use the clarity of his recollections as the defense in Cloud's general court-martial. It wasn't the sergeant's fault, the lawyers said. He's seen and done things under orders you cannot possibly imagine—that he literally can never forget, the defense claimed. The trauma of his photographic memory caused him to snap under the stress of battle, they asserted.

PTSD killed those villagers, and the garish terrorist reprisals in Italy and Iraq that killed those American tourists and service members, the lawyers claimed? Not the fault of their client.

After just seventy-three minutes of deliberation, most of it in *pro forma* review of the testimony and case law, the court of military officers and senior enlisteds called bullshit as one. They could indeed imagine, and remember, their own combat experiences. They knew well the pressures and terrors war imposed, but they denied the defense contention that Cloud had just snapped. One review of his storied combat experience would validate that. They convicted him.

He was sentenced to forfeiture of all pay and allowances, a reduction in rank from Sergeant First Class E-7 to Private E-1, and given a

Dishonorable Discharge from the U.S. Army. He barely escaped a death penalty, and instead received thirty-seven years to life confinement at The United States Disciplinary Barracks at Fort Leavenworth, Kansas, the only maximum-security correctional facility in the Department of Defense.

After a few months of getting the lay of the land at Leavenworth, Cloud befriended a young and impressionable Air Force sergeant unsure of his sexuality, and traded confinement for freedom. Weeks before, Joe had pressed Cloud on how he managed to escape from prison. He said he could tell Joe the story, but then he'd have to kill him.

It wasn't the old joke; it was a matter of fact. Joe was far less curious thereafter.

Large oval plates of steaming Chinese food arrived and covered the top of the table. The two subwaiters who delivered the food stood at attention with the metal trays under their left arms until Cloud looked at them and nodded his dismissal. They bent in unison at the waist and withdrew. Cloud and Joe dug into their meals and ate silently for several minutes.

"When these jokers call me back, I'm giving them the warehouse location for the meet," Cloud said between bites. "We know that space, they don't. We will recover what is ours."

He looked up from his meal with two large shrimp captive between wooden chopsticks.

"You remember the warehouse?"

"That shit ain't funny, man," Joe said. He reached down with his left hand and rubbed his sore knee where it had been violated by Cloud's commemorative ice pick. "I remember where the damn warehouse is. I live here too, y'know."

Joe devoured his food without further discussion and calmed down. It wasn't long before he finished. The military teaches a man to eat quickly and without wasting time better spent in the field looking for bad guys or protecting your battle buddies while they have their turns to eat. Prison teaches the same lesson somewhat differently. Joe had less on his plate than Cloud anyway, so he cleaned it well and pushed it away with satisfaction.

"Okay, you right. That was pretty damn good," Joe said. He swiped at his face with the pristine cloth napkin, no longer concerned about food items that used to drop onto the lush black beard he and his Ranger battle buddies grew each time they went back to Iraq or Afghanistan. Cloud had been right about the beard issue. It had been a bitch when that green Army tape came off Joe's face, so he just shaved off the spotty remainder of his late beard.

"Imma roll," Joe said, gesturing playfully left and right with splayed fingers. "Imma meet that new girl? You know, about that thang?" It was good to see Joe getting his groove back, and Xavier Cloud smiled.

"Yes. The girl. The thang." Cloud rose when his friend did and they clasped right hands at the thumbs and embraced with their left arms, shoulder to shoulder, like men who respect themselves and each other often will.

"As soon as I hear something, I'll call you once I hear from my guy. About my thang," Cloud said.

"*Ahh-ight* then—later," Joe said, grinning and pointing an index finger at his friend. Then he was gone.

Cloud sat back down to finish his dinner. Night had fallen. On the street, the Indian summer evening was still simmering hot and glorious. Like a 1960s buddy movie projected on a giant IMAX screen, perfect flickering memories of cruising Woodward Avenue and westside hangouts on Telegraph in convertibles with high school pals and girlfriends were suddenly immediate and powerful. He missed those days from time to time, more so lately than ever before.

A shadow fell over the table. Cloud had seen the man approach in his peripherals, of course—the Red Flag's owner. He knew of the man, and the man obviously knew of his best customer. But he had never before approached.

"Mr. Cloud, may I join you, please?"

"Yes sir, of course," Cloud replied. The man eased into the booth and Cloud observed that he was lithe and thinly muscular, though he must have been in his late 70s or early 80s.

"Thank you, Mr. Cloud." He extended his hand. "My name is Xing Jianjun. I am the owner of Red Flag."

Cloud took the man's hand and shook it—his grip was like iron. Evidently,

Xing had held more than cooking utensils in his life.

"I know who you are, sir. Pleasure," Cloud said. He gestured to the main eating area, where busboys and subwaiters were wiping tables, refilling sugar packet containers and topping off tabletop soy sauce flasks. It was late now. Xavier Cloud was the last customer.

"You do a good job here," Cloud said.

"You honor us. Let me say how grateful we are that you seem to enjoy our humble place of business. I think you are our best customer. We are indebted to you for your support."

Xing waved at the young staff hustling to prepare the restaurant for closing. "I do what I can to keep our young people on track, out of trouble. Western ways are powerful, and tempt them. But it is the obligation of the strong to protect the weak. Don't you agree?"

Cloud chewed and nodded in agreement.

"They work hard, go to school, study hard. All family here. We show them that investing in their lives now will repay rich rewards later. I am Chinese. I understand well the benefits of hard work and commitment. The profits on our life investments. Work done well may indeed be its own reward." Xing stopped for just a moment and drew a fresh breath. "I trust you know of these things yourself, Mr. Cloud."

"I have always felt I was in the minority of people who believe such profound truths," Cloud said.

"You do not know it, but in this place—in *my* place—you are among kindred spirits in all respects," Xing said. "My work has been my life. It has taken me on many roads along the way. I have succeeded by knowing what I wanted in life and then deciding how to achieve it."

"'Choose a job you love, and you will never have to work a day in your life,'" Cloud said.

A reluctant smile creased Xing's tightly drawn face.

"Confucius also said, 'When it is obvious that the goals cannot be reached, don't adjust the goals, adjust the action steps.'"

This was suddenly beyond polite dinner banter. A tiny surge of adrenalin raised the hair on Cloud's arms. He regarded Xing with fresh appreciation. His senses spooled up to their highest alert.

"You are a wise man," Cloud said. "Also, one who seems to be remarkably well informed."

"One leads a full life, as conditions permit," Xing said.

There it was. Cloud's words to Joe not ten minutes before. The booth was bugged. And then the real slammer.

"A full life, undeniably, such as that clever work you performed masquerading as Unit 61398 in the Pentagon networks some years ago. Very clever. Very clever, indeed."

China's People's Liberation Army Unit 61398 is the military computer hacker unit Cloud had impersonated when invading the Pentagon for fun from his laptop.

Cloud put down his chopsticks and the two men fixed each other in unblinking stares for seconds, waiting for the other to do something, say something. A waiter appeared from the shadows at Xing's elbow and spoke to him in Chinese. His car was ready and waiting to take him home. Xing looked to the waiter and replied in a quiet voice that he would be a few more minutes. The waiter bowed and withdrew. Xing turned back to his guest.

"I apologize for my rude directness, but I believe men such as we must always speak plainly, Mr. Cloud. Don't you agree?"

"I couldn't agree more," Cloud said. He was on maximum alert, every sense near the redline, paying attention to his peripherals. His hearing was attuned to every whisper and footfall, noting that every sound not from his booth was coming from the kitchen. They were all common sounds. No hard metal on metal such as a gun bolt makes, no hiss of a muffled radio, no soft shuffling as careless men might make moving into an assault position.

"If we are to speak plainly," Cloud said, "now is the best time to begin."

"Just so. As I said, I have had several occupations in my life. My restaurant is one of the more pleasant ones. I won't bore you with my resume." Xing reached into his pocket and withdrew an object. "But I wonder if you know what this is?"

He placed on the table a military uniform epaulet, the flap of cloth on a soldier's jacket shoulders that displays his rank. This one bore the gold crest and three gold stars of a general officer in China's People's Liberation Army.

"Yes ... *general*." Cloud kept his eyes trained on Xing and automatically nodded in respect. "I recognize it."

Xing tilted his head. "Thank you for that," Xing said. He stuffed the piece of cloth back into his pocket. "Modern societies often lose their sense of decorum as they age. I no longer wear the cloth of my country on the outside, but I will always wear it on the inside. How do you say it? Once a soldier, always a soldier."

"We also say that the apple doesn't fall far from the tree. And you, sir, seem to have fallen very, very far."

Xing looked out at the darkened restaurant. His demeanor was dark and brooding. "It may seem so, Mr. Cloud. But in fact, the roots of my tree are very long, strong, and nourishing." He turned back to the American. "A caterpillar becomes a butterfly. A cub becomes a lion. A general retires. What have you become, Mr. Cloud? Or are you still becoming it?"

The idea had crossed Cloud's own mind more than once in recent weeks.

Xing placed both hands flat on the table. "I must go, and we must close." He glanced toward the kitchen where anxious young faces peered through the glass in the swinging doors. "Our young people have their own lives to proceed with this evening."

Xing made to stand and Cloud respectfully got up at the same time, grabbing his cellphone from the table and dropping it into his left-rear jeans pocket. Military respect knows no time, boundaries, or uniforms. Though an enlisted man, and a publicly disgraced one at that, Cloud was diminished not a bit to show respect to the former Chinese general officer even if he didn't know the man's history. He didn't know many things.

For one primary example, how did one of the highest-ranking Chinese generals end up in Dearborn running a restaurant—and why?

More importantly, what did Xing want with him?

Both men reached out to shake hands at the same time, yet their eyes remained locked on each other.

"It has been interesting to speak with you tonight, Mr. Cloud," Xing said with a grave smile. Despite the mannerly expressions, Cloud thought something was on the man's mind that he wasn't yet ready to share.

"I believe 'May you live in interesting times' is a form of Chinese curse, sir," he said. He gripped Xing's hand with just an ounce of additional force for emphasis. Not hard, barely more than a reinforcement of the handshake. But a noticeable message. "Shall we live in interesting times together, then?"

"You misunderstand me, Mr. Cloud." Xing responded with a bit more power in his own handshake before releasing it. "We shall be friends. Perhaps even allies." His face changed, rote manners were put aside, and he became deadly serious. "Imaginably, even business partners. You will return for your regular visit on Friday, in two days hence?" Cloud nodded.

"Thank you. We shall speak again then. You are set upon a difficult and dangerous course. You face many challenges. Even you do not comprehend them fully. I believe we have allied goals and can work together for mutual benefit. No matter that the road ahead is rocky. A pessimist sees the difficulty in every opportunity, but an optimist sees the opportunity in every difficulty."

"Confucius?" Cloud asked.

"No, my friend." The general smiled. "Churchill."

Xing nodded and smiled and then disappeared into the kitchen. Cloud pulled a generous wad of cash from his left-front pocket and left it on the table for his bill. The waiter would remember him again when Cloud returned.

CHAPTER EIGHT

*When you ask creative people how they did something, they feel
a little guilty because ... it seemed obvious to them after a while.*
Steve Jobs (1955-2011), American inventor

Tracey Lexcellent sprinted hard on Belle Isle, the Michigan state park on a leafy island in the middle of the Detroit River. Running cleared her head of old memories, opened pathways to fresh thinking—and helped keep her weight in check, because she ate like a junkyard dog.

She wore form-fitting Under Armour like an Olympic athlete, tight on top where it showcased her topography and more elastic below where it demanded efficiency of movement. Tracey ran steady and strong, effortless in execution and long in stride and endurance, a machine powered by focus and determination.

She purged herself of calories, doubt, guilt, and self-reproach while running. The slipstream peeled it back from her in strips to rapidly dissolve, like shards of dry ice, on the hot asphalt pavement.

Guilt was delivered several ways. It swirled about her when thinking about her dead parents and sister, how she had failed to save them. Guilt crept in when her homicide squad colleagues teased her about being "just a girl" in this hard occupation.

Guilt came atop double cheeseburgers laden with bacon. Just guilt. Everyone had it, though most people reject that idea. They deal with theirs as they saw fit. Tracey dealt with hers the same way.

The death of her family wasn't her fault, but she always believed she should have done more to save them. It was as real an expectation as it was unreasonable.

Tracey was only eleven that Christmas Eve when the blue Plymouth sedan spun on black ice on the snowy Belle Isle Bridge, vaulting the low decorative rail and punching through the crystalline ice of the Detroit River like a 4,000-pound bomb. The frigid water may have paralyzed her mother and father; she still remembered them motionless in the front seats. Maybe they had been knocked unconscious by the impact. She couldn't know. She would never know.

The big sedan bobbed essentially flat long enough for Tracey to push open the back door and row herself out. Her six-year-old sister was alive and literally kicking as she too started out of the open rear door after Tracey and toward life. Then, nose down, the car surrendered its buoyancy to gravity and sank.

The force of the water slammed the door shut just as Sammie bobbed through it, trapping her lacy church dress. The car descended, and it dragged Sammie, thrashing and screeching in abject terror and screaming Tracey's name, down into the icy murk along with it.

Tracey kicked hard on the surface, trying to stay above the ice hole as the frigid, fast-moving water below towed her toward doom. The car was gone. Her parents were gone. She couldn't reach Sammie. The water bubbled furiously for a few seconds, only a precious few seconds, and then it was over.

People on the bridge shouted at Tracey. *Hold on, just hold on, help is coming.*

That was twenty-three Christmas Eves ago. Though as confident and self-possessed as any accomplished woman, Tracey harbored foamy reservoirs of doubt. And the guilt scarred her like a branding iron. She still felt failure lurked around every corner of her life.

Like creative people often do, she thought that one day her talent would be exposed as the fraud she often believed it to be, and then she would be exiled to ... she didn't know what. Something else. Some menial occupation and a lackluster life, devoid of excitement and meaning and great shoes.

This constant flight from her own perception of failure was what sparked Tracey's lifelong struggle to seek perfection and, failing that, to embrace excellence.

Tracey's path toward guilt started literally at birth. Her father had named his unborn child Tracey, in a common male spelling, instead of the female Tracy. Then a girl baby was born. He had badly wanted a son. When the girl child arrived, he imposed the male name as a consolation.

Her parents never had another child after Sammie because her father didn't believe he could produce the son he so desired. His personal disillusionment at two daughters was crippling, and not always concealed as well as it might have been.

He had been a loving and attentive father, of course, but by age eight or so, Tracey could see his occasional flicker of disappointment in her gender, as much as he tried to mask it. She could throw a ball with him, and did, and ran track and cross country better than boys, a good basketball player but no football, of course. All A's in school. Excelled in everything she ever attempted.

But like Pinocchio, she wasn't a boy. Unlike Pinocchio, that would never change.

Then her family was dead. That was never going to change either, despite a grief-stricken Aunt Marilyn who loved her and raised Tracey as a member of her own family—as the daughter that she never had in a litter of boys. Tracey's guilt became an artifact frozen in the amber of time, only to be carefully taken out and examined at different angles from time to time. Then it would be discarded once again in a wild run through the Belle Isle woods, or in the *Detroit Free Press* Marathon.

Tracey completed her lap of the island and arrived winded at her duty car. There was nothing better for her to exorcise demons than leaving them behind on a run. She loved Belle Isle, and loved her city of Detroit, downcast as it had become. Her detective talent, skill, and success at solving homicides had created a national reputation, frequently drawing offers of new employment elsewhere.

Not just in affluent Detroit suburbs, but for high-profile homicide slots in New York, Los Angeles, and Chicago, which these days could really use her help, sadly. Even federal offices had courted her for a time, but they had bigger issues than recruiting a *wunderkind*, and they took no for an answer.

Tracey always listened politely to the job offers. Her momma raised no fools. But she always knew when those conversations started that she would turn them down by the time they ended.

Detroit was her town. Detroiters were her people. The Detroit Police Department was her team. She wasn't leaving any of them behind for money. Detroit still faced lots of challenges. Awakening from its stunning and historic bankruptcy, the city was just maybe starting to do a little tiny bit better.

Streetlights in darkened neighborhoods were coming back on week by week. City services were perking up. Citizens occasionally waved at police driving by using their whole hand instead of just a single finger. And the homicide rate was stabilizing.

That usually meant folks were going back to work instead of sitting around angry, strapped with guns or laden with dope. Even the media were saying nice things about Detroit again, and young people were moving back into the city.

Tracey Lexcellent was a daughter of Motown. She was staying.

She pushed the unlock button on a remote key fob and pulled open the door to the black Chevy Impala SS sedan just as her cellphone sounded off with the sing-song theme from the TV reality show COPS.

Bad boyz, bad boyz, whatcha gonna do when they come for you? Bad boyz, bad boyz ... She recognized the custom ring tone as her office reaching out. In her line of work, duty literally called.

Tracey slid behind the wheel, affixed the seat belt, and keyed the powerful V-8 into life. She dropped the cellphone into a console cup holder and thumbed the answer button, reached for the gear lever and pulled it down into Drive.

As Tracey sped away, she could be forgiven if the car drew uncommon attention from looky-loos, joggers, and bike riders. The custom Michigan license plate on the imposing black four-door read *25 2 LIFE*.

The call connected and she spoke into the phone.

"Tracey Lexcellent here."

CHAPTER NINE

It is the mark of an educated mind to be able
to entertain a thought without accepting it.
Aristotle (384-322 BC), Greek philosopher

Tracey walked from the police headquarters locker room for women after showering off the Belle Isle run and putting her school clothes back on. Her wet red hair was pulled back into a tight dance bun and her sleek profile was draped in a tailored suit that was slightly looser under the right shoulder to allow for a shoulder holster holding a Smith & Wesson M&P .40-caliber duty pistol.

She looked more like a millionaire CEO of a downtown tech start-up than a veteran Detroit homicide detective sergeant with twelve years on the job. It was a national legend that Detroit homicide detectives were some of the best-dressed cops in the nation. Tracey did her part.

"You rang, Babe?" she said to the squad's receptionist. Ruth Figelski was a retired street cop from the ethnically Polish enclave of Hamtramck, a pocket city surrounded on all sides by Detroit. Ruth retired from the streets after twenty-two years, and within weeks came into the Detroit homicide section as its civilian administrative boss and den mother.

Ruth took inbound telephone calls, greeted the curious, the lost, and other citizenry, and kept the shifts humming as efficiently as possible. Her nickname was Baby Ruth, after the candy bar, but most everyone shortened that to just Babe.

"Yeah, I did ring," Babe said. She reached forward and grabbed familiar pink message forms tucked under a clip with Tracey's name and badge number on it. "You know a Jeff O'Brien, right? Sergeant-type, uniform, eastside radar cop? He says he knows you, anyway. Left his number. Said he thought he had something for you, from a traffic stop."

She handed the first one to Tracey.

"Then, you got a call from the M.E.'s office. That City-County jumper guy or whatever, the well-dressed one that smashed his head on the pavement last week? Turns out he was cleverly hiding a bullet in his brain."

Tracey took the messages with a tingle of excitement. The call from the medical examiner's office was thought-provoking but not shocking news, and the well-dressed man from Homeland Security was already dead. He could wait until her partner arrived.

"Would you reach out to Amber and ask her to call or swing by, please?" Baby Ruth nodded and reached for her desk phone without looking.

Tracey looked at the first slip of paper and recognized the number. It was indeed Sergeant Jefferson O'Brien, The Grim Reaper. They had been in the same academy class, though she made sergeant earlier; O'Brien occasionally had a little friction with authority. Tracey walked a few steps over to her desk and called him back. He answered his phone on the second ring.

"Hey sarge, what's goin' on over there where the big, ah, you know, *brains* live?"

She snorted. "Yeah sarge, big brains. That's us. I just got your message, Jeff. What can I do for you?"

"Just some heads up," he said. "I stopped a kid two days ago, gangbanger, speed-drivin' a piece-of-shit Monte Carlo. Too bad for him he was speedin' past my spider hole."

O'Brien was nicknamed The Grim Reaper for the shadowy place adjacent to Gethsemane Cemetery, off Gratiot south of Conner, where he lay concealed until the unwary on the street drove too fast into his traffic radar beam.

"I policed him up and we impounded the car. No insurance, bad registration, and so on. He went downtown, the car went out to impound. By the time it had been dragged over there across some of the finest crop of urban potholes in the Midwest, some interesting personal property was shooken loose from under the front seat and into plain view."

Tracey made a skeptical face at the slang and the *plain view* remark, but put the phone between her ear and shoulder and reached forward to wake up her computer terminal. She logged in and opened a notepad page on her computer.

"Go ahead," she said, and started typing.

"Well, turns out my gangbanger had some dope and some guns with him when he decided to blow through a thirty-mile-per-hour zone at seventy-seven miles per hour. Givin' those guys tickets never gets old. I had the POS towed to impound, and a gun was discovered on the floor, a Glock 19. What is it about nine-mil handguns that appeals to gangsters, anyway?"

Tracey laughed. "I dunno, man. I blame Hollywood."

"Yeah, dig it. So, we got a warrant to search the rest of the car, and his front seat had been modified with horizontal pouches. One was for a dope stash, fuckin' idiot. The other was for the prettiest little all-pink Kel-Tec .380 you ever did see."

"Ha," Tracey said, "a petite gun for his ladies. Why do I care about this?"

"The three-eighty smelled like it had been fired. Just wanted you to know Ballistics has the guns in their queue, and I put you down as a contact if any firing results match up. 'Cause, you know, thinkin' a' you, bud."

"Okay bubba, thanks for that. We can use all the help we can get closing cases around here. I'm even taking a couple, and I'm JTF. Jones Two retired in January, you heard that, right? So we're catching more cases since Chief didn't replace him. We only got Baby Ruth because she's way cheaper than Jones was. Budgets are eatin' the man alive."

"Yeah, heard that. How's old Baby Ruth workin' out? I worked with her some when she was still on Hamtramck. She's a tough one."

"Pretty great so far. You wanna not get caught calling her 'old,' though. You know she still gets to carry a gun, right?"

Tracey saw Amber enter the squad bay.

"Okay mister, gotta go. Thanks again. Talk to you soon, okay? You owe me baby pictures."

Jeff promised to post some photos of his newest baby boy to his Facebook account, and hung up.

"Hey," Amber said, ignoring the creaky wooden chair and instead perching on the side of Tracey's ancient wooden desk. "I was headed up here anyway. Heard you were looking for me."

"Yeah. Got a call from the M.E. on the Well-Dressed Guy. They found a bullet in what was left of his brain."

"Yeah? That's kinda interesting in a *wow-I-didn't-see-that-coming* sort of way," Amber said with a grin. "Ask them to email you the autopsy report and copy my office address, okay?" Tracey nodded as she typed.

"I reached out to DHS about the creds and business cards," Amber said. "Man, you'd think those cats were all sitting around their computers dressed like the Men in Black, the way they won't tell you nothing about anything. They admitted al-Taja was one of theirs, but stonewalled anything more. How about they get the TSA squared away before lording it over us real law enforcement types, huh? They said they'd 'get back to me' as soon as they could. So yeah, I'm sitting quietly waiting for my phone to ring."

Tracey laughed. "Or *naw*?"

"Yeah, naw. How was your weekend?" Amber asked.

"Ehh, about the same," Tracey said. "Nothing much."

To Amber, that meant Tracey spent too much time in the Sweetwater Tavern again, her hang-out joint across the street from her downtown apartment building, and then lurched home. Alone. Fridays were the worst.

The Sweetwater was always packed with potential dating subjects after work, especially on Fridays, but the vibe Tracey broadcast from her reserved place at the far end of the bar facing the door was so *don't mess with me* that few dared approach her. All who did were denied, or they excused themselves when they learned she was a cop. So, Tracey drank a little too much, a little too often, and was a little too lonely.

The job was her world. She loved it and it loved her back, by way of a fast promotion to sergeant on her first look, and the kind of autonomy, first in Homicide and then in the JTF, envied by some of the men in the detective unit who had been there longer.

The demands of her job and a few years of finishing her degree at night had already killed a starter marriage. That was a mercy killing, but still. She detested the cliché that she was becoming. It would be time for more Belle Isle therapy soon. She needed more hard runs and fewer hard rums.

"And your weekend was?" Tracey asked.

"Pretty great, actually," Amber said. She leaned back on Tracey's desk and kicked her taut legs in the air. "*Yow!*"

"You. Are. *Gross*," Tracey muttered, but she smiled. The other detectives were all out on cases, but Baby Ruth turned in her office chair at Amber's brief disturbance and looked sternly at the women over her half-eye reading glasses.

"Gross, huh? Really? When's the last time you got some, little girl? I mean, I'm just a poor little college-educated woman, tryin' to make my way alone in the world. I have no babies, no husband, and no time or patience for either. You know my boy makes me feel good. He was able to come down here this weekend, bless his youthful and muscular little heart. If you and I hadn't been stuck with the Well-Dressed Guy last weekend, we'd have had this conversation sooner."

"Great, terrific. Enough with the sharing, please. Separately, what was your buddy Benoit's take on the Homeland Security connection?"

Amber made a sour face. "He pinged on his DHS butt-buddy in town, and they had a long meeting from which I was disinvited to attend. He took my notes and the case file and said he'd let me know where to go from there. If past practice is any prelude, I know where he intends to tell me to go."

"Ha, really. That guy just loves him some spotlight, don't he? How can he keep grabbing cases like he broke them himself and get away with that?"

Amber smiled. "Well, given that I have thirty-one years on the job in one form or another, and given that I dropped my retirement papers last Thursday, I'll give you that I don't give a rat's ass what he does."

Tracey spun to face her friend. "*No* you didn't put in for retirement! You knew this last week and I'm just hearing about it now?"

Amber tilted her head and a wry *oops!* smile creased her face.

"Well, hell!" Tracey said. She looked at her watch and saw that it was past four in the afternoon, her unofficial personal bug-out time when circumstances permitted. "This calls for a drink."

Tracey got up and dropped a preps handset radio into the bank of chargers as the women walked out of the door.

"Babe, I'm out. Text if you need me, okay?"

✪

In the Sweetwater Tavern, Tracey and Amber picked up their glasses and clinked them once.

"*Prosit!*" Amber toasted. Her Army history in Germany was never too far from her thoughts.

"*Sláinte!*" Amber replied with a faked Irish accent. "May ye be in heaven 'aff an' hour bee-far the debbil knows yer gone."

They sipped the drinks, Dortmunder Union draft for Amber and Stroh's for Tracey. Stroh's Beer was a Detroit legend, but it hadn't been brewed in town for decades until a microbrewery licensed the recipe and brought it back to the city. Few places carried it. The Sweetwater had it on tap, and that was one of the reasons Tracey liked the place. Its devotion to things Detroit matched her own.

The Sweetwater Tavern literally was a short stumble across the street to the lobby door of the Millender Center apartment building where she lived. That helped, too.

"So, what's this retirement stuff all about?" Tracey asked.

"It's about putting down the sword and enjoying my life," Amber said. "One way or another, I've been kicking in doors my entire adult life, first in the Army, then ATF, then FBI. Our task force has been a nice change from office work, but even this is getting old." She gently rubbed the glass on her bottom lip, a pre-drink tic. "Like me."

She took a sip of the beer. "And if I have to go much longer working for Benoit, I swear I'm gonna get up on a water tower with a high-pow-ered rifle."

"Yeah, I get it," Tracey said. She doodled figure-eights in the rings of condensed water that formed around her beer bottle. "I hate to see you go, though. I like working with you, and who knows what jerk I may get next? I just got you trained up."

Amber smiled. "Honey, we are friends for life, and I'm a Michigan girl. I'm staying around here. My boy works out of the Traverse City state police post now, up north. I like that place, but it's just too damn far from everything. Plus, I gave the Bureau a ninety-day notice of intent, so it isn't like I'm going anywhere right away. We gotta see where this Well-Dressed Guy thing goes."

"Your buddy Benoit has that now, though, right?"

"Okay, number one? I know you're joking, but fercrissakes please stop calling him 'my buddy.' Second, I'm still the case agent on paper, and you have your case open for now, or until your boss gets a call from my boss. So let's see what we shall see. Separately, I know Benoit has been pushing for a full operation between the FBI and DHS, concentrating on Dearborn. Lotsa suspected terrorist cells there, and now the damned right-wing militias are talking about 'taking action' there. We've been watching them for years. Do you know Dearborn has the largest concentration of Arabs outside the Middle East?"

"I do. And I know a guy who knows a guy who works for Dearborn PD," Tracey said. "If we're going to get any traction, we're going to start getting it sooner over there. Lemme give my guy a ping and see if he can get us an introduction tomorrow."

"Good idea," Amber said. "The Bureau has assets there too, but I'm probably not going to be able to tap them. I don't swing a big enough bat—and pending retirement hasn't strengthened my standing with the team any."

Tracey reached for her iPhone and got into the Favorites menu. "It's okay, fam. We got this."

She touched the listing for GRIM REAPR and raised the phone to her ear.

CHAPTER TEN

When you can't make them see the light, make them feel the heat.
Ronald Reagan (1911-2004), 40th President of the United States

Though it was morning, Xavier Cloud inhabited the warehouse shadows. The black hole of the dead warehouse seemed to always be as dark at any time of the day as a demon's intent, and it reassured him. He was comfortable in the dark because he knew how to use it as a weapon. He knew the building, and knew the score. His visitors did not.

He heard the Saudis clumping up the concrete staircase to the fourth deck. They were not practicing noise discipline, with shuffling in the dirt and debris, talking too loud, and kicking at rats that probably were not there. Cloud knew they were scared. Intrigue was not their business. Violence was not their profession. It was his.

This could be an early end to the day.

Cloud was surprised when two slight men in their thirties appeared from the stairwell. The first one led the way with a cellphone flashlight that was dimming fast. The men came onto the floor looking around in all directions, bewildered. Their gazes centered on two chairs and a table carved from the darkness by a single overhead light, the same light that had illuminated Cloud's conversation with Joe weeks before.

The men approached the round pool of yellow with slow, deliberate footsteps, like actors in a 1940s war movie negotiating a mine field, and no tactical separation. They stopped near the flimsy card table separating the chairs. One man carried the silver Halliburton briefcase. The other kept his right hand concealed under a loose-fitting plaid shirt.

"Gentlemen," Cloud said from his dark place. His eerie voice echoed among the fluted concrete pillars that still shouldered the building's expired legacy.

He walked from the pitch black into the circle of light.

"I am happy to see you."

"Who are you?" the first man demanded. He tried to sound dangerous, but it came off as peevish and uncontrolled. He was young. He might learn lessons today if he lived.

"Did you brought the money from us? *For* us?"

"Who am I? I am your redemption," Cloud said. "I am everything you need. What is your name, friend?"

Cloud's gaze flicked for a microsecond to the other man.

"Please ask your companion to remove his hand from under his shirt."

"I am Ahmad." He nodded to his escort, who then showed both hands empty at his sides. "This is my little brother, Azim."

"So, Ahmad—the *praiseworthy*. And brother Azim—the *defender*." Cloud smiled warmly at the two. He didn't care to cause the pain of a double loss to their mother. This altered the proceedings to come.

"*As-salāmu alaykumā.*" Peace be upon you.

"*Wa-Alaikum-as-Salaam,*" both men said in return. And upon you the Peace. Ahmad was confused, and his eyes narrowed. He was caught off-guard by the traditional Arabic greeting in perfectly conjugated masculine plural form, and he relaxed just a little.

"What do we call you, brother?"

Cloud smiled. "Call me *Naji*." Survivor.

"Naji. We have brought this case for you." He raised it and shook lightly. "Did you brought your money for us?"

"I have indeed brought your just rewards, Ahmad."

Only a few yards away holding a suppressed Sig Sauer P226 pistol, Joe stood in the dark at a ninety-degree angle to the Arabs. He heard the non-lethal cue "just rewards" and zipped two muffled shots into the two men, one .22-cal long rifle round into the meaty part of their behinds.

He could have chosen to shoot them in the legs. That certainly would have crippled them, but the chance of hitting a femoral artery or leg bone was too great to ignore. Pain was an excellent way to underscore serious intent, but Cloud wanted the Arabs left alive and mobile. At least for now.

The two men fell howling to the dirty concrete deck, holding their butts. It would have been mildly comical under different circumstances. The briefcase clattered to the ground and slid over the gritty surface to Cloud's feet as if by command.

If he had used the other pre-arranged cue, the lethal one, both would have been dead before their exploded heads hit the floor.

Cloud and Joe descended on the crying Arabs and checked them for weapons, wires, radios, cellphones, anything that might pose a threat. They found nothing except a cheap little .25-cal automatic tucked into Azim's waistband, gangster style. This troubled Cloud. Could these two birds be as genuinely unprofessional as they seemed?

And yet, Joe positively identified them as the men who had tortured him into giving up the briefcase weeks before. It was all Cloud could do to keep Joe from returning the favor. Joe got in a few hard kicks to Ahmad's ribs anyway.

"*Yeah* motherfucker! Yeah *bitch*! Who the man now, raghead mother-*fucker!*" Joe kicked Ahmad again.

"Joe, will you relax? We need these guys. What they did to you was just business, right? Just business. Don't make it personal."

"Got-*dammit*, when a man threatens to cut off your fucking *dick*, that is not business. When they put jumper cables on your toes, that is not business. That shit is *personal*."

Joe glared at Ahmad, who covered his face with bloody hands. "*Fuck* you, you goat-fuckin' motherfucker."

Cloud put a calming hand on Joe's arm. "Hey, go take a good look at the briefcase, will you? Make sure that's the exact same case you gave them, okay? Let's just get what we came for and get out."

Joe picked up the case and looked back down at Ahmad. When he spoke, the slow cadence of his words chilled the warm night air.

"Back in the day, I used to kill sand-nigger motherfuckers like you for a livin'. And my livin' was damn good."

Joe picked up the briefcase and walked about twenty feet over to the card table where the light was better. He used his hands and the sleeve of his shirt to brush off the dirt and grit picked up from the warehouse floor. He raised the case closer to his bad eyes and examined every scratch and dent. The Halliburton badge affixed to the lid above the three-digit combination lock was etched with a product series designation and five-digit serial number Joe recognized.

"This is it, man. This my briefcase."

Ripping open the seat of Ahmad's pants, Cloud was already bandaging the flesh wounds with QuikClot from a backpack of gear they brought along. The Arabs would live to tell lies about how these minor gunshot wounds were obtained. They probably would charm the clothes off more than one woman in the telling.

"No disrespect to your brother"—Cloud nodded to Azim, who was sitting tilted up on his undamaged butt cheek and crying—"but you seem to be the talker, so you will now talk to me. Tell me how you knew Joe had the briefcase. Tell me who told you to get it from him. Tell me who told you it was okay to sell it back to us."

Cloud turned to Joe. "Open the case, bro. Let's get our stuff and get out."

He half-smiled and turned back to finish Ahmad's bandages. Cloud looked forward to getting this show back on the road. It would be a short night, after all. A hundred million reasons urged him forward, and there were other issues needing attention.

"So, Ahmad. You were saying …"

Joe turned the numerical thumbwheels until he arrived at the combination. He flipped both chrome latches at the same time and they popped free with a metallic clatter.

When Joe raised the briefcase lid, there was a brilliant flash of light and a vicious explosion that threw Joe back twenty-seven feet before dropping him into the dirt like a rag doll.

Cloud was already low to the floor working on prone Ahmad's gunshot wound. When the briefcase exploded, most of the horizontal concussion went over his head. The blast still pushed him down hard onto Ahmad. A fragment of the table clipped the top of his head as it winged past.

Decades of undisturbed dust and other debris was shaken from its slumber and rained down from the warehouse rafters. Time stood still for a few moments. Cloud shook his head to clear the concussion cobwebs and dirt spun from it like a dog shaking off a spring rain.

Cloud blinked rapidly to clear the grit from his eyes. He rolled Ahmad over onto his back and covered his mouth with his hand, shaking his head left and tight—*don't speak.* Then he scuttled into thick shadow behind a concrete pillar in a defensive position to see if anything else happened, or if intruders flooded the space. The only sounds were Ahmad's ragged breathing, low moans coming from Joe, and the sharp, high-pitched ringing in Cloud's ears.

Cloud checked himself for wounds, starting with his ears. No major blood, some minor head trauma that wasn't bleeding much, but no apparent injuries anywhere else. He was satisfied for the moment that no one else was coming in just yet. He couldn't hear well with the ringing in his head from the blast, but he was lucid. He knew he had only a few minutes to get moving out of the warehouse.

An explosion like that would be magnified many times in the echo chamber of the empty space. The metal window inserts in this end of the warehouse had all blown out with tremendous force into the street. Surely some homeless man with an Obama phone was dialing 9-1-1 right now.

Pointing at Ahmad with one index finger and holding the other vertically against his lips, Cloud signed for Ahmad to stay quiet, and then crawled toward Joe by way of young Azim.

A tubular leg from the card table had been blown off and arrowed into little brother Azim's sternum. When Cloud rolled him over, he could feel where the tube pressed a red stain outward against the back of the boy's plaid shirt. Azim would tell no war stories to anyone tonight but the seventy-two heavenly virgins he was probably being introduced to right now.

Cloud scurried over to Joe, who had seen better days.

"I need a damn beer." Joe coughed up lots of red fluid. Bubbly red froth came to his lips as he spoke. Other rivulets of blood cascaded from his eyes and ears. His head was cleaved deeply across the left side by a metal shard from the briefcase. Brain trauma and internal injuries would kill him soon.

"I'm sorry, man," Joe said. "That was our case, bro." Joe coughed hard and a wad of bright red blood and thick mucus landed on his shirt. "That was our damn case!"

"I know, I know." Cloud used the back of his hand to wipe dirt and crimson spittle from Joe's cheek. Then he smiled. "Somebody got us this time, bro. That's all right. What goes around, comes around, right? Next time, it will be us getting them. Ain't nothin' to it but to do it, right? Just hang in there. I'm going to get you out of here."

Joe tried to get up on his elbows. "Well, let's go then! We can't ..." He fell back to the concrete floor. "Ahh, we can't, the noise, we gotta get ... gotta get ... *ohhhh, the fuck* ..." Joe exhaled briefly and died, eyes wide open and staring in disbelief.

Xavier Cloud brushed the grit from his hand on his shirt, and carefully reached out to close Joe's dull eyes. He was not a religious man, but he bowed his head and silently said the Catholic Hail Mary and the Lord's Prayer for his battle buddy.

He laid his friend gently back to the concrete floor. Then he rose and strode toward Ahmad, pulling a suppressed Colt Model 1911A1 .45-cal automatic from a shoulder holster hidden under his loose shirt. He didn't jack the slide to chamber a round. That was a bullshit Hollywood move that only happened in the movies. A round was already in this chamber, the hammer was back, and Cloud's index finger rested against the trigger, not along the slide.

Ahmad's eyes got wide and he raised fluttering jazz-hands in defense as Cloud approached, the dark weapon outstretched before him.

"Mister, please, I don't know this! You believe me now! I don't know bomb! I swear you! The man gave us money and told us how to get briefcase from your friend. Then he told us take phone calls on you, meet you. He said if you brought us money and took the case, we go home and enjoy Allah's blessings, peace be upon Him. I don't know bomb!" He whimpered like a child. "I don't know bomb ... *I don't.*"

Cloud stood over the slender Arab and watched him speak, the weapon inches from Ahmad's head. Joe was dead and that was a damned shame. He was a good man, and a good battle buddy. But he was still dead. The sirens growing ever louder through the faded ringing in Cloud's ears said it was time to go.

Cloud lowered his weapon.

"Can you walk?"

Ahmad seemed surprised at the question. "I can walk, mister, for sure!" he said, wide-eyed and grinning like a maniac. "For sure I can walk!"

"Get up and help me," Cloud ordered.

He holstered the automatic and grabbed his backpack, slung it over one shoulder by a strap and directed Ahmad, who limped with a bullet hole in his ass. Ahmad was in considerable pain, but he counted his blessings and embraced the pain as proof of life.

The two half-carried, half-dragged Joe's body with them down the staircase at the other end of the extended factory floor. They were leaving long trails of Joe's DNA all over the place, but it couldn't be helped.

No man was being left on this battlefield tonight. No American man, anyway. Cloud didn't care if the police found Azim, and Ahmad, sweating like a pig, said nothing about his younger brother as they departed.

In the back of the warehouse, they loaded Joe's body though the side door of a dark blue Plymouth Voyager minivan. It was just the sort of nondescript shitbox the police wouldn't see unless it ran smack into the back of a police car as they escaped. Cloud motioned the sweaty Ahmad into the driver's seat and took the floor behind with Joe. He told Ahmad to drive.

✪

At the nearest of his three safe houses, Cloud closed the unsteady wooden garage door behind the minivan with a remote clipped to the sun visor and Ahmad cut the engine. For a moment both men remained motionless, listening to the hot engine ticking as it cooled. The old garage smelled of sawdust and mold. The soft rustle of a leafy branch scratched against the shingles on the roof. The coppery smell of Joe's blood filled the minivan with its aroma of death and it filled Xavier Cloud with rage and resolve.

Cloud stepped from the van and around to the driver's door, yanking it open and pressing the silenced pistol barrel against Ahmad's left temple in the same fluid motion.

"Out. Now."

Ahmad raised his hands to shoulder height, turned gingerly in the seat and his feet touched the garage floor. He stepped out on legs stiffened by the drive and the field-dressed injury he'd been sitting on. Cloud pointed at the door leading into the house, and the two went inside. He motioned for Ahmad to sit at the kitchen table. He took the opposite chair.

The nightlight from under a microwave oven mounted over the cook-top was all the light Cloud needed.

"Now," he said. He pulled the trigger of his suppressed weapon once and a .45-caliber slug zipped through the top half-inch of Ahmad's right shoulder just above the clavicle, embedding itself in the door of the refrigerator. He redirected the pistol at Ahmad's heart.

The Arab howled at his fresh injury and pawed at the shoulder.

With his free hand, Cloud tossed Ahmad a clean dish towel to cover the new bullet graze. The Arab grabbed the towel and pressed it against his shoulder, grimacing.

"We are going to get better acquainted," Cloud said.

It wasn't personal. It was just business.

CHAPTER ELEVEN

I am not afraid of an army of lions led by a sheep;
I am afraid of an army of sheep led by a lion.
Alexander the Great (356-323 BC), Greek king

Amber Watson and Tracey Lexcellent drove out of downtown Detroit, west on Michigan Avenue toward the leafy suburban community of Dearborn, Michigan. Home to the Ford Motor Company headquarters—the famous Glass House—Dearborn's former claim to automotive fame had been eclipsed by the overwhelming influx of Middle Eastern immigrants who flocked to the neighborhoods seeking a better life.

Not all of these migrants sought a better life from their American hosts. Ever since 9/11, the FBI had blanketed Dearborn with undercover agents and confidential informants seeking terrorist plots, and sometimes finding them. Inevitably, a lot of what these people found ended up being nonsense.

An informant will often tell a cop what he thinks the cop wants to hear, especially if he is getting paid to say things. Nevertheless, there certainly were terrorists hiding in plain sight among Dearborn's population, lions navigating among the sheep.

"Who are we meeting with?" Amber asked. Her Corvette pulled up to a red stoplight at West Outer Drive.

"Dave Lovato is the name Jeff O'Brien gave me. Lovato works traffic for Dearborn PD. He was in motorcycle school with my academy buddy

Jeff awhile back." She looked down at the Google Map displayed on her cellphone. "Hang a right here. We could have turned back there at South Military Road, but I wasn't paying attention, I guess. We're meeting Lovato at the Dearborn Country Club."

"Really?" Amber said. "Country club. He's making too much of that sweet overtime money."

"Jeff said in his off time, Lovato is the club golf pro."

The Dearborn Country Club wasn't the swankiest golf course on Earth, or even in Wayne County, but it was nice, and on this nice day it was buzzing.

Nearly every parking space was filled, often with an expensive sports car, Mercedes sedan, or high-end SUV. When they reached the clubhouse sidewalk and approached the main building, they saw the pro shop humming with customers. Tracey flagged down a course groomsman zipping past on a golf cart.

She dropped a practiced hand casually on the man's shoulder when she spoke. It never hurt to pre-load the prospect's cooperation.

"Dave Lovato, hon." Tracey said. "Seen him around this morning?"

The man squinted toward the building and pointed to the large glass windows of the pro shop. "In there, yellow sweater."

Tracey squeezed and then patted his shoulder in thanks and gave him a dazzling smile, rewarding him like you might a puppy. The groomsman smiled and half saluted, then puttered off in the cart.

The women entered the pro shop and stood for a moment just inside the doorway, taking in the surroundings. The air conditioning might have been blowing crushed ice.

Dave Lovato was across the big room lobbying the merits of expensive Callaway golf clubs with a dark-skinned man about five-feet three-inches tall, dressed in what you expect a golfer to wear in a Bob Hope comedy, all contrasty plaids and colorful polka dots, complete with knickers buckled just below the knees and tall orange socks. The man was a squat pear shape, wide in the butt and narrow in the shoulders. He paid rapt attentive as he took in Lovato's sales pitch.

Lovato noticed the two attractive women standing nearby watching him and he thanked the man, doctor-something, for coming in. He handed doctor-something his business card and encouraged him to come back when he decided to buy those Callaways. The doctor assured him most earnestly that he would do just that. They shook hands and the doctor departed.

Lovato turned and strode directly at the women, expectation painted on his round, possibly spray-tanned face.

"And how can I make your days better today, ladies? Who needs lessons?" he asked with a wide, duplicitous grin.

The yellow sweater draped over his wide shoulders and around his neck was tied with its arms in a loose knot. He wore a white Polo shirt and blue plaid shorts with a yellow pattern that matched the sweater. He smiled so broadly that his acutely bronzed face pulled back into shallow pleats on either side of his mouth, like a Shar-Pei puppy.

Tracey and Amber discreetly displayed their credential holders. "Jeff O'Brien said we could talk to you?" Tracey said.

Lovato's mood changed when he saw the two badges.

"Yeah, sure. Of course." His happy grin slipped a little.

Lovato had been expecting a visit by two cops, but he looked crestfallen that this promised to be more official business than monkey business.

"Let's go into my office."

Zig-zagging around chrome carousels of golf shirts, wild and mild golf pants, and a huge display of golf shoes, Lovato led them through the pro shop to a side door marked EMPLOYEES ONLY and into office spaces behind the retail area. He closed the door behind them as they entered.

"Okay, so how can I help the infamous Joint Task Force today? Here t'help, and all that. Never turn down a request for assistance from a brother officer, I say."

He paused for a moment, walking around them to sit at his desk. "Or sister, either, of course. You know what I mean. I gotta say, you two took me by surprise. When Jeff texted me you were coming, I guess I was expecting ... oh, I dunno. Men, I guess."

"Yeah, we get that a lot," Amber said.

Like children will, cops sometimes lie for no reason at all. The women recognized Lovato wasn't being truthful with them. First, he offered up that they were JTF. This was no secret in the law enforcement continuum, so if he had not known it before O'Brien's call, Amber knew O'Brien would have told the Dearborn cop that the two officers coming to see him were females, not males. He might even have bragged about how great looking the task force was, probably with descriptive physical characteristics, man to man.

Second, O'Brien most certainly would have provided a brother officer the heads up that Amber was FBI, just in case it mattered to the quality of his answers.

And third, O'Brien definitely would have told Lovato he had seen Tracey naked, better for Lovato to fuel his own imagination and envy when the women arrived.

Amber wondered whether Lovato was hiding anything else.

They had decided on the way there that Amber would throw her federal weight around as the lead interviewer, better to underscore to a local cop the importance of his cooperation with a serious case. That sometimes backfired on local police with self-esteem issues, making them indignant, but it seemed to be working all right with the effusively cooperative Lovato.

"We're looking into the homicide of a DHS agent," Amber began, drawing Lovato's attention to her. "This has the highest priority. We hope you can answer a few questions for us, maybe help point us in a direction."

"Sure, anything," Lovato said. He tried to be subtle when his eyes flicked back and forth from Amber's face to Tracey, but failed. Lovato thought he would be completely cooperative, of course—he had nothing to hide, despite his opening little white lie—but he also thought this smelled to him a little like freelancing.

If such an important federal case needed his official input, he wouldn't be providing it on his own time in the golf pro shack with a pastel yellow sweater tied around his neck. His Chief would have his Captain have his Sergeant have him in the Chief's office to talk with the FBI. In any case, Lovato kept these thoughts to himself.

"What was the guy's name?"

Amber produced a composite photo of the DHS agent's business card and his driver's license photo. She had the postmortem photo for a backup. The medical examiner had done a passable job pushing al-Taja's features back into a close resemblance to his former look, but it was never again going to be very good for identification.

"Mohammed al-Taja. DHS confirmed he was one of theirs, but either he was deep undercover and not telling his bosses what he was up to, or we don't have the Yankee White security clearance to know about it, or it isn't Thursday with my head held just right. Jeff O'Brien seemed to think you might be able to shed some light on this. Did you know him? Al-Taja?"

"Jeff is talking out of school a little," Lovato said. He looked at the photo only for a moment. "But be that as it may, yeah, I knew Jerry a little. He asked everyone to call him Jerry. He was sensitive about being called by his first name out here in Dearborn. A lot of the long-time, shall we say, 'European-heritage' members who golf here aren't crazy about the whole Arab thing, though more of them are out here all the time. They're good golfers, too, the Arabs. Decent tippers."

Amber rolled her hands over horizontally a couple times. *Get to the point.*

"Jerry used to golf here every so often with a group of guys. He took a few lessons on a cop's professional discount. I haven't seen him in months, though." He frowned. "Guess I won't be seeing him at all the rest of this season, huh?"

He feigned a weak laugh at the lame cop humor, but no one joined in.

"So, when was the last time you saw him?" Amber asked.

Lovato made a body language move Amber recognized, his eyes defocusing and looking slightly off into space. He was dredging up a memory.

"Um, I think it was early spring. I only work here when I'm not on the road, so I'm not here every single weekend. I can check the records to see if he had tee times or bought anything when I wasn't here. But the last time I personally saw him was about late April, I think. Remember how warm it got so early this year? People were coming out for their first rounds. I think he came out with his usual group and they did eighteen holes. I can look it up."

Lovato turned to his computer and performed a search. "Yeah, here it is. Monday, April 17. I didn't work that day. He was here, had a zero-eight tee time, the big cart, and they played eighteen holes."

"They?" Amber said. "Who was he with?"

"Well, you just missed one of them."

"One of who?" Tracey interjected.

"One of Jerry's group, one of his regular foursome. Doctor Malhotra, that guy I was talking with when you came in? He's looking at buying some nice Callaway golf clubs. That'd be a nice commission for me. He's a cardiologist down at Henry Ford Hospital. Teaches in the med school downtown at Wayne State. Lebanese, I think. Nice guy, though."

Tracey leaned in a bit more so that her red hair draped over her face, as if what she was about to ask was a big secret. Maybe even a sexy one. Lovato's attention was sharply focused as he leaned his ear in toward her lips, as if to receive a whisper. His gaze was fixed on the swell of Tracey's cleavage and his head was clouded by the slightest hint of her perfume.

"Perhaps, big Dave, in your records there, you have a club member phone number for good Doctor Malhotra?"

Cops were sometimes even easier to cow than civilians. Lovato swallowed hard.

"Why, um, yes. I believe I do have that."

✪

Amber and Tracey walked toward the Corvette in its far parking spot and Amber punched Doctor Malhotra's phone number into her cellphone. As she touched the last digit, Tracey laid a hand on Amber's arm and nodded ahead.

"Twelve o'clock," Tracey said.

Parked two empty slots down from Amber's Corvette was a brandnew steel-gray Mercedes S550 four-door. The vibrant Doctor Malhotra was just loading his golf clubs into the spacious trunk when the two policewomen approached him.

"Doctor Malhotra?" Amber said. He turned with a start to face two sets of police credentials thrust into his face, one from the FBI. "Could we ask you a few questions please, sir?"

Doctor Malhotra's lips trembled just a bit and they could see the color drain from his dusky face. Then his eyes rolled up into his head and, with a convulsive moan, he dropped slowly to the asphalt as if he was deflating.

"Hmm," Amber said. "Was that a yes or a no?"

Tracey saw the groomsman from before rolling up to the group on his golf cart. They could use that to get Malhotra into Lovato's office.

"Yo!" She yelled and waved him forward. "We got a clean-up on aisle five!"

✪

Doctor Malhotra sat in Dave Lovato's office chair and sipped Fuji water from the bottle. Condensation collected in the plastic ring left around the top once the cap was twisted loose, and as he drank, a steady drip of water droplets landed on his golfing attire.

The man's color had returned and the sweat was mopped from his face, and his faculties were restored. Tracey and Amber explained why they were there. No, they assured him. He certainly was not in trouble.

"I apologize, officers. I taught eleven hours yesterday and I was in surgery until nearly two a.m. A bad one, that. Traffic crash on the Lodge. Nearly lost the woman, but we pulled her through. I really should be in my bed sleeping, but this was such a glorious day and I couldn't wait to get out on the course. Do you golf here as well? It really is quite highly recommended, absolutely splendid in all respects."

He nodded at Lovato.

"Excellent staff here as well, of course, Mr. Lovato. Excellent indeed. Only nine holes today. Very tired and dehydrated. I think I experienced a slight vasovagal or neurocardiogenic syncope when you surprised me with your identification. Well, you saw the rest."

His diction was precise, pronunciation perfect, English a second language that he mastered with enthusiasm and skill. The women looked at him. This was a talker.

"Again, forgive me." Dr. Malhotra smiled. "I am a teacher and I will rattle on from time to time." Malhotra placed the water bottle on Lovato's desk and returned his hands to his lap. "Now then, the doctor is in. Tell me, how may I help you?"

Amber leaned forward.

"Tell us what you know about Mohammed al-Taja."

✪

Amber drove the Corvette into the small expanse of Dearborn parking lot at Michigan Avenue and Middlesex, found an empty slot close to and facing the side street, and shut down the car. Tracey handed her a small cardboard pouch of deep-fried chicken items and a Diet Dr. Pepper.

"What did you think of the good doctor?" Amber asked Tracey. "I think he was fairly informative, don't you?"

Tracey unwrapped a bacon double-cheeseburger and took a small nibble. "He was. I don't know a lot about golf, though. Before today, I thought a foursome was something else entirely."

Amber snorted into her drink straw. "Christ! Don't make me laugh when I'm drinking!" She covered her mouth while coughing up Diet Dr. Pepper that had tried to go into her lungs.

Tracey slipped off her shoes, slouched and raised both bare feet to rest on the dashboard, then took a more serious bite of the burger and chewed thoughtfully. She peered out across busy Michigan Avenue, seeing no one was noticing them. Directly off the nose of the car was the Red Flag Chinese Restaurant.

"I'm going to have to add 'Jerry' to the case file as an alias, I guess," Amber said. She pulled a misshapen chicken tender from its cardboard sleeve and took a bite that severed the piece in half.

"Me too, in mine," Tracey said. "Don't forget to add the narrative of Doc Malhotra's interview, and the golf partners." Tracey took a short pull on her Diet Pepsi. "Dem golf partners, doh. 'Curiouser and curiouser, cried Alice.' I just emailed you the recording from my phone."

"Thanks. So yeah, ol' 'Jerry' and Doc Malhotra were half of the golf foursome. The good half. 'Jerry' was a power hitter, 'cause he was big. Doc

Malhotra is small and stubbier, but he has the finesse, the real golf skills."

"I looked up 'Muslim golfers' while we drove over here," Tracey said, scrolling the oversize screen of an iPhone Xs Max. "And you know what? Islam has a ton of rules about sports. What body parts must be covered, by whom, what can be uncovered, in the presence of whom. Yeah, lotta rules. Not even one of them prohibits golfing, though, at least for men. Islam says sports are good because they make strong bodies twelve ways."

"That was the Wonder Bread slogan."

"Okay, same difference, though. So there is no religious prohibition for a Muslim leader—say, Imam Sayid al-Waheeb, only the most prominent Muslim cleric in the Midwest, maybe all of America, and your buddy—to play a few holes with Doc Malhotra and, oh, I don't know, maybe an undercover agent from the Department of Homeland Security."

"No, heck no, why not?" Amber said. "And since we need a fourth, how 'bout we just grab this 180-year-old Asian cat who runs a Chinese restaurant?"

It was Tracey's turn to giggle. "Please do not say 'cat' and 'Chinese restaurant' in the same sentence!"

"No, really, he's wiry as shit. You should see his drive. Man hits a golf ball so hard it goes back into time."

Tracey was full-on laughing now.

CHAPTER TWELVE

It is twice the pleasure to deceive the deceiver.
Jean de La Fontaine (1621-1695), French poet

Xavier Cloud sat in the Red Flag restaurant in a booth facing the door. It also offered him a sightline to the swinging kitchen doors. The silenced Colt .45 automatic was in the shoulder holster under his right arm on the wall side of the booth.

There were only couples in the house tonight. Two Caucasian couples and one Asian, each nearly finished with their meals. Cloud ordered green tea and a double potsticker appetizer, chewing slowly. When the waiter returned, Cloud asked in Mandarin whether Xing Jianjun was in the house tonight. The waiter nodded in the affirmative and backed away.

The two Caucasian couples paid their dinner checks and departed. The Asian couple small-talked at their table in quiet Chinese.

Xing Jianjun materialized from the darkness and approached Cloud's table with a tight grin, a thin arm raised in greeting. Cloud rose, the men shook hands and they sat back down in the booth.

"Welcome again to my restaurant, Mr. Cloud," Xing said. He gestured to the half-eaten appetizer. "I trust our work remains satisfactory?"

"Yes, as always," Cloud said. He did not smile. He raised his right hand into the air at about head level and twirled an index finger in circles. A questioning look crossed his face.

"No, we are clear," Xing said. "Please forgive a momentary lapse of courtesy. Some of my old ways die hard. We are all alone here tonight."

Cloud didn't know if he could trust that Xing removed or turned off his listening devices. He had no other choice except to proceed.

"General, we didn't have time to finish our conversation last time. I would like to continue it now."

Xing nodded his head.

"What is it you think you want from me?"

"I am prepared to bring considerable resources in support of your goal."

The waiter brought another teacup for Xing and filled it from the teapot. Xing took a small sip of the brew and sat back against the red velvet fabric.

"And what is my goal?" Cloud asked.

Xing replied without hesitation. "You are attempting to recover one hundred million American dollars, hidden in the Afghan mountains bordering Pakistan."

Cloud remained deadpan, but inside, he was roiling. He considered surprises just proof that he had failed to adequately prepare, and this was one big surprise. What was *really* going on here?

"The Hindu Kush was a very serious place when you were there with your Army, when you had limitless weapons and ammunition. Do you imagine it to be somehow more hospitable should you manage to go there as a civilian?"

Cloud stared at the man. Without the information he needed to locate the hundred million dollars, without his battle buddy Joe, Cloud felt something that was alien to him: Baffled. He had never felt it before, and its uncertain alien presence coiled around his brain and squeezed until his pride couldn't breathe.

"I told you my roots were long," Xing continued. "I can extend my friendship—and my resources—to you immediately. I can also tell you there is little time left, and none at all to waste."

"I don't know how to find the location yet. I was to obtain that information two days ago, but an unfortunate accident occurred." Cloud's eyes bored a hole into the general. He mourned the fresh loss of his battle buddy Joe.

"My friend—the one who was here with me last time—was killed. The information was lost." Better to keep some secrets, if any could be kept from the man.

"I am sorry to hear of this" Xing said. "But you know, our greatest glory is not in never failing, but in rising every time we fall."

Cloud frowned. "Are we to play quotations ping pong tonight, general? I'm not in the mood. I'll take Confucius Quotes for a thousand, Alex."

The general sat quietly without response. The darkened restaurant was nearly silent. The only sounds were those of wicker ceiling fans pushing around fragrant Chinese aromas.

Cloud thought of the Confucius quote that said, *Silence is a true friend who never betrays.*

Xing reached into his coat pocket and withdrew several photographs. The first was a 4x6-inch color print of a beautiful young woman, mid to late twenties, evidently Asian American. She had dark hair, but blue eyes, unusual for a Chinese woman. The woman was sitting on an iron bench with her arm around a slender older woman who appeared to be American, and she had blue eyes too. In soft-focus background behind them was a sign that read STANFORD.

"My daughter and her mother, my beloved wife." Cloud took the photo and tilted it into the light for a squinty look. He would need an eye exam one day soon.

"My wife accompanied our daughter on a Stanford University student exchange trip to Poland. They disappeared while changing aircraft in Frankfurt. We did not know where they were until a friend in the Pakistani ISI sent my colleague an email."

The general looked down at photographs spread across the table, all of the young woman. Now he seemed to be the defeated one.

"Mr. Cloud, my beloved daughter is being held hostage by an ISIS cell in Ramadi."

Cloud looked up from the small pile of pictures. Pakistan's Directorate of Inter-Services Intelligence—the ISI—was well respected among global intel players. If they said the general's daughter was in Ramadi, they could give you the GPS coordinates and a phone number that you could write down in ink.

"Iraq? Crazy bastards. Why? What do they want? ISIS is on the way out over there now, anyway. Ramadi was liberated."

"I must speak frankly. I should not discuss such matters with you, but we must work together to achieve mutual goals. In my military career, I have had the privilege to command some of my nation's most fearsome tactical and strategic weapons." Xing was talking about what the American military often called simply *the specials*.

Nuclear weapons.

"I'm long out of that discipline, but my daughter's captors believe that I can access areas of influence that would help them possess such weapons for themselves. I cannot, of course. Evidently, they intend to use such weapons to try and restore some level of dominance in Syria and Iraq." He paused. "And perhaps elsewhere."

Cloud frowned. "Even crazy ISIS idiots must know they can't convert your knowledge into weapons. They have no infrastructure for that, and they don't seem to be the smartest terrorists on the planet anyway."

"This is true," Xing said. "But I am a military man, not a scientist. They have expressed their interest in one of our most clandestine products. It isn't well known publicly that my nation has developed a series of small, highly portable nuclear devices. Very small, very powerful. Very clean. Any tool may be misused, of course"—Xing gave Cloud a knowing look—"but we *intend* to use them for our large-scale construction projects, moving large amounts of earth for dams and the like. We call them Mad Gophers. Under different circumstances, you might call them suitcase bombs."

Xing reached forward and covered the photos with his hands facing up, in supplication.

"I can do many things for and because of my nation, but I cannot start a war with Iraq, not for my own purposes. I am able to do things for you, help you recover your legacy, even spend my nation's money toward that goal. But I cannot lead an attack on Ramadi to recover my daughter."

Xing trapped Cloud in an icy cold stare.

"You, on the other hand, have the means and the training to rescue her.

First, we will retrieve your money. Second, we will retrieve my daughter. I do not care what it costs."

Cloud was bothered by just one perspective.

"You haven't mentioned your wife but once. Presumably we are we bringing her home as well?"

A look of incalculable sadness darkened Xing's face. "My wife is dead. I cannot bear to show you the horrific photos I received, encouraging the same fate not befall my daughter."

For Cloud, that changed the calculus. After a moment, he nodded. A silent meeting of the minds had occurred.

Xing said, "I trust you have a valid U.S. passport?"

"I do."

"Please pack for a ten-day trip. Bring your identity documents, though you may not need them. Pack as you see fit for any eventuality, including any personal weapons you care to bring along. We will have additional equipment and personnel at your disposal."

"Chinese hospitality is extraordinary, general," Cloud said, "but what else do you expect from me? I know the Chinese origin of your given name, *Jianjun*: It means 'protect the army,' more or less, yes? How prophetic for an infant who grew into the career you've had. But now? You want something more than your daughter, and you haven't told me what it is. Even if we succeed, it can't as simple as an endowment for your PLA retirement account. Can it?"

Xing was deadpan. "What did your General MacArthur say? Old soldiers never die. We just fade away."

Cloud was unmoved.

"Yes, of course. You have a right to know the answers to your questions. It is true that I hope to share in the bounty once the considerable treasure has been recovered. We shall have expenses to take care of from among my partners, all of whom will provide their services, as it is said, 'off the books.' And we will incur certain expenses once you are on the ground in the mountains, principally among Pakistani and other associates. All told, I believe we can get back with more than eighty-five to ninety-five million dollars, to be split evenly between us."

Cloud was skeptical, but he grudgingly admitted the old man seemed to have many answers, if not quite all of them.

"Seventy-five percent me, twenty-five you. Expenses off the top. And we still don't know where we're going."

"On the contrary," Xing said. He reached inside his sport coat pocket and withdrew several more photographs, fanning them out across the table. There were different angles of soldiers picking their way on foot down a mountain pass. A cave opening partially obstructed by a landslide. A darker image taken from deep inside the cave, with the bright center of a camera flash bouncing back off translucent blue plastic, revealing a large cube of dust-covered American money shrink-wrapped to a blue plastic pallet. Behind it in silhouette was another cube of the same shape.

The cubes were covered in small rocks and dirt, but there was no mistaking what they were. A helmeted Chinese soldier in desert camouflage stood grinning next to the pile, holding up to the camera a crisp $100 bill with one hand and pointing at it with another.

"We know exactly where to go," Xing said.

Cloud was discouraged for the first time in his life. Twelve years gone since his Army Ranger team placed the stolen cash in the cave. They all were to share in it after the war, but then the war didn't end, and only he and Joe survived their multiple deployments. Now Joe was dead, too. A grand plan was in disarray. And now the money was in another man's hands. Literally.

He instantly resolved to explain these failures to no one. If it came down to his survival, he would have to disappear before anyone else could differ. Looking down at his custom Suunto Core wrist watch, with its many additional features hidden inside, he wondered if disappearing was even still an option. But Cloud was good at reinventing himself.

"How is this possible?" he asked.

"My former military colleagues in certain offices have many associates in Afghanistan, Pakistan, and other areas in the Middle East. Pakistanis in the mountain regions often are simple people, living comparatively short lives of hard work without anything we in the more civilized world would recognize as achievement. One such animal farmer, a drunken man, chased a goat into the cave where the money was hidden. There was so much of it that, by the next day, the man was certain he had dreamed it up in an alcoholic haze. He told that dream story to his disbelieving friends in a village square and was overheard by one of our informants, who passed the word along. In due time, it met with less skeptical ears. We sent a reliable team to verify."

Cloud was equal parts frustration, astonishment, and resignation. "There is no reason for you to connect me with the money. How did you know I was looking for it?"

Xing smiled and shrugged.

"I am not aware of the precise connective tissue," he said. "Suffice to say China's global electronic eavesdropping is nearly as good as your NSA's. We connected dots until they us led to you."

"How so?"

"Some years back, your playful hack of the Pentagon under the *nom de guerre* of Ghostar was quite elegant, according to some Chinese information warfare people I know." Xing smiled appreciatively. "We have paid low-key attention to you ever since. Our people never did figure out how you made it look like China was at fault in that attack, but they identified you." Xing wagged an index finger at Cloud. "That caused us some little bit of trouble at the time. Well done."

Cloud said nothing.

Xing's demeanor changed, softened. "Mr. Cloud, you must recover my daughter. My nation cannot be seen to cooperate with kidnappers any more than your government can, and China cannot declare war on ISIS for the sake of one individual." The general's face regained its hardness. "We have no friends in the region to whom we could look for help. The Russians are animals on a good day, buffoons on the next, and they are all in Syria, anyway. I do not care for war, but nevertheless, war may be what is required. A private one, perhaps. But war in any case."

"I buried my friend Joe today."

Cloud had arranged with a discreet funeral home in suburban Detroit to prep Joe for burial and hold a brief ceremony. He was interred in Holly, Michigan, at the Great Lakes National Cemetery with full military honors. Cloud was the only attendee. If he was still alive, Cloud would return in a couple months when Joe's headstone was installed.

He became steely. And blunt.

"Did you kill Joe?"

"No," Xing said. "We were not involved with that aspect of your program." The Chinese general shook his head and frowned. "I wish we knew more of that event, in fact. Assassination is a shameful business. We continue to seek enlightenment about it."

Cloud noted that he'd hadn't told Xing *how* Joe had been killed.

"A rescue exercise will require lots of moving parts," Cloud said, relaxing somewhat. "Reliable, trained personnel. Global transportation and coordination. Front money. The logistics alone are daunting enough. I mean, we might do it, but it takes time."

Xing sat impassively.

"Evidently, all this has occurred to you."

"I'm in a position to harvest a lifetime of granted favors. Many are from people who once were insignificant, and who now are …" He paused for a moment to reconsider his next words. "… and now, well, they are no longer insignificant. Something we can count on in all respects is that our people are reliable and well trained. And utterly obedient."

Cloud saw in his peripheral vision the Asian couple from the other table stand and approach. They stood respectfully apart from the booth at Xing's left shoulder.

"These people will see that you are taken care of. Note their faces, and call them simply One"—he motioned first to the man, then the woman—"and Two."

Now up close and in better light, Cloud saw they were much younger than he had supposed, probably late twenties, and extremely well built. More soldiers, probably, from the People's Liberation Army, gifts from the PLA to the people of America.

"You will meet them again on Sunday at the Owosso Community Airport. You will have no difficulty finding it. I use Google Maps," the general said. "Our aircraft is very comfortable and will be ready to take you on your journey of a thousand steps by helping you to make the first one."

"If you already know where the money is, what do you need me for? You can grab that anytime, pay some scrubby mercenaries to rescue the girl, and fade away into the sunset. I hear Belize is very nice. Not many Chinese restaurants."

"Mr. Cloud, friends do not treat friends so. Money is not an end for me, but a means to an end. My country is wealthy, and I am one of her favorite sons. I will accept money that is earned, but do not need to steal money from you. And at my age, a man desires to engage in adventures as he may."

The Chinese general smiled.

"The cave is secured by many of our people and some locals, who will later be paid quite handsomely by their standards. We are able to help you achieve a goal you cannot achieve on your own. Conversely, you are in a position to do something for me that I cannot achieve on my own. Shall we have a deal?"

They shook hands. The simple act was more than enough to seal the deal for such men.

CHAPTER THIRTEEN

The bravest are surely those who have the clearest
vision of what is before them, glory and danger
alike, and yet notwithstanding, go out to meet it.
Thucydides (460-395 BC), Greek historian

The Owosso Community Airport is deserted most Sundays. Xavier Cloud drove the rental car at the speed limit along the town's East Main Street. There was no traffic at this time of the early morning. He hooked a left into an Arby's restaurant at about 0600 and ordered drive-thru breakfast, stuffing the bag of greasy food into his backpack.

There is a 24-hour Walmart Supercenter next door to the Arby's, nearly across the street from the small airport. Cloud drove the anonymous dark blue Ford Focus into the lot and parked in a space nestled among the largest glut of cars, mostly older or beaters. These would be employee vehicles that usually park in the same area day after day. The car he rented with an alternative identification wouldn't be noticed for a long time, if at all.

He wiped down the few surfaces he had touched, then closed and locked the dusty car before heading back toward East Main. It was only about a quarter-mile walk down the entrance road to the building that served as the airport's executive terminal. There was a small plaque on the wall near the entrance that said the airport was owned and operated by Tzu/Chao/Solo Real Estate LLC. It showed postal addresses in New York City and Hong Kong, China.

Most aircraft using this field were light, single-engine puddle jumpers owned by flight hobbyists, local people who had done well in the car companies, or as automotive suppliers. There was a big skydive and flight training facility with an office building and a large hanger at the far east end of the field, and a few business jets were parked on the ramp for a national rental service based in Owosso's slow-speed economy.

In front of the business jet office, one gleaming new Dassault Falcon 7X whined softly, three muscular engines already hot, its anti-collision lights alternating brightly in the morning half-light.

From the nearby hanger trotted out One.

"Mr. Cloud, welcome," One said, bowing his head slightly as he neared. He reached forward and took Cloud's black duffel bag, but he was waved off when the man reached for Cloud's backpack that contained his weapons and his breakfast.

"As you wish, sir. Please follow me."

The young man spoke with excellent English, no Chinese accent at all. He bounded up the air stair into the aircraft with the lithe grace of a Chinese acrobat, his military physical training on full display.

Inside the aircraft, Cloud automatically looked left through the open door into the flight deck. Two Chinese pilots were going over a checklist. They looked up at their passenger, smiled and nodded. Cloud waved and turned back into the plush cabin. He heard the flight deck door close behind him and lock with a muted click.

Cloud found a plush seat wide enough for almost two people and automatically strapped in. Two approached from the galley carrying a tray with a single drink, his favorite: Lagavulin Islay single-malt scotch, about three fingers tall. She bent at the waist and extended the tray.

"Mr. Cloud, I believe this is your drink."

He took the heavy glass and savored the liquid's aroma, then raised it at Two in a silent toast as she withdrew. He sipped the amber liquid and felt its peaty warmth infuse him.

Two returned a few minutes later with a printed schedule of meals and the inventory of other foods and beverages available during their scheduled non-stop flight time of just under thirteen hours. On the back of the card was a detailed floor plan of the aircraft with an office for crew rest and two lounges, one fitted out as a dining room and another as a full-dress bedroom with TV, shower, movie channels, and video games.

"When do the rest of the passengers arrive?" he asked Two.

As if in reply, the air stair rose on hydraulic cylinders and hissed closed, latching automatically. The engines instantly spooled up and the plane turned for the taxiway.

"There is just crew. You are the only passenger, Mr. Cloud."

CHAPTER FOURTEEN

Every bad precedent originated as a justifiable measure.
Gaius Sallustius Crispus (86-35), Roman historian

Foster Heath Benoit III wheeled his powerful Mercedes sedan out of a long, tree-lined Grosse Pointe driveway, turned right onto Renaud and right again at Lakeshore Drive. Once he crossed from the posh confines of his suburb and onto Detroit's broken pavement, it would become Jefferson Avenue.

Heading to his office in the downtown federal building, he realized the FBI finally was becoming the burden his Grammy said it would become when he joined the Bureau. If he was ever going to launch a political career—his real one, not just office politics—he was going to have to get moving.

The al-Taja case, and the plans around it, would be that ticket out of the gray government office and into a wood-paneled Senatorial suite. He would lead the resolution of this case, or even just seem to have led it, and then leverage that public spotlight into anti-terror, anti-immigrant, pro-law enforcement screeds that would ignite his campaign to higher office in America's fractious political climate.

There were plenty of former FBI agents, CIA analysts, and military types who had leveraged their government careers into private-sector executive suites or plush federal offices, even without the smooth skill

Benoit was bringing to bear toward achieving his goals.

Not to mention a virtually bottomless family treasure chest with which to help pay for it.

The wealthy friends who fluttered in Benoit's orbit often pestered him about his shrewd political ambitions. He was a publicly respected senior federal law enforcement agent, if privately scorned by those who knew him well. He had vast personal wealth, plus that coming to him in future years as parents and older relatives finally died.

His public service *noblesse oblige* had been satisfied, his friends said. Why, they asked him, did he want to squander his best years campaigning for a Washington politician's job when he could much more easily stay home and just be rich? Do good deeds if you like, they said. You have the money, they said.

But Benoit's larger plans included something his friends never considered. It would one day be a lot easier to run for president of the United States if he did it from a seat in the Senate, and not his mother's cushy Grosse Pointe living room filled with obscure, hideously expensive art, certificates of thanks from United Way, and uncomfortable furniture protected with form-fitting plastic slipcovers.

He pressed the phone icon on his steering wheel, spoke a dialing command, and in a moment, the ringing was replaced by a pert female voice.

"Federal Bureau of Investigation, Detroit Field Office. How may I direct your call?"

"Frannie, it's me," Benoit said.

"Good morning, sir!" she said. Poor Frannie Demopolis was young and impressionable, fresh from college only a year ago and hoping to apply to the Bureau one day. Her ambition had led the receptionist to make poor decisions regarding the relationship with her boss. Such a poor decision, in fact, had been made again only the night before.

"Clear my calendar today. Reach out to Anderson at DHS and Prescott at ATF, and let's see if we can get a lunch meeting today. My conference room, 11:30? Bring in lunch from the Rattler."

He made the statement casually, but the two local federal agents who never refused a command performance from their FBI colleague would receive it differently. They believed he was going places, and it seemed to them that keeping Benoit happy now might be good for their careers later.

The Rattlesnake Club on River Place in Detroit was probably one of the two top restaurants in the city, neck and neck with The Whitney over on Woodward but without The Whitney's woody charm. Benoit had hosted many parties at The Rattlesnake Club in private rooms, all paid for as office conferences by the taxpayers. He regularly had his office lunches catered in from there.

Even though a month's exorbitant tab for such meals was far less than a rounding error in his checkbook, it gave him a quiet sense of entitlement to pay for them with a G-card, his government-issued credit card. He didn't drive one of those ratty G-cars he was issued, but the credit card was different.

He was the special agent in charge of one of the top four FBI offices on Earth, and as such, he believed that everything he did was in service to his Bureau and his nation. He believed he was never off duty, which was nearly true. Because he was rarely officially off the time clock, the government credit card was used for nearly everything out of Benoit's heartfelt sense of personal entitlement.

With but few exceptions—his car being one of them—in his private financial dealings he was the opposite, exhibiting the penurious spending habits often associated with very wealthy people that were not understood by people without money.

"Tell them we'll go over the al-Taja matter, and to bring anything new they've learned. Remind Anderson that DHS still owes me their file on al-Taja."

"Yes sir, I'll do that immediately."

He paused. "Are you up for another date tonight?" he asked.

"Yes sir," she whispered. "I'd do that immediately, too."

Demopolis looked slyly around her desk to see if anyone was within earshot. Finding no one, her voice turned into molten lava.

"I'd do it right now in your office, if it didn't have a glass door."

"Excellent!" Benoit said, a little too fast. "I believe your energy and stamina can be put to great use by the FBI, both now and in the future."

He was making a lame joke, the kind an older man will make to a younger woman when he's nervous and trying to sound clever, but starry-eyed Frannie failed to grasp the humor.

She rang off the phone with her boss and speed-dialed the Detroit Department of Homeland Security number, then opened a new window on her computer to download an FBI application at last.

CHAPTER FIFTEEN

Many of life's failures are people who did not
realize how close they were to success when they gave up.
Thomas Alva Edison (1847-1931), American inventor

The Dassault Falcon 7X is a large-cabin, long-range aircraft that can be fitted out in any way a customer can afford. If the customer can afford the jet, customizing the interior is only a matter of choosing fabrics and amenities, not budget.

This particular jet had been configured as a flying executive condo. It could seat and accommodate many in the lounge area, as needed, but the spacious stateroom was designed for just one sleeping VIP passenger. The actual capacity of the large bed could be from one to four, sometimes more. It had been used in those combinations, from time to time. Considering the flight forecast of slightly more than thirteen hours, unbroken by fuel or other stops along the way, Cloud found the stateroom to his immediate liking.

When Two's taut, nude form slipped under the soft sheets with him, Cloud liked that as well.

Two was not a romantic name by any means, but this was a business trip, after all. The woman was lithe and warm, lush of body and alternately aggressive or compliant as needs demanded, moment to moment. Cloud didn't think for a second that her being in bed with him was any less a military expectation by her masters than daily exercise drills. Nevertheless, she presented no threat to him at 37,000 feet other than exhaustion. Cloud found the woman completely artistic and genuine in her hospitality role. He aspired to return as good as he got. It was the gentlemanly thing to do.

Afterward, Cloud wondered whether the sleeping cabin had been wired for eavesdropping like the booth in the Red Flag restaurant had been. He supposed it was, but he didn't care. He hadn't divulged any operational information but, in fact, it was their operation, anyway. In any case, whatever activities any eavesdroppers witnessed or overheard was likely to be beneficial to them in other ways when they returned home to their spouses.

The jet touched down at about two a.m. destination time. Cloud saw in a single glance through the cabin window that they were nowhere near his promised endpoint. The deserted Al Taqaddum airfield outside of Ramadi was as sandy and deserted as he remembered it back when he and his battle buddies called it simply TQ.

The plane slowed to the end of the runway and turned toward the taxiway, meeting a battered white Toyota gun truck that materialized from the darkness with soft yellow lights crudely wire-tied on the tailgate. The jet fell in behind and followed it. There is no terminal here.

When Cloud looked out of the window as the plane turned, he saw The Beachhouse still stood off the end of the air strip. That's what the Americans had called it. The signage on the beat-up former American maintenance building had been scrawled over in Arabic graffiti. The scorched hulk of a blackened Chevy crewcab pickup truck crouched on its charred steel wheels in the sand in front of the building. It was covered in more spray-painted Arabic. None of it was complimentary.

The airplane rolled to a halt and the engines were switched off. It was only a few seconds before someone on the tarmac plugged in ground power from a truck-mounted APU and the air conditioning resumed. The gesture was hollow, because even in the sleeping cabin where he finished dressing, Cloud heard the hydraulic whine of the air stair unfolding toward the sun-blasted asphalt.

Cloud came down the steps behind One and followed by Two. There were two American-built Humvees and an old International Harvester cargo truck waiting, and men with ready weapons were arrayed all around the near perimeter facing away from the plane. Facing away was good, the warrior thought.

That meant they were there to protect him, not detain him.

The originally desert tan U.S. Humvees had been sloppily repainted in ISIS white. They didn't look too bad from fifty feet in the dark. Each flew the oversize black and white ISIS flag. A soldier with a slung rifle stepped forward and lowered the checkered *keffiyeh* scarf from his face. He was Chinese.

"*SabaaH al-khayr!*" the man said in Arabic. Good morning. He reached out and shook hands with Cloud with a tight, mannerly grin. "How was your flight, Mr. Cloud?"

"It was superlative," Cloud said truthfully. "*Mutašakkir 'awi.*" Thanks very much.

"I am Commander Xing Chung," the soldier said. "Call me Chuck. Your Arabic is very good, sir."

"Zave. As is yours, commander—Chuck. And your English, too."

"Yes, thanks." His face hardened like a cold wind had swept across it. "Stanford. Like my sister."

The man looked like any other common Arab soldier as long as the *keffiyeh* obscured his face. There is abundant Asian DNA in the Middle East gene pool to account for his somewhat almond-shaped eyes. He could well have been a very passable Kazakh.

His all-black uniform and balaclava marked him as a senior ISIS commander, so that uniform and his language skills would probably satisfy any thinly spaced ISIS rabble they might encounter. If not, AK-47s would.

Obviously, this wasn't the man's first rodeo.

"Commander Xing, huh? I think we have friends in common, but rather poor direction finding. We were supposed to liberate my money before we liberate your sister."

The soldier grimaced with slight guilt. "Yes, my father is a popular *restaurateur* in America. I haven't seen him in many years, though I am the grateful beneficiary of his personal and professional benevolence."

As he spoke, Xing tilted his head forward in respect to his father and senior officer. He looked left and right, waved an arm in the air and spoke in rapid-fire Chinese to his aide, who loudly commanded the group in Chinese, Farsi, and Urdu to mount the vehicles.

"As for your location ... if you please, Mr. Clou—ah, Zave—we must depart this area now. We have secured this airfield for your landing, but the period of assured protection is brief."

Behind them, a soldier disengaged a fuel truck's thick rubber hose from the aircraft's fueling port and the Falcon's engines started turning and burning. Xing gave a crisp salute to the pilot, who returned it just as sharply.

Two scampered into the plane with a smile and a shy wave at Cloud, and the Falcon taxied toward the runway threshold even as the air stair rose. The jet stood on its brakes long enough for the throttles to be pushed forward, and then it accelerated hard, took off like a fighter jet and ascended steeply. In seconds, it was gone.

Xing turned back to Cloud. "We're only about thirty klicks from Ramadi here, but that's as the crow flies. And since we have no helos here, we are not going as direct as the crow does."

He looked to see that all his men had returned to their vehicles as he and Cloud climbed into the back of the second Humvee, then told his driver to radio the move-out command. Led by the first Humvee security vehicle and followed by the fuel truck and the cargo truck loaded with the rest of the soldiers, the convoy moved out smartly.

The vehicles didn't go directly into Ramadi, but to an abandoned fish farm off the main Ramadi road on the outskirts of town where the Chinese irregulars had established their base. When the vehicles approached the dilapidated complex, camouflaged soldiers rose from nowhere like ghosts and opened a gate, admitting the convoy. Once through, they closed and secured the worn gate as if it had never been disturbed and used brush to whisk away the tire tracks. Then they too disappeared back into hiding places where they stood invisible guard.

After the constant wind blew for a few minutes, there would be no trace of vehicles ever passing through here.

The truck and the Humvees drove straight under a wide and deep canvas canopy indistinguishable from the sand. The trucks turned, backed tactically into individual stalls and the drivers shut down the diesel engines. A large cover made from the same sand-patterned fabric was drawn across the broad opening.

Unless someone almost literally stumbled upon the location, Cloud and his new friends were one with the landscape and undetectable.

Around a table made from an old American military cable spool, Xing and Cloud held glasses filled with Maker's Mark bourbon. A bottle stood half empty on the table next to a small and dimmed electric lamp.

"Disregarding that I have a deal with General Xing," Cloud said, using the man's rank purposely, "you are obviously his subordinate in all respects. How do you propose to change his deal with me now?"

"I do not propose to change it," Xing said. "I only suggest that the deal may be changed by you, if you see fit to do so."

Xing looked for inspiration in his glass, unconvinced by his own words, and then sipped its contents.

"My sister is not a soldier, Xavier. She is not a damned *combatant*. She is a college kid who only wanted to have a college kid's adventure with a semester of study in Poland. She was abducted by these ISIS animals and is being held hostage for suitcase nukes."

Xing looked up. Anger and fierce resolve diffused his face.

"*Nukes*. What are these goat-herding assholes going to do with a god-damned nuke? Only something bad. Yes, we are quite a way from the Hindu Kush and your money. Ramadi is just a few kilometers down the road. If you thought it made more sense to get my sister first, since we're here, I would not object to that."

Xing paused.

"However, we are honorable and flexible people. If you prefer your original arrangement, I can have the plane back in one hour. Time enough to finish our drinks." He raised his glass and tipped it in salute to Cloud, then drained the glass. "By this time tomorrow, you could be a rich man. A very rich man." Cloud looked at the man unimpressed.

"You two sandbagged me. This was no navigational error. You know perfectly well that my money is nearly two-fucking-thousand miles from here. Your airplane flew here direct. You and your father knew what you were going to do from the beginning." He took a breath, suppressing anger that boiled up inside of him.

"Everything for the rescue can be made ready quickly," Xing said. "We are almost ready now, in fact. The same people who are going to help us get your cash are helping us get my sister back. We're only changing the order. We can pay them when we get back from Pakistan."

"Pricks," Cloud said. He hated chaos. It was so unreliable. "Were you lying before, or are you lying now? Or both? How do I know you won't slit my damned throat and push me out of that fucking jet once we get your sister back—and then retire on my money?"

Cloud forced himself to become calm.

"And why am I involved in the first place? From what I've seen so far, you have ample resources to rescue your sister without my input. Are you guys just in it with me for the freelance money?"

Xing was impassive. "Yes, in part. It is considerable, after all, and we Chinese are nothing if not a pragmatic people. We will pay our contractors with the money you pay us, because my military superiors would never approve such an off-the-books program. And as my father has discussed with you, if a People's Liberation Army soldier is caught or killed on this mission, it could be considered an act of war by Iraq.

"We don't care if ISIS declares war on us, but they have friends in Iran, even Russia. They are bugs, but still dangerous bugs. Any complications here will make my superiors quite nervous if they must explain our unauthorized actions to our political leaders." He paused. "Or to yours."

Cloud well understood how intractable politicians could be. It didn't matter what language they spoke. They were most often all cut from the same ass-covering, blame-storming camouflage cloth.

"And, we will be there for you because we are still partners. Once we get my sister back alive, nothing on the planet can stop us from retrieving your money."

Cloud noted the subtle qualifier: *Alive.*

"We can't give up now, Zave," Xing said. "We're so close. *So* close. The house where my sister is being held is less than twenty kilometers from here. You could hit it with a decent-size artillery shell. She is there. She is within our grasp. These ISIS donkeys have IQs about three points above plant life, so one of my soldiers equals ten or more of theirs. And we have additional local contractor forces who are well experienced and quite good. We have superior firepower and tactics. And I assure you that I have the will to win. We only need to go in and get her."

Cloud knew he had no choice but to get the sister first, because otherwise he was screwed. The Chinese could just abandon him in the desert or, worse, turn him over to ISIS as an American soldier in exchange for Xing's sister. What a handsome party favor that would make.

"I didn't see a whole lot of manpower out there on the airfield."

Cloud's implied question told Xing that the changed deal was agreed to. Or Cloud would have told him to fuck off, and might even have reached across the informal little table and tried to kill him.

"We can't storm a defended position of that importance with a few exercise freaks, some pop guns and harsh language," Cloud said. "Don't you have anything else?"

Xing smiled a genuine smile at Cloud for the first time. He motioned toward the fabric-covered exit from the enclosure.

"Let's take a walk."

CHAPTER SIXTEEN

It is not a sign of arrogance for the
king to rule. That is what he is there for.
William F. Buckley (1925-2008), American commentator

Around the Detroit FBI conference table sat Conrad Anderson from the Department of Homeland Security and Pete Prescott of the Bureau of Alcohol, Tobacco, Firearms and Explosives, commonly abbreviated as ATF. In the center of the heavy table sat their sumptuous four-course lunch from highly regarded The Rattlesnake Club, now decanted from its pedestrian foam carry-out boxes onto adequate ceramic plates and bowls accompanied by decent cutlery and linen napkins.

The men made small talk while Frannie Demopolis filled their plates with food and served each guest on either side of the long conference table, with Benoit at the end. His colleagues would face the glass windows that looked out upon the Detroit skyline, but Benoit knew the incoming sun glancing off the windows of a nearby office tower would nearly blind them at their seats this time of day, a subtle but effective subliminal reinforcement of his superiority.

The whole conversation would be uncomfortable for his guests and untroubled for only him. The men took their places. Anderson, squinting against the sun, skated a thick manila file across the polished table to his host.

"This is your copy of the entire DHS portfolio on Mohammed al-Taja,

Foster. We provided it to CIA too, by request. But here is the Reader's Digest version."

Anderson reached forward and took a long swallow of a Heineken beer that Benoit provided for the lunch. He flipped open the cover of his copy of the record.

"He joined DHS out of NSA, which he joined right out of the Navy. We had him for six years and change, almost all of it undercover here and there looking for terrorist douchebags. He's ethnic Arab, and speaks Urdu, Farsi, French, German, and some North African dialects like a native. NSA wouldn't say directly even to us, but he was there less than ten years, looks like; and he was seventeen years in the Navy. He's from Dearborn, born and raised, second generation Jordanian; mother was from Cyprus, father from Raifoon but grew up in Beirut. Parents killed in a traffic accident in 1998 ..." Anderson flipped a few pages. "... in DC. Fuckin' Beltway.

"He graduated from Edsel Ford High School, went to University of Michigan on the Dearborn campus for two years and then finished at Ann Arbor. Was Navy ROTC."

Anderson stopped for a bite of his steak. He liked it "black and blue" style—essentially raw, so rare it looked as if it had only been waved over the fire a few times. Anderson thought that marked him as a tough guy, but the tens of pounds of fat around his middle made that a lie.

"He had undergrad and master's degrees in Middle Eastern and North African Studies. Did his postgrad in regional security studies at the Navy Postgraduate School in Monterey. No wonder NSA wanted him. Same reasons we did, plus his NSA time." Anderson dove back into the juicy steak.

"Why only seventeen Navy years?" Benoit asked. "That close, you're really on the glideslope to full retirement at twenty. He must have been, what? A commander by then?"

Anderson raised a blue-tabbed a page and nodded. "Yep, O-5. On the short list for full-bird Navy Captain. He was a fast mover. Probably had a star or three in his future. Navy Intel is a real growth business."

"So why does a hard charger like that dump everything and leave the Navy only a handful of years away from his full and copious active-duty pension, free medical care for life, and the love and appreciation of a grateful nation? Still with plenty of time left to do whatever it was he left the Navy early to do? What pulled him away from all that, after all the time he'd devoted to achieving it?"

Why indeed? Anderson thought. Something in this al-Taja thing didn't pass the smell test, and it might get smellier before long. If Anderson's career arc was going to benefit from Benoit's trajectory, he needed a flexible buffer between Benoit and the potential ramifications of this odd investigation. If it went well, Benoit still was the senior man on the case and would reap the lion's share of the glory and acclaim, as he always did. That would cascade down to Anderson.

Anderson said, "Foster, maybe you might consider leaving the case agent on this a while longer?" Benoit turned toward Anderson. "The street agent can do more excavation, get more solid evidence, and then you can supervise the resolution to its natural and successful conclusion."

Anderson put the "toad" in *toady.*

But if the case went to shit, Benoit needed someone to insulate him—and thus Anderson—from the stench of failure. Some fall guy to take the blame.

And it didn't have to be a guy.

Benoit reached forward to the intercom button on the conference table speakerphone.

"Yes, sir?" Frannie answered instantly.

"Frannie, ask Special Agent Watson to join us, please."

There were three precise taps on the conference room door, and Benoit asked Amber to come in. She walked to the head of the table where the three agency SACs were having lunch and automatically assumed an easy military parade rest position, feet apart at shoulder width and hands behind her back at the belt line, thumb crossed over thumb. Benoit grinned appreciatively at this autonomic show of courtesy.

"As you were, Watson," he said genially. Benoit had no meaningful military background. When he was sent home only four months into his

plebe year at West Point, the Commandant had told him with some consternation, "Mr. Benoit, you are the most *non-military* person I have ever
met." But Benoit still enjoyed using some of its terminology, much of it
picked up from watching war movies on the Turner Classic Movies channel.

"Please join us. We must pick your brain." He gestured at the food still
warm and steaming on the table. "Have you had luncheon? We have plenty."

"Thank you, sir, but no thank you. I've eaten."

"A drink, then." It wasn't a question.

Conceding to his persistence, Amber went to the bar cart and withdrew a small bottle of Dasani water from the oversize ice bucket, drying
it on a red-striped white bar towel hanging from the cart handle. Benoit
waved her over to the chair next to Prescott.

"You know Prescott and Anderson? ATF and DHS?"

"Yes sir, we've met. Good to see you again, sirs." She smiled warmly at
each man as they rose and shook her hand across the table. Amber pulled
out the chair and took her seat.

"So, how may I help you?" she asked.

How indeed, Benoit thought. "The al-Taja homicide case."

Benoit, a lawyer by education but who had never practiced, still adhered
to the first rule of lawyering, policing, and parenting: Never ask a question
for which you don't already know the answer—and never one that can be
answered with a simple yes or no.

But this wasn't a question, really, just her boss's inscrutable way to
open the discussion while remaining above the pedestrian need to ask
his subordinate for anything.

"Yes, sir," Amber said. "As you know, the JTF was on that from the
crime scene. We experienced some small difficulty obtaining information
about the victim from some of his employers"—she avoided looking at
Anderson from DHS—"but we got it sorted out. We were really just getting
the case off the ground when you acquired it for supervisory screening."

The FBI SAC was many things, but one of his most refined skills
was his judgment of character. He knew his street agent was trying not
to sound as pissy as she was feeling about having had her big case taken
away from her.

"Yes, well. I have indeed screened the file and the case documents. There are many aspects of this case that mark it as rather different from a standard homicide, don't you agree?"

No shit, Sherlock, Amber said in her head, but Benoit continued to speak.

"I think you and your DPD partner have done a commendable job with it thus far. Commendable job. I'd like you to stay on this case, in the near term, at least. Keep me in the loop as developments warrant."

Amber sat stock still for a moment, not sure whether this was some elaborate prank Benoit was hatching in front of the SACs from DHS and ATF, more to embarrass her when the inevitable lame point was made.

"Pardon me, sir?"

"I'd like you to resume primary responsibility for the al-Taja case, Special Agent Watson," Benoit said. He smiled, but his tone had gotten a little crispy.

The woman should be jumping for joy over her little perceived victory, he thought, and he hated having to say things more than once. It was a lesson learned from a Mormon father at the end of a leather belt with a thick steel buckle. The middle finger on his left hand still nerve-twinged occasionally, damage from using the hand one time to protect his behind from a vicious beating.

"Log in on the case in SENTINEL and check it back out; I've reassigned it to you. Retain me as the supervisor on it. Keep me informed. Let me know if you need anything."

SENTINEL is the FBI's electronic case management system. Amber had been locked out of the file after Benoit took control of the case.

Benoit looked at Watson as if she was a pet. Why wasn't his employee obeying?

"Please proceed, special agent."

Amber sat for just a moment longer, then jumped up before Benoit could change his mind.

"Yes, sir. Understood, sir," she said evenly, heading for the door. Her fancy water was left behind, unopened, dripping beads of condensation onto the expensive wooden table.

CHAPTER SEVENTEEN

A lot of truth is said in jest.
Eminem (1972-), American musician

"Are you fucking kidding me right now?" Tracey screamed into her phone.

"This is no shit!" Amber screamed back. She was thrilled to know her career would probably end on the high note this case was likely to generate. "We need to get productive before the NTAC changes his mind. When is the goddamned M.E. going to email the autopsy? Wait, screw that. Where is Ballistics on the bullet?"

"Damned if I know," Tracey said. She was as excited for herself as for Amber. If her partner was being allowed to keep the al-Taja case, that meant Amber's boss—the No Talent Ass Clown—wasn't calling Tracey's Chief to demand jurisdiction. That meant she stayed on the case, too.

"Scoot over here and get me and we'll go over to the lab ourownselves," Tracey said.

"On the way."

✪

Since the Detroit Police Forensics Lab closed in 2008 under a scandal of gross incompetence, the DPD forensics work was farmed out to the network of seven Michigan State Police labs, including all the firearms work. DPD used the MSP lab in Northville Township, about twenty-five minutes across I-96 from the DPD headquarters.

Tracey had a contact there and pinged on her by text to see if her schedule could stand an official visit. Within seconds *come on over i have donuts* was texted back, including little chocolate emoji donuts and coffee cups, and a smiley face with heart eyes. Minutes later, Amber and Tracey were headed to the Northville State Police forensics lab and its commander, Lieutenant Adriana Hero.

Growing up, Adri Hero had taken plenty of abuse over her proud Greek name from kids in school—but it was nothing compared to the drilling she sustained once she'd signed up for police work. Just try going to the state police academy in Lansing with a recruit nametag that screams *HERO*.

Lieutenant Hero looked up when she heard three soft taps on the door glass and waved in Tracey and Amber.

"*Hay yooou!*" she drawled, her standard greeting. Adri's Greek heritage had given some ground to her upbringing in suburban Atlanta. The beguiling southern accent bubbled out of her like soft waves of honey and music.

Adri came around her desk, and she and Tracey embraced warmly. Tracey had never been quite sure about the sexual tension that seemed to exist between her and Adri, but she had admitted to Amber that she enjoyed the ambiguity. Forewarned, Amber went in for just a firm handshake of her own.

"Adri, Special Agent Amber Watson, FBI. Amber, Lieutenant Adrianna Hero, Michigan State Police. The one and only. Lab commander."

"Pleasure," Amber said.

Adri nodded and smiled. "Same here. I've seen your name on a case report or three."

"In fact, that's why we came over," Amber said. "You have a ballistics report on a bullet found in the crushed skull of Mohammed al-Taja, a.k.a. The Well-Dressed Guy."

Adri reached for a folder on her desk. "Yeah, I pulled it when Tracey said you guys were coming over about it." She sat back down in her chair and spread the pages out across her desk. "Y'want the short version? He was already dead when he hit the sidewalk, is what the M.E. thinks. Me, too. Have you read this autopsy report yet?" Adri pointed to a page with her longish red index fingernail.

"Um, not yet," Tracey said, using her hand to cover a comical *Oh shit!* smirk to Amber behind Adri's back. "I think it must be in my email."

"Well, no problem, bud. I printed this out for you guys, anyway. The M.E. found symmetrical stippling around a contact wound on the back of al-Taja's head. No exit wound, so that says something about the load. We thought the round was probably custom-made for close-in work, if you know what I mean."

They did: *Assassination.*

"We checked the rounds remaining in the clip, and the low-power theory was confirmed. Doc did find the bullet when he went into the skull. Evidently your killer put his gun to your guy's head, shot him, and then tossed him head-first over the edge of the City-County Building, figuring if he hit the fall right, the crumpled head would cover up the shooting. Almost did, too, seems like."

Adri raised a small clear-plastic Ziploc bag sealed with red evidence tape.

"This is the bullet."

She raised a second bag. It held the prettiest little all-pink Kel-Tec .380 you ever did see.

"And turns out, we already had the gun that fired it."

Tracey swore. "Christ on a *fucking cracker.*"

It was the same weapon The Grim Reaper had recovered from his gangbanger traffic stop.

She lunged for her iPhone and dialed the downtown lockup while looking over the ballistics report on the gun. The name of the gangbanger Jeff O'Brien had arrested on the speeding charge was Liam Cortez Williams. No wonder he used Liam. Who names their kid William Williams?

What she didn't know was whether Williams had been charged with the two guns and weed found in his car at impound.

Sometimes, especially following minor primary charges like a traffic beef, proposed gun or other charges lagged for days or even weeks in the prosecutor's office if the connection to the suspect wasn't perfect, or if the suspect had a bitchy lawyer who was certain to drag out search warrant protests, chain of custody gripes, and maybe the influence of the Moon.

It didn't help that The Grim Reaper was occasionally resourceful in his policing and report writing. All in the greater cause of justice, you understand, but sometimes not as strictly legal as the justice system yearns for.

If he had not been charged with the guns found coincident with the traffic stop, chances were better than even that William Cortez Williams was already in the wind, with or without a lawyer. Non-violent offenders got big slack at the Wayne County jail anymore. Overcrowding was the rule on good days, and there was no overtime money for extra deputies. So, you didn't have warrants or kill somebody, you usually walked.

William Cortez Williams may have either killed The Well-Dressed Guy, or he knew who did. Or he knew someone who knew who did the killing. Tracey had to locate Williams and hold him to find out, and she might already be out of luck.

There were few days on Tracey's calendar when she felt like she was dropping the ball. Suddenly, this seemed like it was going to be one of those days.

The phone rang downtown at the Wayne County Jail on Clinton Street. "WayneCountyJailDeputyFelixHowMayIDirectYoCall?" asked the bored deputy answering the phone in one breathless statement.

"Jesus, Felix, I'm so glad it's you," Tracey said. "You got a guy on a traffic arrest, William Cortez Williams, probably booked as Liam Cortez Williams. Please, for the love of the smiling Christ, tell me you still have him."

"Who this?" Felix said, and paused for a moment. "Naw Tracey, I'm just playin'. I know it's you, hon. Hold on, lemme look."

Tracey could hear thick fingers tapping uncertainly on his computer keyboard. Few sheriff's deputies were notable for their clerical skills. Not even the clerks.

Holding her hand over the cellphone mic, Tracey whispered to Amber, *How fast can we get down to the new jail?*

Corvette Watson reached into a pocket for her ignition key and she smirked. "Are you kidding? We're halfway there right now."

There were some muffled sounds of talking as Felix covered the phone with his hand and told another man what he wanted from Greektown for lunch. He continued to hunt and peck the keyboard with one agonizingly slow hand.

"Oh, okay," Felix said into the phone. "Yeah, here we go. We got him, hon. For a minute, anyway. You know we can't keep nobody but damn serial killers anymore, anyways. He s'posed to be released in, like, fifteen minutes or somethin' like that. Him an' his asshole lawyer doin' the paperwork for his bond-out right now."

Felix didn't know whom William Cortez Williams had gotten as his lawyer. He just thought all lawyers were assholes.

Tracey yelled into the phone, "You *hold* that son of a bitch, Felix, do you hear me? You *fucking hold that man* until I get there!" and then she sprinted with Amber for the door. On the other end of the call, Deputy Felix pulled the receiver away from his head.

"Hello? Hel-*lo?*" he said. "Well, okay then." Then he hung up.

"Uh, buh-bye," Adri said to her empty office.

The two women jumped into the police Corvette. Amber buckled her seatbelt and ordered Tracey to do the same while inserting and twisting the ignition key.

She released the parking brake and shifted into Reverse in one smooth motion, then back into first gear before the car stopped rolling backwards. She dropped the clutch hard and the big Chevy V-8 howled like an angry prehistoric beast.

The smoky burnout she laid in the police crime lab parking lot was as good as any NASCAR victory dance in the last ten years.

Amber ignited all of the Vette's many emergency red and blue lights and ignited the electronic siren. Traffic was light, fortunately. Still, the non-standard police car got many startled looks when it flashed past the obligingly stopped traffic.

Once onto the interstate and headed back downtown, Amber wished she'd had time to raise the convertible top. At a hundred and thirty-five miles per hour, the wind whipping their hair was fierce. Tracey leaned in under the windshield for a little protection and gathered her red hair close around her head with both hands.

This time of mid-morning, the commuters were already at work and expressway traffic was blissfully sparse. As the speedo climbed above one-forty, Amber leaned over toward Tracey and shouted at the top of her lungs, *"This makes my dick hard!"*

They both laughed. Police work could be such a blast.

The Corvette rocketed into the jail's official-vehicle parking area and skidded to a stop, brakes glowing red hot and wisps of smoke rising from the wheel wells.

"Go-go-go!" Amber shouted at Tracey, who vaulted from the car and ran into the Wayne County Jail. Thirteen minutes, door to door. Not too shabby.

Tracey ran directly to the office where Deputy Alvin Felix would be found.

"Fe-Felix," she gasped, out of breath. "My, my guy. Where's my guy?"

"Oh, Mr. Williams? I believe he's waiting for you down in reception. Gimme some, girl."

Felix grinned his best self-satisfied grin and raised a palm that Tracey high-fived.

Cooperation with more important officers in the law enforcement continuum could help get a guy out of dreary lockup duty and onto the street doing actual police work, if a guy played his cards right. Felix was going to the gym and had already dropped twenty-six pounds. He'd had his uniforms taken in twice. He intended to wear them in a patrol car one day soon.

"Thank you, *Jesus*," Tracey said. She gave Felix a powerful hug that he would shamelessly brag about later.

Felix walked Tracey down to the reception area on the public side because it was closer and faster than having to negotiate the internal maze of locked doors and hallways.

The so-called Reception space was a full-duplex room. Suspects were sometimes brought in this way, but it was also used to check in visiting friends and family members who arrived to see prisoners, and it was the route back to the street for prisoners being released or bonded out.

Inbound or out, it was just a big waiting room that still reeked of cigarettes and despair, though smoking there had been prohibited for many years. There still was no way to alleviate the despair.

They appeared at the admin window and Felix rapped on the thick Plexiglas partition with the old Cass Tech high school ring he still wore proudly, though the ring threatened to submerge in Felix's fleshy, sausage-like finger.

"Yo man, where William Cortez Williams at?"

"Who?" Deputy Bobby Stankowski asked. His nickname was Stank because Bobby just stank. Thin wisps of dull, mouse-brown beard failed to disguise the acne that scourged his pale skin. Nothing, evidently, could disguise his body odor.

"William. Cortez. Williams," Felix said, like talking to a child. "I sent you an email about keepin' him until Sergeant Lexcellent got here?" Stank returned an uncomprehending stare. "From Homicide? Your inbox?"

"Email?" Stank said with distrust. "My inbox?"

He poked at his computer. Even from her side of the partition, Tracey could see the tired old terminal was hardly more than a boat anchor. And the deputy was no brain trust.

"I ain't got no damn email, bro," Stank said.

"Hey look, just scroll—" Felix got agitated with his colleague's embarrassing ineptitude in front of Tracey. "Look dude, just buzz us in, man."

A loud vibrating sound told them the door to the admin office was now unlocked and they could enter. Tracey felt an acidic bowling ball mature in her stomach. That was going to stomp her ulcer into a bloody puddle if it kept up.

Felix put his big paw on Stank's shoulder. "Lemme in there, man," he growled. He kept his head turned away from the clerk.

Stank stood back. Felix reached over and pushed a key labeled PAGE DN and a whole new screen of email messages was pulled up. Felix's note was right at the top, the Subject line STOP RELEASE ORDER WILLIAMS,

WILLIAM C in all capital letters.

It had been pushed down and off the screen by other incoming emails. There were other pages of administrative communications that had also never been read, acknowledged, nor acted upon, going back weeks.

"Oh, no shit!" Ivey said. "I neva knew that was there."

"Okaaay, deputy, now you do," Tracey said, leaning in. She wondered how this man was allowed to carry a loaded duty weapon. Fury smoldered on her fair, freckled skin. Ignoring his aroma, her hands trembled when she raised them to caress Stank's round, oblivious face.

"Where is he?" she asked with a fake, twitching smile. "Where the hell is Williams?"

That cartoon light bulb must have winked on in his head.

"Liam Williams? He gone, man. Asshole lawyer took him out just before you two walked up."

Tracey considered lowering her soft hands down to Stank's oily, pencil-thin neck.

"You're that cute girl from Homicide, right? JTF-type? What that's like?"

Amber arrived in the office then from the official side. She took one look at Tracey and put both hands lightly on her friend's right arm, because Tracey wasn't much of a puncher with her left.

Gently, then with increasing volume, Tracey asked, "Deputy Stankowski, may I please see *the fucking paperwork?*"

CHAPTER EIGHTEEN

We are going to have peace even if we have to fight for it.
Dwight D. Eisenhower (1890-1969)
U.S. general & 34th President of the United States

A summer day in New York City is glorious. In Times Square, tourists walk the streets with eyes wide in wonder, pickpockets get paid, and half-crazy people in cartoon costumes extort offerings from anxious tourist parents whose children can't resist having a photo taken with a fake SpongeBob or pretend Captain America or a simulated Statue of Liberty.

Many of the moms preferred the so-called Naked Cowboy, though he wore briefs no smaller than a swim suit.

There is no better location in America, in the very midst of commotion, clamor, and chaos, to have a private conversation.

A stocky, clean-shaven man in an untucked yellow cotton shirt sat on a bench. He read *The New York Post*. A woman approached and sat on the bench.

"A nice day," she said. Her mild Yiddish lilt easily penetrated the background din of the city this close to the man.

From behind his newspaper, the stocky man said, "It is possible that it will rain soon."

"The radio said the sun would rise one day as well, maybe in ten days."

"My daughter-in-law, Cynthia, says the Yankees will win the pennant."

"All things are possible," the woman replied. She heaved a deep sigh, sad and resigned. "But I believe night follows day." She rose and looked down at the man. He regarded her over the top of his newspaper. "Anyway, that's what the radio says."

The woman smiled, nodded goodbye to the man, and walked away. The stocky man finished the comics, folded the newspaper, and tossed it into a trash barrel. He strode to a waiting sedan, its engine running, and spoke to the driver.

"Let's hit it," he said. The car leaped away from the curb while the stocky man punched numbers into a secure encrypted cellphone.

✪

"She said that, huh? Ten days, maybe?" Army General John Glenn McCandless asked. The stocky man in the untucked yellow cotton shirt, CIA senior manager Poppy Benedict, nodded and spoke with authority.

"I used the code word—CynthIA. She friggin' knew I was CIA. When I told her we were ready to drop bombs on all the remaining ISIS locations, she didn't bat an eye about the 'rain.' And she said the bomb-blast 'sun'—the suitcase nuke—could rise in maybe ten days. I told her the Yankees would win the pennant, that we were going to prevail in this thing, but again, it didn't register. She used the code word 'black' for ISIS, that black follows day. ISIS black triumphs over 'day,' over good. Over us. 'That's what the radio says,' she said. They're obviously running a Mossad numbers station and she's getting coded info by shortwave radio."

Benedict paused. This kind of intermural agency cat-and-mouse crap made him crazy.

"But if they are telling us that way, via some random-ass freelance agent on the street, why not tell us directly? It's because there's something they *aren't* telling us—but it might also be because the celebrated Mossad moles have their heads up their clandestine asses. I'm going with that."

There was no mistake. Benedict had recorded the entire exchange. They listened to it a half-dozen times and the message was clear.

The pain was coming.

An ISIS cell in the United States expected to have a nuclear device in hand within ten days, and the terrorists would detonate it. The Americans didn't know where.

"That's all she said, huh? Christ, I hate all this cloak and dagger bull-shit," General McCandless said, pacing the room. "That's what *you* do. I wanna find targets and blow the hell out of them. That's what *I* do."

The general walked over to a large map thrown on the conference room wall by a digital projector hung from the ceiling. The digital map was covered with symbols showing Russian and Iranian forces and proxies in Syria, Americans in a few key locations, Kurds, various warlords and rebel groups supported by either the CIA or the Pentagon, and a diminishing swath of red slashes marking ISIS concentrations across the Middle East. Black stars enclosed in circles marked the locations of every secret ISIS and Taliban training camp, headquarters, supply dump—the works.

There was a growing Russian presence on a few Syrian bases now, and they were a mounting, troublesome factor prone to be uncooperative.

The map changed every day. The red ISIS areas ebbed and flowed, usually smaller, but never absent from the plot. Taliban influence was growing. No U.S. politician had been willing to do more than lob a few bombs at these people, so they and their violence spread like a virus, person to person, village to village, month after month.

And though they were hardly effective today, ISIS business managers had collected gigantic stockpiles of cash from illicit oil sales, most of it still missing. It was only a matter of time before they coerced the Chinese general in Dearborn to give up a Mad Gopher, or paid someone else to sell them a device from a nuclear state's arsenal.

Such transactions were the final validation that money truly is the root of all evil.

The CIA knew Xing Jianjun's daughter had been kidnapped as lever-age on the retired PLA general, intending to force him to use contacts to obtain one of China's small construction nuclear devices, the so-called Mad Gopher.

The kidnapped daughter wasn't even a real factor, just a distraction, though if the gambit paid off in a suitcase nuke, ISIS would certainly make that deal.

Such a convoluted plan was not likely to bear fruit. But there were other avenues for such weapons.

An ISIS cell could put so much cubic money on the table that a key official or military officer in, say, the Pakistani nuclear structure, might be persuaded to give up a really big bomb or two. Such plans were already on the bad guys' to-do list, in fact, General McCandless knew.

McCandless knew which foreign military officers were on the ISIS call-back list, too.

What he and his military-contractor-spymaster task force did not know was how their secret ace in the hole might come through for them. Too many variables, not enough time.

Shit or get off the pot, the general's father had often said to him in times of indecision. It was time to decide.

General McCandless turned to his ever-present aide de camp, Army Major Tommy Crosby.

"Get the car, Tommy. We have places to go and people to see."

The aide vanished down to the parking garage to retrieve McCandless's war wagon and escorts, an up-armored black Chevy Suburban operated and manned by Defense Intelligence Agency body men.

The heavily armed DIA guys were a protective services team to safe-guard the general, but with fewer restrictions these days in their rules of engagement. Every one of them had been former active duty special operators, most of them known to the general personally. They would mess you up and then happily go to lunch.

Their sole obligation was, to coin a phrase, make that other dumb bastard die for *his* country.

General McCandless grabbed his cover and lodged it on his head at a rakish, dramatic angle, and shook hands all around as he made to depart. The man could be a thorn in your ass, but he could be a bigger thorn in the bad guys' asses.

He had the unlimited black bank account of the SECDEF and the atten-tive pink ear of the President of the United States. Everyone in the clan-destine program thought that was a fair trade for his rare cranky days.

"Jeez, ten days. Maybe less," McCandless fumed. "Well, gentlemen, that focuses our intentions, doesn't it? I'm going to see the president, because we have some decisions to make. Either you get your program rolling in one quick hurry, or I'm going to get mine rolling. Mine will be a metric shit-ton messier, but I guarantee you it will be highly effective. One way or the other, we need this thing resolved, and fast."

If Poppy Benedict couldn't use his angles to interdict the ISIS plan to acquire a small nuclear device—and this wasn't the only serious threat Benedict was dealing with—General McCandless and his coalition partners were going to send squadrons of bombers to obliterate every known ISIS and Taliban headquarters, ammo dump, and training camp in one big raid, and Russians and the United Nations be damned.

The plan was called *Operation Clean Slate*. Special forces would parachute in to mop up and secure flattened areas until local order could be restored with follow-on coalition ground troops. McCandless had promised it would be messy—militarily, logistically, and especially politically. It was the understatement of the year.

The general turned and departed, closing the heavy insulated and soundproof door that locked audibly behind him. In the hallway, a red light with the words ROOM IN USE–DO NOT ENTER lit back up.

Benedict slapped the table and spoke to the room full of silent, wondering people.

"Okay folks, you heard the man. That is our green light, and I'm authorizing the Go code right now. Let's get our program rolling—as the general said, in one quick hurry."

He turned to a uniformed Navy lieutenant standing nearby, one of those new Signals nerds whose name he didn't know yet.

"Send our guy the go-ahead tones."

CHAPTER NINETEEN

I know not with what weapons World War III will be fought,
but World War IV will be fought with sticks and stones.
Albert Einstein (1879-1955), theoretical physicist

Chuck Xing put the brown liquor bottle back into a small map case of his other personal effects and led Xavier Cloud outside and down into a hidden opening in the hillside. After fewer than thirty steps, they walked through another door in the hillside that Xing secured behind them. Inside the space was an electronic showcase of breathtaking Chinese might and ingenuity.

The situation inside the below-ground bunker was rather pleasant. The computers and high-tech communication gear needed to be chilled to a consistent low temperature to function at their best, and the long hours the Chinese pilots spent in their combat chairs meant the rest and food areas were first-class, since no one was permitted to leave during the duty shift.

Cloud looked over the shoulders of Chinese drone drivers and watched the crisp video displays showing high-resolution, full-color imagery of Ramadi courtesy of China's CH-4 Rainbow unmanned aerial vehicle. The Rainbow is a powerful armed drone on the order of the American military's fierce MQ-9 Reaper drone, whose physical design and mission profile the Rainbow was designed to mimic. The Rainbow was new to China's inventory. Its secret deployment to Iraq, by way of General Xing's backchannels, was its first combat mission.

The UAV's electronic nervous system was attuned to pick up electronic emissions from American and coalition flights of any kind, manned or unmanned. There was a real chance that an American drone or AWACS airborne surveillance platform would see and possibly act against a strange drone found in Ramadi's dark skies, and that wouldn't do for the Chinese.

The Rainbow was stealthy, throwing back the radar return of an eagle, and it was nearly invisible to the eye due to light-bending optical camouflage technology the Chinese had perfected while America's DARPA still played with it in labs.

If the Rainbow detected the slightest whiff of American or other opposition presence, it would dive to ground-following level—not just tree-top, but house-top level. It was that good—and withdraw until another day. Spies paid to be common workers on the American bases housing Reaper drones and other coalition aircraft provided a short analog early warning.

If an American drone taxied toward a runway, the Chinese would know about it within minutes and the Rainbow could safely scoot away before it risked detection.

The Rainbow idled over Ramadi at an altitude of about four thousand feet. Its powerful unblinking video eyes were focused on a house and courtyard in the middle of the city. It was the house that Pakistani intelligence had identified as the location of Susan Xing, General Xing's daughter and Commander Xing's sister.

Over Cloud's right shoulder, Commander Xing watched the displays intently for signs of life.

"The imagery is really quite good," Cloud said.

"Yes." Xing grinned. "We liberated the sensor design from its American oppressor, a vendor who supplies the same technology to General Atomics."

General Atomics manufactures the American MQ-9 Reaper combat drone.

"You people really must learn to change your passwords more often."

Cloud laughed—but he memorized every switch, button, and move the pilots made in case he needed that information later.

It was easy to be mesmerized by the high-quality displays. The UAV could stream video, audio and data in real time, but in autonomous stealth mode, the Rainbow transmitted its coded signal up to a Chinese communications satellite in a scrambled, high-speed burst at random intervals of three to eight seconds. Then the data was relayed back down to the command bunker buried in the sand at the fish farm.

There always was the possibility that something bad could happen in between bursts, either to the drone or to its surveillance targets, because the burst transmission method left gaps in the continuous view that could be exploited by an attacker.

In self-directed stealth mode, the Rainbow sent its human operators in the bunker a constant stream of buffered video, but it was like watching an American TV broadcast with a seven-second delay. The UAV could also passively detect targeting radar, and if it did so, the data stream would automatically go to real time for defensive purposes.

"Hey, Chuck," Cloud said. Commander Xing turned toward him. "Did you know that back in the 1980s, those first IBM PC desktop computers were not considered fully Microsoft compatible unless they could run Flight Simulator?"

Xing laughed. "In 1980 I was five. How old *are* you, dude?"

Cloud just smiled and turned back to the Rainbow video surveillance. "Are we going to watch the pretty pictures all day, or are we going to do something? Where are all the resources your father told me to expect?"

"The pretty pictures serve two purposes," Xing said. "First, I'm looking for extra or unknown enemy soldiers in and around the house. There do not appear to be any"—he pointed to a secondary screen showing the form of a single individual soldier atop a neighboring structure—"except this overwatch position. The defenders are probably all inside with my sister. Related to that, these geniuses are rotating shifts exactly every six hours, just like clockwork, coming and going in untidy gaggles, always along the same route.

"Second, we've been mapping ingress and egress routes to and away from the house, and watching to see what local structures they are using for safe houses. We found only one other, which seems to be their local headquarters. Our egress coordinates are now being downloaded into the computers and reformatted for our handheld GPS devices. So yes, the answer to your question is we are indeed going to do something. Once you have reviewed the maps, you can tell us what that is."

Cloud smiled. "If you want peace, you don't talk to your friends. You talk to your enemies."

"Who is that?" Xing asked. "Sun Tzu? Confucius?"

"No," Cloud said. "Desmond Tutu."

A light electronic tone emanated from Cloud's wrist, an alternating *bee-beeBeep, bee-beeBeep*. It cycled three times, paused, and repeated. He frowned for just a moment, imperceptible in the dim bunker light. The tone was a meaningful signal he hadn't expected to get yet.

Cloud raised his left arm and showed a black Suunto Core watch to Xing. "I forgot to shut off the alarm."

He pressed the rubber-clad button on the top right of the dial and the tones went back to sleep.

So, it's a go, Cloud thought. *About damned time, Poppy.*

"Okay," he said, "let's take a closer look at those maps."

The assault teams crept through the darkened city wearing the U.S. military-issue ATN/PVS7 monocular night-vision system. They'd been left behind by the truckload for use by the refashioned Iraqi army, but along with weapons, vehicles and ammunition, the goggles had been abandoned in place when ISIS forces advanced on Ramadi.

The city now was considered officially liberated from ISIS proper—indeed, the entire region had been liberated, with the so-called caliphate in tatters—but all that did was allow many left-behind ISIS soldiers to melt back into the populace and hide in plain sight.

Though the Iraqis had a clear numerical advantage and the best training and equipment American taxpayers could buy, they had occasionally still bolted from the battlefield in multitudes if under attack, often stripping off their uniforms and folding back into the population as civilians in the same way the old Iraqi army had when previously overrun by U.S.

military forces.

It was an easy matter for the spies paid by the Chinese to just pick up, literally from the ground, a few dozen weapons and night vision goggles without resorting to bribes. The spies kept the bribe money nonetheless.

✪

Xavier Cloud led one team along the alleyway behind the houses across the street from the objective. Commander Xing led his team behind the objective itself. The plan was timed such that both teams would storm the house before the shift change, before the fresh ISIS fighters arrived and while the tired ones were careless and listless.

The last shift change had occurred at ten the previous night: They would attack the building at 0200 Zulu, before the six-hour changeover expected at 0400 and near the end of that shift when the soldiers would be fatigued. A careful recon had put human eyes on the single drowsy overwatch soldier.

These people, Cloud thought as he crept silently toward the sleeping gunner, *are not professionals*. The terrorist soldier was silently knifed. Sweet dreams.

Cloud carefully peeked around the corner of the building directly across from the house where Susan Xing was a prisoner. He had an unobstructed view across the unfenced yard to the front door. There were only two windows facing the street on each of two floors. It was very likely that Susan was on the second floor.

Cloud pulled off his night vision and extracted another thermal optical device from a pouch strapped to his combat vest. This was a highly modified military version of the FLIR One III, an imager attachment to Cloud's iPhone with high resolution and enough cooled sensing power to tell him where the warm bodies were behind the walls. Combined with now real-time thermal imaging from the Rainbow UAV circling above, the teams would know how many people were in the building and where they were located. Then they got lucky.

The airborne thermal imaging from the Rainbow drone displayed six men sitting or mostly lying around on the first floor. There was no movement, and they all were probably sleeping, because there was no hot spot corresponding to, say, a lamp, a television, or video player. There were two heat signatures on the second floor. One was motionless in a chair in front of a door, and the other was lying in a bed.

"Hello, Susan Xing," Cloud whispered to himself.

Then he turned up the magnification and took a longer, closer look at the door guard. The man's head kept dropping slowly forward and then snapping back, and it looked a lot like the bored soldier was dozing alone in the dark hallway.

They were attacking in less than three minutes, but that door guard had to be put down: First, to safeguard Susan Xing, but second, before the man finished his nap and rose to full awareness. Cloud pointed at the Rainbow imager and whispered in his Chinese team leader's ear. The man nodded and used his throat mic to radio instructions to the sniper on the roof of their building where the ISIS overwatch used to be.

Peering through a thermal sniper scope, the contract Tajik rifleman aimed through the open but shrouded window and took out the door guard with a single suppressed shot, no muss, no fuss. The threadbare curtain covering the open window fluttered only briefly as the bullet passed through it, as if disturbed by a breeze. This breeze had been deadly. The *jihadi* died in the chair without a sound.

A second command sent the two assault teams creeping toward the house front and back at the same time. The teams were prepared to exert overwhelming force against motivated opponents, but instead they entered a shooting gallery.

Theirs.

The muffled staccato of machine guns mercilessly ripping into sleeping ISIS soldiers didn't even make it to the street. None of the terrorists had time to cry out or raise an alarm. There was a moment after the shooting stopped where no sound was heard but the tinkles of expended brass bouncing and settling to the hard floor. Smoke from discharged automatic weapons was swept out an open rear window by the night breeze. It was suddenly remarkably calm, almost serene.

Then Cloud went from man to man and put a .45-caliber slug in each *jihadi*'s head from his suppressed Colt 1911 automatic pistol. Whatever lingering dreams they might have been having suddenly went dark. The ISIS dead were checked for anything of intelligence value, but all the raiders came up with was a half-empty Turkish cigarette pack and some local currency.

One ISIS soldier, wearing the all-black uniform of a commander, like Chuck Xing, was found with a letter in an unsealed envelope. Cloud read the handwritten scrawl to find it was the soldier's letter home to his family, wishing an eight-year-old daughter a happy birthday. It enclosed a few Iraqi *dinars*. Cloud stuffed the envelope into his pocket.

The real danger was still upstairs. The critical task was for Chuck Xing to get up the stairs, wake his sister, and keep her from screaming as strange, armed men powered into her bedroom. Xing crept up the stairs with another fighter to the hallway outside of Susan's room.

He stopped to inspect the dead guard. Nice center-mass heart shot, like a boss. Xing wished all contractors were as effective.

He crossed the man's lifeless hands in his lap and, with a single pull, he yanked a dusty curtain panel off the window and draped it over the dead sentry from head to floor.

The rescue fighter guarded the hallway and stairs while Xing tip-toed into the small bedroom. He clamped a gloved hand over his sister's mouth and whispered, "Susan ..."

She awakened instantly and her eyes went wide with fear until Xing pulled the *keffiyeh* from his face.

"It's me, honey, it's me," he said.

"Chuck ... *Chucky?* Is it *really* you?" The tension and the fear fled from her and, sobbing, she wrapped her arms around his neck so tight she almost cut off his air.

"Yes, it is me," he managed to croak in the darkness. He reached up and gently peeled away her embrace. "Don't cry, honey. I brought friends—we're here to take you home."

His sister flung pale arms around his neck again and she hugged him, desperately and hard. Joyful tears flowed in quiet streams down her cheeks and left streaks on an unwashed face. She cradled his face in her hands.

"Chuck, do you remember all those times growing up when I swatted you with my dolls?"

"You used them on me like big clubs. Hurry up and get dressed. This bus is leaving."

Xing's battle buddy surveyed the street from the hall window, turned, nodded *good to go*, and gave an upraised thumb.

"Well," Susan laughed in ebbing fear, "I want you to know I am *really fucking sorry about that!*" She grabbed a handful of her clothes and dressed as they fled.

The teams exfiltrated with Susan Xing as furtively as they had arrived. The streets were nearly deserted in these early morning hours, but the hint of dawn flirted with low-hanging clouds in reds and oranges, and occasional Iraqis were encountered in the street. They all averted their eyes and hugged the building walls as they edged past, hoping to seem invisible to obviously dangerous, heavily armed strangers they wanted nothing to do with.

The challenge was managing Susan's excited and terrified sobs and squeaks as they quick-marched through the city to their secure vehicle staging area in an abandoned garage. They would hunker down to burn off the day before setting out again that night.

In the city center, just off a town square where the Humvees awaited, the relative order of a reawakening city now featured a sprinkling of municipal offices as the government struggled to reconstitute. Cloud paused before a large, remarkably unscathed building that was the Ramadi post office.

He stopped and pulled from his pocket the ISIS officer's birthday greetings to his daughter. The envelope was addressed and even had a stamp. He opened the flap of the envelope and checked that the money was still inside, then he moistened and sealed the adhesive, and slipped it into the mail drop.

CHAPTER TWENTY

It is a good thing to learn caution from the misfortunes of others.
Publilius Syrus (85-43 BC), Syrian writer

Lieutenant General Najib Waid Gilani was on a daily after-breakfast walk about his base in Rawalpindi, thinking about how his life was about to change so much for the better.

On this morning, a glorious day without a wisp of cloud in the blue sky, the birds sang and his troops bustled about the base after their jobs. It was a picture of managed energy and effectiveness. All troops look busy when their commander is in range, but Gilani enjoyed the spectacle of competence nonetheless.

He was shown on CIA World Data Book organizational charts as commander of Pakistan's Army Strategic Forces Command, which includes direct control of the country's worrisome stockpile of land-based nuclear weapons. No one but him knew it, but this walk was his farewell tour.

His career had been marked by distinction and rapid advancement. It wasn't only the American military that valued rigorous patriotism, an unremitting work ethic and selfless—his family might have said slavish—devotion to duty.

All these characteristics, and some backroom political posturing from time to time, had put Gilani in command of some the most terrible weapons on Earth, Pakistan's growing nuclear arsenal.

Pakistan was a small and sometimes vulnerable nation. It was rife with religious turmoil and official corruption, and her people needed cleaner water and more reliable electricity.

But in the game of global geopolitics, her possession of a large storehouse of deployable nuclear weapons meant that she was a formidable player in a very tough league.

The offensive missiles couldn't be launched without an order of Gilani's civilian political leadership, but his simple directive could disinter the warheads from secret bunkers and move them. And he had moved three warheads that very morning to the military railhead.

The special train would depart in two hours, along with other railcars loaded with conventional military supplies for other destinations. Along the way, one closed boxcar unremarkable from the others—but for its sophisticated locking doors and a bright orange triangle newly painted on its roof—would be detached and left on a remote siding.

In it would be the three Pakistani nuclear warheads, small but robust objects of breathtaking destructive power that were quite technically elegant, contradicting their cruel intent.

The general stopped to relight his expensive Cuban cigar. He mused about his impending retirement to a small Caribbean island that offered more of his favorite tobacco treats and no extradition. He would take with him two companies of trusted Pakistani Special Forces soldiers to serve as his own private island army, against the idea that some methods of justice didn't respect extradition.

Gilani's career had been long and full of struggle, but soon it all would pay off handsomely in the end, *inshallah*. If Allah wills it.

He cared not for what terrorists did to infidels.

At the same time Gilani took his stroll, Pakistan's defense minister sipped his coffee. On his wide desk was a crisp, red-rimmed but otherwise unclassified folder left in the minister's office the night before by an unseen cleaning woman. He opened it, and began reading documents, phone transcripts, and bank records.

The papers detailed a series of deals General Gilani had made with banks and others to ensure the safe and discreet transfer of tens of millions of dollars to a Swiss account in a deceased nephew's name. There were date-stamped telephone transcripts of Gilani discussing with his deputies the movement of nuclear warheads to a railhead, with additional instructions for a transfer to follow. Other records showed the deputies also enjoyed large cash deposits to secret bank accounts in Switzerland and the Cayman Islands.

The minister went cold. His eyes fell upon a framed photo on his scrupulously uncluttered oak desk. His wife and three loving daughters looked back at him, a happy moment frozen in time at his youngest daughter's birthday party last month.

The minister was struck by the sense that their joyous smiles were entirely, utterly out of place.

✪

Gilani's headquarters base at Rawalpindi was not the country garden many American military installations often were, especially the U.S. Air Force bases, with their golf courses and coffee bars, but he loved it in any condition. He looked around and took in the relative spectacle of order from apparent chaos. It felt good to be in charge in all respects, public and private.

His mandatory security detail stood a respectful distance away.

General Gilani took a few more steps up a short grassy rise and stopped again, hands on his hips as he surveyed his domain. His base wasn't much, but it was *his* base. His to command, to do with as he pleased, good, bad or indifferent. His total control was intoxicating, and he would miss it.

In any military on Earth, men and women in charge of troops understand the awesome power of command, of the commander's authority and responsibility to order people to their deaths as well as to make sure they are fed and clothed and paid on time.

His troops were like his own beloved children. A sudden pang of guilt triggered a small tremor and headache on the side of his head. Perhaps he was wrong to go out this way?

He was a genuine patriot. He had not faked his zeal for things military, his passion for his country, all these years. Those Indian frogs would have seen his commitment first-hand if the nuclear attack order had ever come.

But though Gilani was a patriot, his decades of military training had also made him a practical man. He had mouths to feed, image to maintain, even as his service came to an end. A decorated general might not live well forever on a service retirement. And the ISIS had given him so much money, just offered it up on a platter.

It was so much on the first offer that he didn't even feel like he should ask for more, though clearly there was more to be had.

Gilani leaned against the thick base perimeter wall and kicked a bit of mud from highly polished boots. When offered drinks by colleagues in the Officers' Club, he had often joked that he was a man who could resist anything but temptation. When the real test came, he proved that was true.

Then, flying in unseen among the puffs of blue cigar smoke, there materialized a petite object the size of an insect. It made no sound at all. It winged over the ivy-covered perimeter wall and struck Gilani in the back of his head with its sharp nose before flying away without notice.

Gilani first believed he'd been stung by a bee—the security captain later testified he saw Gilani grab the back of his neck—and indeed he had, a deadly variety custom-made just for this specific occasion in a clean room in Ft. Meade, Maryland. The mechanical device even left behind a genuine bee stinger implanted in the general's neck wound.

Gilani dropped to the ground moments later, struck down by a massive heart attack, the military medical officer would later report, tragically induced by a previously unknown allergy to bee stings.

He was instantly engulfed by the screaming security detail. They were still shouting in panic into radios for help when the sound reaching Gilani's ears faded and the light gradually dimmed in unblinking eyes.

At the last, Gilani knew what had happened to him, and why. It was all a game, and he had lost.

His final thought was sadness for his children, who loved to swim.

✪

The Pakistani defense minister closed the red-rimmed manila folder with trembling fingers, the color draining from his taut olive face. He removed thick eyeglasses and fumbled in the desk drawer for a lens cloth, something he always did when he was nervous.

He could never show the folder to another person, or his own fate would be sealed by recrimination and scandal, and probably prison—or even devastating war.

Nonetheless, he would have to act swiftly to ensure nuclear security and isolate his general officer until other measures were appropriate. The minister reached for his secure telephone just as an aide knocked and rushed into the office.

A horrible tragedy had occurred, the aide said—General Gilani had dropped dead of a heart attack.

The minister slowly returned the telephone handset to its cradle with care and dismissed the aide, a junior captain. The aide asked as he turned, Would the minister care to notify General Gilani's family himself? Yes, the minister said. Give me ten minutes, and make the call.

The defense minister had never been a devout man, but as soon as his office door closed behind the aide, he fell to his knees facing Mecca and prayed then to Allah that he was worthy of this Divine intervention obviously intended to save him for other tasks.

From his kneeling position, the minister swung a few degrees right and vomited his breakfast into the trash can. He pulled a bright white handkerchief from his pocket and cleaned his face, rose, and again reached for his desk phone.

Gilani was speedily replaced with a hand-picked successor known to the defense minister since childhood. A fast deconstruct of Gilani's plan resulted in the swift and discreet recovery of the railcar containing the stolen warheads. Their brief absence from the nuclear infrastructure was written up as a training exercise.

The late general officer had an opulent Prime Minister's funeral with the highest military honors, including a meritorious promotion to a fourth star, providing additional benefits to Gilani's oblivious and brokenhearted family. The fifteen-year-old son was awarded a scholarship to the prestigious Pakistan Military Academy at Kakul, walking distance from the Abbottabad compound where Osama bin Laden had been killed.

Several of Gilani's deputies were routinely reassigned out of nuclear programs and, curiously, within months, most died of natural causes, in accidents or various unsolved crimes, or simply went missing.

Like General Gilani, the defense minister believed in pragmatism. In part because he feared what would happen if the bribe money was ever discovered, he discreetly ordered Pakistan's diplomats to plunder Gilani's and his associates' bank accounts in Switzerland and the Caribbean.

The money couldn't be returned to the terrorists and it couldn't be deposited in the country's national accounts without raising red flags, so the minister decided Allah must have intended for him to keep it. The ambassadors who had recovered the bribes were handsomely rewarded for their discretion.

CHAPTER TWENTY-ONE

We want an Islamic state where Islamic
law is not just in the books, but enforced.
Abu Bakar Bashir (1938-), Indonesian activist

There are many Muslim mosques in southeastern Michigan, but none like the magnificent Islamic Center of America on Ford Road in the Detroit suburb of Dearborn, the single largest concentration of Muslims in all the U.S. Dusk was falling as a young bearded man strode from a side door and walked swiftly to a waiting car.

He sat talking with two men for almost fifteen minutes, and then he left the car and walked away from the mosque area on the sidewalk until he was no longer in sight.

Imam Sayid al-Waheeb watched this event from an upper window with dry approval. The young man had come to him for advice weeks before when an FBI agent tried to turn the young man into an informant. *Go ahead*, the Cleric urged. *We have nothing to hide, and we must keep the wolves from our flocks.*

This was a hard choice for the Cleric. He disagreed with almost every knee-jerk move America made in the Middle East—and he left few of those topics unchallenged on those several occasions each year when he was invited to Washington for private consultations with FBI and Homeland Security officials. They always listened attentively to what he had to say, and took copious notes.

There were so many ways a Muslim leader could fail in America. First, if he practiced moderate Islam and negated the *shari'ah* law demanded by Islam's most ardent practitioners, he failed his most zealous believers.

If, on the other hand, he embraced fundamentalist Islam, he risked alienating the moderate Muslims and non-believers in the community—and frankly risked arrest by federal authorities as a possible terrorist, a sympathizer at least. Treading the finest line was his goal, but the line wavered and got thinner with every passing year.

The Cleric had strong roots in Iraq, family and friends, and the ineffable pull of the Holy Land of Allah was powerful, but he held strong affection for his native-born American citizenship.

His devout father had been murdered in a Tehran street by a common robber, and the United States and her people had been kind to his refugee mother when she arrived pregnant in Dearborn in 1960. He was born at Henry Ford Hospital fewer than three months later.

He grew up in tree-lined, sunlit neighborhoods full of other American kids. They all played baseball and football, and rode their bikes, and he was as American as any boy. Only the world changed when he wasn't looking, his life diverted onto a new path before he noticed it had changed.

He was a man with a *najdl* sandal in both camps, Islamic and secular American. This often caused an inconsistent state in the mosque and in the community he served.

He routinely fulfilled the promise of the axiom *You can please some of the people all of the time, you can please all of the people some of the time, but you can't please all of the people all of the time.* Benedictine monk and poet John Lydgate had written those words, but Americans associated them with Abraham Lincoln's alternative use of them. The Cleric wondered if either Lydgate or Lincoln meant those words from experience, or observation. It was probably both, he concluded. Juggling many different and sometimes opposing things was true in the Cleric's life every day, just as it probably had been for Lincoln and every president who followed him.

Muslims in these neighborhoods, especially those who attended this huge house of Islamic worship, were largely Lebanese-Americans and, like the Cleric, they felt their American roots strongly, whether native or naturalized. There were minor fanatics and would-be radicals among them—"bomb throwers" had been a popular euphemism for such anarchists and disruptors in earlier decades, until the term again became literal in some corners of the world.

Islam had its share of such fundamentalists, as did every other stratum of American society. No one could deny that, and the Cleric didn't try. But while the level of Islamic extremism was in no higher percentage in Dearborn than white nationalists or Ku Klux Klansmen in some American states, the Cleric did have to admit his people were potentially just as colorful and, at times, just as prone to violence.

So, from time to time, as any other well-meaning American citizen might be called upon to do, the Cleric, the young bearded man, and a handful of well-vetted others offered to the FBI tidbits of information they might have overheard at Little League baseball games, in restaurants, or in basements during religious holidays or family gatherings.

Dearborn may have the largest concentration of Muslims outside of Tehran, but it remained a close-knit and often insular society that prized its connectivity to one another. It wouldn't do anyone any good if the information got out that Muslims were informing on other Muslims.

In fact, though, Muslims were not informing on other Muslims *per se*, but the small team of information gleaners did report back to the Cleric and the FBI about goings-on that generally seemed threatening. No names were attached; this had been a strict rule imposed by the Cleric.

At the last, in a time of rumor and innuendo being sufficient to warrant scrutiny, the Cleric would not expose even suspicious Muslims to federal hammers. He and his people would pass along occasional leads to law enforcement, but it was up to them to do their jobs thereafter.

This pinpointed the final awkwardness of being a patriotic American Muslim.

Muslim-American citizens wanted to interdict terrorism as much as any other American citizen, and in most cases, even more so. A terrorist attack in southeastern Michigan—by any group—might be a final straw that loosened the choke chains on forces longing to go into Dearborn like an invading army and start burning mosques and homes.

The FBI knew of these people too, and kept watch on them just as closely.

So, the Cleric had been saddened by the killing of Mohammed al-Taja, a Muslim Homeland Security agent with whom the Cleric had become close and occasionally golfed with in their regular foursome. Al-Taja worshiped in the large Dearborn mosque, and his identity was known to most who attended there. Everyone considered him an honorable man with a difficult job no one envied.

He was a man drawn both to his faith and his nation. While some quarreled with that divisive character on religious grounds, the moderate Cleric encouraged al-Taja to be true to both realms. He could be a respectable if not wholly devout Muslim, and a loyal American who sought to keep his country and his faith safe from harm. It was all that could be expected in any case.

Then he was dead. The Cleric would miss him, and their golf outings. He was a powerful hitter and fun to watch.

Rumblings about the murder had quickly traveled up Michigan Avenue from downtown Detroit and into the homes and Islamic religious centers of Dearborn. A Muslim agent in Homeland Security is killed, that is going to make the news. Paradoxically, this also created some anger among far-right rabble-rousers against the Muslim community al-Taja had been a part of.

For a few days, some Muslims in Dearborn loaded their weapons and took quiet positions on rooftops or in upper windows, cellphones in hand. Unfounded rumors told of angry mobs of white people forming on street corners, no different than Klan rallies in early decades that haunted Southern black neighborhoods. The addition of a handful of Sunni protesters to foment more discontent against the mosque's mostly Shi'a congregation briefly created more hysteria.

None of these rumors had been true, though a few white nationalist protesters had circled a single intersection for an hour one day, long enough to draw local TV trucks in time for the six o'clock. These were hollow show-protests, intended for the media. Federal agents hated them as well, because such activity took the spotlight off solving the DHS homicide and other matters.

Nevertheless, the small demonstration had been enough to trigger weapon and ammunition sales in Dearborn for several days, leading into several tense nights. Fortunately, nothing sparked a confrontation. Any Sunni radicals, white nationalists, or redneck militias who tried to do harm in Dearborn those first few nights would have been met with a small but intense war.

After the initial excitement died down, the Cleric directed his information gatherers to pay particular attention to anything they heard about al-Taja's murder. No detail was too small, he said. It was vitally important that no Muslim be blamed—or credited—with the gruesome death of a federal agent, especially a Muslim one.

After a few weeks, bits and pieces of overheard conversation came together to form an idea for the Cleric. He made a few more phone calls, sent a text and received clarifying details, and soon was ready to do more.

He scarcely had to even reach out to law enforcement. They were always near at hand.

Al-Waheeb had always believed that, as a matter of course, his every move was monitored, recorded, and cross-checked. He was one of the most powerful Muslim Clerics in America. A word from him could cause great harm or great good in the United States.

He accepted his physical and electronic surveillance because there was no alternative to acceptance. He disagreed with it, but he understood it. It was just business. He proved conclusively one day that the surveillance was present when he conducted a small but effective experiment that confirmed his suspicions.

He tested the notion by sending a text in Farsi to his cousin in Iraq, something conversational about potatoes arriving at noon. He'd chosen the innocent phrase because it sounded like a coded message. Within minutes, he saw from an elevated window, dark sedans and SUVs were slowly, too-innocently roaming the surrounding streets around the mosque—and two black SUVs bristling with antennas parked brazenly in the parking lot facing the building.

The Cleric laughed at this, but thereafter, he believed he understood his putative allies better.

So, it put a smile on his face to send a text to FBI Special Agent Amber Watson, asking her for a quiet dinner meeting the next night at the Cleric's favorite Chinese restaurant, the Red Flag. He hoped it didn't get her in trouble.

CHAPTER TWENTY-TWO

There is no kind of dishonesty into
which otherwise good people more easily and
frequently fall than that of defrauding the government.
Benjamin Franklin (1706-1790), American politician

Stopped at a traffic light, Amber Watson was on her OnStar cellphone connection with Tracey Lexcellent. She could hear well even with the Corvette's convertible top down. It was almost ten p.m., and though this wasn't a dangerous area and she was armed, Amber habitually looked at her mirrors and from side to side to ensure her perimeters stayed clear. Then she habitually patted her holster and credential wallet.

"Yeah, al-Waheeb. From the mosque. Yeah! The big cheese hisownself."

"That's a little too timely for me. Did he say what he wanted?" Tracey asked.

"No, he was a little sketchy in the text, just wanted to meet again and have a friendly dinner. I'm pretty sure he's not looking for a golf partner. I met him at that agency-community mixer last year. Seems like a decent guy, but not my usual sorta date, y'know?"

She giggled.

"But I wasn't busy, and the boyfriend is on his two weeks of Marine Corps Reserve active duty out at Pendleton. It's funny, too, al-Waheeb acted like he didn't want to say much on the phone when he confirmed, though he must know we record and report his every syllable, slurp, and burp. And for grins, I checked with Surveillance Services and they are still monitoring him. They had his text, and his call to me, and played it. And he knows that I know that he knows this stuff. So, we shall see what we shall see."

"Where are you?"

"At the light at Michigan and Schaefer, just up from the Red Flag. A Muslim who likes Chinese food. Aren't they against, like, pork and stuff like that? Bet he goes right for the rice and veggies. Or the chicken, maybe. I dunno, all that Muslim stuff is Greek to me."

Amber took another look around as the traffic light changed to green, then she depressed the accelerator and took up the clutch slack, motoring off easily.

"Okay hon, I gotta park this thing and go have my non-pork Muslim non-date."

"Yep, understand. Call me after? I wanna know what he has to say. Prolly it ain't a conversion attempt."

✪

Inside the Red Flag, the room lighting was dim, the dark booths were shrouded, and the aromas were heavenly. A young waiter walked up and took a menu from a holder next to the cash register.

"How many? You sit anywhere?" he asked with optimism. She was a few minutes late and looked around the room, spotting al-Waheeb.

"My party is here," she said, smiling to the waiter and walking toward the darkened booth.

He saw her approach but didn't stand to greet her. She was American and non-Muslim, so first, she probably wouldn't expect him to stand. Most American men were not inclined to do so.

But second, if he stood, she very likely would extend her handshake in greeting, and Islam disallows Muslim men to shake hands with a woman. It was better to sit in the booth and let her take her own seat, which is what she did.

"Imam," she said in greeting. *Good*, he thought. *Businesslike*.

"Do I call you special agent, or ...?"

"I can stand Amber if you can," she said. "Shall I call you Imam? I think you preferred that last time we met."

"Yes, please. I appreciate that, thank you." He paused for just a moment, as if gathering his thoughts. Or courage. The young male waiter brought tea on a hammered silver platter and arranged the cups, sweeteners and teapot on the table before withdrawing in a bow.

"You are wondering why I asked you here tonight," al-Waheeb said.

"It crossed my mind," Amber said.

Al-Waheeb's eyes were dark in the daylight, but in the booth they were fiery circles of red that reflected light from festive Chinese lanterns strung around the room. On a religious man, the effect was rather demonic.

The Imam drew a deep breath.

"Mohammed al-Taja."

Amber's neck hairs elevated at the sound of those words. A few seconds later, her specially modified Apple Watch buzzed discreetly against her wrist, letting her know the follow team was in place and recording everything that was said in the booth.

The electronic hands of the grinning Mickey Mouse watch face continued to merrily circumnavigate the device as before, but now it also served as a small and powerful eavesdropping tool. The experimental listening and transmitting function was an operating feature never dreamed of by the engineers in Cupertino, but by those of an enterprising federal contractor in Fairfax, Virginia.

"Did you know him? Al-Taja?"

"I did. He was a member of our mosque, as I expect you know by now." She did, and nodded noncommittally.

Al-Waheeb said, "He was a fine man, a fine American. A fine Muslim."

The Cleric reached for the teapot and filled their cups with the hot liquid. Like a hummingbird, the cup hovered small and delicate in the man's large hands. *You know what they say about a man with large hands,* Amber thought crudely.

He blew briefly across the top of the cup to dissipate the rising steam and took a quiet sip.

"Yes," Amber said. "And he made a fine corpse as well," Amber said.

Al-Waheeb was taken aback by her coarseness, but he kept it off his face.

"Who killed him? Do you know anything about his death?"

The Cleric gently put down his ceramic teacup and gazed at Amber for another moment, reaching a solution to whatever internal discourse plagued him.

"I may." He hesitated again. Though a lifelong patriot and American by birth, al-Waheeb had grown into and embraced Iraqi Muslim traditions by high school. It was sometimes still difficult for him to talk openly to American women.

This was a trait that first appeared while he was in school, such reticence around attractive women. It got no better during the twelve years he studied to become an expert in Islamic jurisprudence and *Qur'anic* commentary. Al-Waheeb was an attractive man. Islam expected its leaders to be fit and present their best public image. But he was not a practicing ladies' man on his best, most charming day.

"Forgive me, Amber." The intimacy of a non-Muslim woman's given name on his tongue was nearly painful. Allah forgave such sins, he knew, but the pain of them was real to the Cleric as they were committed. "I am not entirely certain how I should proceed with you, so let me just sketch it out as I understand it, and you ask me any questions as they occur to you. Okay?"

"Yes, okay," Amber said. "Please go on."

Her gaze never left his face. She couldn't tell if she was looking into the red-reflecting eyes of a holy man—or a cobra.

"Of course, you know that Mohammed al-Taja was a Homeland Security agent engaged in a, say, 'non-standard' investigative process. As we became better acquainted, he asked me, as his Imam and as an American citizen, to help him locate and neutralize certain fundamentalist—*jihadi*—elements he believed were planning a terrorist attack."

"I appreciate the difficulty of this arrangement," she said. Under the dark wooden table, Amber squeezed her taut thighs together to keep from any possibility of peeing in her pants with excitement. The tea wasn't helping at all.

"A man believed to be from Iran was secretly trying to recruit our young people to be martyrs in this attack. Neither Mohammed nor I knew this man's name, nor any recruits he might have acquired, but he was known to us as a figure willing and able to provide significant money and hard resources to achieve his goals. I believe the man responsible for planning the attack is also involved in killing Mohammed al-Taja."

Amber took a calming sip of her tea, which had turned cold and did nothing to alleviate her bladder discomfort.

"Okay, so there's a guy, and he has a plan, but no name. What is this plan? Is there even a plan? This all seems pretty thin right now."

She waved away the waiter who returned for food orders. Her Apple Watch inaudibly buzzed her wrist three times, then once. *Keep it going.* Now the follow team was excited, too.

Amber noticed an older white couple enter the restaurant and sit at a table, facing her. She thought the man's scowl lingered just a half second too long on the booth and the Cleric, and she didn't think her face was the reason why. He wore a baseball cap embroidered with a logo and the words *Operation Iraqi Freedom.*

"Are you a baseball fan?" the Cleric asked. She turned her attention back to al-Waheeb.

"*Ehh*, yes and no. I go to Tigers games when they're at home sometimes, but mostly to hang with friends and drink beer. I like Comerica Park, though. It's as pretty as Baltimore's Camden Yards, and open-air like that stadium is. World Series bein' played here in a few weeks, so that's a big get, right? Why?"

"My information," the Cleric said, "is that a well-developed terror attack is intended to occur during the televised opening ceremonies of the World Series."

CHAPTER TWENTY-THREE

Thinking is the hardest work there is,
which is probably the reason so few engage in it.
Henry Ford (1863-1947), American businessman

Two white-painted Humvees followed by a canvas-covered stake truck packed with heavily armed soldiers roared out of the fish farm and pointed toward the al-Taqaddum airfield.

Slightly farther behind trundled a twenty-one-foot M-1078 truck that had been loaded with the Chinese gear and electronics from the bunker controlling the Rainbow UAV. The Rainbow had been dispatched forward on autopilot to another location where it would be acquired and safely recovered.

All the weapons had not been loaded, though.

The stake truck stopped at the hidden gate to allow the cargo truck through and let four camouflaged soldiers clamber on board after securing the gate. As the truck negotiated the sandy road and turned right onto the paved main drag toward the TQ airfield, there was a muffled *whummp* and bright tongues of flame erupted from the bunker area behind it like holiday fireworks.

The flames lit up the night sky and surrounding sand dunes only briefly before the deadened sound of demolition charges even reached the fleeing truck.

The fires disappeared as quickly as they had risen, extinguished in moments when the sand-covered enclosures collapsed into the bunkers to make the entire area once again a trackless waste. If any ISIS patrols had seen the short flare of light and fire, which was not likely, by the time they arrived to investigate the scene would again be one uninterrupted sand dune.

At the airfield, the Falcon F7 had returned. Its fuel tanks had been topped off and it sat idling on the ruined asphalt tarmac, air stair down and spilling out interior light, waiting to ingest its passengers. The Humvees pulled up next to the big jet.

The darkness was illuminated only by the stars. Even the jet's navigation and anti-collision lights were switched off at present. The white fuselage and swept wings of the F7 shimmered like an impossible dream in the heat waves still rising from the tarmac. Even this close, the engines on idle were quiet whispers of combustion and superheated exhaust. The scene was all the more bizarre because this impossible dream was real.

Commander Xing, Susan Xing, and Cloud dismounted the Humvees. Around the small perimeter, soldiers from the stake truck and the second Humvee raced to security positions without orders. The team had only had enough time to send three men ahead to check the airfield for ISIS soldiers and the *all clear* they radioed back was encouraging, but no guarantee.

"Thanks, man," Commander Xing said to Cloud. He extended his hand with an uncharacteristic huge smile. "I owe you, mister."

Susan Xing hugged Cloud tightly.

"Chuck told me you are responsible for getting me out of that horrible place," she said. Tears traced dirty rivulets down her dusty cheeks. "I'm very, very grateful, Zave." She hugged him again and laughed. "What is your backstory, anyway? I hope to learn more about it on the way home."

Already her terror was receding. She hadn't yet asked about her mother, and no one had volunteered any information. That brutal task would have to fall to others.

"It's a long story," he said. "Maybe I'll have a chance to tell you about it on the flight."

Commander Xing considered the night sky, then looked at Cloud. "Maybe you will, man. Just not today."

Cloud heard the unmistakable turboprops of C-130 Hercules cargo planes at the end of the field. By the time he turned around to look, two unmarked Herks were touching down at the threshold and immediately going to reverse thrust, throwing up clouds of sand and dust as they slowed to a crawl almost instantly, control surfaces all extended into the airstream as air brakes. Those pilots had made short-field landings before.

Commander Xing hooked a thumb at the F7. "This is her ride." He smiled and pointed at the first military turboprop that stopped only a few dozen meters away, its engines shutting down. "That one is ours."

With hand motions and a couple of radios that suddenly appeared, Xing's troops broke down the M-1078 to its air-transportable height and loaded it, the weapons, and Rainbow control equipment into the second Hercules. Several helmeted loadmasters scampered around signaling the rig into a balanced position in the cargo hold, and then they chained it down securely.

While the load-in occurred, a fuel truck materialized and topped off the tanks of both cargo planes.

Susan scampered up the Falcon's air stair with Two right behind. They both turned and waved, and the jet buttoned up instantly. It turned toward the runway threshold and the engines roared up to full power without the courtesy of a brake-stop. It streaked down the runway and into the air, nose high, climbing hard and loud and no longer caring who knew. In moments, it turned northwest, toward Europe, taking Susan Xing the long way home to her father.

The heavily laden second Hercules was right behind. Xing came to attention and rendered a salute to the Chinese pilots, who returned it, and then they too roared off into the black night, pulling up slowly with their heavier load and vanishing into the black horizon.

A few of the team's local contractors were not going ahead to the next mission, but would stay behind and provide after-action intel, if any post-rescue news developed. Xing spoke to them in Farsi, shaking each man's hand and expressing personal and professional gratitude.

He promised their compensations would follow, and they knew the promise was good. Xing gave them the two Humvees and the stake truck, and with a wave, they mounted up and drove away fast.

The muscular form of One appeared out of nowhere at Cloud's right elbow.

"May I escort you to our aircraft, sir?" he asked.

Cloud looked at One and at Chuck Xing, recognizing and appreciating the surreal nature of his circumstances. Around them circled the remaining anonymous soldiers who had secured Susan Xing's release, as well as the airfield, without losing a single man.

Cloud had to admit, in the starlight and the dust, the group looked like it was ready to kick some more ass and take some more names.

"Why, yes, squire," Cloud said in a lilting *faux* British accent. "I think you may escort me to our ride."

As the group strode to the big turboprop military plane in the murky desert, the TQ airfield filled Cloud with nostalgia and a little pride. Good work had been done here and through here, back in the day. He suddenly missed the men of his squad, nicknamed *The Gutter Lilies*, and he was sad that none had survived the war to enjoy the spoils he and his Chinese and contractor battle buddies were headed to liberate.

But Cloud wasn't a man given to brooding soliloquies. They were not out of the woods yet in any case. It was time to get the program rolling into high gear, and bring some stark reality back to his surreal surroundings.

In the darkness, he reached down to a rubber-covered button on his Suunto Core watch and pressed it three times, then two times, then a second button four times. An American MQ-1C Gray Eagle drone orbiting invisibly miles above detected the signal, captured and amplified it, and transmitted the digits to a satellite that relayed the encoded message data to an obscure office in an unmarked tower of the Arlington governmental hive known as Crystal City, just across the highway from the Pentagon. The report displayed a short boilerplate update message with an urgent electronic tone on a computer terminal logged in by Poppy Benedict.

His eyes flicked over the words.

"Well, I'll be a *son of a bitch*," he whispered to the screen. "We are in fucking business!" he shouted to the empty room, his arms triumphantly raised into the air as if signaling a football touchdown. "Take that, Mossad assholes!"

He punched a long string of numbers into a desk speakerphone. After a few odd clicks and tones, a scrambled male voice sounding like it came from a robotic burger joint callbox issued from the other side, answering with the last four digits of the telephone number Benedict dialed.

"Six-four-eight-nine," the smooth monotone responded. "What is your emergency?"

"This is Anvil Control," Poppy said to the man on the secure encrypted telephone. "Inform Anvil One that *Operation Patient Anvil* is underway at this time."

"Yes, sir. Understood." The connection was broken.

"Goddamn, I *love* this job sometimes," Benedict said aloud. There was no one with whom he could share his impulsive excitement, but there would be many faces in the room before long. General McCandless—Anvil One—would see to that personally.

And then the real work began.

CHAPTER TWENTY-FOUR

When I was young I thought that money was the
most important thing in life; now that I am old I know it is.
Oscar Wilde (1854-1900), Irish dramatist

A flight in a Lockheed Martin C-130 Hercules is not usually a first-class experience. For starters, there is no first-class section—passengers long for the airline-style coach seats, not canvas benches and slings hung from brackets. It's loud, and there is no movie unless you brought it in your tablet. If you are given any food, it probably rips open from a brown plastic pouch labeled MEAL READY-TO-EAT, INDIVIDUAL.

The experienced pray for the pork and rice MRE with barbecue sauce, or the meatloaf and gravy, even spaghetti with meat sauce. God loves a good joke, though, and the gelatinous chicken goo with rice or—bad day—the jambalaya a starving man would throw rocks at, crushes hopes.

This bird was a battleship gray and unmarked C-130J-30 Super Hercules, best of the best and new, handled nearly like a fighter jet and fast as a clear thought. The airplane's provenance, and how it and several like it had been secretly acquired by the Chinese military, would never be fully defined.

As he welcomed them on board, the young Chinese pilot bragged in excellent English that his airplane still had that new-car smell. The dash-thirty designator marked the plane as one with a fifteen-foot fuselage extension, which was put to good use. This Hercules carried a custom-built

SLICC—the comfortable Senior Leaders In-transit Conference Capsule executive pod—almost a full mobile home-sized insert that could be pressurized separately from the aircraft, if needed.

The SLICC was complete with comfortable passenger seats, sound insulation, a galley, two modest sleeping quarters, even a small bar and HD movies called up from the seatback video screens. The pod was stuffed into the cavity of the plane's cargo hold and bolted in place, turning this Chinese Super Herk into a very passable airliner.

Flying clandestincly across Iraq, Iran, and Afghanistan wasn't the trickiest part. The terrain-following radar in the sophisticated all-glass cockpit could reliably autopilot the big bird to sand-dune height at 400 miles per hour all day long. Landing safely in the desert near a modestly populous area and getting away with $100 million without getting the aircraft shot up or people killed by bad guys, that was the trick.

The plane could drop into any known or improved airfield, but its specialty was hard-scrabble or less, and they wanted a landing as close to the money cave as possible. Bagram had plenty of American fighter jets based there, and no one wanted them to scramble with their curious radio calls. Jalalabad, more military, and United Nations too. Out.

Landing at any of those places also put the group too far away from their objective by vehicle and exposed everyone to risk of military arrest.

"Look at these plots," Commander Xing said. He pointed with a rubber-tipped stylus on an oversized iPad Pro displaying a detailed Google Map of a landing zone, and everyone leaned in to get a look. It showed a village called Tagab. Soldiers who had been through there, the few that had, just called the place *Teabag*.

"We know a few certain things. We don't want the plane to be on the ground long. We don't want to have to drive any great distance, because the longer we are on the ground ourselves, the greater the chance of running up on a random militia, an ISIS or Taliban patrol, or even some coalition checkpoint. I'd shoot the shit out of some terrorist assholes just for practice, but I don't want to have to shoot at good guys who don't know us just to protect money, when we could have planned better."

Heads nodded all around.

"How about this?" Cloud said to Xing, reaching toward the map. "The cave with the money is just up the mountain from Teabag, just off this little ville called *Alah Say*. Your guys are there, and they have trucks you said, right? Big ones? Each of the two pallets has fifty million bucks and they weigh about eleven hundred pounds apiece. My guys, eight of 'em, carried those pallets up in there by hand."

Xing grinned. He saw where Cloud was headed.

"You have your teams carry those damned pallets outta there and put one on each truck. Then they drive 'em down the mountain and meet us here."

Cloud scrolled the map an inch and touched the sandy plain north of Tagab.

He put his arm around the pilot's neck and pulled him in for a closer look, like a brother grabbing a headlock for fun.

"There's this piss-ant dirt road that runs north and south right here, on the north side of town. See this here?"

Cloud ran his finger along a light brown track.

"*Nǐ néng bǎ nǐ de fēijī jiàngluò zài nàlǐ ma?*" Can you land your plane there?

The Chinese pilot nodded.

"Are you kidding me? At minimum weight, I could drop this plane into the Rose Bowl if you took down the goal posts, and take off again. That road is like 24-Left at LAX to me." He smiled. "So, yeah. My answer is yes, I can land there and take off again, with room to spare. Do a barrel roll out of there for show if all of our stuff is tied down."

Cloud clapped him on the back. "I *knew* that," he said with a wide, approving grin.

Xing spoke to his aide in Mandarin, then turned back to Cloud and the pilot.

"We will radio instructions to the ground team. I know the leader of that group, he's a good man. So listen, we've been in the air about an hour. If they start moving the pallets in the next half hour, drive down the mountain in the next three, three and a half hours, max, figure in some margin for Mr. Murphy's nonsense, we should be just over Tagab by the time they are driving out onto this smooth area north of the village. We'll coordinate all that by encrypted radio, of course. We don't know what warlords or militias or friggin' terrorist morons might be nosing around, so we'll plan to go into a potentially hot landing zone."

Xing consulted his watch.

"Minimum time on the LZ, load the cash and our guys, blow the trucks, and we shall be gone"—Xing's wide grin returned as he looked up at Cloud—"like a turkey through the straw."

CHAPTER TWENTY-FIVE

No legacy is so rich as honesty.
William Shakespeare (1564-1616), playwright

Tracey Lexcellent sat in her cozy home bar, the Sweetwater Tavern, literally across the street from her apartment house, the Millender Center. Stumbling distance for her was a good policy, and she was never a driver when drinking, anyway. Her stomping ground was the downtown area, which made getting around on foot a good idea after some drinks.

Tracey liked her some drinks.

She waved her empty beer glass in a circle at Malik from Malawi, the bartender. That's how the man introduced himself to everyone.

"Hello. I am Malik from Malawi," as if *from Malawi* was printed on his birth certificate as his middle and last names.

He pulled another Stroh's draft for Tracey and a Guinness for Sergeant Jeff O'Brien. Malik brought the round of drinks to the corner where the two police officers sat, put the glasses on the table, and removed the empties.

"Still drinkin' that Stroh's garbage, I see," O'Brien said. "I stopped drinkin' that stuff when they closed the Detroit brewery and sold out to Pabst or Miller or one of those. My motto is always 'read the local papers and drink the local beer,' and Stroh's ain't the local beer anymore."

Stroh's had been brewed in Detroit again since 1996, but she didn't correct him. He took a long, ironic pull on the Guinness.

"Why Sergeant O'Brien, I believe you have become cynical in your advanced age," Tracey said.

"Cynical, my ass—pragmatic."

"Pragmatic, huh? That's a pretty big word for a traffic cop. You been sneakin' in some night classes down at Wayne State?"

The midtown sprawl of Wayne State University saw many police officers in classrooms, most of them at night.

"Do you ever get tired of being a turd?" he asked. But he smiled, and took another swig of his stout. He reached for his cellphone and called up an album of photos he'd shot of his new baby boy, the fifth, and handed the device to Tracey.

"I'm glad we could get together. You ever think, back when we were in the academy, that someday our lives would be where they are now?"

"Aww!" Tracey said at the cellphone photographs. "So cute this baby is! Must be the mother, huh?" She flipped through the rest of the photos and slid the phone across the table back to O'Brien. "No, never. How could we? Two rookies, still got lint on our blues, super-cops out protecting the citizenry and stuff? No one can predict the future, Jeff. Hard as we try."

She had emphasized *no one* just a tiny bit harder. They became close in the police academy pressure-cooker and had relied on each other to make it through. The result was a short, intense relationship that neither wanted but neither could resist. It continued recreationally for most of a year after graduation, but ended badly when O'Brien wanted a permanent deal.

Much later, when the anger cooled and the friendship resumed, they agreed it was probably a good thing they didn't stay together long enough to have kids. The breakup was inevitable, they decided, but at least there were no children to hurt. Only each other.

Jeff gazed away from her and out the bar window facing her apartment building. "I still think about it occasionally," he said. "You know, we really were good together there, for a minute."

Tracey wondered if Jeff was working up to pitch a little reunion. He had hinted at it from time to time over the years. His wouldn't be the first marriage that suffered some postpartum setback, usually in bed.

"Yeah, for a minute," she admitted. She suppressed the urge to smile at the sudden vivid recall of his well-marbled body on top of hers in the dark, always in the pitch dark, sweating and grunting and wet thrusting and *stop!* she ordered. *I will not open that door.*

"But then we were terrible for a couple years, remember? I like it better this way. No drama, mama."

O'Brien half-grinned in grudging acceptance and changed the subject without breaking stride.

"What's new with the al-Taja thing?"

"Well, you know that pink Kel-Tec three-eighty you took out of William Cortez Williams' Monte Carlo was matched to the bullet found in al-Taja's brain case. Williams got sprung from the jail before I could put a *habeas grabbus* on his narrow behind, so we're looking for him. His momma won't return my calls and I can't afford to put guys on his place. Budgets suck out loud. You give him another speeding ticket out there in your damn graveyard, you police him up for me, okay?"

O'Brien nodded in the affirmative. "You bet I will."

She drained the last of her beer. "'Nother for you?" she asked O'Brien. He didn't know how long Tracey had been in the Sweetwater before he got there, but she was getting tipsy.

"Ah, no, thanks. I gotta roll. I'm coming off midnights and I start days in the morning, and there's plenty of work yet to do before I die."

"You know, I always hated that little slogan of yours."

O'Brien looked at his watch and saw it was nearly midnight. Time really does fly when you're having fun, he thought, and Tracey Lexcellent was always fun. But his wife was going to be pissed when he got home. He would be on baby-tending duty all night because of it.

O'Brien rose from the table and leaned over to kiss Tracey on the cheek she offered.

"You be careful driving home, okay?" she said.

"Ha, no, *you* do it," O'Brien joked. On the sidewalk, he turned left toward the rear parking lot.

Tracey had two more beers, and a bonus tequila courtesy of Malik from Malawi, before she stood unsteadily and gave a two-fingered Cub Scout salute to the bartender. He totaled her bill and put it on her account. She always tipped well at the end of the month when she settled the bar tab.

"You are okay, Missy Tracey?" Malik from Malawi asked with his sing-song accent and megawatt smile.

She had to laugh out loud or she would tell Malik how much, in that moment, he sounded like the Jar-Jar Binks character from *Star Wars*.

"Yes, Malik from Malawi, thanks. I'm good."

She laughed and waved at him. Then she thought again of tall, muscular Jeff O'Brien standing wet, nude, and majestic in her shower, and she'd just sent him home to his wife and children when she didn't have to.

"Yes, I am goody-*good*-good. Goin' home, though, so that's good too. G'night, bud."

No one else was in the bar. As Tracey pushed open the glass door to the sidewalk, Malik from Malawi was already shutting off the lights and putting chairs on the tables so he could mop up in the morning when he reopened.

Tracey's attention turned from the sidewalk to the street so she could judge the uncertain step off the curb toward her apartment building. At that moment a bedraggled homeless woman ran around the corner and headlong into Tracey. Both women turned to each other in shock. Tracey's surprised reaction was hardly more than an amplified *ohhh*, but Maggie Prynne's scream was long, screeching and loud, descending into nonsensical moaning and grumbling as she dropped to the concrete sidewalk.

Malik from Malawi appeared and started to shoo the mumbling homeless woman away.

"No, Malik, it's okay. I know her," Tracey said.

Tracey recovered enough composure to suppress the sudden crushing urge to puke in the street. Goddamned tequila.

The homeless woman sat on the curb, arms around her knees, rocking gently. Tracey sat beside her and gently touched her thin arm.

"Maggie, honey, it's me. It's Tracey. When did you get out?"

Maggie had been in a rehab ward since Tracey and Amber had last seen her, weeks ago. She rocked and mumbled under her breath. Tracey leaned in, and what she heard the woman mumbling startled her.

"Force no one," Maggie whispered. "Force *no* one. *Force no one.*" Tracey was struck nearly sober by that.

"What does that mean, honey?" Tracey reached out and smoothed the woman's hair. "Huh? Tell me what that means to you."

Maggie was still clean, and her clothes were fresh. Not new, but new to Maggie. From the rehab stint.

"Force no one. Force *no* one. *Force no one.*"

Tracey asked, "Force no one?"

Maggie turned open-mouthed to Tracey as if shocked back into reality.

"Yes-yes-yes! Force no one! Force no one!"

She nodded her head several times, seeking understanding in Tracey's round face and finding none.

"Force ... *nooo* ... one!" Maggie insisted, and pointed up Brush Street. "Force no one! Force no one!" she said again, then stood and pulled on Tracy's outstretched hand, nodding fast. The two women walked up Brush hand in hand, away from the Sweetwater's canopied front door and to the end of the building, where they stopped short of the rear parking lot.

Maggie seemed nearly lucid for a change and crept up to the corner, peering around it as if she expected to see a ghost. She whipped back flat against the still sun-warmed brick surface of the bar and closed her eyes in fear.

"Force ... no ... one!" she whispered, again pointing madly.

What the hell was this all about?

Tracey strode past Maggie and into the stark mercury vapor lights of the parking lot. Maggie recoiled in terror. But there were no cars there at all, and just one distant set of receding taillights on a station wagon of some kind she couldn't identify at this distance, in the dark, on the outside of eight beers and a traitorous tequila.

Tracey turned back to Maggie, hands on hips. "Force no one?"

Maggie nodded hard and grimaced, afraid. The woman was crazy, but she wasn't stupid. Something real was going on. What the hell was it?

Tracey got out her cellphone and called a girlfriend at Wayne County Hospital. It was all the way up Woodward Avenue to the New Center area where the major hospitals are located within blocks of each other. Too far, her friend said, and they couldn't send an ambulance for a favor, but if Tracey could get Maggie up there in a cab, they'd keep her overnight and settle her back down. *Can do*, Tracey said. *I owe you big, hon.*

Tracey called a Yellow Cab and it arrived from its downtown stand in just a few minutes. She badged the Somali driver, took a cellphone picture of him and his cab license, and gave him thirty bucks to take Maggie to Wayne County Hospital. It would cost less than half that to get her there.

She told the cabbie whom to ask for, said the nurse would be out front looking for him, and to let Maggie out there. The cabbie smiled a lot, all nervous, and said in a quiet English-as-second-language accent he'd do just that. She told him to keep the change.

Tracey crossed the street and walked back up the block to her apartment house entrance. What the hell did *force no one* mean? Did it mean anything?

Whatever it meant to Maggie Prynne, it meant the same thing tonight that it meant when Maggie had uttered it the first time, over and over, when she and Amber saw her last.

At the al-Taja murder scene.

CHAPTER TWENTY-SIX

*The more time you spend contemplating what you should
have done ... you lose time planning what you can and will do.*
Lil Wayne (1982-), American musician

By nightfall, the C-130J Super Hercules orbited the little village of Tagab, Afghanistan, at an altitude of three miles. The drone of its engines, throttled back to just enough power to cruise, didn't register to the young boy on watch over his flock of goats.

It was a very fine flock, raised by the boy himself, and it would make his family enough money to keep them warm and fed over the harsh Afghan winter that would blanket them with snow all too soon.

Even fourteen-year-old Afghan boys dreamt of long summers, hot as they usually were. This boy was having a good summer, by his measure. The goats thrived, and no soldiers or warlord raiding parties had come through in many months. The boy had no cable TV, no WiFi or cellphone, but he knew that there was peace in his small corner of the world, and he liked that tranquility very much.

Suddenly from the hills behind him came the rumble of heavy vehicles. His natural instinct was to hide, but tonight he felt strong and free, like a man who should stand his post and defend his charges. So he did not hide, but wooden staff in hand, he stood plainly visible in the dirt road leading down from the mountains.

The yellow cones of truck headlights backed by a harmony of diesels made a glowing corona behind the crown of the hill, then three large, unmarked military trucks crawled over the rocky crest.

Two of them were the hefty but unarmored cargo trucks the Americans had left behind in droves, his father taught him, that now were used by anyone else who could twist ignition wires together. Each had a tall, covered square of something in its cargo bed. The third truck was a hulking Tatra flatbed, built up around the sides with steel-plate armor some resourceful field engineer had crafted up. It had a large, dark machine gun bolted to the roof of the cab, and the bed was filled with soldiers, their many rifle barrels extended into the air and swaying back and forth like the quills of an angry porcupine.

Suddenly, the boy was frightened and certain that standing his post had been a bad mistake.

The approaching trucks brightly illuminated the boy, who raised an arm to shield his eyes from the glare. The lead truck ground slowly to a stop with the boy centered in the road, paralyzed by fear. The truck stared him down, a black shape behind buttery yellow eyes that seared his retinas.

The engines of all three trucks stopped. The driver's door of the first truck opened slowly and a large, dark shape jumped down onto the stony road, splashing little yellow dust devils in the dirt against the backlighting. The shape crunched forward on the stones into the headlights, lit from behind and throwing a giant's shadow onto the frightened boy.

The man held a large black handgun in his left hand. Under his breath, the boy started saying his prayers. He trusted Allah would care of the goats when he was dead.

A man's form took shape before the shadow when he knelt in the dirt next to the boy. He stowed his weapon up into a downward-facing shoulder holster. Even on one knee, the man was nearly as tall as the boy standing on both feet.

"What's your name, laddie?" the man asked in heavily accented English. He reached out casually for a gentle, precautionary pat down of the boy's front, back, and sides. No bomb belt.

The boy grasped that the man spoke English, but his little bit of education did not extend to understanding it. He looked back and blinked, mortally afraid. But this was no ISIS soldier. With that bushy red mustache the texture of a wire brush, he wasn't even an Arab.

"Shy one then, eh? Well, not to worry."

The man reached into a deep inside jacket pocket and withdrew a Toblerone chocolate bar, the big one, almost the size of a child's baseball bat.

"I've brought ice-breakers for you, laddie."

The boy's eyes grew large. He'd seen such things in the shops in Kabul, but only the small ones, and he had never had one of his own.

The man smiled at the boy. "I have a son about your age at home. I want to see him again. I expect your father wants to see you again too, and well, eh *jimmuh?*"

Former 3 SCOTS Sergeant Major Barra MacPharlain, the leader of the truck team that collected the $100 million, was a proud Scottish warrior. He called people *jimmy* in the same informal way an American might use *bubba.*

Angus presented the candy bar, level to the ground with both hands, an act of submission like surrendering his sword.

"Take this, laddie. It's yours. In good health, yeah?"

He paused for a moment and reached into another pocket, handing a piece of paper to the boy.

"Here y'go, *jimmuh.* Don't spend it all in one place, then."

The boy held the paper up into the light from the lead truck. It was American money. The boy didn't know much more than that, except to note the bill had a one and two zeroes on it. It seemed very important, and a little dangerous.

"You'll want to give that to your parents, yeah? Mummy and daddy, right? You know, parents?" Eyes still on the boy but head cocked toward his shoulder in frustration, he called back to others in the truck.

"What is the hell is the bloody word for par—"and then he remembered it. "*Wālidān,* eh? You know what that means? Your parents are at home, eh? *Wālidān?*"

His eyes bright with understanding, the boy nodded and said, "*Wālidān! Wālidān!*"

"Well done, lad! Well done, indeed!" The man stood and patted the boy on the shoulder, applying gentle pressure to urge him from the roadway. "You take that candy and the money and go see your *wālidān*, laddie."

The warrior watched the boy run off toward his home. The candy bar was raised over the boy's head in one hand and the American hundred-dollar bill held aloft in the other. He screamed for joy in the night as if it were Christmas and the man Santa. Or whatever such holiday they might celebrate here.

"Okay! Let's move out!" the man shouted. He waved his upraised hand in a circle and the three trucks started their engines. He climbed back into his truck, closed the door with a hollow *clang*, and the trucks elephant-walked in unison down the short length of road that spilled out onto the plain north of Tagab.

In the cargo bed of the second truck a soldier spoke into a satellite phone to the copilot of the C-130J Super Hercules orbiting lazily above. In a few minutes, its engine sounds grew louder.

Inside the cargo airplane, the pilots wore integrated thermal-night vision goggles and peered through the windows at the ground rushing up at them fast. The high-resolution ground mapping capability of American APN-241 low-power color radar in the nose of the plane scanned the ground for markers until it found them, two flashing infrared beacons anchored a hundred feet apart on either side of the dirt road, then eighteen more pairs in rows about every hundred feet.

The pilot smiled, rotated the yoke left and pushed forward in a descending bank. He spoke into his voice-activated intercom to the co-pilot.

"No different than last year in ..." He thought better of discussing those mission details. "... in the simulator."

The landing strip the ground team had marked out with the beacons was well north of Tagab, on the smoothest portions of a hard-packed dirt road that was junk to begin with. The ground team had chosen an area about a mile and a half from town, but four six-blade composite propellers make a hellacious noise when reversed to slow the plane.

As soon as the aircraft touched down in the still air and slowed, it taxied to the farthest infrared beacon and turned back toward the way it came, its passengers hoping no one in town would be roused. It was as loud as hell in the plane.

Cloud had done rough-strip landings in backwaters before and wasn't concerned about this one. Anything could go wrong, of course, and Mr. Murphy might invoke his law just for grins and giggles, but everything seemed to be going according to plan.

The Super Herk had rolled to the end of the makeshift runway and the engines went to idle, the propellers feathered but still turning. The ramp at the rear of the plane lowered immediately and the loadmaster pointed an infrared flashlight at the mountain, blinking it three times. Two opaque shapes, M-1098 flatbed cargo trucks, roared into view from the shadows with their lights off.

The third truck took an overwatch position to defend against gate-crashers. The 1098s rolled up dark to the back of the Herk and turned away in opposite half circles, then backing together up to the ramp in the darkness. The helmeted loadmaster waved them in with a small red penlight, stopping them just inches from the ramp. He pressed a button and raised the cargo ramp to meet the level of the truck beds where two cubes of shrink-wrapped greenbacks rested on blue plastic cargo pallets.

Even with the executive pod inside the Super Herk's cargo hold, there was ample room for the men to muscle the bundles across the small air gap and into the aircraft. The loadmaster lowered the ramp again, pounded twice on each of the trucks and they drove off, stopping about three hundred feet away. The overwatch truck joined the group.

All the soldiers dismounted and ran to the plane, scrambled up the ramp, and found seats in the executive pod. The loadmaster raised the ramp and chained the pallets to the floor, then pushed and pulled on the shrink-wrap to convince himself nothing was going to spill out. There were a couple areas where the plastic had been cut or torn through and currency removed, so he duct-taped over the holes. Satisfied, he keyed the A-OK to his pilot on the intercom.

Out on the sand flat, the three trucks blew up without fanfare. No warlords or ISIS soldiers would turn those back into war machines.

On the flight deck, Commander Xing, Cloud, and the young Chinese pilot-in-command were congratulating each other and the teams for super-lative work while the co-pilot conducted his takeoff checklist. Everyone felt like the atmospheric pressure was reduced just a bit, and nervous laughter replaced tension. The men were just now allowing themselves to savor the importance of having one hundred million dollars literally at hand, and it made them a little giddy. Even hardened soldiers and mercenaries can feel euphoria, all the sweeter because it was so rare for such men to feel it.

They were alive and rich. It was a rare combination in this line of work.

The co-pilot reached to a side pocket to stow the checklist clipboard in its place. When he looked up, headlights were approaching from town. Fast.

"Shit!" he yelled in Chinese. "Bandits approaching, twelve o'clock!"

Cloud and Xing knew to get off the flight deck and into the executive pod. "Everybody sit down and buckle up!" Cloud shouted in his best Ranger command voice. "This bus is leavin' right now!"

The pilot set the flaps, shut off all the engine bleed air and stood hard on the brakes while he pushed his throttles all the way forward into full military power, the maximum take-off muscle. When all four engines quickly stabilized, he released the brakes and four scimitar-bladed tur-boprops clawed at the air, taking gigantic bites of thick atmosphere and thrusting it aft.

The co-pilot watched his gauges change and announced velocities while the pilot focused straight ahead. The yoke shook and bounced violently in his hands as the big airplane rocketed down the packed dirt road strewn with rocks and random debris.

The take-off roll wanted at least eighteen hundred feet in most low-weight cargo scenarios to clear a fifteen-foot obstacle—and this plane wasn't low weight. Boeing said 3,290 feet minimum, but this pilot knew eighteen hundred feet or probably less was achievable with the euphemis-tically titled "max effort procedures" he had just employed.

In any case, they were going to find out soon.

The approaching truck was closing and it was eating away at the margins fast. The makeshift runway road was neither really smooth nor much of a road, but while it had been composed enough at taxi speeds, hurtling down the dirt track on takeoff power meant every stone and rock attacked the tough rubber tires and shook the plane. If they lost a tire, or more than one, the decision to press on or abort would literally be one of life or death.

The pilot felt his control surfaces achieving effectiveness, but the truck was so close. At the same time that he pulled sharply back on the yoke and raised the airplane's nose, his co-pilot instantly hit the switch that raised and stowed the landing gear.

He was just a second too late. The plane passed over the truck full of militiamen just close enough for a heavy nosewheel carriage to smash through the truck's windshield and the main gear to strike the truck's nose, but the landing gear continued up into its space, the doors closed, and the plane continued on its way as if nothing had happened.

On the ground, the truck flipped backwards end-over-end for nearly half the length of a football field. It burst into a fireball and spilled out torched human beings that bounced and rolled across the sand to burn into char.

The fires burned brightly for several minutes, cooking off secondary explosions from grenades, magazines full of bullets, and a canvas backpack of RPGs that detonated with ferocity.

It was dawn less than an hour later. Frightened wives and mothers and children came out to find their men who had never returned, to gawk or mourn, and carry away their dead if they could identify them.

A fourteen-year-old boy stood next to a pile of smoldering residue and blackened clothing. He recognized his father's favorite jacket, the one his father said had special plates inside it to withstand the bullets of his enemies. The bulletproof panels were exposed when the Kevlar fabric covering them burned away.

The boy sobbed to himself, hands thrust into the pockets of his own jacket, fists clenched, his mind a lake of roiling anger. The taste of last night's chocolate was still in his mouth. He felt the Toblerone candy wrapper in his pocket and he withdrew the souvenir, turning it over in his hands and examining the alien object from all angles.

He couldn't read the words, but he knew now what they represented. Death. Destruction. Corruption. In fury, he crushed the paper wrapper into a tight ball and tossed it onto a small pyre burning next to the remains of his father. The paper flared once, burned brightly, and was reduced to gray ash.

The boy walked a few meters away from the scene, bent at the waist, and shoved two rigid fingers deep into his throat. A violent cascade of chocolate vomit spewed across the sand for several moments, then subsided. It filled his nose with acrid stomach contents that burned and choked him. It was over as quickly as it began. The boy wiped his mouth on the sleeve of his jacket and stopped crying, smoothing his clothes.

His uncle approached to console the boy, but was stunned to find him no longer weepy. The boy told his uncle where to find the goats, up the road near the crest of the hill. The uncle looked at the boy with questions in his heart, but he did not ask them.

The boy gripped his American hundred-dollar bill tightly in a jacket pocket. Some things infidel were to be destroyed, but others were to be used wisely.

The boy bade farewell to the uncle, turned, and started walking toward Kabul.

CHAPTER TWENTY-SEVEN

He who fights with monsters might take care lest
he thereby become a monster. And if you gaze for
long into an abyss, the abyss gazes also into you.
Friedrich Nietzsche (1844-1900), German philosopher

Poppy Benedict had been in the Central Intelligence Agency since college. It had been twenty-seven years since his last kegger at Southern New Hampshire University, where he'd played a little intramural lacrosse but mostly just studied, drank, and didn't date much.

His undergrad degree was in data analytics and his master's in operations and project management, so when—through a howling hangover one Sunday—he saw a subtly worded ad in *The New York Times* for employment opportunities with the CIA, that little cartoon light bulb went on over his head.

He'd never known another employer. If he could describe his work to someone with the requisite security clearance, he wouldn't know what to say. He was no James Bond, but he finally had achieved his career goal of being an operator—a spy. These days, the well-muscled kids who graduated from their training at The Farm were no longer its only poster boys.

Poppy's work as an operator had more to do with running computer programs than running from enemies in Moscow or Beijing or Tehran. He had grown in the CIA from an entry-level analyst poring over electronic intel, or high-altitude surveillance imagery with a large magnifying glass, to managing that section, then directing the entire department and its emphasis on high-resolution satellites and, later, adding remotely piloted aircraft and unmanned aerial vehicles—RPAs and UAVs, or drones. With no field experience nor aspirations to have any, Poppy's professional interest drifted to the agency's management side.

He was paid well at the deputy director level, but he was a free agent, a swing man, a jack of all trades though a master of them as well. He lent his expertise and executive skills to many understaffed offices on a project basis, and he was a hot commodity. But even within the CIA, his true mission and activity was need-to-know. If an org chart was printed out, Paul "Poppy" Benedict would be listed as just another random mission manager under the Science and Technology Directorate.

He was much more.

✪

U.S. Army General John Glenn McCandless stood at the front of the room holding a waxed paper coffee cup and surveying the space now filled beyond a fire marshal's nightmare with milling people. Of course, it would be a rare fire marshal who got this far into the unremarkable glass building in Crystal City, the nickname for the Arlington hive of leased federal government office towers across from the Pentagon's south parking lot beyond I-395.

The conference room had been designed for occupancy by fifty-five or fewer people, according to the mandatory government sign in the hallway with its hand-drawn-in-red-Sharpie arrows pointing the direction to fire exits. That didn't include the square feet consumed by the long but narrow conference table dotted with speakerphones and the gallery of hard chairs snaking around it, nor the conga line of additional chairs lining the walls for the deputies and seconds. Today there were seventy-two people in the room, and it was getting stuffy fast.

At the card table refreshment stand shoved against the walls in a front corner of the room, General McCandless drained the last cold drops of black coffee from the vending machine cup and turned to his ever-present *aide de camp*, Army Major Tommy Crosby.

"You ever miss Germany, Tommy?"

McCandless had been the three-star lieutenant general commanding all of U.S. Army-Europe, at Wiesbaden, Germany. Crosby had been his aide there, too. When McCandless was tapped to lead the secret military-CIA hybrid task force and given his fourth star, he brought Crosby along with him knowing it would be the best possible pathway to accelerated promotion for the man.

"Yessir, I do, from time to time."

The general was a lifelong bachelor—few occupations were as hard on relationships as a military career—and he had come to refer to Crosby in private conversations as "my kid," though the major was thirty-five and had been in the Army for twelve years. The last three had been with McCandless. He'd made major fast, and McCandless intended to see him continue promoting early.

"We always had fun in the fall," Crosby said with a subtle smile. "*Fasching. Oktoberfest.*"

Crosby was also single, but always seemed to have a spectacular date when he wanted one for a beer carnival or *volksfest* on local Army kasernes or out in town.

"I liked it, too. Maybe we'll get back there one day," McCandless said.

He loosened his black uniform tie and unbuttoned the top shirt button. He handed the empty coffee cup to the junior officer. "Let's get started."

Crosby spun smartly and tossed the cup into a nearby government-gray trash can lined with a clear plastic garbage bag: Nothing but net. He turned back to get the room's attention and introduce his boss, but General McCandless already stood at his podium. The room fell silent by the time the general ritually cleared his throat.

Crosby made a knife-hand motion to his Signal Corps staff sergeant dressed in the popular new World War II-throwback "pinks and greens" uniform. The woman lowered the room lights and brought up the ceiling-mounted projector at the same time.

Outside the room, a red light reading ROOM OCCUPIED–DO NOT ENTER went on over the door and an electronic lock clicked softly.

"Okay, I presume you all have seen the early briefing deck, but here is the updated version as of one hour ago."

McCandless pointed a ruby red laser pointer at the screen showing a map of the Middle East. In the center was Iraq, Iran, and Afghanistan.

"At about 2330 last night, we received an action notification from our asset embedded with a Chinese People's Liberation Army force conducting a hostage rescue operation in Ramadi, Iraq."

He paused and turned toward the darkened room. The powerful beam shed by the overhead projector illuminated the general's face with shadows and light, appropriate considering the context of this discussion.

"These are honest-to-God PLA soldiers. We think they are being led by a young Chinese Special Forces commander named Chuck Xing, a man with a lot of enterprise and impressive access to resources."

Chuck Xing's photo was put on the screen.

"This is an image from an old Stanford student ID card, so it's about twelve years old. The kidnapped woman is Susan Xing, a dual-citizenship American/Chinese person living here legally, currently also a Stanford student. Xing and his team are working freelance, because the kidnapped girl is Commander Xing's little sister."

The screen displayed driver's license photos for Susan Xing and her mother.

"While changing planes in Germany en route to Poland on an exchange student trip, Susan and her mother, Catherine, a native-born American, were lured out of the Frankfurt-Main Airport security zone and snatched by ISIS assholes. ISIS is—or was—holding Susan for ransom. Catherine Xing hasn't been seen since they were abducted. We are aware that she is dead."

He made the statement without emotional topspin. She was a minor factor in the equation, nothing more. Just business.

A hand in the back was raised tentatively to ask a question. The man thought better of his timing and the hand disappeared in the gloom. Better to not interrupt.

"They may just want cash, maybe information, maybe more. That 'more' part is the troubling bit. There is a considerable body of circumstantial evidence from other sources suggesting they think they could have traded

Susan Xing for some kind of Chinese miniature nuclear device. That's when *Operation Patient Anvil* was initiated. We have waited a long time, spent a lot of money, and made many sacrifices to get our man inserted into this Chinese operation, and he has worked his angles hard, domestically and in Iraq. Now it is time to start hammering the Anvil part of the program. Next."

The image on the screen changed to a recorded satellite video feed. The video had been shot at night from space, but it was as perfect and detailed as if the onlookers were watching it happen in the parking lot two stories below. Of course, this secure room had no windows. The telltale lack of color in the gray, black and white imagery established that this orbiting overwatch was infrared.

"This angle is on the al Taqaddum Air Base outside of Ramadi. It's largely unused anymore. Watch: Here, a white business jet takes off"—McCandless pointed his laser at the aircraft. It rose lazily at this high viewing angle and disappeared to the northwest. Digital details in an onscreen window flickered as changes in azimuth, direction, altitude, and other vectors, even ground temperature, were analyzed and displayed.

"Then an M-1078 is loaded into this aircraft." The general circled a Hercules cargo plane with his laser pointer. "As soon as it buttons up, it rolls out and takes off. The Humvees and a third cargo truck depart together. Then, this group of men carrying weapons"—another laser point—"walk toward an unmarked C-130J Super Hercules. The Herk turns toward the runway threshold and immediately takes off."

The scene jump-cut to another clip, also at night. A dark C-130 taxied along a roadway lined at regular intervals with infrared markers. It turned around where the markers ended and faced back toward the village of Tagab.

"About five hours later, a little less, maybe, the same Herk lands outside of a little place called Tagab, near the Pak border. We watched it the whole way across Iran and Afghanistan. AWACS directed our coalition aircraft to give the plane an uninterrupted flight path—and we had assets ready to help out discreetly if the Iranians got frisky, but they never saw a thing.

"This pilot is really good. The plane flew way south and low, keeping

off Iranian radars as they overflew the entire friggin' country. We kept
the coalition AWACS birds apprised and the C-130's pilots had no idea
they were being followed. It turned east just here, below Basra, and then
went flat out across Iran and Afghanistan to Tagab."

Haha, Teabag, we called it, a voice whispered from the darkness, followed
by suppressed laughter.

Without turning around, McCandless said, "Yep, that's what we called
it, too."

More laughter. The room was cooling now, and people were leaning
comfortably, attentively forward in their chairs.

The general's pointer moved to the right of the screen while the video
continued to play.

"Here, three trucks run down from the hills toward the plane. They
are not challenged. One takes a defensive position and the other two turn
away, then back up to the plane's tail."

The imagery changed to another angle, nearly close-up and evidently
shot not by the spy satellite, but from a drone or other atmospheric platform, because the picture slowly panned from left to right as the camera
platform winged by.

"Two large shrink-wrapped pallets are man-handled onto the plane,
then the trucks are driven away and blown up."

Most of the viewers in the room had seen many such surveillance
videos before, or the many gun-camera posts that show up on Facebook,
LiveLeak and YouTube, but the lack of sound as the trucks transformed
into silent, expanding clouds of smoke, dust, and flying metal flipping
end over end through the air was still surreal.

The general circled the aircraft's ramp with his laser pointer as the
ramp closed, a signal to the staff sergeant to pause the video. Two dark
cubes were clearly visible in the gloom.

"Each of those pallets has about fifty million American greenbacks
stacked in bundles of one hundred dollar bills." A low wolf-whistle of
appreciation rose from the back row of chairs. "Yeah. That's a nice retirement package, huh?"

McCandless gestured again with the laser and the scene changed to another view.

"Note the infrared markers along here," he said, tracing the length of the road serving as a runway. "If that's what we think it is, that's about as minimum a takeoff distance as you're gonna find. Watch the Herk."

The scene changed back to satellite infrared. McCandless pointed to a whitish blip rolling out of the adjacent town of Tagab. "At about the same time the plane starts its takeoff roll, this truck here comes rolling hot out of the town."

The Army officer stopped talking and let the soundless action unfold. It was clear that the speeding truck was full of armed men, likely militia from the village. In just seconds the two white blips merged, but then in slow motion the plane rose into the air without a bobble and flew out of the frame.

Magnification increased. On the ground, the truck burst into a hot blotch and flipped backwards, end over end, like a circus acrobat. Along the way, men on fire were ejected from the truck and spilled across the terrain, sometimes flopping and rolling around briefly as they burned hotly in the infrared, but most were already dead and motionless when they came to rest.

On the video feed, spectacular secondary explosions burned in splotchy white orbs that bloomed fast and faded slowly. It seemed like a Hollywood special-effects movie, making the lack of sound all the more profound.

"Scratch one truck full of militia," McCandless said. Light applause filtered into the air. "Lights, please." Instantly the windowless room brightened, and people blinked away the sudden change.

"We believe that second C-130 is the team that rescued Susan Xing in Ramadi." Her smiling driver's license photo again appeared on the projector, its color washed out from the overhead fluorescent room light. "As I said, she is the sister of the Chinese Special Forces commander who helped free her, but that's not even the punchline."

The photo on the screen changed to a dignified Chinese man in a PLA general officer's uniform.

"They both are the children of General Xing Jianjun, a retired PLA three-star who, as incredible as its sounds, operates a Chinese restaurant in Dearborn, Michigan, just outside of Detroit."

A murmur of *whaaat* and *no way* disbelief circulated around the room. The general half-smiled in wry agreement.

"Yeah, inconceivable, but true. I hear the food is good, too." Another ripple of laughter.

"What does all this have to do with anything, you're asking? Well, to start with, our asset embedded with the Chinese freelancers is a former U.S. Army Ranger, convicted of war crimes, who busted out of Leavenworth about seven months ago."

Sharp intakes of breath and shock came from the direction of several chairs. There was only one of those guys.

"He left thirty-seven years to life on the table, but here is the material thing: Those horrific crimes we accused him of? That we publicized so widely to show the world how judicious our government is, serving up truth and justice and The American Way, all that crap?"

Heads nodded all around the room. The sordid ordeal had been in the news cycle hourly for months.

"We made it all up."

CHAPTER TWENTY-EIGHT

If the trumpet give an uncertain sound,
who shall prepare himself to the battle?
Corinthians

Not a sound littered the gently moving air in the packed conference room. The general's thoughts, and those of many in the room, instantly went to the seventeen Americans and scores of Europeans killed in the *jihadi* terror pandemonium that followed the faked murders of a small village of Iraqi civilians.

The cover story Cloud's bosses had asked him to submerge into made him fully despised at home and abroad—and thus attractive to certain circles about which U.S. intelligence services wanted to know more.

"It was a tricky setup," McCandless said. "I'm betting most of you in this room are too young to remember the My Lai massacre that occurred in Vietnam back in 1968. Soldiers went crazy and killed a village of civilians, more than five hundred people. Some soldiers were punished, even some generals, and it left a stain on military service during the Vietnam Era that still hasn't subsided. We set up the same atrocities, but faked this time.

"We used satellites to find a long lost town in the Iraq desert. CIA para-military special forces and military intelligence operators descended on the place far enough away from other settlements that even most locals had forgotten it was there. Under strictest secrecy, a special unit of soldiers and local fighters shadowed ISIS killer teams before they could do their work. We obliterated those killer teams, of course, and added them to our ghost cast. Then the deceased, and sometimes just their parts, were used to populate the ghost town.

"Photographs were made of the carnage, videos were recorded, and then our B-1 bombers annihilated the place. Staged photos were made of our guy and his 'battle buddies' holding aloft horrible trophies of war."

Not all the trophies were captured weapons or flags.

"At no time did it seem to occur to anyone that only our guy's face was identifiable in the imagery."

The general reached for a bottle of water on the podium, cracked it open, and took a small drink. He and the rest of the room were lost in thoughts about the aftermath of the faked war crime.

Innocent civilians had been caught in punishing extremist reprisals in Europe, mostly tourists killed by a single terrorist with an AK-47 and some hand grenades on an Italian passenger train. It had wadded up in spectacular fashion just as it entered a mountain tunnel, splattering train cars full of screaming people into the rock face and then spilling them down the mountainside into a fast-moving river hundreds of feet below.

Other deaths, the worst ones, were American military, captured or kidnapped, despicably mutilated alive and then beheaded on video, the results distributed throughout the world. Real and horrible deaths, in angry retribution for faked ones.

Anyone who witnessed the video execution of Navy SEAL Chief Special Warfare Operator Atticus John, held down by four *jihadis* and writhing and screaming obscene death threats in handcuffs while he still fought them and bellowed out the National Anthem as he was slaughtered, was never the same.

"Yes," McCandless said quietly. "We did not foresee the terrible unintended consequences. For that I shall pay dearly when accounting for my actions one day to my Maker. We compensated the families of the victims— our own American martyrs—but no compensation substitutes for a human being, a family member, a spouse, a father. They are heroes all. Each gave their life for their nation while not knowing they were doing so. May God continue to bless and keep them."

The general surveyed the crowded room. The expressions on many faces were uniformly melancholy. People in this line of work, clandestine work, were sometimes forced to confront the terrible ethical ambiguities of their profession.

They were just as important to protecting the nation as a Marine lance corporal standing an embassy checkpoint in Kabul, or an Army military intelligence officer interrogating a terrorist prisoner—but the nature of clandestine service is necessarily not above board, open to public scrutiny neither for blame nor acclaim. They answer to their bosses, like any other government employee, but when they go home for the day, they answer to their consciences.

Sometimes, to Jack Daniels.

And just like a lance corporal who mistakenly kills a civilian in the dead of night when a car approaches his checkpoint too fast, the spooks too sometimes made mistakes, hidden behind glowing computer screens and the polished glass eyes of armed robots patrolling skies half a world away, or dissecting plans of action in fortified conference rooms.

They were usually estranged from the carnage they caused, these "chairborne commandos" as other, dustier warriors referred to them from the ground in sandy places. But they were not disconnected from the suffering they caused, nor from the consequences. Nor the bad dreams.

"So, the asset, formally U.S. Army Ranger Sergeant First Class Xavier Cloud, was pilloried, publicly scorned for war crimes he did not commit, and following a show trial, sent to federal prison just so he could 'break out' and go underground to find a connection to domestic terrorism.

"We helped get word around that his highly desirable skill sets were for lease to the highest bidders. We stumbled into the kidnapping plot, and we had Cloud offer to pay for the rescue out of the hundred million. That got us closer to the Chinese, who seem to know about a terror attack plan on American soil. But Cloud indeed is neither a war criminal nor an international fugitive. He is one of ours."

The on-screen photo changed to Cloud in his Ranger beret and Army dress blue uniform.

"His mission was to get next to these Chinese folks, to see if he could first employ them in his recovery of the girl and the hundred million, thus gaining their trust. He succeeded in this. And yes, that is real money. Cloud and his former Ranger team stole those dollars from us—the taxpayers—back when we were cementing our deals for OEF support from warlords in Afghanistan literally with cubic money. I was in-country at the time as the 513th M.I. Brigade commander, and I can tell you, the Vigilant Knights were slinging those pallets of money around from our CH-47s like hash browns at a Waffle House—smothered and covered—all the *cucamarangas.*"

McCandless took another swing of his water.

"It was a hectic time in those early days and the accounting was sometimes theoretical. If the helos went out with a team and the money, and they reported it delivered when they returned, we wrote it down that way. If some random warlord complained about not getting his graft, we either wrote him off as greedy, or sent out more friggin' money."

McCandless gestured a knife-hand to Benedict, who rose.

"We are letting Cloud keep the money, by the way. Whatever is left after his ordeal is over. It is long off the books now, and I think he has earned a bonus from his country for all the nonsense we're put him through."

The general waved Benedict forward.

"This is Poppy Benedict. Many of you have worked for him and with him in the past. I have put him in direct charge of *Patient Anvil*. It is a very short chain of command, people. Any order or instruction issued by him has my complete authority behind it, and the direct authority of the President of the United States behind that. Poppy."

General McCandless took his seat as Benedict approached the polished wooden podium. He would oversee every aspect of the crucial operation, but that didn't make him nervous in the slightest. As a long-time CIA operative in Washington and a serial husband with four ex-wives—two drunks, one cheater, and one saint; he'd screwed up the good one on his own—he'd had tougher bosses before than this general.

"Thank you, sir."

Benedict picked up his own laptop remote, nodded to the Army staff sergeant and the lights went back down.

"Someday you must tell us what *cucamarangas* are."

He punched the button that began the PowerPoint slideshow with a map of metropolitan Detroit.

"We believe a terror attack is being planned for somewhere in the metro Detroit area. We don't know much more than that yet, but two possibilities assert themselves. The first option is an attack on the peaceful Muslim population in the Detroit suburb of Dearborn, the largest concentration of Muslims outside of the Middle East, and by far the single largest in the country."

The map perspective dissolved into a video feed of the giant primary mosque in Dearborn. The feed was identified on-screen as being from an MQ-9 Reaper hunter-killer drone orbiting high above the American city. This was no recording. According to the geopositioning and timestamp data on screen, the video feed was live and in color and being streamed into the meeting in real time.

Some in the room noted the sea change: For the first time, an armed American drone was surveilling an American city on a combat air patrol, and it wasn't a drill.

"We have information of a credible threat that was dug up by someone we placed in the Department of Homeland Security, and DHS had him working undercover in Detroit. Regrettably, the guy was murdered a few weeks ago. We're monitoring that investigation, but right now, it isn't clear whether his murder is related to the undercover, a suicide, or just one of those random Detroit things, frankly. I'm still waiting on the autopsy.

"There are both foreign and domestic issues on the threat board. One domestic terrorist goal, apparently, is to kill large numbers of innocent Muslims, specifically targeting children, schools and heavily trafficked areas such as the Fairlane Town Center shopping mall"—the scene changed to several more video angles on the busy Dearborn shopping mall parking lot—"provoking an Islamic insurrection leading to a regional race war with far-right American militias who we know are preparing to respond in relative force. This is a plan by domestic extremists—white nationalists, basically Hitler Youth without the education."

The screen changed to an overhead infrared view of armed, uniformed men spreading out through a forested area at night. The warmer human bodies glowed as white silhouettes among the cooler, darker trees and vegetation. When the magnification was enhanced, many of the figures appeared to be overweight.

They were too bunched up to be tactically effective and, in the darkness, their weapons often were pointed at each other. One plump figure seemed to trip and fall flat on his face. His cronies just flowed past him in the darkness, none offering to help.

"This is surveillance of a group of white nationalists calling themselves the Michigan Wolverines. Not the football team."

In the back of the darkened conference room, a lone female voice piped up with *Go Bucks*.

"There is considerable evidence of American militias, white nationalists and other far-right radicals performing these lame training 'maneuvers' in preparation for a confrontation. With our FBI colleagues, we've been watching these birds for some time. Someone or some group is rattling them with nonsense about an 'Islamic break-out' from Dearborn into the surrounding secular areas. I don't know what the hell that's supposed to mean, but there you go.

"Right-wing talk radio and alt-right websites have been particularly shrill about it in recent weeks. The militias in Michigan, Ohio, and Indiana are loosely coming together under Wolverines' so-called leadership to literally fight it out with innocent Muslim-Americans over this bullshit.

"We do not believe any such 'revolution' would be successful—but it would be very messy, and probably cause serious and persistent damage to relations with Muslim communities domestically and abroad."

Benedict pressed the remote and the scene changed again to a high, real-time angle on Detroit's downtown open-air baseball stadium from another drone.

"This is Comerica Park, the stadium where the Detroit Tigers baseball team plays. Incredibly, the Tigers are in the World Series this year, with the Cubbies again." A few weak *yaaays* came from around the darkened room.

"There is chatter out there suggesting an attack by foreign terrorists may be in the cards for the World Series this fall during the opening ceremonies there. Perhaps the revolution will be televised after all."

If anyone understood the reference to Gil Scott-Heron's famous rap rant, no one appreciated it out loud.

"And coincidentally," Benedict said, "just to add some real excitement to the mix, we got word through a Mossad back door that ISIS assholes are trying to coerce Xing Jianjun"—the file photo of former General Xing in his PLA uniform returned to the screen—"to use his connections to the PLA to obtain a 'Mad Gopher.' It's a small, modular, very clean Chinese nuclear device designed for large earth-moving needs, like dams and mountain highways."

The screen displayed an aerial video of a mountain pass that suddenly rose into the air in slow motion, dropping dirt and rocks on both sides of a newly excavated trench two hundred feet wide and a mile long.

"That's why ISIS kidnapped Xing's wife and daughter, but the wife has been killed, and our guy and the Chinese Special Forces freelancers rescued the daughter, so we don't know what they have up their sleeves now. We continue to prosecute these opportunities."

The screen displayed a regulation Samsonite suitcase, one of the really big ones, with stout wheels and a thick handle.

"This is not the device, but it's the sort of container we think a Mad Gopher will fit into. The device will be light in weight and high in yield, configurable, throwing anywhere from a half kiloton to upwards of five kilotons. I'll remind you that fifteen kilotons was the yield of the device the United States dropped on Hiroshima to end World War II—so five will make a big-ass dent in a city."

The darkened room was deathly quiet, silence broken only by the soft whir of the cooling fan in the ceiling-mounted projector.

"Ladies and gents, the suitcase nuke. Our worst damned nightmare."

CHAPTER TWENTY-NINE

Act boldly and unseen forces will come to your aid.
Dorothea Brande (1893-1948), American writer

Xavier Cloud climbed into the flight deck of the Super Hercules to find the pilot's hands flying over the controls. He plugged his headset into the ICS and vox piped his voice into the intercom.

"Is this a bad time?"

"Pressure's still falling," the copilot announced in Chinese.

"Copy pressure's falling," the pilot responded in Chinese. "You have the airplane." The copilot acknowledged.

He turned to Cloud and spoke in English. "That little incident with the truck on takeoff was more than a bird strike. We have big damage to the landing gear hydraulics. It was all we could do to get the wheels up and the doors closed on takeoff. Primary and backup systems were damaged and we're hemorrhaging hydraulic fluid like crazy. We can replenish it in flight to a certain extent, but by the rate we're losing the fluid, I don't think we can keep up."

The Engine Instrument Display Panel showed the hydraulic pressure dropping—a red box around it indicated pressure was out of limits and underscored the urgency. There had been horns and other crisis sounds too, but those signals had been cancelled.

"Will we be able to land?" Cloud asked. The Chinese pilot grinned without mirth.

"I don't know. I mean, gravity will not be denied at some point, after all. You haven't told me where we're going yet, but I think that Rose Bowl option is out."

He reached forward and tapped a readout on the instrument panel.

"Oh, by the way? We need gas. A lot of it—and soon."

CHAPTER THIRTY

If you want to go fast, go alone. If you want to go far, go together.
African proverb

Amber Watson and Tracey Lexcellent sat in Amber's yellow Corvette on Belle Isle Park, the convertible top down and early evening summer glory flooding in. The beautiful leafy island in the midst of the Detroit River had been ceded to the state park system during Detroit's bankruptcy days, and the state had restored the place to verdant eminence.

Wide avenues used for the annual IndyCar racing festival made plenty of smooth surfaces for drivers, bicyclists and, of course, runners. Safety had returned with regular patrols by a small state police contingent that included park rangers with full-dress police powers.

It had been a sunny day, warm in the high 70s. Now, as the sun headed west, the women sat in the Vette facing a glittering downtown cityscape come alive with lights, eating drive-thru food out of a grease-stained carry-out bag.

"*Ohh*, that's really good," Tracey moaned through a big bite of sloppy double-cheeseburger. "I think I'm having a mouthgasm."

"I swear I don't know how you can eat like this and still look like—like *that*," Amber said, waving an airy gesture at Tracey's curvy form.

She swirled the ice in what was left of a Diet Pepsi in a fast-food cup featuring Captain America and other Marvel characters, and nibbled at a cold deep-fried chicken wad of dubious nutritional value.

Tracey mumbled through the burger bite. "It's not my fault. I have the metabolism of a horny ferret."

It was harder and harder for Amber to keep her weight in check, even though she mostly ate reasonably and worked out some. Exercise had never been a best friend, even in her Army days, where she often skated around the MP company's routine physical training workouts with some duty-related excuse, real or imagined. The MP investigators enjoyed such leeway in those days, and the company commanders mostly didn't care all that much if the PT paperwork was clean and nobody dropped any dimes to battalion.

Tracey habitually chewed and talked at the same time, and only occasionally spilled something on her blouse. She tried harder to spill less after Amber started calling Tracey's ample chest a snack ledge because all the dropped food bits collected there.

"We gotta find that damned William Cortez Williams. He is the answer to a buncha questions." Tracey ticked them off on her greasy hand, finger by finger. "Did he actually kill al-Taja? If so, why? How did the little jerk even know him? And why isn't DHS helping us at all? Al-Taja was their guy. You'd think they'd want to help us find his killer." She examined an index finger and then licked some sauce from it.

Amber snorted. "Well, that DHS moron, Anderson, was in the meeting with the NTAC last week when he gave me permission to keep working the case with you. That probably means something."

Tracey giggled. "NTAC! No-Talent Ass-Clown is funny. Does FBI Special Agent in Charge Benoit know you refer to him with such affection?"

"I dunno. I s'pose not. Who gives a shit? He insists we use 'Benoit III' when we refer to him, by the way, number and all. Says it's part of his name. 'That asshole' is part of his name too, but we don't use that; I mean, not in front of him. I'm retiring in less than ninety days, he can't do jack to me."

Amber took a pull on the drink straw and it returned the icy gurgles of an empty cup.

"What's the deal on Williams' momma, anyway? If she's not returning your calls, whyn't we just mosey on over that way and pay her a little social call ourownselves?"

"I love it. Nobody has answered the door yet, but it's worth another try." Tracey grinned and nodded. "I mean, we're friendly people, right?"

Amber turned the sports car's ignition key and was rewarded with a throaty V-8 rumble. She backed the Corvette with care off the grassy area facing a picture-postcard Detroit skyline twinkling with light and headed for the park exit.

Tracey took a last look at the lovely downtown skyline view through the passenger-side door mirror as they departed, and smiled.

✪

The screaming-yellow Corvette was not inconspicuous parked down the street from the Williams residence on Detroit's east side, but it was after sunset now and that helped some. This was one of the many neighborhood avenues whose dark streetlights had not yet been restored by a reawakening city still punch-drunk from bankruptcy, so some cover was realized.

Nevertheless, the porches were jammed with people smoking or drinking or making out in the warm night, here a charcoal grill glowing red under steaks and sizzling hamburgers, there old men gathered around a giant prehistoric radio perched on a windowsill listening to a WXYT replay of the Tigers pennant game that clinched the Series berth in their improbable triumphant year. They cackled in glee at every crack of a bat.

There also were abandoned houses and charred husks dotting the block, communal voids that used to be filled with families, but no longer homes to anything but tall weeds, rodents, homeless people and junkies—random, insignificant humans who lay on newspapers or dirty mattresses stained with bodily fluids, chemically dreaming of better days, past and future.

Soon the highs would dissipate and so would those dreams, and the cycle would start again.

"Sixteen seventeen, right? The address?" Amber asked. She habitually touched her credentials wallet and her holster.

"Yeah, down there," Tracey gestured, looking around, "six houses on the left. With the gaslight in the front yard."

She had prowled the neighborhood solo before looking for William Cortez Williams, but it looked different at night and she had to reacquaint herself with known landmarks. That was one of the earliest lessons taught in the police academy: Everything is different at night. Places, colors. Sounds, smells. People.

The two women walked up the street on the sidewalk opposite the Williams home. Citizens on the porches didn't need spider sense or to see badges to understand these were police officers. Two nicely dressed white women walking in this neighborhood did not mean Avon was calling.

They stopped behind a large white Sprinter work van directly across the street from the Williams house, and peeked through the van's tinted door glass. The house lights on the ground floor were on in the front and on the side, and one was on upstairs in the back. The window was small, and they suspected it was a bathroom. The front door and windows were open, curtains fluttering gently in the night breeze. It looked a lot like someone was home this time.

"I'm just going up to the front door like I own the joint," Tracey said. "Will you go up the driveway and watch that side door for me?"

"You bet."

Amber checked her weapon and credentials wallet. She looked up to see on the unlit porch behind them a middle-aged man wearing a bright white wife-beater and a dark blue ball cap with the Detroit Tigers' white olde English D, taking it all in. The muscular man was dusky brown and nearly invisible on the shadowed porch, making the T-shirt and the olde English D hover in space like a Hollywood special effect.

When Amber's eyes locked with his, he grinned a knowing Cheshire grin, nodded and gave her an upraised thumb in a hand holding a cigarette. Amber smiled back, grateful for the show of support, and returned the gesture.

"Okay," she said to Tracey. "Ready-set-go?"

The women strolled casually from behind the large work van and crossed the street. Amber went to the right rear corner of the house, where she would have eyes on both the side door into the driveway and the windows and back door into the yard next to a detached garage. Her left arm was across her midsection and her hand rested on the butt of her handgun in the cross-draw holster.

Tracey walked up creaking wooden front porch steps and knocked calmly on the screen door. The interior door and a decorative iron security grille stood open, letting in a breeze that ruffled lavender sheers before making a left turn back outside through the open front windows. Tracey didn't pound on the door like cops do, just knocked politely, like a next-door neighbor would.

The lightweight screen door of old warped pine rattled in its frame with every hit. Soon an attractive black woman in a casual sleeveless print shift came to the door. When she saw Tracey, the wide smile that had been forming faded.

"Miz Williams?" Tracey asked. She held up her badge in a leather holder. The woman took a deep breath before answering.

"Yes," Carla Williams said, exhaling in a discouraged rush. Resigned, she pushed open the screen door and its rusty spring made that happy summer-memory sound screen door springs often make.

"Come in, child."

Tracey and Amber sat in comfortable, overstuffed chairs in Carla Williams' tidy living room. They declined her offer of lemonade, but Tracey accepted a second offer of sweet tea.

"My own momma used to make swee' tea," Tracey cooed.

She accepted the sweaty gas station-premium glass emblazoned with Detroit Lions football logos, and a brown Arby's napkin to absorb the condensation.

Amber looked at Tracey sideways: Was there just a tiny hint of fake Southern accent in there just then?

Carla Williams sat back and ramrod straight in a large wing chair that faced not the television, but the street. Floor to ceiling shelves of books lined an opposite wall, with a large Master of Science in Nursing degree in a handsome frame on a shelf. Next to her on the floor in wicker baskets was a knitting project on one side and a large stack of the religious magazine *Guideposts* on the other side. The cover of the top magazine was filled with an American flag photograph and the simple headline "In God We Trust."

"I know who you are," she said to Tracey. "I've seen you on the news." She fanned her hands across her dress to smooth invisible wrinkles, a nervous and pointless effort. "I'm sorry I never returned your calls." She was quiet and seemed sad.

"Miz Williams, we think your son can help us solve a homicide," Tracey began. "He may not even be involved in it, but I gotta talk with him to get him cleared. He was legally released from the jail on his traffic stop the other day, but I can't find him anywhere to clear him of this other thing. Can you tell me where he is, ma'am, please?"

"How do I know you would treat him right?"

She wasn't quite angry, but she was tense, wary, a mother lion protecting her cub. The Detroit Police had earned every iota of such circumspection in some precincts. The Williams boy was seventeen. He was in danger just being a young man in the city, exposed in the streets and the schools to thugs and athletes, sons of drug dealers and sons of car dealers.

There were a thousand ways and more that a young man's life could go sideways in Detroit, but only a few ways for it not to. Parental oversight usually made all the difference.

Except for occasional traffic beefs, Tracey had seen in the files, the boy's record was clear. He didn't come off as a dangerous kid at all, she thought, so a homicide was way out of character. In fact, there was no mention in the kid's jacket of any gang pedigree that Jeff O'Brien claimed when he busted Williams for speeding past the cemetery that day.

Carla Williams stared down at the floral print fading in her dress. "I am old. I am tired. I have lost one son to those God-forsaken *streets*," she said, tipping her head toward the unlighted street outside her windows.

Tracey had seen the records of Williams' oldest son's death by heroin overdose. EMS had already been in the dope house, called to help another skank who was crashing, when the Williams boy, Elder by name, crashed too. Neither of them would be saved that day.

The mother looked up and pinned Tracey with a fierce stare.

"I do not—I do *not*—intend to lose another one."

"I understand," Tracey said. The soothing Southern pretense had left her voice. Now she was speaking to Carla Williams woman to woman. "I do understand. I'm a Detroit girl, too."

Williams looked up.

"Yes, born and raised. I am from our city." Williams drew breath to object. "But no, I am not of these streets. Your streets. I won't tell that lie." Williams settled back down in her chair.

"I love our city." Tracey said. "I do. I know you do, too. So please help me help you, and your son. I must talk with him soon. Nobody needs your boy to be run up on by some street cop who doesn't give a sh—who doesn't care about him, only sees him as a faceless Want in the computer. Let me protect him. Let me help him.

"Let me talk to him."

Neither Tracey nor Amber could tell whether Tracey's plea had struck a nerve or been remotely successful. They waited patiently while Carla Williams quietly mulled it over in her mind. Then she decided.

"You know, a mother always knows what's best for her baby," she said, looking up. This was the moment of truth. "Cortez?"

Amber heard a soft rustle from the kitchen only inches away. She spun and pulled her handgun faster than any cowboy in the history of Western movies.

In the doorway stood William Cortez Williams himself, hands away from his sides and palms facing forward.

"Yes, Momma?"

Outside, as if on some impossible celestial cue, the dark streetlights all winked back on at the same time.

CHAPTER THIRTY-ONE

There is nothing so strong or safe in
an emergency of life as the simple truth.
Charles Dickens (1812-1870), English writer

I thought you guys had all your logistics lined up," Cloud said. The pilot shrugged. "You didn't think we'd maybe need some in-flight refueling?"

"As a matter of fact, I *did* plan for that," the pilot said, testy. This was as edgy as the man had been the entire trip. He looked up to Chuck Xing.

"We burned additional fuel coming across Iran and Afghanistan fast and low to avoid radar. That was a long flight to begin with, but low altitude means more drag, and I swear we might have clipped a few camels on that flight. We burned up more fuel with that high-energy departure from Tagab. So we're low on fuel right now. Really low. And still flying under the radar, which will have to change soon."

He gestured out of the windscreen to the low, black sawtooth silhouettes against the far-off dawn.

"Those are mountains ahead."

"What does that mean in my language?" Cloud asked.

"Well, in short, I think we have about twenty minutes. And then we must be hooked up to an in-flight refueler, on the ground next to a fuel truck—or jumping out of the aft door."

Cloud had seen parachutes stowed in the executive pod. There weren't enough of them for everybody. But as a precaution after the hydraulic failure, he had the loadmaster rig the money pallets with cargo chutes and reinforce the eroded plastic shrinkwrap with round after round of duct tape. If they had to eject the pallets before a crash, the shrinkwrap was likely to shred in the wind blast almost instantly anyway, amplifying a pennies-from-heaven theme unheard of among desert-dwelling tribes.

All you can do is all you can do, Cloud thought.

"How far can we get?" Xing asked.

"Not far. I'm nearly on fumes already. Twenty minutes is well inside my reserves. That means we ought to be looking for a flat place to put down right now. I'm not sure the landing gear will go down and lock one more time. I'm positive it won't come back up."

"We had our tanker lined up to meet us," Xing said. "Where is it?"

"They radioed that they couldn't make the rendezvous," the pilot said. "They got bottled up by combat air patrols we didn't expect, and they never got off the ground. They are too far away now to reach us in time. And listen, if we can get in-flight refueling, we can't do it down here in the weeds. We'll have to climb. That means we show up on everybody's radars, friends and foes."

He looked up at Cloud. "And we have damned few friends in this neighborhood."

The Russians were flying combat patrols all over the region, especially around Syria and its borders, and the Russian shoot-down of a commercial airliner in Ukraine was well documented. No one wanted to bump into a random flight of Russian fighters and risk a shoot-down here. A regular Hercules is pitifully undefended.

"You're right about that. I know the maps of these countries perfectly, and there are no places around here on the ground friendly enough for us to land for fuel with a hundred million bucks on board," Cloud said. "I don't want to have to explain our payload."

Some cash American might grease a few palms for a freelance refueling on the ground somewhere, but God help them, Cloud thought, if anyone got a glimpse of the pallets. People will do crazy, suicidal stuff for a crack at a couple of pallets of money.

"We can't just fly around until we run out of gas," Cloud said. He looked around the all-glass aircraft cockpit until he spied the radio stack. A wild idea formed.

Could it work? he thought. *Ain't nothin' to it but to do it.*

"I'm going to give you a radio frequency," he said to the pilot. "You dial that in and let me do the talking."

✪

In a darkened and cooled air traffic control trailer parked outside of the American Embassy in Kabul, Afghanistan, drowsy Air Force Reserve air traffic control Airman Tom Orlando was on twenty-four-month recall orders to active duty. He was tilted back in his office chair playing Fortnite on an iPad. His radio headset covered just one ear so that he could hear game play in the other.

This was a slow night. No white flights—the ones that were known—were scheduled, and the one or two unscheduled black missions that occasionally flew by had not materialized so far. Nevertheless, two Air Force KC-135R Stratotankers and a KC-10 Extender aerial refueling jet orbited in large thirds of the sky to service anyone who needed a jolt to get back to a distant base or aircraft carrier.

Orlando was happy to have this break. They come few and far between in a war zone.

Then the radio crackled in his ear, heavy with static.

"Aspic One, Aspic One. This is Acrobat. Aspic One, Acrobat."

The airman had leaned so far back in his chair that the sudden radio call, with a secret callsign on a secret frequency, caused him to fall backward and complete the arc. The iPad hit the floor hard, the screen shattered and it went dark.

It was the first time Orlando had ever received a call for the dormant master callsign of the American Embassy—and he had never gotten a call on this never-used secret wavelength. No one he knew had ever received one, either.

Scrambling back into his swivel chair and repositioning the headset over both ears, he keyed the mic and responded. At the same time, a new radar contact was painted on an unidentified target to the southwest, climbing hard out of nowhere. It was too slow to be a missile and it was going away, so first things first.

He thought he knew what it was in any case.

"Uh, Ac-Acrobat, Aspic One." His voice was shaking. He had to notify somebody about this. He fanned through the soft-cover operations ring binder to the ACROBAT tab and scanned the procedure, then keyed his radio.

"Change frequency to ALT-seven and ident." The airman's lips moved silently as a finger traced down the bullet points of how the secret procedure was to work.

Black flights like this sometimes popped up from thin air, and they sometimes didn't have the daily sheet of radio code words for positive identification. They were black flights precisely because they wanted no identification.

But this was a hot war zone. The wrong answer from a mystery guest could be bad for everybody. The operations binder gave the procedures to follow to identify such mystery radio calls and radar contacts.

"Ah, Acrobat, Aspic One." Orlando's finger stopped midway on the page at the communications codes. "Authenticate *Bernardo.*" What the hell was going on here, man?

In the Hercules, the pilot started a countdown-to-empty clock ticking backwards from fourteen minutes. The copilot changed the radio frequency to a secure encrypted channel Cloud provided from memory. He handed the copilot a scrap of paper with a squawk code written on it that would identify the plane to air traffic control radar.

The copilot punched a keypad to read 2700 before pushing down a Send button, transmitting the Identify Friend or Foe code to the U.S. Air Force ATC computers.

Every air traffic controller in the U.S. armed forces knew Acrobat and its variants was a priority CIA callsign, and 2700 was a primary CIA special air mission IFF that had precedence over anything that wasn't Air Force One, the command aircraft of the president of the United States. Especially over Fortnite.

Few remembered any more that SAM 27000 was the callsign for a former back-up Air Force One, the second of two Boeing VC-137C aircraft in service from 1972 to 2001. The CIA just loves Easter eggs like that.

The challenge-response authentication was an additional security protocol. A random incoming radio call is no different than a cellphone ringing with no Caller ID. Except in the war zone, the caller probably wasn't going to be a telemarketer.

The Air Force controller had asked Cloud for the correct response to the challenge code word *Bernardo*. Anyone could spin up a radio call and ask for things, in good English and sounding legitimate. Authentication assured the airman that the mysterious radio call wasn't from some bad guys trying to lure good guys to a spectacular ambush.

If the caller provided the correct answer, his identity as an American or ally was confirmed. If not, he just might get a visit from fighter jets on combat air patrol, and a missile up his tailpipe.

However, Cloud had not had to authenticate more than an internet purchase in over ten years. Code words were changed daily—sometimes hourly—and he obviously didn't have the daily comm card known to some aviators as a bat decoder, with the roster of current communication codes.

"Acrobat, Aspic One, contact, I have you Special Air Mission two-seven hundred, southwest and climbing out of angels one-nine. Authenticate *Bernardo*. Copy?"

Orlando was a bit more insistent that time. He noted on his radar display a three-plane flight of U.S. Air Force F-16s on combat air patrol only about four minutes away on afterburners from his mysterious caller. Just in case.

"This is Acrobat. Copy that, southwest, angels one-nine. Standby." Cloud turned to the Chinese pilot.

"Can you line up on an American aerial tanker?"

The pilot smiled. *Did nothing bother this guy?* Cloud wondered.

"Yes, I can," he said, and presented a thumbs-up. The man's wide, sincere grin in the dim light reminded Cloud of George Takei as Mr. Sulu in *Star Trek*.

"But what are you going to do about the code word?" the pilot asked.

Cloud smiled with confidence, but he wasn't entirely sure.

"I'm gonna do what I do," he said, but even as he uttered the words, for a rare change, he didn't immediately know what that was. Cloud gazed out of the cockpit windows. Blooming morning sun backlighted a looming orange horizon well-defined by craggy mountains. War was often gorgeous at altitude.

Bernardo, huh? *Bernardo* ...

"Acrobat, Aspic One ..."

Cloud keyed the radio mic and spoke with confidence and authority.

"Aspic One, Acrobat. Our fuel state is *chicken*. I say again, *chicken* fuel state. Request a direct vector to ARCO 3."

Cloud took a deep breath. It could only be one thing.

"I authenticate ... *Long live the king.*"

On the instrument panel, the pilot's countdown clock reached nine minutes. *And this is not an exact science,* Cloud thought.

There was a long silence. The military brevity code *chicken* identified them as requiring urgent tanker support. The whine of four hungry turboprops sucking down their last gallons of fuel at a prodigious rate was all that broke the silence while men crowding the flight deck waited nervously for the radio to come back to life.

They were running out of gas fast, and there was no fallback position—only *fall down.*

One way or the other, without a successful authentication the aircraft would run out of fuel at 21,000 feet above the sand just about the time the combat air patrol arrived to send the mysterious Hercules back to the taxpayers in pieces.

"Acrobat, Aspic One." There was a long burst of sudden radio static that threatened to drown out the airman's transmission. "... support required. I say again, copy *chicken* fuel state, urgent tanker support required."

There was a pause and another burst of static.

"Copy authentication, sir—standby for vector."

There was a stunned moment of silence before loud cheers and clapping erupted in the Super Hercules cockpit. Chuck Xing stared up at Cloud in open admiration.

"Man, I was standing right here—*right here!*—and you pulled that code phrase straight out of your ass! How did you *do* that?"

Even Cloud was amused by his achievement.

"Well, I have a pretty good memory. Perfect, in fact, but we needed some dumb luck. From the odd challenge code word, I was counting on the code writer to be a Shakespeare fan with a sense of humor. Bernardo is a character in the opening lines of Hamlet, and sentries challenge him as he approaches in the fog. Classic call-and-response. In the play, the soldiers demand Bernardo to 'Stand, and unfold yourself,' meaning to identify himself in the dark with an expected response. He answers simply with a loyal soldier's reply, 'Long live the king,' and they recognize him as Bernardo. I was counting on our radio exchange to be similar. He asked 'Bernardo,' I answered, 'Long live the king.'"

The men on the flight deck regarded Cloud in silent, open-mouth awe. Turboprops droned in the background.

"C'mon," Cloud said. "Life is a crapshoot. This time the dice rolled for us. Next time, they might roll *on* us. Besides, James Brown did a better call-and-response in '68, with 'I'm Black and I'm Proud.'"

Airman Orlando saw all three refueling aircraft, callsigns ARCO, on his radar screen. Two tankers, ARCO 1 and ARCO 2, were well northwest and northeast of Acrobat's position, but ARCO 3, the KC-10 Extender, patrolled the area southwest of Kabul where Acrobat was flying low on fuel.

If this obviously black flight appearing out of nowhere was *chicken* fuel state—nearly dry—it was a damned good thing this cagey man on the radio knew what he was talking about. They were probably only about four minutes away from the flying gas station and the pause that refreshes.

The airman was thrilled to have something to do that for once seemed important—the C-I-*mother-grabbing*-A was on the horn, baby! He would tell carefully parsed war stories about this encounter later, but he was all business now.

"Acrobat, Aspic One," Orlando radioed. "Vector two-two-three degrees and descend to angels one-seven. Contact ARCO 3 on two-two-six-point-seven. I will advise them you are inbound. And you sir, you have yourself a *fine* Air Force day."

Cloud smiled. "Acrobat, copy heading two-two-three, descend angels one-seven." Listening on his own headset, the Chinese pilot heard the instructions and nodded wordlessly. He started turning the aircraft toward the tanker's place in the sky and the co-pilot reached forward to change another radio to the rendezvous frequency.

"Contact ARCO 3 on two-two-six-point-seven. Thanks a lot, bubba. You made damned good money today. Out here."

Cloud pulled one side of the headset off his ear.

"And that," he said to Chuck Xing with a flourish, "is how we do it around here."

He turned to the Chinese pilot, suddenly realizing he had never asked the man his name. The pilot's flight suit had no nametape.

"Hey man, you do good work. What is your name, anyway?"

"Call me Bob. I always liked that name. I found a sweet vintage garage mechanic's shirt on eBay with a blue oval on the left chest, and the name says Bob. I've been Bob ever since." He extended his hand to Cloud, who grabbed and shook it with a smile. "How the heck are ya?"

"Well, I'm okay, Bob—I'm damned great just about now, thanks." The two men laughed at each other's nervous elation that disguised the anxiety now evaporating away inside.

"Let's find that tanker and get us some gas," Cloud said. "I suppose you've done in-flight refueling before, yes? That's a pretty small gas door you got up there."

He pointed to the top of the Super Hercules. The inflight refueling port was directly over their heads. Bob would follow radio directions and maneuvering lights up to the tail end of the American tanker. Then the boom operator in the flying gas pump would take over, actually flying the boom with his own control stick right into the fuel inlet of the Hercules. About forty-six thousand pounds later, they could go nearly anywhere within twenty-four-hundred miles with good reserves.

"It's not impossible," Bob said, eying Cloud with a sideways glance. "I used to bull's-eye womp rats in my T-16 back home, and they're not much bigger than two meters."

Cloud took only wry comfort at that line. It was word-for-word what

Luke Skywalker had uttered in *Star Wars* just before leading the attack on the Death Star.

✪

Thirteen months later, Tom Orlando's feet were propped up on the arm of his mother's sofa while he watched a *Ridiculousness* re-run on MTV. It was getting spring-like in San Diego, and after two years of Air Force recall, he was anxious to resume his life and his dispatcher job with the San Diego County Sheriff Department.

There was a knock at the door and his mother answered it. A few words were exchanged and his mother laughed. Then he heard a heavy truck engine as someone drove away.

His mother stood in the hallway looking at him with an astonished look on her face. "Tommy?"

Orlando didn't look up. "Yes, mom?"

"Come here, please. I think you have a delivery."

Not expecting any FedEx today, he thought. He rose and walked to the front door. His mother handed him a boxed object in a sealed bubble envelope. He tore it open to find a brand-new iPad.

"What's this?" he asked, hugging his mother. "You are such a sweetie—did you buy me this?"

"No, honey. But it was delivered with that." She pointed out of the open door. Orlando stepped around the corner and saw a brand-new Air Force-blue Corvette convertible in the driveway.

He ripped open the envelope and found a card stamped simply *Thank You* in silver on the front. Written inside, it said, *Thanks again, bubba.*

It was signed *Acrobat.*

CHAPTER THIRTY-TWO

Extremism in the defense of liberty is no vice.
Barry Goldwater (1909-1998), 1964 presidential candidate

Poppy Benedict pushed his slideshow button one last time and the screen filled with the seal of the CIA. He placed the remote control on the podium and leaned forward on his arms.

"Look, folks, I'm not going to blow sunshine up your skirts. This is a no-bullshit evolution. We gotta find out who's doing what to whom here—in three different directions—or we gotta go down to the U-Haul store and start moving our families to the hills."

He looked around the room and saw two things: determination, and a bit of fear.

"Because if Dearborn goes up in flames in some Muslim-Skinhead race war, or the World-fucking-Series gets 9/11'd *on television?* Well, the game is over. We won't have to wait for the ISIS assholes to blow up DC next, because the American people will haul us out by our necks and kill us in front of our children *for not doing our goddamned jobs.*"

In his chair, General McCandless had nothing to add. Benedict had read his mind.

"So, here's what we're gonna do, people. Science and Tech?"

"Yo!" Two voices called from the back of the room, and two short-sleeved arms rose in the gloom.

"Mine first, then DHS. Let's heat up our proprietary cellphone towers in the Midwest, say Illinois, Ohio, Michigan, and Ontario. I'll take care of the Canadian coordination. Start sifting the metadata for relationships with our known actors, including the Chinese *restauranteur* and extended family. Unleash all the surveillance you got. I want the USA-186 satellite repurposed over Detroit and made exclusive—and armed drones on 24/7 overwatch on Dearborn and Comerica Park in twelve hours. Copy armed, correct?"

The CIA Science & Tech manager, Tom Hughes, raised a single thumb into the air over his head, and kept typing on a tablet with the other hand.

"Source 'em where you got 'em for now—is that Nellis or Battle Creek, or where?"

"Ah, both, sir," Hughes said, nodding without looking up as he continued to type on his tablet.

Poppy nodded. "We'll figure out area logistical and operational support shortly. I don't want to shoot anybody in an American city, but if we see a thing going down and we're even pretty sure, we're going weapons hot and we will sort out the public relations later. Better to be excoriated for blowing up terrorists on an American street corner than for not blowing up those pricks at all and dealing with the aftermath of what they do."

Hughes raised his hand again. "Sir, we have a new MQ-9L SuperReaper and three Avenger UCAVs out at White Sands right now, equipped for testing in the laser upfit program. Two Avengers have the 150-kilowatt beams and the SuperReaper has that new experimental 300-kilowatt unit. Those both are well powerful enough to deal with most hard targets, like cars, but it's literally overkill for soft targets—for individuals. If we have to shoot at people in an urban environment, this approach would help us contain the collateral damage."

Hughes grinned wryly.

"I mean, a human target will just instantly burst into flames, or pieces. You should see the cows we've shot out at Dreamland." He made two fists and extended the fingers all at once, making an explosion sound. An engineer sitting next to Hughes made a disapproving face.

"What?" Watson protested. "They were euthanized first."

Dreamland was a common shorthand for the old Area 51 test range in Nevada—classic location of recovered aliens, UFOs and more—and where weapons platforms were still sometimes tested at night. All the real secret aviation stuff and artificial intelligence research had long ago been moved to Area 51-Delta, sometimes referred to as Dreamland-D, or more commonly *Winghaven.*

"Do it," Benedict said. "Lay on conventionally armed backups, though. I'll get PRISM and XKEYSCORE assignments for this operation to zero in on Midwest phone, internet, and email traffic. Anyone in this room can forward keywords for us to look for, but I think we'll have it covered."

Watson spoke up. "Sir, do you want FIVE EYES coordination?"

The FIVE EYES group is comprised of the United States, United Kingdom, Canada, Australia and New Zealand. It's a coordinated faction of intel sharers that goes back to the end of World War II, when they watched the developing and disturbing activities of the Soviet Union and its client states. Today, in a broader contemporary threat window, its activities covered the planet with communications surveillance of all kinds, mostly within the CIA's ECHELON signals intelligence collection and analysis network.

"Ahh, not generally, Tom," Benedict said. "Let's do ping the Brits on this. They can help with oversight of some Middle East regions, especially while *Patient Anvil* is underway out there. I'm going to talk to the Canadians anyway, so I'll brief them in, too. And Tom, get someone to adjust our parameters in BOUNDLESS INFORMANT, please. I'd like our new attention focused on Michigan to not show up red on the activity heat map until we're ready, okay?"

Benedict took a deep breath and exhaled.

"We must go correct on this, people—cool, calm, and collected. I'm pissed about having to chase down assholes trying to do another attack on a par with 9/11, but I don't make decisions based on that anger. I'll email delegation of authority to some people who also can authorize trigger pullers, if need be. Quiet as it's kept, I do not work around the clock. Not effectively, anyway, after the first seventy-two. But when the time comes to move on something, chances are you can't wait for the information to go up the chain of command. That means your asses are on the hot seat—but if you screw it up, rest assured my ass is going to be on the hot seat right next to you.

"Cross-check *everything*. You need more analysts, just wire them in from other sections. Highest priority, and I'm buyin' the overtime. Nothing gets past us on this, okay? Your people have questions and you have time, you staff 'em up the chain. Anyone who doesn't know what they're looking at, moment to moment, you ping somebody *fast* who does."

Benedict tapped the podium with an index finger three times. "We're definitely working without a net here, people. If you're on the bubble for a decision, you act first and ask questions later. That's official."

The room was as quiet as a cathedral. The prospect of combat shooting at targets in a populous American city with Star Wars weapons required some moments of introspection.

"Homeland Security S&T?" Benedict said.

"Here, sir," a woman replied.

"I need you people on the ground in the three counties of southeastern Michigan—Wayne, Oakland and Macomb—with radiation sniffers, our own cell towers, and with at least one NEST team. Two is better."

A Nuclear Emergency Support Team is made up of nuclear physicists and scientists who work in the nation's weapons labs, but when their encrypted pagers alert them—and sometimes commandoes—they become an investigative unit tasked with finding and dealing with a terrorist's nuclear weapon before it ruins everyone's day.

Poppy didn't think the *jihadis* were going to succeed in getting a Mad Gopher via General Xing, but he was paid to assess risk. And there were other sources of such weapons and essential components on Earth.

This risk was unknown, so as the saying goes, hope for bon-bons and rainbows if you must, but plan for an ambush.

"DHS OPSO?" The Homeland Security operations officer raised his hand. "I want you to get me every scrap of paper and pixels you have on Mohammed al-Taja, and somebody who knows how to talk about him intelligently. He had a handler—get me that contact info, please. We're going to open this cat up wide and find out if he is anything more than a guy in the wrong place at the wrong time. My guess—well, my guess is he was killed on purpose, but I ain't guessing. Let's find out. I need that in two hours, please. That damned autopsy report is overdue, too."

"Roger that, sir," the DHS OPSO said.

"DOD?"

General McCandless cleared his throat just a little. "Poppy, I guess that's me."

Benedict had forgotten his boss was sitting quietly in the background shadows.

"Oh, sorry sir. Well, I'd like to have some DOD assets on standby if we can get them. CIA—sorry, 'FBI,'—probably doesn't have enough drones, ordnance, or operators to make a full-court press work in the Midwest. Can you move aircraft and people to operate from Selfridge or Battle Creek, as needed?"

The Selfridge Air National Guard Base in Detroit's far suburb of Mt. Clemens, Michigan, was not a secret location. The sprawling former active Air Force base was a fixture in the Midwest, and military air traffic routinely flew into and out of the big airfield all day long. A few extra aircraft and transient personnel would raise no red flags outside the base, and anyone on the inside was on the team.

Plus, it was literally minutes to Dearborn and downtown Detroit if aircraft had to scramble suddenly. The Battle Creek ANG base in Western Michigan already had a wing of General Atomics MQ-9 Reaper unmanned aerial vehicles in the 172nd Attack Squadron stationed at Kellogg Field. A few more UAVs, airplanes and staff there would not be suspicious.

Poppy would have to trust blind luck that flying additional aircraft and surveillance drones around the clock would not trigger interest from the nosy cellphone cameras of airplane buffs and the general public.

"I will provide whatever you ask for," McCandless said.

"Thank you, sir. Got that for action, Tom?" Hughes again raised a thumb high in the air.

"DOJ?"

"Justice here, sir," a man said.

"I want the FBI to coordinate with DHS and be sure you send me everything you have on this al-Taja case. Has the SAC taken over that file yet? Last I heard, he had a street agent and a Detroit PD homicide detective working it. Who is this genius SAC, anyway?"

"He's Special Agent in Charge—" the man started to say. Benedict chopped him off.

"Yeah, that was a rhetorical question, sir," Benedict said, a little testy. The pressure was starting to ramp up on him. He could feel his afternoon sugar deficiency starting to poke him. This often resulted in an edgy response when dealing with people to whom he had to explain the obvious.

"Please get the FBI case files and computer records to me soonest. I'd like to see them in two hours, please."

Poppy Benedict was one of those people who could use the word *please* in a sentence, and you fully understood it was an order.

Even respectful meetings sense when they are about to break up, and the people in this one started the commonplace end-of-meeting rumble of muted talking, chairs rolling back from the table, papers and folders rustling, and so on.

"I think that's it for now. Daily meetings in this room at the same time until otherwise directed." Benedict craned his neck to see the institutional analog clock on the wall above the screen behind him. "Check that, make it 1500 daily, in here. That's three p.m. for you genuine civilians in the group. Our Detroit field office will be established in the next few days and I'll lead a team to work from there."

The lights in the room came back up all the way.

Benedict reorganized his briefing materials with a little practiced difficulty. As a child, his left hand had been accidentally crushed in a car door by an angry stepfather who slammed it without looking. The man had been remorseful, but the episode broke the back of a strained marriage that was already faltering. The hand had healed slightly askew across the knuckles.

When Benedict used the bent index and middle fingers of his left hand to point at the reps from Homeland Security and the Department of Justice as they rose from their chairs, the fingers looked like a snake's fangs.

"Al-Taja," he said. "Two hours." They both nodded and hurried from the conference room.

General McCandless rose and shook Benedict's hand. "Great briefing,

Poppy."

"Thanks, boss." He held the general's gaze for an extra moment before releasing the man's hand.

"But you gotta tell me: What the hell are *cucamarangas?*"

CHAPTER THIRTY-THREE

New beginnings are often disguised as painful endings.
Lao Tzu (605-531 BC), Chinese philosopher and poet

William Cortez Williams was a cool character. Sitting all Mirandized and lawyer-waived in the Detroit Police Headquarters interrogation room, he looked every bit the seventeen-year-old proto-man. He was a calm, collected, and experienced street character who had escaped a serious criminal record only through the grace of God and the oversight of a strict mother still grieving for the tragic loss of her first son.

His façade was cracking just a bit, though, Tracey saw, when small beads of sweat started to form at his hairline.

In Michigan, seventeen-year-olds go to big-boy jail, with no need for parental presence in interrogations or even any notifications. William Cortez Williams had waived his right to remain silent. Whatever happened next was up to him.

"Do you need another pop, or a snack?" Tracey asked the boy. He'd already downed a can of Vernors ginger ale and a small bag of Better Made potato chips.

"No ma'am," he said. "I'm good." Behind a one-way mirror in the observation room next door, Amber Watson and Carla Williams watched the interview proceed. *You damned well better be 'good,'* the boy's tight-lipped mother thought.

"Cortez, tell me about an all-pink Kel-Tec three-eighty," Tracey asked, mustering up a sisterly concern.

Williams didn't flinch. "Three-eighty? I don't mess with no guns." Realizing his mother was watching, he added, "Ma'am."

"Tell me about when you were stopped for speeding a few weeks ago. The arresting officer said he found a pink Kel-Tec three-eighty under your seat, a nine and some dope. Some marijuana. Big bag of weed?"

"Yeah, he stopped me, all right. He said I was doin' sevenny in a thirty-five or some crap like that. Man, I just got that car, and I'm workin' on it, right? But that hooptie can't do sevenny if you drop it off a cliff. It only has two gears, plus reverse. When he pulled me over by the cemetery, he said he arrested me for speeding, but no way I was speeding, man. Ma'am. No way. I'm tellin' you."

Tracey leafed through the folder containing the printouts of the arrest report, the impound sheet, evidence photographs of the guns and marijuana, and the affidavits and the warrant to search the car once the gun had been found in plain view.

At least, "plain view" is what the police report said.

"What about those secret pouches under the seat? You had the gun in one and the dope in the other, didn't you?" Tracey hoped she didn't sound as skeptical as she was beginning to feel.

A sudden annoyed expression fading to expressionless scrolled across the boy's face.

"First off, there ain't no stupid 'secret pouches' under my seats. That car is a 1984 Chevy Monte Carlo and it still has the original cloth seats. They just split at the seam 'cause that cloth is older'n me. Man, even the foam pokes out. That don't make it any stupid 'pouch.' No ma'am, I did not have no gun and no weed. It is not true. No."

Williams' hands were flat on the table as he spoke. When he raised them to self-consciously pass them across his short hair, the boy left moist handprints behind.

Then Williams drew an uncertain breath.

"Somethin' like this, maybe you better look at your boy, is what you better do."

Tracey's face contorted in rage and she leaped to her feet. She knocked back the old office chair that caught a raised seam in the chipped and cracked tile floor and it tripped over with a loud metallic clatter in the enclosed space.

It was time for an episode of Bad Cop Theater. Just now, Tracey thought, it was easy to be convincing.

"Are you telling me," Tracey shouted, "that a Detroit police officer planted a *gun* on you, Cortez? That he planted a Ziploc bag of weed in your car nearly as big as my *head*, Cortez?" She smacked the metal table with the flat of her hand so hard that, behind the glass, Carla Williams was startled and jumped back from the one-way mirror.

"What kinda *bullshit story* is that, Cortez?" Tracey placed her hands on the table. She leaned across just inches from the boy's round face and his suddenly wide, shocked eyes. She spoke in a voice that was scarcely more than a soft, scary whisper.

"You need to tell me. Because that is some kinda *bullshit story.*"

The boy was suddenly terrified and afraid he'd pushed the detective too far with his swagger act. Tracey was triggered, in fact, but in a way Cortez couldn't suspect.

Tracey was roiled by the growing suspicion that Cortez wasn't lying. The consequences of that truth would be as wretched as they would be actionable.

It was the nature of those consequences that Tracey dreaded.

Cortez sat straight up in the chair and in a clear voice enunciating every word, said, "I don't know anything about no gun and no weed, ma'am. Therefore, I cannot tell you if that officer placed that stuff in my car, or found it on the roadside, or pulled it out of his buttocks. I cannot tell you any of these things because I don't know jack about no gun or some weed. I swear on my *mother* I don't."

Cortez stole a quick glance at the mirrored surface of the window over Tracey's shoulder.

"And now, I think maybe you need to let me, ah, see my—my lawyer, please."

He looked down at the table and a bead of moisture dropped onto its surface in a wet starburst of adolescent dread. Tracey couldn't tell if it was sweat, or a tear.

"If you don't mind."

William Cortez Williams was a lot of things. Not great in school, didn't attend church as often as his momma liked, and he sometimes stayed out too late. He also loved thinking about how much fun a career in military service would be. He even toyed with the notion of becoming a cop after the service, if-when. And he always believed he might someday have to pass a polygraph.

William Cortez Williams was a lot of things, all of these and a few others, but a liar was not among them.

Tracey looked at the boy with dismay. If he was lying, she thought, his shit was weak. She would find out and Carla Williams would lose another son to the streets while he burned off twenty-five to life in Jackson State for the murder of Mohammed al-Taja.

But Cortez probably *was* telling the goddamned truth. It angered Tracey to think it, but she felt it in her cop's bones. That meant Cortez didn't kill al-Taja. That also meant her traffic-cop academy fuck buddy Sergeant Jeff O'Brien was not truthful. Any other conclusion just disregarded facts that she would not ignore in any other case, one with a different cast of characters.

There was no ambiguous middle ground here. No gray area.

After a few moments, confused by Tracey's inner timeout, Cortez said, "Miz ma'am?"

"Huh? Oh. No, Cortez, that's okay," Tracey said slowly. She reached out and squeezed the boy's shoulder, like a supportive big sister might, then slowly turned and picked up the discarded chair.

"You don't need a lawyer today, Cortez. You're going home now."

She walked the few steps to the interview room door, twisted the knob and pulled it open. Light flooded into the dimly lit chamber like rays of God's own grace, and Carla Williams already stood bathed in the middle of it like some angelic, redemptive figure descended from an unlikely Heaven.

She rushed into the room and wordlessly wrapped her son in a fierce maternal embrace, rocking him back and forth for nearly a minute, her arms engulfing his head. By the time she stopped and pulled back, the mother and the son both had fat tears of euphoria and exhaustion rolling down their faces onto their shirts.

"Miz Williams, you can take Cortez home now," Tracey said. She was dog-tired and suddenly certain that her life had been wasted doing police work.

"We're done for tonight."

Then a harder, commanding tone infiltrated Tracey's voice.

"But stick around, okay, Cortez? No more creepin' and stayin' away and stuff. I need to see you when I need to see you, got it?"

The boy grinned and nodded. He wiped at his shining eyes with the back of a chocolate-brown hand and it came away wet. "Yes, ma'am. I got that."

Tracey nodded at Carla Williams.

"C'mon son," Williams said. She wrapped her arm around the boy's neck. "I made cupcakes."

Tracey watched Cortez and his mother, arm in arm, walk away down the stark corridor. Its many layers of paint were chipped and stained with institutional indifference to aesthetics and the previous decades of heartbreak witnessed there, and the flickering overhead fluorescent tubes were impassive eyewitnesses to what had transpired. Tracey was suddenly inflamed by the repetitive futility of her occupation.

She was so utterly tired of it all.

I still have Ronnie Clark's phone number, Tracey thought, *maybe even his email. I should reach out to him, see what he's doing. He liked me a lot. I could stand to be a rich bitch, drive a Mercedes, live in Grosse Pointe, have cute babies. Ronnie was cute as hell. Bet he'd make some damned fine babies. He did like me a lot. He was a boob man.*

Then Tracey paused and shook her red mane madly for a moment, as if shedding an infestation of insects and bad juju. But it was her guttural growl that sold the frustration.

"Oh, Jesus, Mary, and *Shlomo!* What—what fresh *bullshit* is this?" she said aloud.

Amber's head spun around, caught by surprise at her partner's outburst. "What, hon? Cortez?"

In her reverie, she'd forgotten where she was for a moment. She desperately needed a hard run, and Belle Isle beckoned to her by name.

"Who? Oh, no. It's nothing. I was just thinking about something really stupid for a sec." *Grosse Pointe sucks anyway,* Tracey said in her head.

"C'mon," she said to Amber, lunging for the door to the elevators.

"Where we headed?" Amber asked, trailing Tracey down the dingy hallway.

"We are going to talk to my old friend The Grim Reaper."

CHAPTER THIRTY-FOUR

In preparing for battle I have always found that
plans are useless, but planning is indispensable.
Dwight D. Eisenhower (1890-1969), 34th American President

Owosso Community Airport is a sleepy place most days, but the activity picks up some on weekends. The sole commercial business jet operation only works a couple times each month, but the place is kept bustling enough with the recreational flyers and the business execs who work all week and come out to play pilot for a precious few weekend hours.

Sometimes they wouldn't even turn the key in the ignition, just push the bird out onto the ramp for a wash and wax, or to tune avionics, or vacuum the interior and check tire pressures. Anything to be close to the airplane. Some folks just had the sky in their bloodstreams.

Charlie Bird was one of those people. Even his family name always hinted that his destiny lay in the sky. He served twenty-six years in the U.S. Army, first as an enlisted Airborne Ranger in the 75th Ranger Regiment, and later as a commissioned officer, a mustang. They sent him to Officer Candidate School to learn which spoon went with which fork, which fancy dress uniform went with which fancy dress ball—and how to lead men into the screaming face of Hell with honest smiles on their faces.

He had led a succession of commands in a career distinguished by superlative OERs and early advancement. By the time he pulled the ripcord as a lieutenant colonel on his last, ceremonial retirement jump, he had 514 drops in his logbook—including three rare mustard stains, the small bronze stars on his Master jump wings representing combat jumps. He insisted on taking the 514th military jump because he didn't want his record to end with the ominous thirteen.

His old boss, Lt. General John Glenn McCandless, back home from Germany for assignment to some hush-hush new command and a fourth star, was thrilled to be invited along on the last "knees in the breeze" jump with Bird as he went out the door of a C-130 one last time as a soldier.

Charlie rolled into his office at Owosso Community Airport at 0700. It was Friday, and the weekend training roster had been posted the day before to the usual pattern of groans from instructors who had to work on the weekend.

Charlie's Michigan Drop Zone, a flight training, skydiving club, and parachute training facility based at the airport, was staffed only with former military-trained parachute and aviation veterans, mostly Army, but a handful of Navy and Marines, with a sprinkling of former Air Force and Air National Guard. That meant daily complaining about almost nothing was standard operating procedure.

This Friday was light duty, but the kind the instructors mostly disliked—tandem birthday jumps. All the birthday jumps seemed to come on weekends, and many of those on Fridays, because people whose birthdays fell mid-week had work or school or whatever to contend with. They waited until Friday to celebrate their birthdays with adventure.

All the MDZ members were people-oriented, they understood the joy of free-fall on a birthday, and they did well with clients. But they mostly did not like the gleeful, blissful birthday jumps.

Birthday jumpers started coming out in force after President George H.W. Bush—Bush 41—started making tandem jumps in his eighties strapped to the chest of jumpmasters from the Army's Golden Knights parachute demonstration team. People saw that on CNN and thought, *If he can do it at eighty or eighty-five and ninety, I can do it at forty, forty-five and sixty.*

"Don't make me, Top, I'm beggin' ya. Please don't make me do it," Kerry Baker pleaded to Kathie Murphy, the company's chief operating officer who kept all the trains running on time. And the duty rosters written. She was typecast in the troop management role after twenty-two years in the U.S. Army, retiring as a command master sergeant out of the 8th Military Police Brigade in Hawaii.

Baker, a former Army Jumpmaster with 445 military jumps and nearly 350 as a civilian, had twice been power-barfed on in the five previous birthday jumps he'd been assigned. The memories of the last one, with its thick and copious stream of wine, chunks of undigested Italian food and birthday cake from only hours before streaming across his facemask in HD helmet-cam video footage, still haunted him. There is just no defense for that.

"Look, Kerry, it happens to everybody. Your duty is out of my hands now," Murphy said. She was forty-four and looked twenty-five, but cute as hell did not dislodge the command steel in her voice.

"It's *your turn* in the barrel, man. I cannot help that. You are free to try and swap with someone else, but, you know. Nobody else wants those tandem birthday jumps, either."

"But Kathie!"

"No," she said with finality. "Just no. Find someone to change with or go forth and execute." She flipped up the blue cover sheet on the guest clipboard and squinted. "Your birthday party will be here in about an hour."

She grinned her killer *I'm done* grin at Baker and said, "You're dismissed, bubb."

Baker turned away from the raised main lobby desk to find former Navy jet jock and flight instructor Cindy "Candy" Clark reading the whiteboard assignment roster. He only took one step toward her before she spoke without even looking in his direction.

"Don't say it, bro. Don't you do it. I ain't even here."

"Candy, please. I can't do another birthday. I'll do anything."

"Regrettably, my brother, there nothing you *can* do for me." Just then a stunning brunette pulled up outside the big lobby bay window in a new Camaro ragtop. "She, on the other hand, *can*."

She waggled her fingers at Baker in an exaggerated wave. "*Ta,* baby! You was the Ranger—now go lead the damn way."

MDZ's prized possession was its 1982 Lockheed C-130H Hercules, a nearly pristine low-time aircraft that had long been in deep storage in the Arizona desert—and it was the only former military C-130 known to be in civilian hands.

Usually, civilian parachute trainers used commonplace Cessna 182s, and larger schools often deployed the SC-7 Skyvan or DeHavilland Twin Otter. MDZ had two 182s used to provide flight instruction and drops for small parties, and one Twin Otter for slightly larger skydive groups. The Herk was used for very large skydive groups. And other missions.

A Canadian company had restored the plane, and because the owner was a former Canadian Forces colonel Charlie Bird had known while on active duty, Bird arranged to buy the plane and navigate the strict rules of the U.S. Munitions List governing military sales to American civilians to import the aircraft into the States. It was certainly not normal for a civilian drop zone operation to have such an aircraft. But there was an important additional reason why the purchase was easy.

Once back on American soil, Charlie was recruited to sign a sole-source Indefinite Delivery-Indefinite Quantity contract to provide "transportation services" to the federal government, which proceeded to further upgrade the C-130's avionics and communications gear even more thoroughly, notably with some highly specialized laser defensive equipment being tested for wider use in future military applications.

Charlie created a new subsidiary for the plane and its business titled MDZ Global Initiatives to administer the IDIQ assignments and personnel—most of whom already worked for the drop zone—and the dual-hatters also got big pay increases for their new extra responsibilities. Charlie Bird was still a commander who took care of his troops.

At the office party celebrating the new government contract and both the revenue and excitement it was expected to provide, a tipsy Kerry Baker suggested the motto for the new division should be *Operator as fuck!* Everyone present, most of whom already on the outside of a considerable intake of adult beverages, thought that was catchy and certainly appropriate, but possibly troublesome on a business card.

Cooler heads prevailed, and the slogan became *Around the clock. Around the block. Around the world.* But near the top on each side of the aircraft's vertical stabilizer were three small letters painted in haze gray that read OAF.

Consequently, the freshened C-130H, its hanger and the arms room were subtly and continuously protected around the clock by a sophisticated and comprehensively armed and equipped security force, all former Air Force and Air National Guard people with extensive flightline security pedigrees.

MDZGI subsidized the expensive jump school plane in part by conducting refresher and specialized training for certain government jumpers who did not appear on military personnel rolls. The team pioneered new and innovative uses for its own custom-designed wing suits, and trained operators to use them. Sometimes, the company rented the aircraft back to the federal government for even more critical missions than the contract specified.

Occasionally, Charlie's team went along as contractors for, well, one thing or another.

They scored the biggest coup by finding Christa "Christmas" Kieszek to drive it. She was a lieutenant commander in the U.S. Navy Reserve—and a long-experienced Hercules pilot as the operations officer at the Navy Reserve's VR-53, the "Capital Express," located at Joint Base Andrews outside of DC.

✪

"Skipper," Kathie Murphy called from her glass-walled office next to Charlie's. She held the desk phone receiver off her shoulder. "Pick up line two, please."

She could see Charlie was immersed in the C-130's manual. He was studying hard to learn to fly the beast as pilot in command, because Christmas Kieszek was not always going to be available if she was serving a Navy Reserve weekend or the required annual fortnight or often more of active duty.

"Busy," Charlie said without looking up. "Take a message?"

Murphy did her best Tina Fey eye-roll and snorted her senior-enlisted *I don't think so* snort. "I think you wanna take this one."

Charlie frowned at her through the shared glass office wall as he closed the aircraft manual over a bookmark and picked up the phone, punching the flashing button for line two.

"Charlie Bird here," he said, making a rude face at Murphy. "What can I do for you today?"

"Sir, this is Ellen Park MacLemore calling. Please hold for the vice president ..."

Charlie automatically sat more upright in his swivel chair waiting for the connection to go through. He punched the speakerphone to life and waved Murphy over to listen in. She sat down in a guest's chair with her notebook open, a black Skilcraft ballpoint pen at the ready, and a curious, inscrutable smile.

"Charlie!" the voice boomed from the phone. "How the hell are ya, boy? We haven't seen you all year."

Only slightly relieved, Charlie relaxed at the sound of Steve Harris—vice-president of marketing for the Detroit Tigers baseball club. Murphy had been in on the joke, and her eyes crinkled at the corners in a knowing grin. She silently mouthed, *Stay or go?* Charlie waved her down to stay.

After a wild and wildly improbable regular season this year, and playoff magic only slightly less confounding than the Chicago Cubs winning it all in 2016, the Tigers found themselves in baseball's World Series. In just a handful of days, the Tigers would host the first game, and the televised opening ceremonies, in the team's gorgeous open-air Comerica Park planted in rebounding downtown Detroit.

"You know, I hate that damned 'vice president' trick you pull," Charlie said. "I should know better by now, you moron."

Except Charlie Bird really did know the genuine vice president of the United States—and his boss—so he was trapped either way.

"Yeah, it's a good one. Hey, Birdman, I have World Series seats for you and your people, free to a good home. Good ones, no obstructed views! I hadn't seen you in a while—you missed the 75th Regiment's reunion blow-out last year—even Cory Remsburg made it, but not *yooou*, nooo ..."

Charlie flipped a rude finger gesture at the speakerphone.

"... so I thought I'd see if you were still fogging a mirror up there in that playground of yours."

"We stay busy," Charlie said, smiling.

All battle buddies were good buddies, and this one went all the way back to when the two men were both Army privates, about the time the Earth cooled. But while Charlie stayed in and made the Army his business, Harris had gotten out after his second enlistment to return to college on his G.I. Bill and get a marketing degree. His first job out of school had been with the Tigers baseball organization, and he never left.

"I'm sorry I didn't make it, but I was out and about." The former active duty Ranger in Harris intuitively understood what that meant without additional detail. Charlie had been on a government mission that hadn't made the newspapers.

"Listen, though, really, I got something for you besides amazing box seats. You know we're hosting Game One of the Series, and thus the friggin' opening ceremonies, right?"

"Yes," Charlie said. "I think I read about that in the last couple hundred *Free Press*'s I read."

"Yeah, well, me bein' the shit-hot v-p *del* marketing around here, I have an idea that probably only you can execute for me."

"What's this going to cost me?" Charlie asked. The drip of caution and suspicion in his voice was intentional.

Kathie Murphy looked at her watch and tapped the face with her finger, motioning to her boss that she had to leave. He waved, and she departed.

"Cost *you?*" Harris said. "Hell, nothing—this is a paying deal, son, as in me paying you. I want to get your C-130 shrink-wrapped up all pretty with Tigers' colors and logos and stuff, and have you HALO a team of thirty-five jumpers into Comerica Park for the opening ceremonies."

A High Altitude-Low Opening parachute jump meant the team would exit the Herk from very high above and upwind from the stadium, and free fall down close to the open top of the ball field. Then the jumpers would pop chutes all at once, appearing in the sky as if from nowhere.

"Each of these folks will trail an American flag as the National Anthem is played and drop red-white-and-blue confettis over the crowd. Then, you time your flight to our cues and roar over the stadium in a low-and-slow fly-by just as the anthem concludes. It'll kill everybody, believe me."

"I'm choked up already," Charlie said, but he was kidding. It sounded like a fun program to be associated with *and* it was a paying gig—featuring the incalculable bonus of untold free national TV airtime for MDZ and its big airplane. "Am I recruiting for this, or do you already have a team?"

"I have a team. Quiet as I'm keeping it, this wasn't my idea. These guys came to me with it and, as my football colleagues over at the Lions might say, I took the hand-off and I'm runnin' with that ball. When the spectacle is over, you land over at City and we limo you all down here for VIP seats, food, and *draaanks*. I'll put you all up in the Athenaeum for the weekend. If you don't get drunk again on Sunday, you can hop back to Owosso Monday morning."

Charlie mulled it over briefly, but he didn't see any downside. He would bring the flightline security flyaway team with them in the plane, along with their self-contained deployable galley and sleeping quarters module. It would be a lot more comfortable a situation than the security people ever had when deployed to Bagram Air Base in Afghanistan. The aircraft could easily base out of Detroit's small urban Coleman A. Young Municipal Airport that everyone still referred to by its old simpler name, City Airport.

"Waddaya say, buddy?" Harris asked. "I'll buy if you fly."

"That's funny," Charlie said. "But I think we're in. Yeah, I think we're in all the way, bro. Thanks."

Even as the innocent words left his mouth, Charlie knew he'd made a classic mistake.

"Ha, *that's what she said!*" Harris retorted with obvious glee. "Rangers lead the way!"

"Okay brother, send me the info. We'll talk, all right?" He hung up the phone.

On the overhead public address system, Kathie Murphy could barely keep the delight out of her voice when she keyed her desktop microphone.

"Kerry Baker, please meet your birthday party in the ready room. Kerry Baker, please!"

CHAPTER THIRTY-FIVE

When the power of love overcomes the
love of power, the world will know peace.
Jimi Hendrix (1942-1970), American musician

It was dark inside the Islamic Center of America. Lights were on here and there, but the large building had alcoves and corners where darkness pooled like water. In one of these voids stood Hamzaa el-Shafei.

Twenty-eight, tall because of a Syrian father and slender because of a Somali mother, he nonetheless exhibited a curious historical genetic quirk that had surfaced from deep in the familial woodpile to cause his skin color to be perfectly Caucasian. If he didn't resort to the accent he used at home speaking in Arabic, his American accent and appearance guaranteed he could pass as any random white junkie on the street.

Because Hamzaa el-Shafei was a committed meth head.

This let him travel through many social circles that would not otherwise have embraced an Arabic man. El-Shafei was an unemployed sometimes-student who needed money for his dope habit—one who, in history, had done shameful things to get it. His health was poor. First crack cocaine and now meth had made him a scandalous person, and so far, all of Allah's might had not yet freed him from his chemical shackles. Imam Sayid al-Waheeb would keep trying, nevertheless.

Part of restoring the boy's self-respect, the Cleric often thought, was to give him meaningful work, and reward him for doing it. It was a childish American custom to give children praise for doing that which they already knew should be done on their own responsibility, but the Cleric knew el-Shafei had grown up in America, and so the boy probably was familiar with the concept.

The Cleric approached the boy in the shadows, ensuring he rustled and scraped a foot on the floor in order not to startle him. El-Shafei had become a different, more nervous person since he'd been spying for the Cleric, and the drug use had already made him paranoid. It would not do to scare him into shouting out in Allah's house.

"*Assalamu 'alaikum wa rahmatullahi wa barakatuh,*" al-Waheeb whispered to the boy. May the peace, mercy, and blessings of Allah be upon you.

"*Wa'alaikum assalam wa rahmatullahi wa barakatuh,*" el-Shafei replied. And peace and mercy and blessings of Allah be upon you.

They looked at each other for moments. Finally, el-Shafei spoke. "I have something for you."

"I expect so. This why you left your mark in the dirt next to my car, to signal a meeting. So, here we meet. What is it?"

"I was right!" el-Shafei said. His eyes gleamed in the low light, but whether it was from excitement or the drugs, al-Waheeb couldn't know. "Those white nationalists I met definitely are trying to recruit me. They say big things are coming, and I better 'get right with the Lord' and get on the winning side. They don't say whose side that is yet, but I see them talking to men in uniforms about stuff. Every time we have these horrible conversations, I pray so hard in my head that I think the prayers will surely reveal my true nature to them. They don't, though. Not yet, anyway."

The boy looked uncertain for a moment. "Perhaps I'm the only one who can hear them."

"These are ... military men?" the Cleric asked.

"I think, yeah, I think so. I mean, they wear those camouflage clothes like you see in the war movies, the green and brown leaves and stuff, and lots of them are fat. Cam-cammies, you know. I don't think they are ruh-real government military peep-pee-people. Not, not the federal kind, anyway. Militias, like hob-hob, hobby, hobby soldiers, you-you know?"

The boy had a wicked stutter when he got nervous and couldn't keep it together. He had been taunted mercilessly in school, where the ethnic Arab kids blamed his stutter on his "demonic infidel genes" and called him other less-civil names. Just common bullying, but thereafter, he stuttered even more easily.

"He s-says they've been doing urb-urb, urban druh-druh-drills up in the woods with instructors who just got back f-f-from Afghanistan and got out of th-the Ah-Ah-Army. He says because this is Ah-Ah-merica, they have m-many guns and much ammunition." He swallowed hard. "*Many* guns"

"Who else knows of this?"

"No one, Imam. You said to tell only you whu-what I learn."

"Of course, you are right," the Cleric said. "Continue to meet with these men. Find out more details of this plan, who is involved, and so on. And for sure, listen closely to any discussion about the murder of the Muslim Homeland Security agent."

Al-Waheeb feigned poor memory.

"What was his name? His name ..."

"Yes, yes!" the boy said. "You mean Mohammed al-Taja, right? Al-Taja. I have seen him on the news."

"Yes, that's him. If we can learn anything about him or his killer, we can protect our own community from harm. Al-Taja was Muslim—and yet we cannot risk lives if some rabble-rouser comes forward to say he did the deed for, or with the blessings of, other Muslims." He leaned his extra height forward. "That would not be good for anyone."

"I understand," el-Shafei said, cowed. "I haven't heard a word of this, but I'll keep my ears open."

He discreetly extended his right hand in the dark to accept something, but looked away as if it would be a surprise.

When he felt the object touch his palm, he reflexively closed his fingers around it. He wouldn't look at it again until the Cleric departed.

It was five one hundred dollar bills in a paper clip.

They spoke for a few more minutes, then the Cleric told him to be well, keep learning new things, and to report back often.

"*Ma'aasalaama!*" the Cleric said as he departed. Peace.

✪

The Cleric did something he almost never did. He changed out of his traditional Islamic garb and into casual American clothes. Grabbing a plastic key fob from a board in his office, he strode to an outbuilding on the mosque grounds where the groundskeepers kept their equipment. His golf cubs were in there as well, but he wasn't headed to the golf course.

He pressed a button on the key fob, raising the aluminum garage door to reveal his very own surrender to secular pride and personal enjoyment: a perfectly restored 1967 Ford Mustang GT.

The Ford Motor Company had presented the muscle car to the Imam during his community welcome ceremony. Such gifts were inappropriate in some eyes, but once al-Waheeb had taken hold of the mosque and started doing such good things for his congregants and their community, no one even remembered his little automotive prize.

He took it out infrequently, and usually after dark, better to not arouse the ire of the envious. He loved driving the car on warm summer nights, thinking about how his life might have evolved differently if he'd owned it in high school. The thought itself was slightly blasphemous, but the Cleric also believed Allah understood the value of his greater intentions.

Then the iPhone laying on the passenger seat rang. Caller ID said the call was from Amber Watson.

"Good evening," he said.

"I got the photo you texted of that sweet car," Amber said. "Are we meeting to, ah, exchange car stories, Imam?"

"I think that would be fun and educational for all concerned," he said. "There is a gas station at the corner of South Woodward and Orchard Lake Road. Do you know it?"

"Yes, sir. I have cruised Woodward before," she said.

Al-Waheeb laughed appreciatively. "I'll bet you have. Only a few times for me. That cruising-street racing scene was mostly over by the time I was old enough to care about it, and then I was in religious study for many years. I go out there in this car occasionally, just to drive and daydream. See you up on Woodward in about twenty, twenty-five minutes?"

✪

By the time the Cleric pulled his car into the gas station, Amber was already there. As always, her yellow Corvette was showroom clean from bumper to bumper. Al-Waheeb stopped next to the Corvette.

"Nice ride, lady—wanna run it?" he asked, and laughed.

"No, thanks. But I do want you to show me that gem of yours."

She got out of the Vette, locked it even though the top was down, and got into the passenger side of the Mustang.

"Yikes man, this is *sweeet*," she said, respectfully touching the interior pieces and turning radio knobs.

"Let's take a drive," Al-Waheeb said, and pulled into the intersection to take a Michigan left up North Woodward. Traffic was light, and they would not be disturbed. Amber's Apple Watch buzzed her wrist three times, alerting her that a follow team was on them. The watch would record their conversation just as it had in the Red Flag.

"I'm sorry I couldn't be more forthcoming the other day in the restaurant," al-Waheeb began. He casually rowed through the gears of the manual transmission with smooth efficiency until they cruised in fourth at the speed limit.

"I wasn't completely sure of what I'd suspected, but new information about a different topic has come to light." He looked in his rear-view mirror. Seemed like traffic had picked up a little, he thought. What he couldn't know was that many of the following cars were occupied by FBI agents.

"There seems to be a growing—what do you call it?—'white nationalist' movement in southeastern Michigan that may intend to do harm to Muslims in Dearborn. I have a guy the group is trying to recruit, and they really want him because he speaks Arabic. He told them he learned it in military service. They have many guns, lots of bullets, and trainers with military expertise. My guy has seen the weapons and spoken to the recruiters. They tell him he has to be ready to act, because some big event is coming."

Amber listened intently but masked her excitement. "Did your guy have any details? Names, places?"

"No, not yet. He said they are waiting for him to join their team. They want to use him as an intermediary between their group and the Muslim community, but he didn't say more."

"A Muslim ambassador from the Skinhead Nation!" Amber said. "That's priceless, even if they aren't in on the joke."

CHAPTER THIRTY-SIX

Three may keep a secret, if two of them are dead.
Benjamin Franklin (1706-1790), Poor Richard's Almanac

Poppy Benedict, General McCandless, and Tom Hughes from CIA Science & Technology were gathered around two men seated in large chairs that resembled pilot's seats from a fighter jet. In a sense, this is precisely what they were.

The men were in a Ground Control Station trailer parked in a backwater of Selfridge Air National Guard Base watching the pilot take his prototype MQ-9L SuperReaper UCAV—Unmanned Combat Aerial Vehicle—through its paces. Though the UCAV station had very high-resolution screens in front, the pilot and his sensor operator wore the new experimental flight helmets with 3D virtual reality displays built into them.

The system was designed such that the pilot and sensor operator felt they were sitting in the drone as it conducted its mission. Poppy, McCandless, and Watson followed along watching the high-definition display screens.

"If Americans ever knew how occasionally well we spent their tax dollars," McCandless whispered, "they would beg us to take more. I mean, just look at this. Hollywood doesn't have it this good."

The SuperReaper flew in long, lazy figure-eights over Dearborn and downtown Detroit, centering on the big mosque in Dearborn and Comerica Park downtown. The pilot monitored his flight instruments and the sensor operator tracked various electronic receptions to get a visual and digital familiarity with the topography and its spectrums.

The drone was relatively lightweight without its customary Hellfire missiles or JDAM bombs and metal ordnance racks, and it handled well, almost with the swift control responses of a jet fighter. The addition of the long centerline pod for a 300-kilowatt experimental combat laser hugging the bottom of the fuselage added no practical performance penalty at all.

"How's it going for you, pilot?" McCandless said. "Because it's looking pretty good out here to us."

"Very well, sir. The SuperReaper is a great airframe to fly. The new software updates have added and refined control feedback, so it's more like a flying cockpit than ever. They've shaved a few more hundredths off the command-to-satellite-to-airframe time, but it's still nearly a full second round-trip, and we fly for that. This bird is the test bed we flew over from Dreamland-D, so the big fiber laser is still the one 300-kilowatt prototype. We flew it up to Grayling and did some calibration yesterday"—the big national guard training center in mid-Michigan—"so we think we have the laser zeroed. We identified a small cooling issue, but we think that was solved."

The panorama of metro Detroit the aircraft's vision displayed on the monitors was breathtaking.

"This particular Reaper still has the new Increment-2 GORGON STARE wide-area surveillance system on board, so our look-down covers about thirty-nine square miles. The air distance between the Islamic Center of America in Dearborn and Comerica Park in downtown Detroit is only ten-point-four miles, so we're watching both objectives, and many miles around them, in a single look."

"Not too shabby," Poppy said.

"No, sir. Not too shabby at all," the pilot said. "Anything happens we need to respond to, we are rockin' on ready, sittin' on go. We've even left the conventionally armed drones on standby at Battle Creek, because the SuperReaper can cover both primary objectives at the same time."

The pilot smiled, and banked left over the Detroit Opera House to wheel around the ball park and head back to Dearborn.

"This downtown is spectacular all lit up at night," the pilot said.

General McCandless, Poppy, and Tom Hughes looked up at the trailer's displays to see what the pilot saw. They each nodded in cynical agreement.

It was their job to keep it that way.

CHAPTER THIRTY-SEVEN

Be careful who you trust. The Devil was once an angel.
Unknown

The western-most precincts in the Detroit Police footprint are the Eighth and the Sixth, but the Sixth shares a border with the suburb of Dearborn.

The swelling immigrant community was surging out of Dearborn's confines as new arrivals found bargain-basement housing in the Detroit city limits that was still close to their ties within Dearborn itself. Like new arrivals from anywhere unfamiliar with new rules and laws, and often coming from countries where many laws were situational, their traffic offenses soared in the Sixth, which classically is understaffed on its best day.

Crashes, speeding violations, hit-and-runs, all were out of control. Sixty-year-olds with no English skills were getting driver's licenses for the first time—some from nations where they drive on the other side of the road—and chaos ensued on Detroit's west side.

Sergeant Jeff O'Brien had taken his traffic enforcement magic out of his usual area for some custom swing-shift overtime in the Sixth. After a ten-hour stint creating revenue for the city, and hopefully making its citizens a bit safer, O'Brien dragged into the precinct to cash in his chips for the day.

He was tired, but more importantly, he was troubled. Things were moving too fast—much faster than he ever believed they could.

"Sergeant Oh-*Brien!*" Desk Sergeant Jayson Ivy bellowed officiously as O'Brien entered. "That JTF hottie from Homicide has been trying to reach you all afternoon. Sarnt Lexcellent? Why don't you leave your damn phone on once?"

He grinned knowingly. "I know I'd take her damn call."

He wadded up a pink message slip and bounced it once, beer-pong style, over the top of the elevated desk. It ricocheted off O'Brien's chest and dropped to the floor. He didn't pick it up.

"Thanks, sarge. I'll take it from here." His phone had been on all day.

As he walked back into the locker room to change into civvies, he pulled the cellphone from his pocket and thumbed it out of standby mode.

Seven missed calls from Tracey in short intervals. No voicemail.

He slowly unbuckled his duty belt and hung it on a hook in his transient locker. Sitting down on the bench seemed like a pointless gesture, as an idea already percolated in his head. How many calls did she make to the desk? At least several. And she's not looking for a date, he mused. O'Brien wasn't a math major, but he could see when two plus two equaled his shit was weak.

He had to send a text to the contact with some fake emergency need and arrange a meet. It was high time to put this thing to rest before it got even crazier. Then, face up on the wooden locker room bench, his cellphone buzzed again, this time with a secure Whatsapp text from unknown.

Meet me there. One hr. $$$.

How timely, O'Brien thought. He reached down and deleted the text, and then punched the neighboring locker door, leaving a sizable depression behind. *I have kids, and a wife who loves me. And this job.* How many times in history had good intentions been derailed by unexpected outcomes?

There was no redemption for him, O'Brien thought. Not now. But there might be retribution.

He took a deep breath, held it for a moment, and exhaled his demons and carbon dioxide at the same time. If retribution was all that was available to him, he'd take that.

He put his civilian clothes back into the battered locker, buckled his Sam Browne duty belt back on and performed the habitual check of his weapon, even though it had never been out of his holster ever since he started the shift. He left the body cam and microphone modules shut off and hanging in the locker when he closed the door.

His trepidation fled. Most anxiety in life leads up to the threshold of decisions. After decisions are made, all that remains is execution.

Ha, O'Brien thought. *Execution. That's pretty damned funny.*

✪

The desk sergeant was mildly surprised to see O'Brien emerge from the locker room still in uniform.

"I think I'm goin' back out for a while," O'Brien said. "Got me a second wind."

"Yeah, takin' a big dump always works for me, too," the desk sergeant growled. He was aggravated by all the goddamned paperwork, and his admin had not been replaced when budget cuts claimed her position. Now this overtime freelancer, not even his guy, wanted to add more paperwork to the tsunami. And he was good at that.

"You did a big shift, man. You sure you don't want to bail and get some Miller Time or something? It's slowed down out there."

"Naw, sarge, I'm good," O'Brien said. His tone telegraphed something odd, but the desk sergeant was blinded by O'Brien's happy grin. "There's still plenty work left for me to do before I die."

"Yeah, well," the desk sergeant said, turning back to shuffling arrest reports and coordinating prisoner transportation needs, "I know you think that's your catch-phrase an' shit, but don't be dyin' out there until after twenny-three-hundred, hear? I'm off at eleven and don't need the damn paperwork keepin' me over."

Then he looked up and pointed an index finger. "And call that Homicide detective back! I don't need her pestering me."

"You got it, sarge," O'Brien said. He stopped at the sally port and turned back toward the desk. "Who's your relief?"

"Tina Beach," Ivy said without looking up. He moved papers from one side of the desk to the other.

"Tell her I'm still out if I don't get back before you check out tonight, okay?"

"Yeah-yeah."

O'Brien spun the patrol car keyring around his upraised middle finger as he headed for the sally port and his ride. In his pocket, the cellphone buzzed insistently.

✪

Tracey tried to hurt her phone stabbing the disconnect button.

"Where the fuck *is* this fucking guy?"

The two women were headed out to west Detroit and Sixth Precinct, where an online duty roster said Jeff O'Brien was working his overtime swings traffic shift.

"Ever had this much trouble reaching him before?" Amber asked. The night had gotten cooler and the Corvette's top was raised for a change, making conversation at speed easier.

"Never. Ever since we were fuck buddies in the academy, every time I call him he thinks he's getting a rematch, so he always picks up. Always."

Tracey's eyed went wide then and she turned to Amber.

"He knows, doesn't he? You and I and *his* fucking ass know he knows." Her anger grew with every word.

"He has somehow figured out that me trying to reach him is police business, not monkey business. He flaked that weed and those guns on Cortez to push the al-Taja murder onto that innocent boy—that dumb-ass son of a bitch! How in the hell and *why* in the hell is he wrapped up in this, fercrissakes? What the *actual fuck* is going on here?"

"All good questions," Amber said. The Corvette pulled into official parking at the Sixth Precinct. "Let's go ask them of your buddy."

The desk sergeant was slightly startled to see two women in civilian clothes enter the desk area from the police-only entrance, their badges and credentials held aloft, just in case. He knew who they were, but this was an out-of-context moment amid his paperwork swirl that took him slightly aback.

"Well, if it ain't the famous JTF theyownselves," he said with a laugh. He stood with a wide grin and put his inner wrists together theatrically, extending his arms forward.

"Y'all just put the bracelets on me now, hear? I don't wanna finish my shift, anyway." He relented when he saw the women smile. "Y'all outta your AO some, huh?"

"Hey, Sarnt Ivy. Turns out the whole city is our area of operations," Tracey said with a tight smile. She had worked with Sergeant Jayson Ivy before, in her first posting as a rookie in the old Ninth Precinct, and again later in her street career in the Second.

Tracey approached the elevated desk and extended her red-tipped hand. Ivy reached down to shake it.

"Do you know FBI Special Agent Amber Watson?"

"Don't think I've had the pleasure," Ivy said, grinning. He reached over and shook Amber's hand too.

"So," Ivy said. "What's up out here in the metropolitan boonies for the JTF?"

"Jeff O'Brien off yet?" Tracey asked.

Ivy frowned. "Ehh, yes and no. He was in here fifteen-twenny minutes ago and went into the locker room to change. Then, not five minutes later, out he comes again, fresh as a daisy, says he's goin' back out for a while. I gave him your messages."

He pointed down to the floor in front of the desk where the pink wad of message slip still lay.

"Does he have any favorite spots over here to run radar?" Tracey asked. She didn't think O'Brien had gone back out to write speeding tickets. But she still didn't know what he was up to beside staying away from her.

"None that I know of. He's pretty wiry, though. I'm sure he'll find some trouble to get into."

Tracey nodded noncommittally. Of this she was certain.

"I can reach out to him via dispatch radio. So can you. You can reach out to him on your preps handset, then get him over on channel five if your thing is private."

He motioned them around to the half-door on the side of the desk. "C'mon up and check him out in the CAD. I can call him up on the locator in my laptop and you can see where his car is."

Tracey and Amber walked through the opening and up a couple of steps to the desk sergeant's level while he opened the Computer-Aided Dispatch system on a Toughbook laptop.

This version of CAD featured a software update being field tested, with a full mapping display on the screen just like downtown in the OpsCenter instead of a spreadsheet-style columns and rows display most station laptops could access.

Within it, represented by blue cars and the radio code, were the three District Six patrol cars on duty then. In this software update, if a car responded to a call with emergency lights and sirens, the blue dot would turn red. If it stopped for longer than two minutes without calling in, the car icon turned into a red square and a timer began counting how long the car was stopped. Longer than ten minutes without checking in meant a signal automatically sent a flag to the precinct and the OpsCenter.

On the screen, O'Brien's cruiser was moving.

✪

Jeff O'Brien prowled an upscale Dearborn neighborhood with his headlights off. A Detroit police car in Dearborn was not out of place, especially with the social turmoil of the shouting Skinheads and militias choking the news day after day. The television stations in Detroit were nearly at a full scream about insurrection in the streets. It was nonsense but made for good ratings.

A T-intersection, and O'Brien stopped and peered ahead into the darkness. At almost eleven at night, no moms with infants in strollers would be in the Dearborn city park, and as far as he could see, no one else, either. This was their usual meet-up spot and O'Brien had never seen another person in the park this late. His contact was supposed to be there alone, but the shadows among the trees and playground equipment could hide half a battalion of federal agents.

Fuck it, he thought. *Dicked if I do, dicked if I don't.*

O'Brien reached into his holster and withdrew his service weapon. He laid it on the seat next to him, then gently depressed the accelerator. The car rolled through the intersection and into the murky park. Showtime.

On the passenger seat, next to the handgun, O'Brien's black iPhone vibrated.

CHAPTER THIRTY-EIGHT

Don't tell people how to do things. Tell them what you
want them to do and let them surprise you with their results.
General George S. Patton (1885-1945), American warrior

Bob, Chuck Xing, Xavier Cloud, and Barra MacPharlain, the leader of the ground team that recovered the cash, sat under a huge desert camouflage canopy draped over and beyond their crippled Hercules.

Passing among them was Zave's chrome-plated flask filled with Lagavulin Islay single malt scotch. It was nearly dark, and a small campfire reduced to glowing coals sputtered uncertainly. Sentries with night vision goggles stood perimeter watches and a few more sat in the cargo hold as money guards, weapons cocked and locked.

"I'm sending a customer-satisfaction email to Lockheed," Bob said. The Chinese pilot tipped his head back and took a long nip of the liquor. "I would have bet the title to my Lotus that our landing gear would not have locked when we set down here."

Thanks to the literal last-minute gas stop from the American KC-10 Extender, the rescue C-130J-30, its happy crew—and one hundred million dollars—were not spread across the Afghanistan desert floor. Flying their low radar-avoidance profile, they found an unpopulated area near the Iranian border a few miles southeast of Mirabad in Chahar Burjak province to land and make repairs.

It wasn't more than a *wadi* in a small mountain valley. Bob set the

Herk down on the smooth, hard-packed sand field as gently as he could. If there had been a single pothole or rut, a wheel strut might have collapsed and their mission would have been over in spectacular fashion now with a full load of fuel.

But Mr. Murphy was off that day and the gear stayed locked, no obstacles were encountered, and they could radio to their support team to meet them with a full company of Chinese PLA maintainers and parts to put the aircraft back in reliable service.

When Xing Jianjun told Zave he could bring resources to bear, he was not joking.

The Chinese repair team met the crippled money plane at its makeshift combat airfield in Russian helicopters and trucks with Iranian markings, carrying tools, parts, and Chinese aircraft maintainers who bitched loudly about the team not taking care of their government's expensive equipment. Zave noted those gripes are the same in any service.

Bob took another small sip and passed the flask back to Zave, who grinned. There had been a lot of grinning and laughing and back-slapping since the money plane had landed successfully. Everyone was bleeding off pressure and anxiety, thinking about richer lives that now looked like they would continue on for a while longer.

"Aren't you driving?" Zave laughed at the pilot. "Maybe you shouldn't be drinking."

It was Bob's turn to laugh. "Well, I won't overdo it, but I think we all have earned it. If you want to report me to my chain of command, I think I can find you a radio."

Zave reached out and the two men clasped hands at the thumbs. "I think you're good, bro. You had me convinced that landing was a lost cause, but at least we were surrounded by thousands of gallons of fresh av gas, y'know? I was crossing every digit I had when you put the gear down and got green lights. Then that left one started flickering, and man, I'll tell you what. I grabbed onto something, including my unit."

He took a drink and passed the flask to Barra.

"Wait," Zave said, "you have a Lotus?"

"Yes," Bob said, "a sweet '95 Esprit S4s Turbo I found on Hemmings.

British Racing Green. Stick. It would be a tight fit for a larger guy like you. I'm smaller, and it still fits me like a Mercury space capsule. Kinda boggy until you tip in the turbo, but faster than a scalded dog after that. I keep the idle turned up a couple of clicks to keep the turbo lag manageable. I love driving that car. I don't get to much, lately." Bob grinned. "Been busy at work."

"Is it difficult to keep a fancy Western sports car like that back home? Aren't they twitchy about such Western affectations in China?"

Bob laughed. "Not really. We have capitalism too, you know. Chinese merchant class is as adept handling politicians as America's, but we hide it better. You should see streets full of Buicks and Benzes fighting for right of way with old men on even older bicycles. Besides, my car is in San Diego, where the air is fresh, the women are blond and bulbous, and the skies and water are blue. Except when there are fires."

Bob grinned again and waited, expecting further interrogation from Zave. The idea of a Chinese PLA pilot seeming to live in Southern California was no more amazing, Zave thought, than a retired three-star general running a Chinese restaurant in suburban Detroit. Zave only raised a single approving thumb.

"I'm conventional," Zave said. "I have a box-stock '63 split-window Corvette at home. When I get back, I might look at a new 911 RS GT3. Signal Orange. You can't call yourself a car guy unless you've owned a Porsche at least once in your life. Overkill is just enough."

It was Bob's turn to raise his thumb in approval.

Barra swirled the scotch around in the flask, mesmerized by the fading campfire.

"I had a '67 Sunbeam Tiger Mark II, with the Ford 289 in it, when I was at uni in Edinburgh." A smile creased the Scottish soldier's face with the memory. "I truly wish I still had that wee motor, it was so bleedin' fast. And bloody hot. Nearly roasted my shoes in that footwell."

He looked up at Bob. "Hemmings, you said? I saw a car on there bloody exactly like mine, and the cheeky bastard was asking a quarter-million dollars!"

Zave asked, "How did you manage to get hooked up with this crew,

Barra? Your Chinese heritage definitely is not showing."

"Ha, nay indeed. I'm a working mon, mi laddie. Retired from 3 Scots…"

"Black Watch, huh?"

"Aye. Regimental Sergeant Major. Those poxy English bean counters chucked a bunch of us out a year before we would qualify for our immediate lump sum retirement payment, fucking wankers. Now we have to wait until we're bloody sixty-five to collect."

The loathing was visible on his craggy face. A reddish handlebar mustache the texture of a Texas tumbleweed danced as he spoke.

"All bloody pen-pushing English bastards must *fucking die.* Two tours in Iraq, two more here in the Stan. Tours in the peacekeepers in Cyprus. London Olympics. Airborne training with your people at Ft. Bragg." He smiled. "I loved Fayetteville, mon. Aye, indeed Fayetteville loved me back. It was a symphony of accents at times, laddie, I can tell you that."

He took a drink from the flask. "But a man needs a job. When this mission was dangled before me, it seemed to fit my training and inclinations. Plus, the money is bloody good, mon." He raised the flask to Zave in appreciation and handed it to Chuck .

In the nosewheel housing, technicians repaired the Herk's hydraulic system damaged by the truck impact departing Tagab at combat speed. A small tank truck waited in the background, ready to top off the hydraulics with warm fluid. It was dark now, and the area was ablaze in work lights on stands, run by generators on a nearby flatbed the maintainers brought with them.

By the next morning, maybe sooner, the aircraft would be one hundred percent, and they could all head back to wherever.

"I'm a ground soldier for a reason," Chuck said. He looked at Zave. "You American Airborne guys, jumping out of perfectly good airplanes. That is just crazy."

"No, that isn't crazy," Zave said. He flashed back to the faked carnage of his desert cover story, with its mutilated human cadavers, dead enemies and people killed by ISIS gathered up by the CIA to create a fake massacre out of whole cloth.

"I've seen trophy-class crazy. Jumping out of an airplane isn't it."

Chuck gazed into the small fire burning low. A campfire will mesmerize fighting men just as easily as Boy Scouts.

"Have you thought about what you will do next?" he asked the three men. "I mean, after the fast cars and the fast women? Do rich people no longer heed the call of their nations?" He took another drink and passed the flask back to Bob.

"You are such a wet blanket!" Bob said in rapid-fire Chinese. Zave laughed and translated for Barra, who guffawed.

The power of the scotch was warming their blood now, so even serious topics could be raised along with the frivolous ones. They felt themselves among friends, among brothers in arms.

"I'm a freelancer, mate," Barra said with vigor, but then he emphasized, "but *not* a mercenary. I may bear arms for money, it's true, but this be nay different than in the Black Watch. A mercenary will do any job for money. There are jobs I wouldn't do for any amount of pay. So, my answer is I bloody well don't know what I'm doing next just now, but it involves warm weather, mon, tall drinks, and tall women."

"I am serious," Chuck said, frowning. "Bob and I are warriors. We have superiors to whom we report, even if the chain of command occasionally is a little fuzzed. Fuzzed?" The booze infused him now, and he smiled. "*Fuzzy.*"

"As do I," Zave interjected. It started to irk him that the Chinese PLA officers seemed to think he was merely a mercenary. He couldn't reveal his true role to them, of course, and he frankly didn't care what they thought. He was confident enough in his own skin, in his job, and in his service to his nation that he owed apologies to no one.

"I have bosses. Everyone does. Your bosses have bosses. There are orders, rules, requirements. We all work for someone else." He gestured to Chuck. "Your sister is rescued, and by now she is probably filling her belly with your father's good cooking. We also have recovered the lost money. Current mission complete."

Zave turned to Bob. "You didn't really have skin in the game like we did, but you and your crew performed flawlessly from the beginning of this enterprise. We only succeeded because of you. I, for one"—he bent his head in respect—"am grateful." Bob nodded in return.

"So, hereafter. You two will go back to your secret lives and I will return to mine," Zave said. "Barra will go on vacation, evidently. After we have paid everyone we owe for our little freelance thing, and I'm back in the States, I have other tasks to complete. Other missions to conduct, other work to do. You both go back to your day jobs a little richer, but as you said, you are warriors. You must heed the call. I too heed a call. Sometimes, I am the one making the call."

Bob took a drink from the flask and handed the nearly empty container back to Zave.

"We live in perilous times, especially in the States," Zave said. "The very freedoms my people fought to preserve threaten to overwhelm us at home. Jack Nicholson was right: No one can handle the truth. Political tensions among nations threaten us all, not least of which are those between my country and yours—and what in the name of the nautical Christ do you people think you're doing in the South China Sea, fercrissakes? Who makes these bad political decisions for you people?"

"'You people?' Who are you kidding?" Chuck said with a sneer and a laugh. "Here is your truth, brother—you people elected Donald Trump as President of the United States. That shit-show is still getting started. We are not ignorant people. Do you think we have any cause to fear that political development?"

Zave raised the flask and conceded the point. The man was entitled to his opinion. "Touché, mon frére."

The mood turned suddenly chilly, despite the outer warmth of the fire and the inner warmth of the scotch. Politics will do that even among friends. As an independent, Barra had no horse in this race, though he did look forward to the prospect of full Scottish independence.

Bob and Chuck just frowned and shrugged with resignation. *Above my paygrade, man,* was the vibe.

And they were correct. It was the same in Zave's tradition. In the afterglow of the team's dangerous and ultimately successful twin missions, the realities of life in the real world were starting to creep back in their awareness.

Zave spoke what they were all thinking. "I know we've had fun these last few days, and we are and will remain friends, I believe, for the rest of our lives. But we also realize that timeline is infinitely variable. The four of us sitting half-drunk around a campfire is unique, produced by an artificial situation unlikely to be repeated. Next week, next month, next year, we might well find ourselves back to our regular professions, and maybe looking through gunsights at one another." No one spoke in opposition. It was the basic truth of warriors.

"It could happen. If it came to that, I'm sure we would all feel bad about killing each other. But we would shoot, and afterward, whoever survived would sleep like babies, later to raise a glass in honor of the fallen."

"Zave, the supreme art of war is to subdue the enemy without fighting," Chuck grinned. "We—China—already own most of your country. Perhaps we will just call President Trump and foreclose before he can declare your entire country officially as well as morally bankrupt, and restructure our loans. You see? Bob told you our merchant class was more powerful than our politicians."

"Jesus, I see the source of your quote ping pong. Do you play this game with General Dad, too? Sun Tsu also said, 'He who knows when he can fight, and when he cannot, will be victorious.'"

Xavier Cloud swung the flask in a half-circle at the fire. The last ounce of scotch discharged onto the coals, erupting in a brief but vicious flash of hot flame.

CHAPTER THIRTY-NINE

Terrorism has once again shown it is prepared
deliberately to stop at nothing in creating human victims.
Vladimir Putin (1952-), Russian President

Abdul Fattaah Saladin considered himself a man of God, of Allah, but he recognized two important facts. First, that he was indeed a man in all respects, and second, that Allah would forgive the sins of his warrior.

He wanted to conclude this meeting quickly to meet an infidel woman to whom he'd been introduced. Muslim women often had too much religious pride to do the messy things in bed that Saladin enjoyed, and they certainly did not take alcohol. American women, infidel women, seemed to bathe in their sinful damnation, especially when drunk, as they often seemed to be.

He turned to face Ahmad Jabara sitting gingerly next to him on the park bench.

"I was sorry to hear about Azim. How are you feeling, brother?"

Ahmad shifted uncomfortably. The bullet wound in his buttocks gave him pain even through the street pain killers he ate like Reese's Pieces, and the shoulder wound, so close to his face, smelled badly and was becoming infected. He didn't dare go to a hospital with gunshot wounds, so he visited a retired Iraqi doctor he knew, who looked at the injuries and changed the dressings. The man was often drunk, and he didn't wash his hands.

"Thank you, *sayyd*. I will live, *inshallah*," Ahmad said. If Allah wills it. Ahmad believed Allah must know a lot more about his prospects for survival than he did, because Ahmad wasn't sure of them at all.

"Indeed. Allah willed that Azim reap his heavenly rewards," Saladin said. "We are sorry for his death because we are human. Yet it cannot be denied that we are happy for his ascension into Paradise because we are Muslim. *Allāhu Akbar!*"

"*Allāhu Akbar!* The other man, the large white infidel, survived. I was afraid of him, *sayyd.* As you instructed, I told him of the police officer, and what he did. I told him I knew nothing about the man that paid us to get the case, just that I got an unknown call on my cellphone offering money to question the black man. We did that, and the black man told us where he had hidden the briefcase, which I gave to you. You gave it back and we met the men. The white man did not bring the money from us—*for* us—as he promised. And then the case exploded, and killed the black man."

Ahmad looked down at his Nike tennis shoes.

"And it killed my brother, also. I am confused, *sayyd.*"

Saladin had indeed harvested the briefcase's treasure, the grid coordinates to a hundred million dollars hidden in a Pakistan cave just across the border from Afghanistan. If he had not been in the right club at the right time, he would never have overheard the drunken American black man boasting outrageously about his enormous treasure, and bemoaning ever having a chance to recover it.

Saladin hardly believed the story, but such money would do wondrous things in service to Allah, and terrible things to infidels. He had to find out for sure. And when the story was not only true, but he could get the location of the money, he praised Allah mightily. Ahmad and his little brother, Azim, were not soldiers. They were poor substitutes for real soldiers, but with Saladin's instructions, they performed well enough to get Joe to give up the briefcase.

When Joe and his partner came back into the picture seeking return of the case, Saladin decided to send them a little present instead. The bomb-filled briefcase was supposed to have killed them all—Joe, Cloud, and the Jabara brothers, too. But evidently Allah had other plans.

Saladin had passed the money coordinates along to his *jihadi* brothers in

Tehran, but this government worked no faster than some others, and even slower than most. By the time the bureaucracy had turned sufficiently to mobilize a Quds Force team to the location, the money was gone. The locals told stories of a big American airplane that landed in the night, leaving tragedy and dead militias behind. The tales of goatherds interested no one. All that mattered was that the money had eluded their grasp.

Saladin put his arm around Ahmad's shoulder on the uninjured side, careful not to jostle the bullet wound. Despite the evening warmth, Saladin wore thin gloves. This fact eluded Ahmad.

"I know you are confused, Ahmad. I know. But be assured that you are doing the work of Allah Himself, peace be upon Him."

Saladin reached into a soft laptop case filled with paper and withdrew an unremarkable white envelope purposely no different from billions of others available at any office supply store. The flap was tucked into the envelope, avoiding a DNA smear on the adhesive.

"This is a token of appreciation, Ahmad. I do not take the blasphemy of speaking for Allah, peace be upon Him, but as we are all directed by Him in mysterious ways, my giving you this means it is from Him."

Ahmad took the thick envelope and pried it open. It was neatly filled with hundred-dollar bills. The boy's eyes went wide. Even the first payment, retrieved from its hiding place when he had been recruited into the briefcase scheme, had not been so much. And that payment had been more money than Ahmad had ever before seen on Earth in one place.

"Thank you, *sayyd!* Thank you!" Ahmad's chest quivered as he tried to keep from crying with joy, but the sobs bubbled out of him. Now he could get his wounds properly treated, and possibly even send his mother to visit his sister in San Diego.

"Th-thank you, *sayyd*," the boy stammered through his sobs. "*Allāhu Akbar!*"

"Yes," Saladin said gravely. "*Allāhu Akbar!*"

Then his cellphone rang, which was unfortunate.

CHAPTER FORTY

A military man can scarcely pride himself on
having smitten a sleeping enemy; it is more a
matter of shame, simply, for the one smitten.
Isoroku Yamamoto (1884-1943), Japanese Navy admiral

Foster Heath Benoit III left Frannie Demopolis's Dearborn apartment a few minutes before eleven, as was his practice. This was a casual affair for him—more and better regular sex than he'd ever had before—but he noted of late that Frannie had become a lot more serious about developing "a relationship."

He was intent on that not happening. Reinforcing his lack of commitment, he felt that if he left before the stroke of eleven, it left adequate margin to avoid spending the night at her place.

She told him of her Bureau application in the days prior, which he had happily endorsed. Behind the scenes, he had made a few calls to expedite the paperwork. The sooner she was gone to Quantico and the FBI Academy, the sooner she would cease to be an irresistible obstacle in his life. He would miss her enthusiasm and creativity in bed, but she was distracting him from larger goals.

Though Benoit wasn't an unattractive man, his mother, whom he revered and still lived with, always told him women would only ever like him for his wealth, of which there was a vast and perpetually growing amount. His poor self-esteem would have shocked anyone who knew him professionally, where he always appeared to be in charge and slightly larger than life, even to those who disliked him. His personal conviction that he was unworthy as a man, a view always intensified by his mother, was about to get a gigantic and kinetic turn-around.

He swung his suit coat over his shoulder like he'd seen a jaunty Don Draper do a dozen times in *Mad Men,* Benoit's favorite TV show and one he watched On Demand over and over. Benoit imagined himself to be a combination of Draper's unflappable cool and James Bond's terminal efficiency. He was neither.

He used his AMG-Mercedes electronic key fob to unlock the S65. He pulled open the driver's door, tossed in the suit coat to the passenger seat, and folded himself into the powerful car, fastening the seatbelt.

Igniting the six-liter V-12 and revving the engine gave him another mild erection. He thought of going back up to have Frannie take care of it. He knew she always watched him from the upstairs window until he left, and she would welcome him back into her bed.

He stole a glance at his Breitling watch: 2256. Only four minutes to eleven p.m. He lowered his window and bent low enough to see Frannie leaning out of her bedroom window. He gave her a little wave, changed the seven-speed transmission from Park to Drive, and roared away from the curb.

He used a new cellphone to dial a number. The burner phone wasn't paired to the car because Benoit knew that was another way, yet another electronic bread crumb someone could use to trap him one day. These burners all were single-use phones for him, anyway. After each call, Benoit destroyed the phone and distributed its parts all over the city. He had a box of new ones in the trunk of his car.

"Hello," came a deeply modulated voice on the other end. This man also had a box of burner phones. He gave the new number to Benoit at the end of each call.

"Glasser here," Benoit said. The codename was his little joke. Harold Glasser had been an infamous Russian spy in America after World War II. Benoit wasn't a spy, but what he was doing was close enough for government work.

"Update," he ordered.

"We have made the arrangements with the baseball team for the tele-vised opening ceremonies at the World Series," the voice rumbled. "It was shockingly easy. The ignorant marketing manager embraced the idea of skydivers parachuting into Comerica Park as if it was his own. I think he passed it along to his superiors as that, too. All the better. No vetting, no background investigations—it's an Official Tigers Program now. It is amazing what a sincere smile and a well-designed business card can get you in this country, especially when what you offer is free."

When the deep voice laughed, it boomed from the cheap cellphone speaker like a special-effects Lucifer.

"I guess," Benoit said. He wasn't interested in the mechanisms, only the results. "And the deliverables?"

Benoit knew the NSA's ECHELON signals intelligence program routinely sniffed the air for keywords in cellphone conversations monitored in real time, and it often made for awkward conversation. For example, the word "ignorant" was substituted for "infidel." Benoit didn't want to use any language that flirted with detection. He was so close now to breaking out, to breaking free. To victory.

"They are being prepared right now, but it is slow, as I foresaw. Thirty-five black chestpacks, each equipped with twenty-five kilos of shaped product."

The product was Semtex, a powerful construction and military explo-sive, another keyword the NSA computers were sure to zero in on.

"The metal parts are already soaking in the compound."

The compound was Compound 1080, a viciously poisonous toxin that would coat and infuse the metal fragments layered in the backpack bombs.

"Our people must work with the liquid with great care, lest they kill themselves and everyone around them."

✪

In a deep sub-basement of a large unmarked building in Crystal City were thirteen Cray CS-Storm GPU-accelerated cluster supercomputers working in an integrated network dubbed COLOSSUS. They were dedicated solely to the anti-terror task force operating in Detroit. They constantly sifted communication channels of all kinds for keywords, and they took instant note of a cellphone call containing the word combination "kill themselves."

Colossus sent a flag on the cellphone call to the CIA office in Detroit's Greektown, where Poppy Benedict had established the team's local working base. In one of the second-deck cubicles, a red light winked on in a new computer window in analyst Deb Hemme's signals intelligence laptop.

✪

The dark voice on the call continued. "The layers of projectiles will go over the product, with an energizer installed. We will ignite all the chestpacks at once with a single signal, better to coordinate the outcomes. It should make quite an impression on national television. Regrettably, I think the game will be cancelled."

"And the airlift coordination?"

"Also simple—the ignorant Tigers contact arranged everything on our behalf. *Allu*–thank the Lord."

✪

Colossus noted the partial word *Allu*—and indexed it instantly against all English words beginning with those four letters, coming up with more than two hundred. Then it searched for all words in all languages that could be expressed in Roman letters that began with those letters. Many more.

But the algorithm knew to look first for context that implied the most danger.

✪

It pained the man to abuse God's name with a Christian expression for Allah, peace be upon Him, but it was for God's own glory, he reasoned.

"We will board the C-130 at Owosso Airport about ten o'clock that morning, and they will fly us to the baseball park. We will do a HALO jump at eleven a.m., and activate the witnesses"—*martyrs*—"as they parachute into the park at about the VIP box level. The blossoms"—*explosions*—"will be extremely impressive by themselves, but the compound will activate"—*kill*—"everyone it touches many times over. Then the infected dead and wounded will activate anyone else who touches them—and then anyone who touches *them*. It could go on for a long time. The bodies infected could remain poisonous for a year."

Benoit just listened. He was concerned that the man was using too much plain—and dangerous—English to not trigger an alarm on a CIA desk somewhere.

"I also will arrange to leave behind a special present in the aircraft that will make it part of the celebrations. That part of the mission is a no-charge bonus. The airplane people, they are all former American military, enemies of Islam."

"Understood," Benoit said at last. Time to wind down this call. "Proceed as previously directed. The payments will continue as before, with the final installment due after the festivities, as agreed. Give me a new phone number."

The man with the deep, accented voice rattled off a ten-digit number on his next burner phone. The man paused. "Wait one."

Benoit guided his Mercedes into the right lane, and then turned into an alley, shifting into Park. He popped his trunk and retrieved a five-pound hammer. He was nervous about the contact asking him to wait, but the man wouldn't have asked without a reason. Benoit knew him to be quite methodical.

The call was open, and Benoit muted his cellphone mic to be safer. When the call was over, he would put the burner phone on the concrete alley surface and smash it to bits with the hammer. He would pick up most of the large pieces and toss them all into a nearby dumpster.

Always so careful.

Who was the man on the other end of Benoit's phone talking to? Benoit knew the location of that meeting and had declined the man's offer to attend and see the work first-hand. That was too much like getting hands dirty for Benoit. But if something was going on at the meeting that jeopardized his plan, maybe he needed to be there after all.

It wouldn't hurt, he rationalized, to just drive over that way while listening in.

✪

Poppy Benedict was tired tonight. The new Detroit offices in Greektown were humming around the clock—and the Old Shillelagh Irish bar was only a block away, the delightful Fishbone's Cajun restaurant only across the street—but the World Series thing was going nowhere. He was beginning to think that was a dry hole.

There hadn't been a single peep about it since the initial chatter out of Dearborn weeks ago. Maybe their time was better spent putting coverts into the Michigan Wolverines, the white nationalist militia group.

They were the apparent lead organization in the so-called rebellion, and the Ohio and Indiana rabble were coming up to Michigan for their so-called training. Poppy had viewed some of the UCAV video of these people in their training maneuvers. He thought they could use a few good drill sergeants, but he also knew that every one of those bozos still had a working trigger finger.

And he needed another Starbucks. Whoever was making the office coffee was trying to give him an ulcer. He rested his face in his hands for a minute. Just a fatigued minute. Or two.

"Boss?"

"Umm, yes?" Poppy rose groggy from his handheld perch. It was that signals intelligence kid from S&T, Deb Hemme. Her last name was pronounced like the big V-8 engine from Chrysler.

She got teased about her name only one time, from a car guy in the group. He'd eyed her butt in tight blue jeans in the breakroom and asked with a laugh, "That thing got a Hemi in it?" after the old Dodge muscle-car commercials.

In less than an hour he was escorted to the sidewalk by bad-tempered Army CID criminal investigators laid on for site and team security. He carried a box of his few belongings and a zero-tolerance handout that described how human resources would contact him about his hostile-workplace termination.

"Yeah, what's up?" It was late. Everyone was worn out. Life was sucking out loud, the coffee was crap, and the terror shot clock was ticking more loudly every minute.

Hemme smiled. Even her eyes may have sparkled in the half-light of Poppy's office. What she said next sat Poppy up straight in his chair.

"I think I have something."

✪

"Okay, okay, everybody wedge in, wedge in," Poppy shouted. "We need to get started. General, can you see and hear A-OK?"

Though it was nearly one in the morning, General McCandless was in the team's Crystal City headquarters on a high-speed satellite video link. Poppy saw he had other teammates in the room as well. McCandless gave a thumb's up to his camera.

"We're good to go here, Poppy," he said.

Benedict turned back to his group and everyone settled down. All the chairs were filled, and a dozen or more excited staffers lined the conference room walls.

"Okay, this is a Prime Flash One update, that's why I've invited our whole team in for the briefing." He turned to Deb Hemme and smiled kindly, like a proud father. These young people were the new principal guardians of the nation, and they didn't even carry guns.

Well. Some did.

"You all know Deb Hemme, from SIGINT." He stepped away from the lectern and waved her forward. "Okay kiddo, tell 'em what you got."

She stepped forward confidently, but Poppy knew the young woman's bones must be shaking inside like dice in a cup.

"Thank you, sir. General McCandless." She nodded to the 8k display screen where the officer's face hovered. It was like he was looking through a window into the room.

"At 2303 hours tonight—*last* night, technically, less than two hours ago—we got a funny hit in the ECHELON system monitoring communications channels for keywords. We're programmed to look for a broad range of suggestive words, patterns, and terms, especially any that have what we think is 'war-like' flavor. English, of course, but anything in about any language, anything about the World Series, or bombs, explosives, and so on. As you can imagine in this tri-county area, we get lots of general hits on Arabic words and World Series chatter, so at the minor risk of missing something, but the major benefit of sifting out the most garbage, we fine-tuned the program to consider combinations of common keywords first.

"Everything is recorded for computer review. The sheer volume of content makes it impossible for human staff to monitor in real time—but if a recording is flagged by the system for certain keywords, the computer serves it up to us for immediate review."

She looked at Poppy, who nodded. *Keep going.*

"Miss Hemme," General McCandless said from the Arlington conference room, "your text said you thought you had such a conversation we should hear?"

"I do, general," she replied. Hemme held her secure work iPhone to the lectern's hot mic and her finger hovered above the Play button on a top-secret app that interfaced with the SIGINT system. "Listen to this."

She touched the button and the room fell as quiet as a cathedral. There were a few pops and beeps as the computer racked the recording, and then two clear voices filled the room.

Update.

We have made arrangements with the baseball team for the televised opening ceremonies at the World Series ...

The call unspooled in the Greektown and Crystal City conference rooms in perfect reproduction. It was like the two talkers were sitting at the table.

... We shall ignite all the chestpacks at once with a single signal, better to coordinate the outcomes. It should make quite an impression on national television. Regrettably, I think the game will be cancelled.

The deathly silence in the room was only broken in everyone's heads by the sudden intense pounding of accelerated heartbeats. They were listening, nearly in real time, to an actual plot to attack the opening ceremonies of the World Series. It was like finding a unicorn.

... We will do a HALO jump at eleven a.m., and activate the witnesses as they parachute into the park at about the VIP box level. The blossoms will be extremely impressive by themselves, but the compound will activate everyone it touches many times over. Then the infected dead and wounded will activate anyone else who touches them—and then anyone who touches them. It could go on for a long time. The bodies infected could remain poisonous for a year. I also will arrange to leave behind a special present in the aircraft that will make it part of the festivities. That part of the mission is a no-charge bonus. The airplane people, they are all former American military, enemies of Islam. Wait one.

Hemme stopped the playback. "The curious 'wait one' is classic military radio lingo for standby, at least for American forces, but does it mean the same thing here? We don't know."

The chill in the room was palpable. No one spoke. The attack plot on the World Series was real, after all—and it was moving forward.

"You don't have to be Inspector Clouseau to figure out this conversation is intentionally trying to evade keyword detection. It suggests a level of sophistication, or information, uncommon to general terrorist cadre. They dropped the ball, though. There were several important partial clues, but the system also picked up on the sentence containing 'former American military' and 'enemies of Islam.'"

General McCandless asked, "What do we know about all the phone numbers? Is there any targeting—I mean, localizing data? Can we find these bastards and scoop them up?" McCandless always got spun up at the prospect of blowing something up, and he was smelling an opportunity.

"Well sir, yes and no," Hemme said. "First, we did track the phone numbers of the two active phones and the numbers stated immediately; they are all burners, probably sold in a downriver liquor store about ten days ago, so no joy on that. As to localizing, COLOSSUS realized the call was important almost immediately and the computers reached out to the remotely piloted aircraft on combat air patrol over Dearborn and Detroit. It first instructed the drone to search for the transmission points based on the signals' relative distances to three of our own mission cell towers. COLOSSUS then sent to the pilots at Selfridge a PF1 WINGHAVEN PROTOCOL request for operational control of the SuperReaper, which they granted."

She noted a few confused faces around the table. "Everyone in this room has a clearance level for this, but until now, no need to know." She turned to Poppy Benedict and raised her eyebrows. *Okay to proceed?* He nodded in the affirmative.

"Now that's changed. Our top-secret WINGHAVEN PROTOCOL is a very advanced experimental autonomous aircraft control method powered by artificial intelligence. Science and Technology has been working on it for about ten years at Area 51-Delta—we call the base *Winghaven* because our smart drones are based there."

People in the room leaned forward.

"The protocol can monitor everything the mainframes process and make its own decisions based on the calculations. Effectively, it's a dynamic extension of COLOSSUS in the field: COLOSSUS is the brain, the drones are its body, or at least its limbs. Once invoked—and it isn't automatic—the protocol can launch, operate, and recover UCAVs, acquire drones in flight, and more. If so instructed, it can plan, fly, execute, and debrief a full combat mission with no additional input from us at all, just making decisions based on what it has monitored. It has certain programming rules, of course. It can't listen in on a kid's cellphone who says something like '*This is the bomb,*' and then shoot him. At this level of development, it's basically as mature as a forty-year-old air force pilot in the grade of full colonel."

Somebody whistled low.

"This mission was its first real-world deployment, and it worked like a boss. COLOSSUS ordered the RPA to orbit over Dearborn at a higher altitude for a broad look-down. We could only get the search down to two five-block areas within which the computer thought the callers originated before the call ended."

Poppy said, "General, we have the mainframes processing all the video takes in those two areas right now. We're cross-referencing addresses, vehicle license plates, crime databases—even facial recognitions, if we get any—to see if anything floats to the surface."

"Okay," General McCandless said impatiently. "How long before these turds float to the surface? Can we match any voiceprints?"

"No telling, sir. Our Crays—COLOSSUS, if you will—are better than anybody's, but it is what it is. And at the end of the run, they might not turn up anything." He rose from his chair and stepped to the lectern. "For now, we wait."

"Very well, damn it. Keep me informed," McCandless said.

The general's image in the ultra-high-resolution display monitor then turned to Deb Hemme.

"And you, little lady, will find a tangible expression of your nation's gratitude in your Direct Deposit very soon." He half-saluted at his camera. "Good night, all. Damned superlative work. Let's nail these people. Um, Poppy? FYI, I think I know who the 'former American military' are. And they happen to have a C-130, just up the road from you, too. I'll be in your office at zero-seven for breakfast and we'll go drop in on them. Out here."

His screen flickered, and the live Crystal City video feed was replaced by the large official CIA seal floating around the monitor in screensaver mode.

Poppy turned to the room. "Okay everybody, night team stays. Everybody else not on actual duty-roster duty get outta here, get some rest."

Chairs and feet shuffled as the team rose to depart. The mood was electric but ominous. More and more, it was looking like they were probably going to have an actual shooting war right here in Detroit.

To Deb Hemme, he said, "You did some pretty great work here tonight, Hemme." He reached out to shake her hand and she took it. Her hand was cold and sweaty with anxiety, and it shook ever so slightly.

"Thank you, boss," was all she said.

Poppy smiled wistfully. If he had stayed with his second wife and if they had a baby girl early on, she might have been just about this woman's age now. Life is funny, he thought.

Not often the *ha-ha* kind, mostly.

"I think the general will want to thank you tomorrow in person. What are you doing for breakfast?"

CHAPTER FORTY-ONE

You can't cross the sea merely by standing and looking at the water.
Rabindranath Tagore (1861-1941), Indian poet

Jeff O'Brien sat in his quiet Detroit police car for fifteen or twenty minutes, just letting his eyes get accustomed to the darkness.

He pulled straight in under a large overhanging tree branch full of leaves, camouflaging the short LED light bar on the top of the unmarked black traffic car. His windows were all down and there wasn't a sound, no late summer breeze to stir the turning leaves, not even crickets.

In Hollywood movies, that was supposed to be a sign of danger.

He unbuckled his Sam Browne and quietly eased the rattling equipment belt off and to the rubber floor mat on the passenger side. Habitually ensuring the iPhone was on vibrate, O'Brien unbuttoned his right shirt pocket, tucked in the flap and inserted the phone upside-down, with the mic facing up. He had preselected Tracey's *call back* number from her last inbound call. All of her questions would be answered tonight.

The phone buzzed again. He didn't need to look at it to know who was calling. *Patience, honey,* he thought to himself, silencing the vibration. *I'm moving as fast as I can here.*

He picked up his service weapon from the passenger seat and popped his car door as quietly as he could. The interior light in his squad car had burned out months ago and wasn't replaced. He stood next to the police car and pressed the door closed until it clicked once, just enough to not risk it blowing open if a random wind arose.

He reached up with his left hand and pressed the *Call Back* button on the phone.

✪

In Amber's Corvette, Tracey's phone rang. She saw who was calling.

"Hey, Jeff," she said casually. "How the heck are ya?"

"Hey sarge," O'Brien said. His voice was low, but clear. "S'up? Saw you were trying to reach me."

"No kiddin', huh? You know why I'm trying to reach you, you little shithead."

"Oh Trace, is that any way to talk to the man who might have been the father of your children?"

O'Brien could hear her plainly in the still night with the phone volume up to about half, but his speakerphone function was not on and the sound didn't carry more than a foot or two. With his phone upside-down in his shirt pocket, the small mic was pointed just about directly at his face. Tracey could hear everything as clear as a bell.

"Not a chance in hell, man, but that's a topic for another time. Why did you kill al-Taja? Why did you flake that weed and guns onto poor Cortez? He ain't got enough of life stacked against him already?"

Tracey was getting angrier by the word. She was bitterly disappointed in her friend, and separately, in her police colleague.

"You're a cop, fercrissakes! You're supposed to look out for people, not screw them over. Not friggin' *kill* people."

"Assumes facts not in evidence, sergeant. I expect better police work from you than a slavish devotion to the superficial."

O'Brien walked slowly and noiselessly through the freshly mown grass, keeping to the shadows. His dark blue police uniform made him nearly invisible in the night.

"I didn't kill al-Taja. If you knew all the facts, you would understand like I do."

"Then try telling me the fucking facts!" Tracey yelled into her phone. "Believe me, I have a few thousand questions I need to ask you. Where are you right now?" Her voice took on a quieter but harder tone. "We'll come to you."

"Well, I'm kinda busy right now, but I am, in fact, going to help you get your case file right, and I need you to shut the hell up for a miraculous change and just listen, okay? Promise me you will stop talking now. You'll hear everything, but you really gotta shut the hell up now. Or you're gonna get my ass killed."

"Where are you? Do you need backup? We're in Dearborn. Just tell me where you are."

"I'm meeting the guy who got me involved in all this crap. All shall become clear soon. I want you to hear what goes on, so mute your phone but leave the call open, okay? You'll understand. You won't approve, but you'll understand. I guess that's the best I can hope for now."

"Amber," Tracey said. "Get your phone out and record what comes out of my phone, okay?"

"You got it." Amber reached into her purse and withdrew her cellphone.

"All right, Jeff, we're listening. But don't get friggin' murdered out there, because I intend to kill your ass myownself."

The two set their phones up. Tracey muted her mic, placed the speakerphone to Amber's mic, and Amber secured the phones with a length of duct tape from a roll behind her seat. She opened her voice memo app and pushed record.

"Amber, please stay here and listen? Imma step out for a sec."

"Hell of a time for a potty stop, hon," Amber said.

Tracey got out of the car without responding, taking her Detroit Police handset radio.

"Two-six-six-three calling radio," Tracey said into the device.

"Go ahead two-six-six-three," dispatch said.

"Yes ma'am, could you please have D-Six-Seventy change to echo-five-bravo, please?"

"Radio calling Six-Seventy. Change over to Echo-five-bravo for two-six-six-three."

"Six-Seventy, radio. Copy."

Tracey changed the radio frequency to an encrypted off-dispatch channel so that only she and the Sixth Precinct desk sergeant were in on the conversation. Anyone else hearing the call with an encrypted radio could also listen in, but at this time of night, that level of interest was unlikely. And it didn't matter, anyway. She counted to five and keyed her radio.

"Two-six-six-three."

"D-Six-Seventy here, go ahead, sergeant."

"Jay, I need a fast favor. Please call up Jeff O'Brien's location on your CAD and send me a snapshot of his coordinates? Just grab a photo with your phone and text it to me ASAP, okay?"

She gave the desk sergeant her personal cellphone number. Receiving the photo on her phone wouldn't interfere with monitoring Jeff's broadcast with her work phone.

"Copy that. Standby."

"Thanks, Jay. I owe ya," Tracey said.

A moment later Ivy came back on the radio.

"Sending it. His icon is red, so he's been stopped longer than ten minutes and that also means he hasn't checked in to OpsCenter."

He paused, unsure whether he should ask anything more.

"Hey Tracey, what the hell's goin' on out there? You guys need cavalry? I ain't got much to send, but I can send what I got."

"Not sure yet. I'll let you know more when I know it. Thanks, though. Out here, brother."

CHAPTER FORTY-TWO

To act is to be committed, and to be committed is to be in danger.
John A. Baldwin (1924-1987), American author

Hamzaa el-Shafei was uncomfortable outside of Dearborn. Detroit was all right, because it was a big city, full of diverse ethnicities, and he blended in, for a drug addict. More directly, he was invisible. He blended in because he was just average enough to not be remarkable.

In Dearborn, he was literally among his own people, Muslims of all sects and colors. They spoke the same language, ate the same foods, appreciated the same faith, and often had the same goal, especially these days: *Stay alive.*

It was becoming as bad in some places in Dearborn as in any Middle East city filled with dissidents. White kids had started driving fast down Dearborn streets, screaming epithets, throwing paint-filled balloons at old women wearing *hijab* on the street, and spray-painting foul slogans and swastikas on mosques, homes, and businesses.

The mood in the country was not the immigrant's dream it was when the old people came to Dearborn. There was more uncertainty, more division. More ignorance. More fear.

The new and growing popularity of an anti-immigrant mood in the Detroit area was troubling to el-Shafei. His conversations with his Imam did not make him feel better. But Imam had said el-Shafei's work was going to keep people alive. He said the work would bring him additional glory in Heaven, would help make up for a life wasted on Earth by drugs, petty crimes, and other abominations. El-Shafei hoped it would be a long time before he learned what those incentives were.

So, he was hardly frightened at all when he sat in a Fishbone's booth, waiting for his crazy white nationalist militia recruiter to respond to his call. Then, when he was looking elsewhere, the man slid into the booth across from him with a sly grin.

"Oh, *hi* ... I didn't see you coming," el-Shafei said, startled.

"Well shippie, that's the point, isn't it? Swift, silent ..." He leaned forward and his voice deepened. "... and *deadly*."

Rudolph Wolf was a recruiter for the Michigan Wolverines. He was former active duty U.S. Navy, and he called everyone he had a passing acquaintance with "shippie" or shipmate—even those he'd never shipped out with. After ten years in the Navy, he angrily declined to reenlist and got out when his Engineering Department head, a Jewish woman, took over as CHENG and became his chief engineer.

Since then, Wolf had picked up about thirty pounds and a defiant long ponytail hairstyle that, because of his receding hairline, made his whole head look like it was being pulled back.

His simple flirtation with ultra-right politics then became a full dedication to the Wolverines, believing that armed resurrection against ghostly "government factions" was the only solution. Solution to what, he could never say with clarity.

He was never certain who his enemy was, not fully read in on the extremist politics or ramifications of his actions by his militia bosses. And as a former Navy snipe—an enlisted man who worked on the gas turbine engines in the bowels of the ship—he brought no pertinent war-fighting skills to his battle beyond hate and enthusiasm. That was enough.

But he was certain of a few things: If he and his band of malcontents could wipe the Arabs, the Jews, Big Government, the fags, and decaf coffee from the face of the Earth, it would be a happier place.

"So, you decided to join our happy little band of warriors," Wolf said, nodding approval. "I'm glad, man. Patriot nation! Things are movin' forward out there, shit's been happenin'. You knowin' how to speak that raghead jibber-jabber makes you a valuable addition to our outfit."

"What happens next?" el-Shafei asked. "I mean, I was never in the 'real military,' just the reserves, but there was, like, a procedure and stuff. Is there any paperwork, like, I sign something, or whatever?"

"Oh, we'll take care of you, for sure." Wolf's grin was more like a leer. "I was in the U.S.-goddamn-Navy, shipmate, and the Michigan Wolverines are at least as good as your 'real military' jerk-offs. But yeah, we have our little induction ceremony when you join up officially. We'll schedule you for some training, get some uniforms issued, all that jazz. You gotta get your own weapons, but our guys are upgradin' all the time. Somebody always has something good for sale at a family price. Then you'll be a militiaman, just like the Founding Fathers intended. Protectin' the Constitution and shit."

"I'm planning to go whenever you say," el-Shafei said.

Wolf reached across the table and shook el-Shafei's hand. Wolf smiled broadly, but his smile slipped just a tick and his eyes narrowed when he spoke.

"Patriot nation, brother! That's good to hear. Because we got big plans for you, too."

CHAPTER FORTY-THREE

Heroism is not only in the man, but in the occasion.
Calvin Coolidge (1872-1933), 30th American President

Jeff O'Brien was less than a flicker among the dense black shadows. The Dearborn park was the perfect meeting place. Removed from the neighborhoods, unlikely to be occupied by others, and quiet as a tomb.

How appropriate.

He stage-whispered from time to time toward the phone in his shirt pocket transmitting to Tracey and Amber. His weapon was extended down at his left side.

"In case I don't get to say this to you later, I want you to know I was always sorry we never worked out."

In Amber's Corvette, Tracey drew breath to respond. She reached to unmute the device, but Amber laid a restraining hand on her arm.

"Just let him speak," she whispered.

"We were on another break when I met Jill. We had a bunch of breaks back in the day, remember? You and me? Everything about us was so intense then. Then she got pregnant the first time, and we started having our boys and, well, life ensued, y'know?"

O'Brien stopped behind a thick maple tree to look around. No moon, no stars, and no safe margins, he thought. *Two outta three ain't bad.*

"Okay sweetie, real quiet now ... shit's about to get real."

He spied two men sitting on a bench about thirty meters away, facing the playground. The larger man reached into a briefcase and withdrew something, handing it to the smaller man. The smaller man seemed happy about that. They exchanged *Allāhu Akbar*'s, and the larger man opened a flip phone and took a call. He spoke for only a few minutes and then set the open phone down on the park bench. The smaller man got up and turned toward an adjacent parking lot.

He only got about three meters away when the larger man pulled a silenced Russian Stechkin APS automatic pistol from under his jacket and shot the smaller man three times in the back.

Well, that must be my guy, Jeff thought.

The larger man rose and went to the body motionless on the fresh grass. He poked the prone figure with his foot, then shot him two more times in the head. He reached into his briefcase again and pulled out a few pieces of paper, dropping them on the body, then retrieved the object he'd given the man, returning it to his briefcase.

Abdul Fattaah Saladin dropped the flyers on Ahmad Jabara's body. They told of a white nationalist militia group called the Michigan Wolverines that hated Jews and Arabs, that screamed America was for Americans. The flyer claimed Ahmad's murder was the group's response to the escalation of immigration in this country and erosion of American values. The flyers promised more reprisals in the coming days and invited membership inquiries to a website.

Intentional poor spelling and a rough, photocopied appearance made the flyers look even more grassroots and menacing. Saladin reached down and retrieved the envelope of cash he'd given to the late Ahmad, removed his gloves and stuffed them into his thin briefcase with the envelope.

The mission could not possibly be this easy. Tonight's next phase would be a bigger challenge.

Then he felt something hard press against the base of his skull.

"Freeze, asshole," O'Brien said quietly.

Saladin automatically tensed, thinking he could spin right, elbow his attacker's head and raise the handgun in his left hand in the same fluid motion. It would be over in seconds.

"Don't flex on me, bro. You're a big guy, and you ain't faster than this hollow point that will sever your fucking brain stem if you even take one more deep breath."

Saladin relaxed. There were always going to be more chances in life, *inshallah*. "Sergeant O'Brien, I presume."

"Throw your weapon to the left in one motion."

Saladin slowly raised his muscular left arm—*"Easy, big fella,"* O'Brien warned him—and flipped the gun into an evergreen. "Well done, asshole. Let's have a seat."

O'Brien stepped back from Saladin and circled around in front of him, pointing to the bench with his free right hand.

"Sit." He reached down and retrieved one of the flyers without taking his eyes from Saladin.

"Why must you Americans always be such cowboys?" Saladin said with a smirk. "This language is offensive and unproductive. Please, lower your weapon and let us just talk. Like businessmen. Like *colleagues*."

He looked down at his burner phone to see if Benoit was still listening in, but the call had been dropped. There was no telling what Benoit had or had not heard.

✪

Tracey felt her personal phone vibrating and she pulled it from her pocket. Her work phone still conducted O'Brien's conversation with his mystery man into Amber's phone, and now he had someone at gunpoint. She awakened her private phone and saw the text photo Sergeant Ivy had sent of the CAD screen map showing O'Brien's mapping. A hot red square glowed against the map's white background. Hovering above it was O'Brien's radio call sign.

Amber leaned in for a look. "That's only a few miles from here," she said, shifting into first gear. "Let's hit it."

✪

"So, *Saladin*. I looked up your name. It means 'peace through faith,' right? Something like that? What a crock'a shit. Abdul Fattaah *Saladin*, that's quite a mouthful. Probably just your fake terrorist stage name anyway, huh?"

Jeff grinned without humor. He hoped Tracey was getting all this. He sat at the opposite end of the bench from Saladin, his Smith & Wesson M&P .40-caliber service weapon leveled at the man's chest. Easy heart shot from here.

"What is the point of all this?" O'Brien eyes flicked back and forth off Saladin as he scanned the flyer promising white revolution. It had a recruiting website address for a militia group called the Wolverines.

"That's actually pretty funny," O'Brien said, dropping the paper to the grass. "Drawing a line between those high school freedom fighters in the *Red Dawn* movie and a pathetic attempt to foment your little white nationalist uprising shows some passing understanding of current events. I don't expect that kind of basic awareness from *sand niggers*."

Saladin smiled and didn't rise to the insult bait. He just shrugged his shoulders.

"I do what I can."

This was still just business for him, not personal. Not yet.

"But really, what is the angle with all this batshit revolution stuff? I see more businessman in you than religious nutlog. Where is the money for you?"

"I can't tell you, of course," Saladin said. "Whether I live tonight or die, our revolutionary movement perseveres. *Allāhu Akbar!*"

O'Brien laughed out loud. "Yeah, I'm calling bullshit on that, bubb. You could care less about some fucking *jihad*. Neither do I, simple fact. I should never have done any of your dirty work, but I was weak. Yeah, I admit it to anybody."

He emphasized *I admit it to anybody* for Tracey's benefit.

"I'm a busted-ass traffic cop. That's all I'll ever be. I'm going to die a sergeant. One minute I'm handing you a speeding ticket, the next minute you are handing me twenty-five grand. Flat out, just pulled it out of your little briefcase like it was a business card. Your line of work, maybe that *is* your business card, huh? I mean, who carries around that kind of money, dude?"

O'Brien knew that answer.

"How long had you trolled for a cop to bribe, anyway?"

"There was some risk, for sure," Saladin said with that Satanic grin. "You could have arrested me for that. I would have killed you where you stood if you tried. But my research suggested you would take the money. You don't seek all those overtime hours because you are a dedicated public servant, do you, Sergeant O'Brien? It wasn't like I offered you a hundred bucks: A hundred bucks is a bribe, an insult to the giver as well as to the receiver. But *twenty-five thousand dollars* is a business deal, not a crime."

O'Brien sighed deeply. "Babies cost money I don't have, and all the overtime on Earth can't make up for the pissant pay scale. But at least I get to deal with quality people, right? I know you, or somebody you know, killed that DHS agent, because we know that Kel-Tec you gave me to plant is the murder weapon. Including the other gun and the weed wasn't much of a dodge. That Tracey, man. She figures out shit more complicated than this all the time."

"We did find you at the right time," Saladin said. "Al-Taja was getting too close. He was good, *and* he was Muslim. I should have killed him the night he swapped my vehicle plates, but we didn't know him yet, didn't know what he knew. He should die for doing the infidel's work. You are right, though. There are other interesting things going on about which you have no idea, and this was only a part."

Saladin adjusted his position on the bench, calculating whether he was close enough to spring on O'Brien before the officer could hit him with a fatal shot. Saladin had sustained many gunshots before, and the prospect of another in service to Allah was just a prize.

"You are small, my friend. A *nobody*, a *cog* of so little consequence that it defies explanation. You are another miserable, failed American infidel who would fuck a swine in the ass in Hart Plaza if I paid you to do it." He chuckled knowingly. "You know this is true."

"Too bad you won't live to see the revolution, bubb."

O'Brien raised his weapon an inch and tightened his grip. *In for a penny,* he thought.

✪

"Fuck!" Tracey said. "That sounded like a gunshot. Amber, was that a gunshot?"

Amber said, "We're only a couple miles away."

She reached down and cancelled the flashing blue and red emergency lights, downshifted to third gear and nailed the throttle to the floor. The V-8 wailed in anger and the car leapt forward, drowning out the phone conversation for Amber. Tracey raised the two conjoined phones to her ear to listen more closely.

✪

"You're right on time," Saladin said to the darkness.

Foster Heath Benoit III materialized from a shadow and reached down to take the gun from O'Brien's limp hand.

"And you, my friend, are *damned careless,*" he said. "We were not to meet again. Let's get out of here."

Saladin found his discarded weapon in the bushes. "He was right. He died as a sergeant."

The tall Arab raised the weapon, switched it to full automatic fire, and emptied the magazine into O'Brien's neck, close and above his bulletproof vest. The force of the shots nearly severed O'Brien's damaged head from his torso. It lolled to the side on a thin strip of skin before what was left of it fell into the grass.

Saladin spat forcefully on O'Brien's brain-covered badge. Now it was personal for him.

"*Jizyah!*" he screamed passionately. *Infidel tax.*

Saladin and Benoit walked across the park until they were again swallowed by the darkness. Saladin reflected on the benevolence of Allah that had matched him with Benoit, making all this possible. In fact, Saladin had met Benoit at the same Dearborn mixer where Amber Watson met Sayid al-Waheeb. Only a few minutes of conversation had revealed Benoit's hollow self-esteem and susceptibility to suggestion. Saladin had only to plant visions of grandeur.

Benoit departed in his Mercedes. Saladin drove off in a black Dodge Magnum R/T station wagon bearing the license plate IMHOT4U.

CHAPTER FORTY-FOUR

*A great deal of intelligence can be invested
in ignorance when the need for illusion is deep.*
Saul Bellow (1914-2005), American novelist

Charlie Bird studied his C-130 manual and tried to cram his head full of Hercules facts, but he wasn't succeeding. He'd gotten a cryptic official email from his government contract administrator to stand by, but the message had no mission profiles or timing attached. "More follows" was all it promised.

Could be a mission, could be an inspection. Could be about any damned thing. This was vague even by government standards of vagary.

He fervently hoped whatever was coming down the pike wasn't going to interfere with his plans to work with Tiger Baseball on the World Series opening ceremonies. He looked up from daydreaming over the flight manual and saw behind him a classic—and familiar—silhouette outlined in the harsh backlight reflecting from his rear glass office wall.

Charlie spun in his office chair to face the grinning countenance of General John Glenn McCandless.

"Jesus H. Christ," Charlie said, springing up from behind his desk. "Could you give a guy some warning?" Charlie and the general exchanged enthusiastic hugs.

"Well bubba, y'neva know when some itinerant military officer is going to show up on your doorstep," McCandless said. "That's why you must be ready at all times." He slapped his former subordinate on his back. "How the hell are you, Birdman?"

"I'm damned good, sir, thanks in no small part to you." McCandless had vouched for Charlie and his enterprise in the run-up to the IDIQ contract award. "We've done a few things since signing our contract. Training mostly. But we're rockin' on ready, and those retainer checks keep coming in like clockwork."

Charlie thought about what he'd just said.

"Hey … you aren't my warning order, are you? Air Mobility Command said we should get ready to get ready for something, but they didn't say what. And then here you are."

"Yeah, I might be," McCandless said, grinning. "I wanted to make sure you weren't off on some other thing when I got here, so I had AMC send you that WARNORD."

Charlie was visibly disappointed. The Tigers mission probably would have to wait on the next World Series in Detroit. And good luck on that. But his contract with the government came first.

"Good thing you pinged us when you did," Charlie said. "We are just about to sign a big contract with the Tigers to play a role in the World Series opening ceremonies. That was going to be a big deal for us—but you come first, boss. Always."

McCandless said, "And your nation is grateful, colonel. I know about that Tigers deal, though. In fact, that is precisely why I'm here."

"You do?" Charlie's confusion was plain on his warrior's face. "You are?"

"I'll bring you up to combat speed, brother," McCandless said. He motioned to the people who had accompanied him. "Do you know Paul Benedict, CIA?"

"Pleasure," Charlie said, shaking hands.

"Same here, colonel. You can call me Poppy, though. I only get Paul when I'm in trouble with my mother or my ex-wives." The men laughed appreciatively.

"Poppy it is," Charlie said. "Charlie for me, please. I only get 'colonel' when the general wants something from me."

He craned his neck around General McCandless to see a short, blonde woman standing timidly in the doorway.

"And who is this?" Charlie asked.

"Charlie, meet Deb Hemme, SIGINT superstar," Poppy said. He stepped slightly aside and Hemme strode forward with a measure of confidence that she wasn't feeling inside. Charlie and the CIA analyst also shook hands.

"She is kind of the reason why we are here."

Out in the lobby, McCandless's aide, Major Tommy Crosby, was already in laughing flirtation with MDZ's highly attractive chief operating officer, Kathie Murphy. McCandless pointed at him.

"You know Tommy Crosby."

Crosby heard his name, looked up and waved at Charlie, then leaned back onto the tall lobby counter to continue flirting.

"Well, general," Charlie said. "What is it we can do for you?"

"Birdman, let us tell you a war story you haven't heard yet," McCandless said. He turned and closed Charlie's office door. "You probably want to sit down for this."

✪

Forty-five minutes later, General McCandless and Poppy had briefed Charlie in on the full World Series terror attack profile that depended on MDZ's cherished C-130H to succeed. At the end of the briefing, Poppy asked Deb Hemme to play the cellphone recording the ECHELON surveillance system had made.

"... I also will arrange to leave behind a special present in the aircraft that will make it part of the celebrations. That part of the mission is a no-charge bonus. The airplane people, they are all former American military, enemies of Islam. Wait one."

"I bet that's us, right? 'All former military, enemies of Islam.' What's the 'wait one' for, do you know? Sounds like trained military to me."

Charlie Bird had more time in intelligence briefings than some soldiers had in the Army, but the incredible idea being floated here still struck him with its utter bravado, cunning—and sheer creativity.

No one in the Tigers, he knew, had even asked one question of the mysterious skydiving marketing scheme, beyond ensuring the skydivers had current jump licenses. *And my bad,* Charlie thought. *Because the idea came from my battle buddy, I didn't ask enough questions, either.*

It would be far-fetched except for one thing—MDZ already had the contract with the Tigers, ready to sign, to provide the HALO drop and ceremonial fly-by. To hear that his passengers intended to ensure the plane and its crew would be destroyed as part of the attack was additionally chilling. And enraging.

"We weren't their enemies before, but by God, we are now," Charlie said. "They killed that Detroit policeman, and defiled his corpse? How did you match the DNA to Saladin?"

"We have considerable resources," Poppy said. "It was obvious O'Brien had been spit on, and we collected that for analysis. It even surprised us when we got the match to DNA taken from a weapon Saladin dropped on his way out of a prison he escaped from in 2005. He'd been grabbed by Mossad after a Tel Aviv bus bombing, but he fled back to Iran after his escape."

General McCandless just nodded in agreement. "Yeah, we thought the voice showed a military background in the recording, based on that 'wait one.' That says he was talking to someone and didn't hang up, though we determined the call was interrupted right after that by a signal failure. Much as I want to roll these pricks up right now, there are larger related issues we're contending with, too. We want you to continue to play ball with these guys"—Charlie shot McCandless a look, but the general just smiled—"pardon the expression. We want to catch them all at once to make damned sure we can neutralize them before I shoot them all in their fucking heads."

Charlie flipped open a manila file folder on his desk and pulled out a stapled pack of papers. He turned to the last page where Kathie Murphy had affixed a pointed red sticky tab imprinted SIGN HERE. He took a jet-black Mont Blanc fountain pen, a retirement gift to himself, and signed the Tigers World Series contract with a flourish in wet black ink.

"Okay. We are literally in business with terrorists. Let's get this party started."

CHAPTER FORTY-FIVE

No trait is more justified than revenge in the right time and place.
Meir David Kahane (1932-1990),
American-Israeli founder of the Jewish Defense League

Xavier Cloud sat in his usual booth, facing the entrance to the Red Flag Restaurant. His tea had already been served. He sipped the sweet, steaming hot liquid and thought about being home again, some of his mission accomplished.

A thin man strode forward from the swinging kitchen door, both arms outstretched.

Cloud automatically rose and accepted the embrace of General Xing Jianjun. Xing had the height of a middle-schooler but the grip of a bear, and he didn't release the much taller American for many seconds. When Xing finally stepped back, his eyes were glistening wet.

"Forgive the indecorum of an old man," he said. "I am often an emotional fool in my advanced age."

Cloud smiled. "I understand completely," he said. "I trust your daughter is well."

"Indeed, she is," Xing said. He grinned widely, almost uncontrollably. "She was here with me for ten days. I fed her too much and loved her fiercely, such that perhaps she was finally happy to go back to school two days ago."

"No more studies abroad?"

"Ha, no indeed! Only Stanford." Xing clapped Cloud on the back, but his tone turned slightly darker. "And, for peace of mind, I have arranged for her discreet around-the-clock security for a time."

He gestured back to the booth. "Let us sit and talk, my friend."

A subwaiter immediately appeared with a tea set for Xing, placing the pot and cup on the table before departing backward in a respectful bow.

"I cannot be more indebted to you, Mr. Cloud. I will say this many times for the rest of my life. My son has briefed me on the rescue of my daughter as well as the recovery of your treasure. You were quite generous with him, with his team—and with me. He and I both are grateful." The general nodded respectfully.

"I could never have retrieved the money without your help. I am grateful to you. He is a good man, your son, as I'm sure you know. I hope to always have him on my side. Once the repair team got the C-130's nose gear fixed, we flew to Abu Dhabi. Your people on the ground had everything in readiness, including UAE arrival stamps we never got for our passports before we left the States for TQ. I got off the Super Hercules, said farewell to your son, transferred our cargo to the Falcon, and we were wheels up. I may have slept all the way back to Flint. We cleared Customs and hopped over to Owosso. Those men—that entire team—earned every dollar I paid them."

"We have used that team from time to time. We keep them together on standby, training, acquiring and honing skills that may be needed in the future. As you know, good help often is hard to find."

Cloud raised his teacup in salute. "You are right about that." The men clinked cups and drank.

"General, since we have achieved such a good working relationship, perhaps there is something now that you can help me with locally."

"The entire world is yours for the asking," Xing said sincerely. "My answers to you will always be yes. You must only ask me the questions." Xing sipped his tea. "How may I help you, my friend?"

"Mohammed al-Taja was a friend of yours." It wasn't a question. "A golf partner, along with you, a heart doctor named Malhotra, and Imam Sayid Al-Waheeb."

Xing's smile may have slipped a little.

"Yes, I knew him. A good and honorable man. Passionate. Patriotic! All honorable men respect such sentiment. Not much finesse on the golf course, but a powerful driver. Doctor Malhotra is the finesse in our foursome. And the Imam? A genuinely interesting man. We have many engaging conversations about, well. About all manner of things."

"I'm sure. He too is a patriotic American. He cares deeply about his country, and for his people. He has told friends of mine that he knows some things about al-Taja's murder. No names, not many actual facts, but he knew al-Taja was investigating a terror plot to attack the World Series when the man was killed. My friends think we are close to locating this killer. He also corrupted a Detroit policeman to plant evidence on an innocent boy, but the plan was discovered—and he turned my briefcase into the bomb that killed my friend Joe. We think this man is a key to understanding who is plotting the terror attack."

Cloud sipped his tea and let the general think for a moment. Not a word of anything he said seemed to surprise Xing at all. After a moment, Cloud pulled from his pocket a sharp color photograph of Abdul Fattaah Saladin, the same photo captured by Mohammed Al-Taja's camera lapel pin the evening he changed out the license plates on Saladin's car.

"Do you know this man?" Cloud asked.

Xing took the photo and tilted it into better light, squinting. The man was tall, well-built, with long, dark hair in a man-bun, and short facial hair in the Islamic tradition. In the photo, the man wore a white tank tee that accented his broad chest muscles and thick arms.

"I do not know him," Xing said.

Cloud said, "We believe this man is a principal player in a plot to attack the World Series. Can you use your resources to help me find more information on him? We think he must operate in Dearborn in plain sight, or know people here. Perhaps al-Waheeb knows something? Knows someone who knows something, who might be afraid or unwilling to come forward? The Series opening ceremonies are only a few days away."

Xing looked at Cloud with his customary impassive stone face, but he was having an epiphany.

"So, you are indeed more than you appeared, Mr. Cloud. You are

perhaps more, then, than a simple man trying to recover his lost property."
Again, not a question. "I suspected as much, in truth. And all the stories
about your crimes? Your imprisonment?"

Cloud returned the deadpan stare.

"Yes, of course. All along, then?" Xing smiled admiringly. "Masterful.
I am happy that the stories of your so-called war crimes are false. They
did not befit the honorable warrior I believe you to be. It is true that real
knowledge is to know the extent of one's ignorance," he said.

"Truly," Cloud replied. "But Confucius also said, 'To know what you
know and what you do not know, that is true knowledge.' We know some
things. We need help knowing the rest."

Xing looked at Cloud with a blend of consternation and pride. He
had always before been at the top of his game his entire career. He was
chagrined to find Cloud had fooled him, even with the general's access
to China's global electronic eavesdropping nearly as good as the NSA's.
If this had occurred while still on active duty, Xing might have been
reassigned, if not demoted.

That danger no longer applied.

✪

Because Xing's integrity had been undisputed, China's political leaders
took a chance when the Ministry of State Security came to them with an
enterprising blueprint to put General Xing Jianjun in secret retirement
in Dearborn, Michigan, operating a Chinese restaurant. He would be the
deepest of MSS moles, available for recall from his sleeping circumstance
at any time as conditions required. But conditions had never required.

Years passed. China's relationship with America generally improved.
Her gaze turned to the South China Sea, to forging new alliances in Asia
and Africa, and the retired general was left sleeping.

Xing exercised his remote military connections regularly, better to
keep those tendons supple and responsive. That's how he had coordinated
the assets deployed to recover Cloud's money, and Xing's own daughter.
But no commands had ever flowed down to him from above.

Now he would come to the aid of the American government in tribute to the man who rescued his daughter. Xing felt no need to notify his erstwhile superiors.

He was retired, after all.

✪

"Yes, I think I can reach out to some people and see what is being said here and there."

"That would be more helpful than you can know," Cloud said. "You have my cell number. You can reach me on that day or night."

Xing looked at his wrist watch. "Allow me to excuse myself now, Mr. Cloud. I must make some inquiries." He reached across the table for a fast handshake. "I shall be back in touch with you soon, I believe."

Xing stood, bowed quickly, and before Cloud could rise from the booth and return the courtesies, the man was gone with Saladin's photograph in his hand.

CHAPTER FORTY-SIX

The sorrow for the dead is the only
sorrow from which we refuse to be divorced.
Washington Irving (1783-1859), American writer

Skipper!" MDZ's chief operating officer Kathie Murphy yelled from the breakroom to the kitchen. "That policeman's funeral is on TV."

Charlie Bird, Carlos Benavides, Kerry Baker, and Candy Clark came out of the kitchen holding coffees. The rest of the team was either working, training, or off. Candy sat on the couch next to Kathie and they all watched the broadcast in silence.

A gleaming black Cadillac funeral car was at the curb of Most Holy Trinity Church, on Porter Street west of the Lodge Expressway near downtown Detroit. A couple thousand reverent spectators stood quietly under black umbrellas in the soft gray rain as Detroit Police officers carried Sergeant Jefferson O'Brien's coffin down the concrete steps from the church.

The TV cameras zoomed in on a close-up of the six officers carrying the traffic cop to the car that would take him to a burial inside of the same Gethsemane Cemetery where he used to hide with his traffic radar.

The pallbearers wore crisp dress uniforms for their somber task. The rain fell on them as they walked in ceremonial lockstep. It soaked into their clothes and dripped like tears from the bills of their uniform caps.

Five men, one woman.

✪

Six hours later, back in dry, comfortable clothes and sitting at her table in the Sweetwater Tavern across the street from her apartment building, Tracey gazed into her beer glass. Amber Watson sat across from her.

"There was nothing you could do, honey. You know this," Amber said. "Jeff was on his own trajectory from the moment his fingers touched that jerkweed's bribe money."

The television behind the bar, its sound turned down to a whisper, replayed the live coverage of O'Brien's full-dress Chief's funeral. Hundreds of police departments from around the nation had sent officers and patrol cars to escort and participate in the melancholy procession, and Porter Street was clogged with police cars, people, and media. At one point, the TV camera zoomed in tight on Tracey helping carry the coffin down the church steps to the funeral car. It captured a close-up of her face, her tears blending with the rain.

The news anchor babbled cluelessly about evidence recovered from a second body at the homicide scene that authorities thought pointed to terrorist plots, and possibly even armed domestic insurrection. The anchor said Dearborn homicide detectives were working together with their Detroit counterparts on the case. Interviews were being conducted, surveillance cameras were being checked, all the usual things, *blah-blah*.

No one paid much attention to the report. It was sad enough the first time when it was live.

Tracey shrugged. "I suppose. Jeff was a conflicted man. But that doesn't speak to the fact that I had to comfort his widow at his gravesite a few hours ago, while she held her sleeping infant and consoled four adolescent boys sobbing for the death of the father they adored."

"Yeah, it's tough all around on this deal. Still, what I'm saying is, don't you take responsibility for this. It isn't your fault. His death is not on you."

"I am a creature of guilt, y'know." She raised her draft Stroh's in a weak salute and took a small sip. When she returned the glass to the table, she took obsessive pains to place the glass in precisely the same wet circle of condensation it occupied before.

"My buddy in the Evidence Tech Unit sent me a transcript of the phone recording we made." Tracey looked up at Amber. "I sent it along to you, FYI. But we already know what was in it."

Amber looked away toward the large windows facing the street. "My buddy the NTAC also yanked the al-Taja case back from me again. I'm locked out for good, looks like. He must smell a resolution in it that we don't detect at our level. He wouldn't have pulled it back unless he thought there was something in it for him. Jungle drums say that other body, that Jabara cat, and those Wolverines flyers, stink of a wider terror plot known only in the rare air Benoit occupies. The World Series thing, is what I think."

She took a swallow of her drink.

"My guess is the next time we see anything about it will be when he goes public with his genius. You know that fucker is asking around the office for volunteers to stand up some damned political campaign? We think he thinks he's going to be the next Gary Peters."

Peters is the junior U.S. Senator from Michigan.

Amber's eyes drilled into her drink. "I would vote for *Satan* before Benoit." She took a sip of her beer and looked back to the bar's front windows, streaked with steady rainfall that looked like tears on the glass.

"Did I tell you I broke up with my boyfriend?"

Tracey's head rose from her reverie in surprise. "No. Why? I thought he made you feel good."

"Yes, he does. Did," Amber said. "But I broke the boy's brain. He wanted to friggin' get married. Ain't nobody got time for that. And I'm a city girl—city bigger'n Traverse City, anyway. I am too young to move up north."

She smiled meaningfully.

"But he retains visitation privileges."

The door to the Sweetwater opened and in strode three men. One was short and kind of dumpy. One was tall, very handsome, and looked to be in great shape. And one was an older but handsome military officer of some kind who automatically reached up and removed his cover when he entered the bar.

Before the door closed, an observer could see another younger military officer sitting outside behind the wheel of a black Suburban. There were dark silhouettes of other occupants in the truck.

The short dumpy one looked around the tavern as his eyes adjusted to the dim light. He spied Tracey and Amber sitting in the corner, and the three men walked directly toward them.

Amber noted the tall man and smirked.

"Hmm. Looks like my rebound just got here. Yours is kinda short, though ..."

Then the three stood next to their table and the short man drew breath to speak.

"Tracey Lexcellent?"

She looked up with a frown from brooding over her drink. She did not have the time or disposition for any interviews about the funeral or her friend. Or anything else.

"Who wants to know?" Her disapproving stare took in all three men standing before her.

"Detective, we need to have just a few minutes of your time, if you please," the military man said. Amber saw he was Army, four-star at that, and that got her attention. Then she was surprised when he turned to her.

"Special Agent Watson," he said, and smiled inscrutably. "Good to see you again."

He extended his hand and Amber shook it timidly. She was certain she didn't know any four-star Army generals.

"Sir. Have we met?"

"You don't remember me, do you?"

"Ahh, no, sir ... I do not remember you," Amber said.

The officer waved Malik from Malawi over from his place behind the bar for drink orders.

"Ladies, do you mind if we get that larger table over there?" He pointed to the opposite side of the room. "Next round is on us."

He turned to Malik.

"Three large diets for us, and whatever they're having."

Once settled in around their drinks, the short man spoke first.

"We know who you are, obviously, but please let me introduce us." He pointed around the table. "That's Xavier Cloud. This is General John Glenn

McCandless. And I am Paul Benedict."

He extended his hand to Tracey. She ignored it.

"Call me Poppy."

The general raised a small wave.

"Zave," Cloud said.

"Okay, now we know who you are," Tracey said. Her contempt was genuine. "Who gives a shit?"

"We are a federal government group looking into a number of related matters," Poppy began. "We think you can help us with some of that. How long did you know Jefferson O'Brien?"

Tracey instantly bristled.

"Are we going to have that fucking song and dance now? You knew who we were when you came in here. Now you are wasting everybody's time asking bullshit questions that I know *you* already know the answers to. So why don't we just suspend the bullshit segment of the program and get down to what the actual fuck this is all about."

The funeral replay of the live TV coverage droned on in the background.

"I've already had a really shitty day."

Out of the corner of her eye, Amber thought she detected General McCandless trying to suppress an inappropriate laugh.

"You know I was in the academy with Jeff, right? You know we had a short relationship at that time. So, you probably also well know that today, and for many years, he was a happily married man raising a now fatherless boys basketball team, and he was a long-standing veteran police officer in the Detroit Police Department. I don't give a flyin' fuck right now what he's done, frankly, or what you think he's done. He was a good cop for a long time, and he was my friend. And I helped bury him today." Tracey's eyes welled up. The last line barely got out above a sob.

Poppy laid a color photo on the table and slid it over to Tracey.

"Do you know this man?"

She sniffed, and took a fast glance at it. "No. Am I supposed to?"

"He's an Iranian named Abdul Fattaah Saladin. He's one of the men implicated in the homicide of Sergeant Jefferson O'Brien."

Tracey clearly remembered Jeff purposely saying the man's name on the recording of his homicide. She picked up the photo and memorized it.

"Hmm. Still no." She handed the photo to Amber. She too memorized it, then shook her head, left-right, in the negative.

"Well, what would you say if I told you I knew where this man was right now?"

Tracey powered down the last of her beer. "Okay, I would say, 'let's go.'"

"Not so fast," the general said. "We understand your eagerness, but there are other issues involved. Would you come with us to our offices? Just over in Greektown." He looked around the sparsely populated bar. "We can't really talk openly here."

Tracey stood. "I say again, let's go."

In the CIA task force offices on Monroe in Greektown, the four men escorted the two women through a series of magnetically locked doors requiring keycards and numerical codes to get through the portals. Once on the second deck, the six walked through a busy cube farm to a conference room where a young woman waited with paperwork.

Poppy entered first.

"Come in, come in," he said to Tracey and Amber, who took seats on the far side of the long conference room table, facing the door. General McCandless, Major Crosby, and Cloud followed and sat opposite with Poppy and a woman. Poppy closed the door, which automatically locked. A light on the keypad next to the door changed from green to red.

"This is Deb Hemme. She's one of our intel operators here, but I've pressed her into admin duty for this meeting. She has some paperwork for your signatures."

Hemme slid copies of Standard Form 312—the Classified Non-Disclosure Agreement—across the table to Tracey and Amber.

"There is no time to do the background investigations on you two for the kind of field security clearance I'm about to grant, umm, meritoriously," Poppy said. "As an FBI agent, Special Agent Watson has had a comprehensive SSBI, of course, but her clearance level doesn't approach what we need today. And Ms. Lexcellent, you don't have any clearances at all."

Amber and Tracey scanned their forms briefly, but they were long familiar with mindless paperwork drills. To them, this was just another one. They inked their signatures at the bottoms of the SF-312s. Curiously, their full names, the date, their organizations, and their social security numbers were already pre-printed on the documents. Deb Hemme witnessed the forms and Poppy signed his acceptance on behalf of the United States of America.

"Basically, for the record and your information, your signature on the form affirms that nothing you learn in this room, or about topics we will discuss, can ever be revealed to another person without specific written approval—which will never be given. Or I will put you *under* the jail."

Tracey and Amber stared back unimpressed.

"*Oooh,*" Tracey said with contempt. "So badass. The short ones always think they're the tough guy."

Poppy ignored the taunt. He faced issues more pressing than an angry young woman's misplaced disrespect. Over his CIA career and four ex-wives, he'd been dissed before by experts. Tracey was not one of them.

Poppy stepped to the lectern and pressed a button. The room lights went off and a projector suspended from the ceiling threw an image of Saladin's Michigan driver's license on screen; he lived on Beaconsfield near the Detroit-Grosse Pointe Park border, was six-three, weighed 257, brown and brown.

"This man, Abdul Fattaah Saladin, was in the park in Dearborn when Sergeant O'Brien arrived. Through information we've developed, we believe O'Brien was there specifically to see Saladin. We also think O'Brien intended to kill him there."

Poppy turned to Tracey.

"We know about the bribe, the twenty-five thousand. We agree with your own suspicions about O'Brien falsely implicating the Williams kid by planting the al-Taja murder weapon in his car. That was among a number of bad calls on O'Brien's part."

Tracey's eyes widened in anger and she drew a forceful breath to protest, but Poppy cut her off with an upraised hand.

"Don't get spun up. I know he was your friend, but he's gone. These are just the facts, and we've got work to do now."

The imagery on the screen changed to dark, grainy video captured at night. It was a long, wide-angle look across the darkened Dearborn park dotted with the hot globes of streetlights and a traffic signal.

"This was video recorded by a Comerica Bank ATM machine about two blocks away. You can just see O'Brien's scout car in the shadows on the very far left. After several minutes, two men walk toward two cars on the other side of the playground, then the cars drive away. We know one of the cars was Saladin's Dodge station wagon, but there's nothing on the second car. That's all there is. No real useful information came out of this, regrettably. There are no pictures of the shootings at all."

Just as he stopped speaking, the video showed Amber and Tracey arriving in the yellow Corvette. Neither would ever forget the horrific crime scene they walked onto next.

The video changed to late afternoon, on a high angle of the City-County Building in downtown Detroit.

"This is footage accidentally captured by one of our global surveillance satellites while it was being repositioned for our use here. As it was being stabilized over the city, the sweep of the optics as the platform's azimuth changed happened to cross over downtown. This important accidental footage was discovered by Miss Hemme over there."

Poppy gave her a nod and a paternal smile, then turned back to the room. He never got tired of viewing this part.

"Watch."

The building rooftop was in twilight as shadows from the downtown office towers blocked the waning sun. Tracey and Amber immediately recognized the scene as the City-County Building. Data snippets in the margins of the frame noted the time was 2044 hours, 8:44 p.m. The video unspooled in jerky snatches, frame by frame, like old black-and-white silent films do.

It had obviously been recorded as the satellite's lens swept across the city, because it was still streaky and poorly exposed. Manipulation in a computer had enlarged the images, slowed the frame rate to nearly stop-action, and the clarity and contrast had been enhanced.

What unfolded next took Tracey's and Amber's breath away.

"I would kill for some audio here," Poppy said with conviction. In fact, Deb Hemme had put COLOSSUS on the case of trying to lip-read from the images, but in the twilight, the pictures were too grainy and indistinct to read at the magnification required to get a decent close-up of the faces.

✪

Two men were on the City-County Building's roof. They walked casually in a random pattern, evidently talking calmly in the complete privacy the rooftop provided. The erratic walking around ended up taking them to the edge of the building that faced Woodward, on the same side as the *Spirit of Detroit* statue. The thinner man wore an overcoat and gloves in the chill afternoon air.

He gestured wildly, as if upset, and the second man, wearing a dark suit, stood listening with his hands in his trouser pockets. The second man shook his head in a negative manner.

The thinner man looked over the side of the building and pointed at the *Spirit* statue several times, as if making a point. The second man then looked, too.

The first man took a long-barreled handgun from his coat pocket, stepped back, and pressed the weapon up against the second man's skull. The second man's arms instantly shot away from his sides.

Poppy said, "We think that gun is a pink Kel-Tec three-eighty with low-power assassin loads, but here, it has an obvious custom-made silencer on the end of it."

Amber and Tracey sat bolt upright in their chairs.

The thinner man seemed to say a few more words, only a few, and then pulled the trigger of his gun. The dark-suited man collapsed instantly in a heap, but was held at the edge of the rooftop long enough for the thinner man to put his weapon back in his coat pocket. Then, with both hands on the second man's shoulders, the thinner man carefully pushed the body over the edge of the building.

"I will just be *goddamned*," Tracey said under her breath. Amber sat electrified by what she had seen.

Mohammed al-Taja—The Well-Dressed Man.

The thinner man looked around, and up and across the neighboring streets, as if to see whether he had been observed by anyone in surrounding office buildings. It was unlikely this long after close of business. Evidently satisfied that his crime was safe from prying eyes, he straightened his tie and walked casually back to the rooftop access door, opened it, and disappeared inside.

The stop-action images progressed a few more yards across the top of the roof before swinging out across the city toward Windsor on the Canadian side of the Detroit River.

The video stopped, and the lights came back up.

"Does any of that ring any bells with either of you?" General McCandless asked.

"Ah, no … no. None here, sir," Amber said, but she was wide-eyed and still thinking about something she wasn't ready to share.

"Yeah, I got nothin'," Tracey said. "But I'll tell you what: You people have some damned fine toys."

"Al-Taja was a CIA undercover in the Department of Homeland Security," Poppy said. "He was investigating a serious plan to attack the World Series during the opening ceremonies, real 9/11-type stuff."

Amber's head swiveled up in recognition.

"We have since learned a few things about this plan, but we still have had no luck with identifying most of the perpetrators."

"Perpetrators is a big cop word from a spy," Tracey said.

"Yeah, I see movies and stuff."

Poppy tossed Saladin's color photo back on the table. "This guy, Abdul Fattaah Saladin, is believed to be a principal behind the terror plan, and we think he was also present at O'Brien's homicide; he was the other side of the conversation you cleverly and helpfully recorded. Al-Taja got the photo when he impersonated a state police detective investigating a fake vehicle license plate matter. The sole goals of that play was to get an image of Saladin and put a GPS device under his car.

"Two days later, al-Taja was dead. But as you can probably see looking at this photo, Saladin was not the thin man on the City-County roof who killed al-Taja with a bullet in his head. The effort to crush al-Taja's head to disguise the gunshot wound was a pitiful failure, if that was the intent. You'd think that was a rookie mistake, but players in this league lost their rookie standings a long time ago. We think it was just spur-of-the-moment to drop our man over the side of the building, causing a commotion on the street while the shooter disappeared in the chaos."

Deb Hemme rose from her chair and placed a tape recorder on the center of the table.

"We're going to play some voices for you," Poppy said. "The first two were recorded from a cellphone call we intercepted. The second two voices were pulled from the recording you two made of O'Brien's last moments. We have done voiceprint analysis of the voices that aren't O'Brien's. It proved conclusively that the unknown men talking on the O'Brien recording are the same ones recorded on the first cellphone call. Listen to this."

Deb Hemme reached forward and pressed Play on the device.

Something unbelievable was causing Amber's spider sense to itch. She leaned in attentively.

The call from the ECHELON intercept played in its entirety, then the recording made during Jeff O'Brien's Dearborn playground event spooled out. The playback stopped and everyone around the table was quiet.

Tracey had only heard her dead friend's voice. She would mourn his passing for a long time, despite the circumstances of his death. He'd made a mistake. He tried to make it right at the end, even though he would never know whether he succeeded.

But he had.

Amber looked up irritated and said to Poppy, "Is this supposed to be some kind of bullshit test?"

"Why?" General McCandless asked.

"Well, I presume you think the Arab-sounding guy is this Saladin cat, right?" She reached out and tapped Saladin's color photograph.

"Yes," Poppy said.

"Well, then why don't you already know who the other guy is?"

Poppy leaned slightly forward in anticipation.

"What do you mean? Do you think we *should* know who he is?"

"I'd say so," Amber said. "That's my boss—Special Agent in Charge of the FBI Detroit Field Office, Foster Heath Benoit III."

CHAPTER FORTY-SEVEN

The true sign of intelligence is not knowledge, but imagination.
Albert Einstein (1879-1955), theoretical physicist

Poppy looked at General McCandless in open stupefaction. McCandless seemed dumbfounded. Neither man was quick to surprise nor struck speechless by very many things, but Amber's statement had left even these jaded operators thunderstruck.

"Are you *absolutely certain?*" Poppy demanded.

"Dude, stand in a hallway with this no-talent ass-clown trying to ask you out on a date, and see if you ever forget what that sounds like. I've heard his voice just about every day for the last four years. Yeah, I would say I'm damned sure."

Then she laughed without humor.

"I always joked that you could see his fucking bald spot from space. I'll be goddamned if you didn't just prove that's true."

Tracey looked at her partner in astonishment. Only Amber was less shocked than anyone.

"Yeah, look, let's everybody just take a deep breath." She stood and paced the rectangle of the conference room. She had her game face on now.

"I'm in the motive business, all right? I always need to know *why* people do things, and we"—she gestured to Tracey—"figure stuff out for a living. So, bat this around. Why in unholy hell is a senior FBI boss seeming to mastermind an extensive criminal enterprise whose goal appears to be killing thousands of people in a terror attack? How does that guy even get to that place in his head?"

Amber shoved her hands deep into the pockets of her black leather jacket and walked slowly around the conference table. *Why indeed?* she thought.

She stepped up to an empty whiteboard and took a red dry-erase marker from a cup. At the top of the board she wrote SAC BENOIT. Below that, she drew a numeral one and a couple of dollar signs.

"Benoit has more than twenty years on the job. He's probably topped out at his paygrade, but he's stupid rich, cubic family money, so there is no apparent financial motive."

She drew a horizontal line through the first point and wrote a numeral two followed by the word *acclaim*.

"His public and media reputations are excellent, but his professional reputation around the country, and especially in Washington, is, ah, imperfect. Plus, personally, he's a fiasco. He has no friends that I know of who aren't out there among his gaggle of Grosse Pointe circle jerks."

Her brow furrowed.

"Wait. Everybody thinks he's screwing Frannie Demopolis."

"Who is that?" Poppy asked.

"Our office manager. She just applied to the Bureau. Benoit endorsed it with everything but a sperm sample."

Poppy nodded at Deb Hemme, and she began tapping on a tablet. Amber underlined *acclaim*.

"He has a paper record of closing a lot of cases, some of them mid-to-high profile, but it's common knowledge everywhere that he doesn't do the work. He's an office queen, an administrator weenie, just grabs cases from agents at crucial points in the investigations and hogs the credit. He grabbed the al-Taja case back from me, in fact."

She double underlined *acclaim*.

"So, he could be looking for a big score to burnish his rep for … for … *really?*"

She drew the numeral three, wrote *politics* next to it and scribbled furious underscores beneath it. Then she extracted from her jacket pocket a trifold paper flyer Benoit had spread around the Detroit FBI office inviting people to a planning committee meeting to assess his viability to run for the U.S. Senate.

Amber tossed the folded flyer onto the table. It slid over to Cloud, and he scanned it.

On the cover was a posed photograph of Benoit at a staged crime scene, looking tall and earnest and pointing up at something out of the frame. The soft-focus background was a sea of police cars and red and blue emergency lights; a stock photo his designer found. Around him were a half-dozen earnest white actors dressed as FBI agents in raid jackets, bathing him in adoring gazes.

Under the photo was the slogan BENOIT FOR AMERICA and an internet address.

General McCandless said, "Christ, I think I see where you're going with this."

In his Army time, he'd seen his share of officers and enlisted alike not beyond burnishing a record or taking credit for the work of others to further their own careers. But what Amber proposed was breathtaking in its scope and effect.

"You think Benoit is going to bust out the terror plot *he devised himself,* and use the glory and public recognition to go off and run for the Senate."

Amber crossed her arms over her chest. "Yes, sir. That's exactly what I think."

✪

No one spoke for moments. The flyer was passed around to McCandless and Poppy, then across the table to Tracey. She ignored it.

"Well, what's next?" Tracey said. "In my business, when we identify a suspect, we roll in hot and hook his ass up."

She picked up the photo of Saladin.

"Whyn't we start with *this* asshole?"

She flicked the photo across the table to Poppy and pointed to a high-resolution monitor labeled SALADIN. A red circle indicated the GPS tracker was stopped at an intersection, then moved off. Tracey didn't know that Saladin was also under active 24/7 surveillance as well, with a dozen vehicles of differing kinds always hop-scotching in trail.

"I see your point, Ms. Lexcellent," Poppy said. "Please see mine. Here is some more information you don't have that I want you to appreciate. We know the plan to attack the World Series involves a few dozen skydivers dropping into the opening ceremonies and blowing up chestpacks filled with metal and toxins into the crowd. The whole point of the exercise is to fulfill the *jihadis* fondest dreams—to have another 9/11-grade attack on television."

"No shit, huh?" Tracey's response was harsh, but her face softened just a little.

"No shit. Almost twenty million people watched game one of the Series on TV last year. So, yes, it's a big deal. The initial live attack coverage will be raw enough, but think back to 9/11. That tragedy and its aftermath were the focal point of news coverage *for years*. The bad guys have been looking for something like that for a long time."

The room grew cold.

"We can go get this fucking Benoit anytime." Poppy looked at his watch and saw it was early. "He's probably still in his office. And we always know where Saladin is. That's how we confirmed he was in the playground when O'Brien was killed. He killed that Detroit policeman, and defiled his corpse."

"How do you know for sure?" Amber asked.

"Besides the car being there, we matched the DNA to Saladin," Poppy said. "It was obvious O'Brien had been spit on, and we collected that for analysis. It even surprised us when we got the match to DNA taken from a weapon Saladin dropped on his way out of a prison he escaped from in 2005. He'd been grabbed by Mossad after a Tel Aviv bus bombing, but he fled back to Iran after his escape.

"He's a certified badass, but he isn't working alone. Who are the thirty-five skydivers? Where are their explosives and poison? Who else is involved? Where is the funding coming from? Who else can hurt us when the shit hits the fan?"

Tracey noticed the far end wall of the windowless conference room was covered with investigative items. Like she and her colleagues often would do for their important cases, photos of people and evidence, print-outs of reports, surveillance photographs, and anything pertinent to the investigation was tacked up in open view.

The display reminded everyone of where they were in the case, and offered hope that anyone looking at the items with fresh eyes might draw a new conclusion or investigative angle.

Tracey rose from her chair and stood before the board, hands on hips, taking it all in.

"This is what you got right now?"

"Right up to the point where Amber identified Benoit, yes, it is," Poppy said.

Tracey's eyes roved over the wall. There were photo stills pulled from the ATM video, a DPD identification photo of Jeff O'Brien, and other photos of Saladin; on the street, in bars, from an aerial viewpoint with data panels blacked out, sometimes driving his Dodge Magnum R/T station wagon. A couple maps, a photo of a big military drone of some kind. A large Samsonite suitcase on wheels, and photos of a young Asian woman and an old Chinese man. Tracey turned to Amber and tapped a photograph of Imam al-Waheeb.

"Amber, your buddy." She turned to Poppy. "What's the Imam's angle?" she asked.

"Unknown connection to the terror plan," Poppy said. "He appears to be looking for information on the Skinheads thing, and he told Amber he might have heard about the World Series attack plan from al-Taja."

Amber chimed in. "I've had a couple conversations with him. He has a Muslim kid who looks Caucasian sort of undercover with these Michigan Wolverines morons. The kid's being recruited because he speaks Arabic, and the Wolverines see him as some kind of go-between to the Muslim community if the militias someday get some balls to attack the place."

Tracey lifted large aerial photographs of the big mosque in Dearborn, and others of Comerica Park only blocks from where she stood.

"Amber, see this?" Tracey pointed to a rear three-quarter surveillance photo of Saladin making a turn in his station wagon. His license plate was clearly shown.

"IMHOT4U?" Amber said. "That's a hoot, though. Too close to my plate for comfort. A little forward for a terror suspect, don't you think?"

Poppy said, "Not that it matters to the investigation, but Saladin spends a lot of time in clubs. Fancies himself a ladies' man. We have surveillance of him in some bars. We hoped to find him recruiting skydivers in them, but he went home with women he picked up, and they always left his flat the next morning. Alive."

Poppy crossed his arms and sat back in his chair.

"We know the skydivers are planning a HALO jump—High Altitude, Low Opening—so they will leave the aircraft at maybe 28,000 feet. That means bailout bottles, ballistic helmets, thermal suits, and the kind of hard-core training most sport jumpers don't have. That tells us his team is or was serious military. We think Iranian, but at present we don't know."

Tracey saw a metal Michigan vehicle license plate peeking out from under overlapping paperwork. She popped the plate free of its pushpins and turned back to the room, displaying the plate in her hands.

"What is this?"

"That registration was on Saladin's car when al-Taja changed it out. The plate is nothing. DHS only sent al-Taja in there on the plate-change ruse to get Saladin's digital photo. Al-Taja dropped off the plate that night when he reported in to his supervisor."

Tracey held the plate in her hands and stared at it. *This means something,* she thought. She tapped on the painted metal surface with a long red index fingernail.

What is it? What are you trying to tell me?

She angled the plate toward Amber.

"Does this mean anything to you?"

"No, hon. Why? What are you thinking?"

"I dunno, but there's … there's *something* …" Then Tracey went rigid, as if having a seizure.

"Oh, *hell* no … it *can't* be …"

She strode to the whiteboard and propped the plate up on its ledge. Everyone could see that it read 4CE N01. Tracey pointed at the plate.

No one in the room moved or spoke. Amber shrugged her shoulders. "Yeah, I got nothin'."

"Amber, for God's sake—don't *you* see it?"

Amber shook her head, wide-eyed. *No.*

Tracey picked up the red marker and drew on the whiteboard in large capital letters the words FORCE NO ONE.

Amber looked like she'd been smashed in the head with a Detroit telephone book.

"Oh, for the love of the smiling Christ," Amber said. *"Maggie Prynne."*

CHAPTER FORTY EIGHT

Action expresses priorities.
Mahatma Gandhi (1869-1938), Indian independence leader

General John Glenn McCandless looked across the table at Amber. She rubbed her face with both hands in frustration.

"Maggie Prynne?" he asked.

"Homeless woman, kinda lives on the economy downtown. We think she witnessed al-Taja's death, but all she can say—*all* she can say—is 'force no one,' over and over. This license plate from Saladin's car has the combination of letters and numbers that, on a vanity plate, could suggest those words if spoken."

"What does it mean?"

"Can't say," Tracey interjected. "Ol' Maggie is a little pixelated, y'know? She's not what you might call a reliable witness. At that, the homicide was committed *after* al-Taja got the plate off Saladin's car, right? So, what does it mean to Maggie?"

McCandless and Poppy Benedict both looked down at their vibrating cellphones at the same time. Evidently, they had received the same group text. They looked up at each other with unconcealed alarm on their faces.

"Ladies, Zave," Poppy said. "Come with us."

✪

Poppy mag-carded the security door and opened it, ushering everyone out into the cube farm. In the center bullpen was a larger open space
occupied by a duplicate of the MQ-9L SuperReaper control trailer console
parked at Selfridge Air National Guard Base. This duplicate was unoccupied, but it remotely mirrored in real time everything that occurred on the
manned station. The high-resolution monitor screens showed the remotely
piloted aircraft had diverted course from its intelligence-surveillance-
reconnaissance pattern over Dearborn and Detroit. It was now headed
north-northwest at a speed of 287.5 miles per hour—one hundred and
twenty-five percent of rated capacity.

Like a storm warning on television, a large red information crawl
repeated across the bottom of the screen.

MISSION DEVIATION PAPA FOXTROT1 ALPHA SCORPION WINGHAVEN
PROTOCOL ENGAGED.

General McCandless reached forward. He keyed the desk microphone
for the encrypted radio link to the manned control trailer at Selfridge.

"Dragonite, this is Anvil One."

Dragonite was the SuperReaper pilot's callsign. In the remotely piloted
aircraft world, it wasn't uncommon for some youthful Air Force drone
drivers to have callsigns named after flying Pokémon characters.

"Anvil One, Dragonite, go ahead."

"Dragonite, what's your status? What's going on with your RPA?"

"Anvil One, Dragonite. Sir, we were flying a normal ISR race-track
pattern over the objectives when we received something called a Priority
Flash One Alpha Scorpion autonomy zinger from COLOSSUS. I didn't recognize that protocol, but before I could ask for clarification, he just took
over without waiting for an acknowledgment."

COLOSSUS, the unofficial callsign for the bank of Cray supercomputers
specifically engaged in ECHELON communications monitoring on the Detroit
anti-terror project, was another little CIA Easter egg. In history, COLOSSUS
was a futuristic supercomputer character from a 1970 movie where the
computer took over all automated defense programs on Earth and enslaved
the humans.

McCandless watched the RPA with more than passing interest. A computer-controlled experimental Reaper armed with enough Star Wars laser power to melt a car should not be loose in the air without his authority.

"Dragonite, Anvil One. Have you tried all the overrides?"

"Anvil One, Dragonite. Affirmative sir, we have. Colossus responded with a repetition of the Papa Foxtrot1 Alpha Scorpion flash traffic. It asserts it has taken control for an emergent mission need relative to saving human life. Uh, wait one … message inbound …"

In the CIA cube farm, a window opened on the number three monitor. It displayed the real-time transcript of a cellphone call originating in western Michigan outside of Marshall near Battle Creek, to a land line in a house in Taylor, downriver from metro Detroit. Colossus played the voice recording over the scrolling transcript.

"Hey bubba, it's the Wolfman. I got ol' Hamzaa up here in his little squirrel cage. He thinks it's part of his militia initiation—and I guess it's really gonna be once I initiate that gasoline."

Deb Hemme tapped on her tablet computer for a few seconds and showed the result to Poppy.

"Hamzaa el-Shafei is the Imam's undercover with the Wolverines," Poppy said.

Hemme tapped a few more times on the tablet, then handed it back to Benedict.

"'Wolfman' seems to be an alias for Rudolph Wolf. He's ex-Navy, a snipe, an engine guy. Not an operator. A known recruiter for the Wolverines."

"All right, then," the unknown voice said to Wolf. "You don't need us up there for that. You just light his fuckin' ass up and make sure you get good video. Use the damn tripod, that's why I give it to you. Don't worry 'bout no audio, we gonna overlay that with our disguised soundtrack over here anyways. We'll just see how the ragheads like getting back some'a they own medicine. Since Hamzaa look white, our *jihadi* voiceover will make it look like the terrorists abducted a white man and burnt him alive, like ISIS do to Turks and them in the sandbox. And that's the end of the A-rabs in this country, starting with Dearborn. Burn that motherfucker, Wolfman! Patriot nation!"

"Patriot nation, skipper! You got it. Little bastard is soaked in the gasoline, all around the cage, too. He's gonna go up like a Christmas tree, man! More as it happens, boss. Out here."

Wolf terminated the call, but not before COLOSSUS had analyzed the content of the conversation and decided on its own that human life relative to its mission was at stake.

The computers had located Wolf's cellphone out in Shelby County and sent the SuperReaper, with its fearsome beam weapon, to try to save el-Shafei.

All on its own dime.

"Poppy, did you know about this PF1-Alpha Scorpion protocol? What is this all about?"

"I did, general, but to my knowledge, it was an AI command module that wasn't in the released master operating system."

Poppy squinted at some of the fine print in a corner of the high-resolution monitor.

"The drone appears to be running under a beta OS version we hadn't released yet. I wonder if it updated that itself, too."

"We're going to figure all that out later." McCandless turned and yelled over the cube farm for his aide. "Tommy!"

Major Crosby's head popped up over the partitions like a groundhog from a hole.

"Get on the horn to Selfridge Ops and scramble the alert-five F-16s. Get 'em vectored out to wherever the hell Shelby County is. I want them in position to shoot down the SuperReaper if push comes to shove."

Crosby's head disappeared again as he reached for the desk phone in his cube.

"Hey!" Deb Hemme shouted to the room and pointed at the monitor.

"You'd better get serious. Look at these readouts," she said.

One hand pointed to the number one screen and the other rose to cover her mouth in shock.

"The drone is descending."

CHAPTER FORTY-NINE

*It's my firm conviction that when Uncle Sam
calls, by God we go, and we do the best we can.*
R. Lee Ermy (1944-2018), Gunnery Sergeant, USMC (Ret.)

Kathie!" Charlie Bird yelled out of his glass-enclosed office. She poked her head around the corner of his doorway.

"Yo."

"Is everyone ready to greet the clients?"

She smiled her saccharine *You already know this answer* smile and said, "Yes, skipper, I believe we are ready."

Charlie and all MDZ were still stunned by the information that they were planned to be pawns in a 9/11-style terror attack on the World Series—and that plan didn't provide for their survival.

General McCandless put Charlie officially on the meter for interdicting the plot from his end. This was attractive to both sides. One, McCandless had full confidence that Charlie and his team of former military special operators could handle the task. Two, this meant MDZ was now billing for roles they would gladly have played for free.

But it would be no consolation at all if the wrong people were hurt or killed.

Today was originally planned to be a full-dress rehearsal for the World Series skydive into the opening ceremonies. Thirty-five jumpers and all their equipment were arriving separately in their own transportation.

Tigers marketing vice-president Steve Harris was also bringing the leader of the ceremonial jump team, known to him by the name of Albert Saladin.

"Call me Al," Saladin said with a wide grin in their first office meeting downtown.

"Al Saladin it is then," Harris replied.

Harris and Saladin would drive up to Owosso Airport in Harris's black Cadillac Escalade, leaving Saladin's car—and its GPS tracking device—in the Tiger's executive parking lot. Federal agents would sit surveillance on the lot for hours without knowing Saladin had departed in Harris's darkly tinted SUV.

"When Steve gets here, let's be sure everyone is standing by in the ready room," Charlie Bird said. "I want a full-court press this morning, full DV visit prep. I don't care if it is just a show, they must be convinced we consider them distinguished visitors, our clients, and our esteemed guests. They don't have to know they aren't really getting a training jump today. Although, we *are* taking them for a ride."

Kathie Murphy came around the corner of Bird's office to join the meeting with a pad in her hand and a concerned look on her face. This was no time for jokes.

Charlie turned to Christa "Christmas" Kieszek, the Navy Reserve C-130 pilot and MDZ's plane driver.

"Weren't you scheduled to drill with your unit this weekend?" Charlie asked Kieszek. "Couldn't get to Andrews?"

"We're going to string together a few duty weekends onto our two weeks of annual active duty training and get maybe three weeks out of a deployment to parts unknown. With our maintenance issues, it's more flying than we've done in a year, so we're getting ready for that. Prepping for this HALO mission has me busy enough. And there's never enough time out here with you folks. I mean, I appreciate that you pay me. I just don't think your ROI is too good with my Navy Reserve obligations sucking all the air from the room."

With the up-tempo operational posture in the world these days, and the long-standing integration of the Reserve components into the active forces, most Navy Reserve jobs anymore were nearly full-time gigs at part-time pay, especially for leaders. Kieszek was sometimes in the field when needed at MDZGI.

Everyone thought Kieszek harbored a small crush on Charlie Bird. At any other time or place in life, that might have been a grand idea. Kieszek was smart, funny, warmly attractive, and you could bounce a quarter off her abs. But Bird had a strict policy of not fraternizing with people he paid to sometimes risk their lives on his orders.

"Okay, so, they think they're getting a familiarization jump, but once we corral them in the ready room for the mission brief, we all kinda slip out casually. Then," Charlie pointed at Baker, "you're supposed to get the jump on them."

"You ain't kiddin'," Kerry Baker said with an evil grin. "They probably won't be armed today, but remember that Saladin asshole is a spitter." The reference was meant to be lighthearted gallows humor, but it failed miserably. The MDZ team had gotten the full post-homicide brief on Jeff O'Brien's case.

Chastened, Baker continued. "The joke is totally gonna be on them. I coordinated a ground force with General McCandless and the Michigan State Police. Between the state's Special Operations Division and the Army Reserve military police Special Reaction Team we laid on from 303rd MPs in Jackson, snatching up thirty-five stinkin' goatherds shouldn't present a big problem. All those SRT MPs have been to the sandbox on recalls. They will be just fine."

"Yeah," Kathie Murphy said, "I spoke with the sarnt major over there. We were in Germany together my second time. Confirm, he and his people know their stuff, for sure."

"*Posse Comitatus*, for the MPs?" Charlie asked.

Baker shook his head in the negative. "Doesn't apply."

The *Posse Comitatus* Act of 1878 prohibits U.S. military from performing civilian law enforcement functions on American soil.

"General's officially declared our guests as enemy combatants. This isn't a police action—in fact, the state police are actually supporting the MPs in a combat action." Baker raised a thumb. "We're covered."

He leaned back in his worn leather arm chair. Few in the group were ever more laid back than Kerry Baker.

"These tangos don't know this is their bust, obviously," Charlie said, "so Crimmas, you still gotta get the Herk warmed up and over here in front of ops as a big, impressive display for our distinguished visitors to see and be awestruck by on their way in. The shrink-wrappers finished up late last night and the thing looks great with the Tigers colors and team logos on it."

Charlie took a long look at his people. He hoped they would all still be looking back at him tomorrow.

"Once all the MDZ folks are clear of the ready room, the ground force will bust in and take them all at once. They won't have their jump gear on, so they won't have a hard time running away—though we're leaving the east and west bay doors open so nothing looks suspicious. But if they try to escape, let the SRT MPs handle it. They will be ready for anything, and we'll just get in their way. Remember their motto: No cuts, no bruises, no scratches."

No one spoke for a moment. Then the stillness was broken by Christmas Kieszek.

"Okay. I gotta go get the plane ready."

CHAPTER FIFTY

Patriotism is when love of your own people comes first;
nationalism, when hate for people other than your own comes first.
Charles de Gaulle (1890-1970), French general and president

Rudolph Wolf stood triumphantly with his hands on his hips before the iron cage imprisoning a terrified Hamzaa el-Shafei.

The fall day was hardly more than late afternoon, but among the thick pines that surrounded them, the darkness crept in faster. Both men were beset with chills that had nothing to do with the air temperature.

"Rudy, you are going to initiate me now, huh? We'll be teammates? Patriot nation, brother, right? Patriot nation?"

Eyes wide, el-Shafei gripped the bars of his cage to disguise his shaking hands. He was scared to death, and on top of it he hadn't had his mid-day meth. This didn't look right to him at all.

"Where are the other men, Rudy?"

"D'yuh think we're all *stupid?*" Wolf began. An evil leer spoiled his face. "D'yuh think nobody but *you* knows anything at all? Never underestimate my ability to find shit out, shippie."

"What are you talking about? I'm here to learn from you, not to be smarter than you in any way. What do you mean?"

El-Shafei sneezed forcefully and coughed into his hands. Gasoline fumes invaded his nose and irritated it. Wolf had led him into the cage blindfolded, locking him in. El-Shafei pulled off the blindfold in horror when the buckets of gasoline were thrown on him, but Wolf reassured him it was all just part of the initiation. Nothing to worry about, he said.

But there was.

"*I* think *you* think we're all *stupid*," Wolf repeated. "D'yuh think we just welcome every new fucker what asks to join us with open arms? D'yuh think nobody was gonna to check into you? We have people everywhere, man. *Ev. Ree. Where.*"

Wolf's eyes narrowed.

"You didn't learn that Arabic jibber-jabber at DLI, didja *hadji?*"

The Defense Language Institute in Monterey, California, had taught thousands of military members to speak Arabic dialects for many years.

"No. You were never in the Army at all, you little bitch—no reserves, no nothin', right? You learnt that shit at your momma's knee, didn't you, boy?"

Wolf looked at the ground for a moment. He believed it made his rant look thoughtful.

"America has had enough bullshit from *you* and *people like you.*" He was angry and getting angrier as he spoke. "*American* people have *rights.* Our rights are in the fuckin' Constitution of these United States, and they don't apply to people who wasn't born here."

"What do you mean? I was born in Dearborn!" El-Shafei sweated freely and felt like he would defecate in his pants.

"Yeah, I guess so," Wolf said.

He reached into his back pocket and withdrew a long-nosed butane barbecue lighter. He picked up the bucket used to douse el-Shafei with gasoline and walked backward with it upside down, dribbling the remains of the fuel along the forest floor.

"But your momma wasn't."

"Don't do this, man! Please don't do this! I didn't do nothin' to you, man, don't burn me man *fuck don't fuckin' burn me!*"

He let go in his pants then and powerful rivers of liquid feces flowed down his legs.

"Oh, you beggin' now, huh? I *love* that." He pointed to the video camera only a few feet away on its tripod. It was trained on the tiger cage. "Your raghead-ass bonfire will serve to burn down all of Dearborn next. So *fuck* you, and fuck everybody *like* you."

Wolf depressed the trigger safety lock and flicked the lighter to a long tail of hissing yellow flame.

"Buh-bye, *hadji*."

A small pink dot the size of a quarter appeared on Wolf's chest and he looked down.

"What, what the fuck? What the—*OWWW fuck that shit's hot what the goddamn fu ...*"

He swiped madly at the pink dot with both hands as if he thought he could brush it off. This caused him to release the lighter, which started falling toward the gasoline-soaked forest floor.

Every time Wolf's hands passed under the pink dot, it left blistered, blood-red stripes across them.

But when Wolf dropped the lighter and released pressure on the trigger, the lighter flame extinguished itself and became harmless.

The very moment the lighter flame went out—before the now impotent lighter had fallen even inches from Wolf's grasp—the pink dot on his chest irised open to encompass the width of his shoulders, and the color changed from pink to an angry red. There was the slightest hint of ozone in the air and a small hum that was overlooked, like the sound of overloaded electrical equipment.

Then the superheated Rudolph Wolf exploded from the waist up, showering el-Shafei and the surrounding evergreens with red fluids, random flesh, bones, and body parts out to about fifty meters.

The sudden massive pressure increase in Wolf's chest cavity launched his head clean off at the third cervical vertebrae. Days later, the state police crime scene processing unit found it high up in a nearby White pine, devastated by birds and small animals.

The boy in the cage fell to his knees, sobbing into his hands. He was in too much shock to notice the insignificant whine of a small airplane engine and fighter jets crossing his location, high aloft.

All he could think was *Allāhu Akbar*, and he repeated the phrase over and over.

CHAPTER FIFTY-ONE

The backbone of surprise comes from fusing speed with secrecy.
Carl von Clausewitz (1780-1831), Prussian general

On the second deck of the CIA task force offices in Detroit's Greek-town, people stood around the remotely piloted aircraft station and watched the MQ-9L SuperReaper and its 300-kilowatt laser weapon roll over into a screaming inverted dive from 20,000 feet, arrowing toward a small clearing in the trees below.

In the magnified streaming gun-camera video the drone provided, the pink targeting reticle was centered on a man standing in the clearing before a tall, square cage holding a second man. It was dark in the forest to human observers, but the drone's infrared glass eyes were locked on the first man and they did not blink.

The forest clearing was growing fast as the SuperReaper dove almost vertically toward the small opening in the canopy and the man in its crosshairs.

The team watched the scene unfold on the control station monitors. Something in the man's hand produced a flame, which caused the drone to turn up the power behind the targeting dot.

The flame in the man's hand went out, and the drone instantly boosted laser power to the full three hundred kilowatts for just one-point-two seconds and the man disappeared in a soundless explosion of red mist and steam. The drone pulled out of its dive, climbing hard away from the trees and only clipping the top of a single pine.

The SuperReaper's sensor suite also noted and automatically tracked the presence of the Air Guard F-16s in its recognition zone, but it knew them as blue friendlies and it was not moved to attack them.

A red crawl on the bottom of the monitor that read PAPA FOXTROT1 ALPHA SCORPION WINGHAVEN PROTOCOL disappeared and was replaced by a green scroll reading MISSION DEVIATION COMPLETE AUTONOMY CANX READY FOR ALL COMMANDS.

General McCandless reached forward and keyed the radio link to Selfridge Air National Guard Base.

"Dragonite, this is Anvil One."

"Anvil One, Dragonite."

"Dragonite, acknowledge primary control over your RPA."

"Anvil One, affirmative sir—positive control has been restored."

"Anvil One, copy. Return that bird to your base *now*. Out."

The aerial view off the SuperReaper's nose swung left as the pilot banked into a wide right turn east toward Lake St. Clair and the Air National Guard base.

"Tommy, call Selfridge and ensure those F-16s escort our enterprising RPA all the way down to the deck and a confirmed cold-engine shut down. They are not to land until the drone is shut down and the hanger door is closed, copy? Just for drill. Then they can go back on battle stations."

"Roger that, sir," Major Crosby said.

McCandless turned to Poppy, who thought he certainly was going to be arrested. Instead, the general said, "I *like* that fucking thing. Let's sort out the command-and-control issues, though, shall we?"

"*Fuck me*," was all Poppy said. But he was relieved beyond measure. Cloud stood with Amber Watson and Tracey Lexcellent.

"We should think about getting that kid picked up."

"Yes," Poppy replied. "Yes, let's … let's do that. I want to talk with him." Benedict was distracted and still surprised he wasn't being frog-marched to a detention cell by the Army CID agents hovering in the room.

"Um, how about you …"

"Yes, I'll get him," Cloud said. He turned to McCandless. "General, can I borrow your bird?"

McCandless and the team had their MV-22 Osprey tiltrotor on standby parked at Coleman A. Young Municipal Airport, though everyone still called the airfield by its old name, City Airport.

"Yes, of course. Whatever you need."

The Osprey's crew was at City with its aircraft. Major Crosby heard the conversation and automatically got on the phone to the crew to get the aircraft ready for flight.

"Amber, do you know if your FBI folks are still watching the Imam?" Cloud asked.

"I don't know directly." She reached for her cellphone. "But I can't imagine why not. What's on your mind?"

"Can you get him in a car ASAP and get him over to City? I want to take him with us when we recover his man. I imagine that kid in the cage will appreciate seeing a familiar face."

"Absolutely." She punched ten digits into the device and raised it to her ear. "I'll text the Imam to be ready, too. He should be at City by the time you are. What about us?"

Cloud smiled at her.

"Care to come along for the ride? It's pretty fun."

✪

Benoit left the office before lunch. Climbing into his S65 AMG-Mercedes, all he could think about was his upcoming date night with Frannie Demopolis. The woman was a sex machine.

His car rose from the federal building's underground parking, stopped at the top of the ramp, and turned right onto Michigan Avenue. The midday sun had left promises of Indian summer lingering in Detroit's air. Benoit turned right again at Woodward and followed the avenue all the way downtown to Jefferson, headed toward home.

He was in a great mood. He loved it when a plan came together as designed.

Sitting at the red Jefferson traffic light, the soft turn signal tone sounding, Benoit thought about the pleasure of leaving pedestrian police work behind and the glory of a Senate seat. His campaign awareness meeting had gone well, with the local DHS and ATF SACs present and promising money and help. A few agents from the three federal offices attended, but most had not. He understood completely. They were not his caliber, anyway.

He had imposed his control over the al-Taja case again and Benoit would soon "solve" that homicide by blaming it on Saladin, who would not survive his arrest attempt. Then, the Director would know of his work interdicting the World Series attack and the perilous gunfight that he and a few of his unwary stooges would have, resulting in the regrettable deaths of the remaining terrorists before they could be interrogated.

Benoit felt certain he'd be put up for an FBI Medal of Valor. The path to the Senate would then become clear.

In Benoit World, all things were right and in order. Just as he had always planned. Then, out of nowhere, Mr. Murphy and his duffle bag of tricks checked in just as the traffic light changed from red to green.

Benoit drove into the intersection and turned north onto Jefferson. He drove under the elevated walkway connecting the GM Building and Renaissance Center complex with the Millender Center across the street but was stopped again at the crosswalk light directly in front of the glass General Motors Building lobby.

A man on a motorcycle came roaring up northbound Jefferson and stopped briefly next to and slightly back from Benoit's car. He reached into a belly bag and attached a magnetic device to the top of the Mercedes. Benoit saw and heard nothing because the second movement of Wagner's *Symphony in C Major* was playing loudly in the car, and he hummed along with his eyes closed, his euphoric mood carried aloft by the powerful music.

The crosswalk light changed and the man on the motorcycle powered forward all the way into the left turn lane, continuing an unbroken arc against the intersection red light and disappearing back down southbound Jefferson to merge onto the Lodge expressway and vanish.

The engine sound opened Benoit's eyes. He watched the deft motorcycle maneuver with a bit of envy at the man's skill but dismayed that he was an FBI agent and not that traffic cop, that O'Brien. *There is never a cop around when you need one,* Benoit thought.

Hey, was there no license plate on that motorcycle?

Benoit's Mercedes exploded from the top down with such power that it dismembered the car and its occupant. The concussion shattered the glass front of the GM Building entrance and reverberated down the office buildings on the west side of Jefferson for blocks in either direction, causing window glass to crash down onto the sidewalks.

The car disappeared into a vivid fireball of yellow and blue. The trunk lid flipped end-over-end through the air and crashed through the window of a passing People Mover railcar. The door mirror on the driver's side was propelled across the street into the DuMouchelle Art Galleries, where it crashed through a fine Chinese ten-panel coromandel screen from the estate auction of a Grosse Pointe Farms designer, and shattered a full table of rare Chinese porcelains and a hand-painted Eli Terry mahogany eight-day wall clock.

The blast just missed a tourist couple, Scott and Barbara Killeen, crossing the street for the GM Building tour. Fortunately, they were shielded from the blast by one of the massive concrete columns holding up the elevated People Mover track. As soon as the concussion passed, even before debris stopped falling, Scott, a retired Navy public affairs officer now living in Las Vegas, spun around the pillar and started taking dozens of high-speed digital images that the next day would grace the front pages of newspapers and websites around the world.

At the Michigan Drop Zone, Steve Harris introduced Al Saladin to Charlie Bird.

"Pleasure," Charlie said, shaking hands. "Looks like all your people are with my people in the ready room, and my folks have checked and cleared their equipment. Why don't we go in there and watch the mission brief? Al, are you jumping with them too, or …?"

"No, indeed not," Saladin said amiably. "I'm afraid I've given up such pursuits for less dangerous endeavors."

Saladin glanced at his Rolex. The Benoit problem should be resolved by now, he thought. *All infidels must die.*

"Coffee first?" Charlie asked. "My briefer is still in the can, so we do have a few minutes."

"Yes, thank you."

Saladin turned toward the breakroom led by Charlie, with Steve Harris and Kerry Baker just behind. As they passed the ready room door, Benavides stepped out of the room and casually slid the pocket door closed.

At the lobby desk behind the men, Kathie Murphy reached into a drawer for her favorite handgun, a WWII-era Remington Rand 1911A1 .45 ACP pistol, then she spoke quietly into her desk phone.

"This is quite an operation you have here, Mr. Bird," Saladin said.

"Yes, thanks. We will surprise you from time to time."

Charlie stepped slightly aside so as not to be directly in front of Saladin. Just in case.

Kerry Baker came up from behind and thrust a Taurus Judge 4510 revolver loaded with .410 shotgun shells against the back of Saladin's head hard enough to get his immediate attention.

"Okay, *right there*, pal."

Saladin froze and slowly raised his arms away from his body. Charlie stepped forward and patted Saladin down for weapons. He was unarmed.

Next door in the ready room, Michigan State Police and the Army Reserve MP Special Reaction Team, weapons cocked and locked and off safe, flooded the ready room through the open west-side bay door to the outside. The thirty-five terrorists were caught by surprise, as planned, but surprise can result in fast responses from trained men.

Two of the terrorists instantly bolted through the open roll-up door on the east side of the ready room. While MPs and State Police shouted thirty-three captives to the floor with their hands clasped behind their heads, a squad of MPs ran after the two who fled.

There were repeated shouts to stop in English, Urdu, and Farsi, evidently unheeded. This was followed by several short bursts of M4A1 automatic rifle fire, then a bellowing MP staff sergeant yelled *cease fire-cease fire-cease fire!* Then silence.

Charlie took Saladin's coffee cup in his right hand.

"I'm sorry you won't be having coffee after all. We do make a really strong pot here."

Before anyone could respond, Saladin spit in Charlie's face. Without a conscious thought, Bird's instant reaction was to lash out with a powerful right that pulverized Saladin's jaw and facial bones, dropping the man to his knees. Unfortunately for Saladin, Charlie was still holding the ceramic coffee mug in his right hand as he swung. Saladin coughed blood and teeth onto the perfectly waxed tile floor as he collapsed in a heap to his knees.

"That's a really bad habit you got there," Charlie said. He reached to the breakroom countertop and retrieved a dish towel to clean his face.

Steve Harris stood dumbfounded at the spectacle unfolding before him. Baker and Benavides pushed Saladin face-down on the floor, Flexi-Cuffed his hands behind his back and slapped a six-inch length of green Army tape across his bloody mouth.

Six heavily armed, unsmiling military policemen bulled left and right through the breakroom door, clearing the room. They grabbed Saladin up by his elbows and dragged him away with them when they left. It was all over in moments.

Harris's astonished face communicated his feelings to Charlie better than his words.

"So, Birdman. Was there anything you forgot to tell me?"

CHAPTER FIFTY-TWO

True patriotism hates injustice in
its own land more than anywhere else.
Clarence Darrow (1857-1938), American lawyer

When thirty-six bad guys are rolled up all at once, the odds are that one or more of them will be willing to sing like B-list rock stars for the prospect of a lesser prison term.

In this case, not even one of the thirty-three surviving terrorists was eager for an extended stay in Guantanamo Bay to live in a military prison forever—and none of the so-called martyrs wanted to die for their country anymore.

General McCandless and Poppy Benedict had their most experienced interrogators debrief the terrorists who survived. Once the first round of information was extracted, they cross-checked and indexed the information obtained, and then went back at them with clarifying questions.

Even Abdul Fattaah Saladin was given his chance to do the right thing. Regrettably for him and his longer-term prospects for freedom, he remained mute. Of course, his shattered face was wired up tight at the time. He did, however, use traditional and universally understood hand gestures to indicate his unwillingness to cooperate.

Saladin was still using such gestures from his maximum-security cell in Camp Three at Guantanamo Bay, where he would have ample time to reconsider his position.

✪

After a couple of days, a clearer picture of the terror organization was formed. Saladin was a senior officer in Iran's so-called elite Quds Force, the unit of the Iranian Revolutionary Guard Corps responsible for "extra-territorial operations." He had been sent to the U.S. three years before to establish a quiet base of operations and prepare for a World Series attack, wherever it would be held and with whatever teams were in it.

The thirty-five jumpers were IRGC paratroopers specially recruited and trained in airborne operations to be martyrs in the terror attack. They filtered into the country over the Canadian and Mexican borders in ones and twos, and occasionally on student visas, during the thirty-six months it took to design and prepare the attack plan.

Over the forty-eight hours it took for the intelligence debriefs to be collated and analyzed, it became clear that the weapons, explosives for the chestpacks, identity documents, money—and the personnel—the Quds Force had provided everything, and thus the State of Iran itself. This culpability would be dealt with later by the United States at a time and place of its choosing. But for now, the current mission had one more piece hanging fire.

✪

In the downtown Detroit CIA task force conference room on Monroe, Poppy, General McCandless, Major Crosby, Xavier Cloud, and Tracey and Amber sat around the conference table. A new S&T programmer kid brought in a cardboard box filled to the top with foam carry-out orders from Fishbone's across the street. As the containers made the rounds and everyone scooped portions onto plastic plates, the room filled with heavy Cajun aromas and light conversation.

Tracey and Amber had signed fresh SF-312s and were now using them as lunch placemats.

"Okay, we don't have all the time in the world," Poppy began. "Our new terrorist pal Abd al Jabbar just can't stop talking, looks like. He makes the other thirty-two tangos look mute by comparison. He gave up the daily code words they use to keep the warehouse and the terror cell safe house calm, so they have no idea their team has been policed up."

Poppy stole a sideways glance at Tracey, sitting to his left at the table. "Policed up" was a term he'd picked up from her. She noticed and smiled back.

"With all the statements and confessions and outright pleading our skydiver pals have puked out since we rolled them up, what's the warehouse plan?" Cloud asked. He poked at his fast-congealed Shrimp Creole with a plastic fork, then pushed it away. Amber, sitting to his left, saw his distaste.

"That's better when it's still hot, believe me. Here," she said, sliding her plate over to him. "Try some of this Snapper Beausoleil. You'll thank me later."

"Thanks. I will thank you later, in fact, given the opportunity. I'm a German beer drinker, too."

Amber may have blushed for the first time since high school.

General McCandless took a sip of a Starbucks vanilla latte. Two extra shots, no whip.

"I brought the RPA drivers down from Selfridge to operate the Super-Reaper from here. I know we can see everything on our Waldo console, but after the incident with COLOSSUS going a little off-narrative, I feel a little better having the human operators directly at hand. Poppy and Deb Hemme assure me a new operating system—without the WINGHAVEN PROTOCOL AI module—has been downloaded to the RPA and confirmed operational." He took a pull from his coffee. "Now I want to get in the warehouse bomb factory these people set up downriver *yesterday*, but I do not intend to just barge in there after what we learned from the interrogations."

High above far downriver Detroit, the MQ-9L SuperReaper orbited in lazy, high-altitude circles over River Rouge, a gritty Detroit suburb distinguished by sharp air pollution from factories and petroleum refineries to which residents had long ago become nose-blind.

Even a cursory glance at a Google Earth projection of the area would confound anyone with a passing knowledge of municipal zoning objectives. Elbow-to-elbow residential neighborhoods, all timeworn and on small lots, competed for space with expressways and wall-to-wall industrial presence.

The gigantic Ford River Rouge Complex pickup truck assembly plant, designed by Albert Kahn in 1917, extended from the river all the way up to Dearborn. The city has steel processing facilities, operating and empty warehouses, maritime terminals, auto suppliers, oil plants, and train yards. Always in the air hangs a pungent, dusky pall that mirrors the desperation radiated by many of the neighborhoods.

In the Monroe Street bullpen, the drone control station was now occupied by the pilot and sensor operator who had previously been working from Selfridge. The station's high-resolution monitors displayed what the drone saw. The pilot and his sensor operator wore the 3D VR helmets that made them feel like they were in the drone's cockpit.

They looked down at a specific warehouse with a brighter white roof, making it easy to spot. While an attack plan was being formulated, the pilot had no orders to do anything but remain on station over the tango warehouse headquarters and await instructions. He pinned digital cross-hairs to the roof of the building and engaged the drone's autopilot at max fuel conservation until he could get orders on how to proceed. The drone would orbit that dot until otherwise directed, or until the fuel ran out about a week later.

"Our anxious prisoners said the place only has six full-time guards, but that seven to ten others live in a nearby safe house and can mobilize to the warehouse in only a minute or three," Poppy said. He took a bite from his Lagniappe salad, chewing thoughtfully. "General, you're the tactician here. What does the Army field manual say about an urban assault on a secure building filled with bombs and highly infectious poison?"

The general snorted. "Well, I don't know for sure, but I imagine it says something along the lines of, 'Don't assault buildings filled with bombs and poison. Call in air strikes.'"

"We know air strikes are out, even without our concern for the toxin," Cloud said. "I saw the interrogation debriefs. You gotta give these people their due: The setup is virtually impregnable if you don't care who dies. They have all the perimeter windows and doors secured, with watches posted up front around the clock. The ground area around the warehouse itself has been cleared for a hundred, hundred-thirty meters or more. There are overlapping and unobstructed fields of fire. It's pretty noisy during the day with that steel processing plant right up next to the perimeter fence, which is good for us—but we can't just power in there, because they will still see us coming. Notwithstanding that the neighborhood butts right up to the warehouse property. We can't have terrorist assholes sprayin' and prayin' when we don't know where the rounds are going. I saw kids' bikes in those neighborhood yards in the satellite photos."

Everyone around the table mulled that over. Cloud took another bite of Amber's lunch. Urban assault was out of Tracey and Amber's wheelhouse, and the people at the table with operating experience were stymied, too. Minutes elapsed.

"So … how 'bout them Tigers?" Tracey said to the meditating room with a humorless grin.

Just a moment later General McCandless snapped his fingers and looked up from his plate to push a button on the intercom. Deb Hemme, sitting adjacent to the drone controllers out in the cube farm bullpen, answered up. She was working a solid crush on Dragonite.

"Hemme."

"McCandless. Can the RPA pilot hear me?"

"Yes sir, I can," the pilot replied.

"Captain, get me some detailed roof imagery of our target warehouse. One long full-frame of the entire roof, a series of the grounds surrounding, and tight close-ups of any HVAC equipment, roof access hatches, vents, ladders, anything like that at all."

"Yes sir, on the way."

The pilot took the control stick and thumbed off the autopilot, banking left into a turn that would take the drone's sophisticated cameras over the warehouse along differing vectors for high-resolution passes.

McCandless released the intercom and spoke to the lunch group. "I have a killer idea."

"Play on words, sir, or ...?" But following right along with the general's thinking, Cloud was already smirking. And shaking his head in disbelief.

Considering the imagery the general had just ordered up, his idea could only be one thing.

McCandless waved to the room. "You folks should finish whatever you're eating. We're taking a trip. Tommy."

"Yes, sir," Major Crosby answered.

"Call our crew out at City and tell them we need to be wheels up in the Osprey in one hour. We're going to MDZ."

"Roger that, sir." Crosby rushed from the room dialing numbers into his cellphone.

McCandless picked up his own cellphone and dialed in the numbers for the Michigan Drop Zone. Kathie Murphy answered on the first ring and put the general right through to Charlie Bird.

"Charlie Bird here, general. How can I make your day better?"

"Birdman, brother, you are not going to believe the deal I got inbound for you."

CHAPTER FIFTY-THREE

If you aren't able to look after yourself and each other, people die.
Bear Grylls (1974-) 21 Regimental SAS, Irish survival expert

The enhanced warehouse imagery came in before the MV-22 had even taken off for Owosso Airport. General McCandless forwarded the files to Kathie Murphy's email account and asked her to output the imagery on the large plotter MDZ used to plan missions.

By the time the Osprey settled to the ground in front of MDZ, Christmas Kieszek was already hand-directing a tractor operator towing the drop zone's Tigers-adorned C-130H out of its secure hanger flanked by armed flightline security escorts.

As he stepped from the tiltrotor, Cloud looked downfield at the hanger housing the airport's commercial jet lease corporation, and smiled.

In MDZ's ready room, General McCandless stepped up onto an elevated platform in front of an oversize corkboard holding the warehouse surveillance photo series and a paper area map. He held an old-school wooden pointer with a black rubber tip and a metal eyelet screwed into the other end.

He paced a few steps back and forth while additional chairs were set up and occupied by the full MDZ crew. Even Steve Harris had been summoned and sat in the second row, watching intently.

The scene looked like nothing less than an assault briefing in a World

War II squadron. Even the general's scrambled-eggs officer's hat was tilted at its customary jaunty angle.

"Let's get started," he said to Major Crosby. The general flipped the long wooden pointer to tap the eyelet on the diamondplate metal surface of the platform where it rang hollowly and echoed around the tall and wide room, getting everyone's attention.

"You all know me and you've heard the overview of our plan. Here are the specifics." He used the pointer to slap the long photo printout of the warehouse's entire rooftop.

"We know this building in River Rouge is where our terrorist friends told us they holed up their bomb factory and the toxin they were going to distribute over the World Series opening ceremonies. Well, the Series is secure."

A ripple of applause scrolled across the audience, with a few ragged cheers.

"Okay, settle down," McCandless said. "Now we gotta go get the rest of these assholes and their bad juju."

McCandless aimed the pointer at a large image of white powder in a capped lab flask. No one could read the tiny words printed in the margin that read CBRNE/DUGWAY.ARMY.MIL/MASSCASDECON/TOPSECRET/NOFORN.

"The toxin is something called Compound 1080, a stone-cold killer even in small amounts. It's actually some kind of sodium fluoro-*razz-matazz*—I don't what it is chemically, but normally it presents as an odorless and tasteless flaky powder. We know the terrorists have reduced it to a concentrated liquid to coat the shrapnel the exploding chestpacks were to blow into the baseball fans. Our experts say it's a horrible killer that usually also kills the next two or three people who encounter the dead bodies it produces."

He used the pointer to circle the warehouse and point out some features of the area.

"This place doesn't look like much, but it's a damned industrial fortress. Clear fields of fire all around. The east end butts up to the river, the west end faces the residential neighborhood. Doors and windows all locked down and sentries on watch, so we can't just bust in there, guns blazing—and because the neighborhoods are so close, we can't do anything more kinetic, like put a cruise missile through a window."

McCandless paused to consider what he was going to say next.

"The solution? I intend to conduct a daytime combat airborne assault on this objective. These two places seem to be our best chances for unobserved—and likely undefended—ingress." He tapped a large air conditioning enclosure and what looked to be a roof access hatch.

"Why daytime? First, the steel processing plant next door generates a metric ton of noise during the day, but they only work a day shift there, so there is no concealing noise at night. Second, we think the terrorists' alert posture will be lower in the day than in the night, when they might expect to be attacked. Third, with the clear fields of fire here, here, and here"—he pointed to the three open areas around the warehouse—"and the back wall of the building only meters from the Detroit River, going in from the top is the best option. Even with armored vehicles, a daytime ground assault would have these people shooting blind all over the place, and the neighborhood is right here."

He drew his pointer along the treeline west of the long structure.

"We can't have them shooting into the citizens. So, here's the deal. We can do a HALO jump from your C-130 maybe as high as 30,000 feet, because we'll have no load on board at all but our butts and fuel. Weather is supposed to cooperate, so we'll free-fall in with the morning dew and pop chutes at eight hundred feet. We'll drop onto the warehouse roof on little cat feet, making as little noise as possible."

Candy Clark elbowed Kerry Baker. "Like he had to say that, right bro?"

"This old heating unit enclosure is empty." He circled a dark oval in the side of the big metal box the size of a garden shed. "This is an opening where an exhaust fan used to be, but the metal strippers pulled the fan and the heater out of there for scrap long ago. These big rooftop units often had catwalks under them, so that maintenance people could work on them without having to climb onto the roof. That catwalk may still be intact, and if so, it will lead to a ladder down to the floor. But we will go into this ready to rappel down, if necessary."

"The other ingress point, general?" Charlie Bird asked.

"Here." McCandless tapped a large white square. "For reasons lost to time, this roof access panel is locked from the top."

He pointed to an enhanced enlargement of the hasp area that showed a large, unmistakable industrial padlock.

"Thirty-inch RAT bolt cutters. I'm sending you with three." He smiled dryly at the assembly. "Try not to drop them all."

The crowd murmured appreciatively. There wasn't an Airborne Ranger alive who had never dropped and lost something important somewhere between the airplane and the ground.

"Questions, comments, concerns."

A hand came up in the front row. "Once we get inside, how do we know what we're looking for?" Carlos Benavides asked.

Candy Clark leaned in and poked his shoulder.

"I'd go for the pricks firing machine guns at you first." The assembly laughed, breaking the tension. Military gallows humor.

Even General McCandless grinned, and it didn't hurt Benavides' feelings. Brothers and sisters will poke.

"He makes a point, though, smart ass," McCandless said, pointing at Clark with a dry smile. "We have a rough idea of what the floorplan looks like from construction blueprints we pulled from the city archive, but the place was built in the 1930s as a textile mill, and who knows what's in there today. From infrared scans, we think there is a well-lighted work area where the Semtex chestpacks were to be assembled, so that should be easy enough to find. The concentrated Compound 1080 was liquefied and the shrapnel is soaking in it, so, what? Tanks of some kind? Vats? Whatever, I think they'll be in the assembly area. We'll play it by ear."

McCandless laid the pointer down on the corkboard's ledge and crossed his arms over his chest. He stood center stage and looked at the crowd until the minor chatter abated.

"No bullshit, though, we gotta find and contain the toxin, at all costs. Every drop. We can't shoot the tanks, or let them be shot. We can't cause an explosion, or allow one to occur. Because we cannot have a spill of that stuff. This is very serious. We'll have HAZMAT teams, the Michigan State Police, and our MP Special Reaction Team battles with their MRAPs prepositioned about ten blocks away, inside the River Rouge Board of Education bus barn. Once we've done our thing, state police will support the MPs in swarming the warehouse location and securing it. A second MP/SP team will breach the tango safe house where the off-duty turds are holed up. Hopefully sleeping, but whatever. The HAZMAT people will have the unenviable job of getting the toxin secured and removed. But at least they are trained and equipped to do it. This stuff gets on us? It's lights out."

The general paused. "Oh, and ah, just for the record? Don't shoot the damned Semtex, either."

McCandless turned to Charlie Bird and waved him in. "That's all I got. Here's your skipper."

The general stepped down from the stage and leaned in to Cloud. "How'd I do?"

Zave gave him a thumb's up. "Outstanding, general. Scared the shit outta me."

"I hope I scared everyone else, too."

Charlie ascended the platform and conducted brief sustainment training. This is especially important for the non-Rangers, with less formal combat training.

Sustainment training is where jumpers got redrilled into their heads all the proper steps and procedures for conducting airborne operations that they learned in Airborne School. Unless you never went to Airborne School. There wasn't enough time to do the full-day refresher and tower falls, so the *do-this-don't-do-that* would have to suffice. Everyone jumping had fairly current military experience or lots of civilian jumps—except Steve Harris, who was only an observer here, anyway—so they hoped Mr. Murphy was on leave this week and everything would be fine.

"Everybody get some rest tonight," Bird said in conclusion. "This is a morning raid, and we will be arriving from the sun side. We'll muster in this ready room at zero-five for prep, suit up, and draw weapons and ammo. Final brief at zero-six. Load up at zero-six-thirty, and wheels up at zero-seven. We'll have knees in the breeze at or about zero-nine-hundred or so."

He gave a thumb's up in Christmas Kieszek's direction for confirmation and she nodded in the affirmative.

Charlie looked down from the platform at General McCandless, who shook his head. *Nothing more from me.*

"Okay, dismissed everybody. See you in the morning."

CHAPTER FIFTY-FOUR

Avoid any action with an unacceptable outcome.
Nichols' Fourth Law

The next morning, the airborne assault team assembled in the MDZ ready room. There wasn't much playful chatter, just men and women quietly preparing for battle, checking each other's parachutes, oxygen bottles, and more as they geared for up war.

Weapons were drawn from the Global Initiatives armory in the C-130 hanger: ammo, suppressed MP4s—even Tasers—but no grenades or flash-bangs on this mission.

Charlie was surprised to see General McCandless and Major Crosby in the ready room getting into thermal suits and parachute harnesses along with the rest of the team. He raised his eyebrows at Crosby, who shrugged.

"I go where he goes," Crosby said with a playful grin.

Charlie bent and turned to Crosby's boss sitting on a bench. "Leading from the front today, general?"

"I'm an Airborne Ranger, Birdman," McCandless said. "My place is in the air with the team. Plus, I'm paying the bill for this show. I buy, I fly."

Charlie couldn't resist a little poking, though. He leaned in and said, "Uhm, how old *are* you, general?"

McCandless raised his head and smiled without slowing his preparations for combat. "Uhm, how old are *you*, colonel?"

The protocols satisfied, Charlie said, "You are welcome on my teams in perpetuity, sir." The warriors clasped hands at the thumbs.

"No," McCandless said, grinning, "*you* are welcome on *mine*."

✪

Steve Harris had pleaded for permission to go along, but as much as everyone liked him, the answer was a resounding *No*. "Once a Ranger-Always a Ranger" is a truthful slogan, but Harris hadn't strapped on a military parachute since leaving the Army twenty-five years before.

Charlie playfully poked his old battle buddy in his stomach like he was the Pillsbury Doughboy. The finger disappeared in Harris's belly.

Harris raised his right hand, extending first his middle finger, then the index, curled into an arc. His trigger finger.

"Brother, you know it requires more than that," Charlie said gently. "You haven't trained for this. You haven't had more than a handful of civilian jumps in the last fifteen years, and no HALOs at all. Do you want me to have a shitty Thanksgiving because you killed yourself dropping into the Detroit River instead of on that warehouse? C'mon, man. See it from my perspective."

"See it from mine, Birdman. Look, these bastards were gonna 9/11 people in *my* ball park and kill *my* friends—and probably kill *my* baseball team," Harris argued. "Okay, so I'm not as fit as I was twenty-five years ago *when I was friggin' twenty*—sue me—but I keep a pretty strong average, and I'm tellin' you I'm as combat-ready today as I was then. And I need to be on this mission."

Charlie looked at Harris with a blank expression. This was going to be a no-kidding daylight airborne assault on a tough, defended target, and they needed all jumpers to be on their A-games. Charlie had initially balked at taking former Navy jet fighter pilot Candy Clark, because her role at MDZ was principally flight instructor, not trigger puller. But she had military jumps in her logbook from her Naval aviation days, over a hundred civilian jumps—seventeen training HALOs—and had qualified with the weapons inventory, so Charlie fleeted her up to operator.

Plus, she was just a badass in all respects.

She wouldn't make this drop, though. Charlie would vacate the second seat up front to lead the team, and Candy Clark would climb in to co-pilot the C-130 in his place.

Harris was different. Military free fall, shooting familiar weapons, combat focus—all that would come back to a former Ranger like it never left. Those training chops always loiter just under the skin of such people anyway. Charlie wasn't concerned about that. But the physical demands of a high-altitude jump, running around dodging bullets, maybe even hand-to-hand combat if it came to that, all presented risks.

That's why Rangers train constantly and stay in great shape.

Steve Harris was not in great shape. A less charitable person would describe his shape as *thick*. No one wanted him to drop dead of cardiac arrest when he was supposed to be shooting bad guys.

Charlie looked over Harris's shoulder to General McCandless for help. McCandless just shrugged. *Waddaya gonna do?* Then he nodded. *All right with me.*

Charlie's focus returned to his old battle buddy. He suspected there had only been one legitimate answer.

"Okay brother, welcome back to the suck." Charlie smacked Harris on the shoulder and sent him off to the armory to be issued weapons.

Poppy, Deb Hemme, Tracey, and Amber would also go along on the plane ride because, as Charlie told them, they too were part of the team, but they would stay in the plane. Without any experience to guide them, the civilians had arrived not dressed nearly warm enough for a flight in an unevenly heated airplane five miles in the sky, where the air temperature could be forty degrees below zero.

Kathie Murphy helped them change into thermal suits and fitted them with O2 bottles, ballistic helmets, and noise-cancelling intercom headsets.

Jumpmaster for the assault was officially Kerry Baker, but Charlie and General McCandless pitched in checking everyone's gear and equipment to ensure no one rigged themselves all sorts of messed up.

Everyone was ready early. It was time for the bus to leave.

Outside the building in her C-130, Christmas Kieszek turned over the first engine.

☻

Charlie spoke. "All right, bring it in."

The entire group came together and gathered in a tight team huddle, fists extended forward. Everyone bowed their heads.

"Heavenly Father, we ask you to put upon us the full armor of God that we may take our stand against our enemy's schemes, for our struggle is against evil powers in this world. We ask to don the full armor of God, that when the time of our enemy comes, we may be able to stand our ground, and when we are finished, to stand. In Your heavenly name."

Not a sound spoiled the moment. Tracey thought she had understood camaraderie from working on the Detroit Police Department for more than a decade, but these men and women took the concept to another level.

Her eyes filled with a watery flood of pride, blurring the image of the huge American flag that hung on the wall of the ready room. Tears dropped from her pert face to make dark circles on the concrete floor.

General McCandless drew a deep breath. When he shouted into the room it shook the walls.

"Rangers Lead the Way on three—one, two, three … *Rangers Lead the Way!*"

☻

Christmas Kieszek taxied the drop zone's C-130H down the Owosso ramp to the west end of the east-west runway. The *pro forma* instrument flight plan she filed had the assault team flying south-southeast to Lake St. Clair, then following the water down to River Rouge. Poppy Benedict had coordinated with his Canadian counterparts in the Security Intelligence Service to fly in Canadian airspace without running afoul of Transport Canada, their FAA.

Air traffic controllers at Flint, Detroit Metro, Windsor, and Cleveland were also on board to manage the traffic in the sky, because the team would need expedited travel priority and cleared airspace for miles around the warehouse target. Dropping a parachuting person onto a random passing aircraft is bad policy.

Owosso's community airport is too small to be FAA tower controlled, so Kieszek pulled the radio transmit button and announced her intentions on the public-broadcast Unicom channel for other aircraft possibly in the area.

"Owosso traffic, MDZ one-three-zero heavy on one-two-three-point-zero, taking off runway eleven. Owosso."

She turned to her new co-pilot, Charlie Bird, with a raised thumb, pushed her intercom button on the yoke and her voice crackled in his headset.

"Good to go, boss?"

"Good to go." He returned an upraised thumb. "Checklist is complete."

The aircraft staged at the end of the runway for one last look around and above for other airplanes. Kieszek pushed the four throttle handles all the way forward and the C-130 roared down the worn asphalt runway.

"Owosso traffic, MDZ one-three-zero heavy, departure runway eleven. Owosso," Kieszek radioed.

In the back, Cloud elbowed Amber Watson and tapped his headset, and they both lifted a noise-cancelling earcup off their ears. Cloud leaned in to her, yelling above the powerful drone of four Allison T56-A-15 turboprops.

"You ever fly this way before?"

She tilted toward his uncovered ear and shouted. "No—but I like the way you people do things!" She patted his left thigh in her enthusiasm. Cloud was pleased when she squeezed and left the hand in place.

The mission profile called for an easy eight hundred feet per minute climb rate while heading east out of Owosso. Kieszek was driving, so as pilot in command, she had Charlie practice his radio procedures.

"Flint Departure, MDZ one-three-zero heavy out of Owosso with you at three thousand," Charlie radioed.

"MDZ one-three-zero heavy, Flint Departure, radar contact. Squawk two-seven-zero-zero, climb to ten thousand, turn right two-zero-two degrees, clear to fifteen thousand. Contact Cleveland Center on one-two-zero-point-three-two-five."

Charlie twirled the plane's IFF transponder to 2700 and pushed the button sending the CIA Special Air Mission code to the air traffic control computer.

"Copy squawk two-seven-zero-zero, climb to one-zero thousand, right two-zero-two degrees. Clear to one-five thousand, Cleveland Center on one-two-zero-point-three-two-five. MDZ one-three-zero heavy."

"MDZ one-three-zero heavy, Flint Departure. I have your clearance, sir. Proceed IFR as filed, have a safe day."

"IFR as filed. Thank you, sir, you have a good one. MDZ one-three-zero heavy."

The MDZ plane had been updated with the full Multifunction Electronic Display Subsystem and other improvements, thanks to General McCandless. The upgrades meant a flight engineer was no longer required, but Kerry Baker sat in the former engineer's jump seat singing his favorite departure jingle to himself.

On the intercom.

"C-one-thirty rollin' down the strip
Airborne Rangers gonna take a little trip ...
Stand up, hook up, shuffle to the door
We're gonna jump right out and gonna count to four ..."

The difference on this hop was that the free-fall time would be considerably more than a count to four.

CHAPTER FIFTY-FIVE

Our cruel and unrelenting enemy leaves us
only the choice of brave resistance, or the most abject
submission. We have, therefore, to resolve to conquer, or die.
George Washington (1732-1799),
American general, first President of the United States

The sky was sparkling clear and deep blue at 29,000 feet over Canada. The wind speed and direction were variable at altitude but demanded a HALO release miles east of the warehouse objective, well into Canadian airspace. Poppy Benedict's coordination with Canada's CIA ensured that air traffic control hand-off went smoothly.

The team would free fall nearly to the deck, pop the canopies at about eight hundred feet, and in seconds, all things going well, their boots would touch down on the white rooftop of the warehouse.

Kieszek keyed her intercom to Charlie. "Okay boss, time for you to go join the party."

"Yep, it is." He reached out and squeezed Kieszek's right forearm. "See you when I see you, bud."

"Copy that. Keep that big water-head down. Send Candy up front, please."

"Will do."

Charlie unbuckled the seat harness and unplugged his headset from the intercom system, removing the aircraft's quick-don oxygen mask and putting on the smaller O2 mask from his bail-out bottle. Then Bird climbed out of the position. Kieszek's gaze may have lingered just a second or two long on her boss's rear end as his form-fitting thermal suit edged between the seats.

Once in the back of the plane, Charlie tapped Candy Clark on the shoulder. He gave her a thumb's up and pointed forward. She unplugged her headset from the ICS, nodded, returned the upraised thumb, and clapped him on the back for luck as she left. Charlie got into the rest of his gear for the jump.

Kerry Baker doubled as jumpmaster for this mission. When a bulkhead red light winked on, he stood and raised two thumbs in the air. *Stand*.

On the flight deck, Candy Clark announced on the intercom, "Oxygen on, one hundred percent for all crew."

The team formed a single line. Then, starting at the back, every jumper checked the equipment of the person in front of him, patting the person on the butt to say *You're good*. This procedure was repeated up the line until it reached Charlie, who said, "Okay, Jumpmaster!" Baker turned to face aft and Charlie checked him over. All jumpers were now breathing through their bailout bottles.

A few minutes later, the red light in the cargo space blinked rapidly and the aft ramp started its slow yawn open. It let in a torrent of wind, bright sunlight, and a panoramic view of the Earth that was crystal clear and breathtaking. There was precious little time to enjoy the view.

Baker turned toward the team and yelled, "One minute!" He raised an index finger into the air where everyone could see it because no one farther back than Charlie could hear him through the mask and the noise.

The entire team turned to face the open ramp as a group. The morning light reflected into the cargo hold and illuminated the plexi facemasks and white jumpsuits brightly against the dark cavern. When the green light came on moments later, Charlie led everyone off the end of the ramp at a dead run as they flung themselves into their destinies.

Last man in the stick, Carlos Benavides held back a moment, then ran toward the open ramp rotating in the air as he pitched himself into space. He wanted to snag a slow-motion video of the receding airplane on his helmet camera as he departed. It would be a fun addition to the debrief the next day. But as he spun in the air, the plastic buckle holding his thirty-inch Rapid Assault Tools bolt cutter snapped and one-third of their bolt-cutting capability was flung away into space. A few minutes later, it dropped unnoticed with a large splash into the Detroit River.

In the plane, Amber, Tracey, Deb Hemme, and Poppy all clapped and roared their approval.

✪

A free fall from five miles up happens frightening fast. At the terminal velocity of about 124 miles per hour, it only takes a few seconds less than two and a half minutes to get to eight hundred feet, and the ground comes at you so fast it can be deceptive. That's why the team used digital altimeters and an automatic ripcord release mechanism to open maneuverable RA-1 special operations parachutes at the correct time and height. The team was working literally without a net and the margin of safety was anorexically thin.

The team's ram-air chutes all popped within seconds of each other, causing enough noise that it would have been well noticeable on the ground without the powerful industrial din produced by the steel processing plant next door to the warehouse. With just a breath of wind at nearly ground level, all seven of the assaulters landed on the rooftop with the gentle impact of a leaf, safe and sound.

So far, so good.

Even Steve Harris, who had not trained on the new ram-air chutes, alighted as if he had just graduated from Airborne training. Fortunately, the new SPECOPS RA-1s are quite like the civilian free-fall parasails he'd flown before. Harris had no trouble steering his to the roof and an easy stand-up landing as if he had done it dozens of times.

Everyone shucked off their parachute harnesses, helmets, oxygen bottles, tool packs, and thermal suits, stowing the gear under some pieces of weathered plywood found on the roof so nothing would blow around. The air was tranquil in any case.

Under the thermal suits, the team wore black tactical ripstop with hoods and Taclite2 gloves. They stuck out like sore thumbs on the white rooftop, but they would be nearly invisible once inside the shadowy warehouse. Even their faces were obscured by Carbomask blackface camouflage paint—it's easier to remove than a NATO camo stick, and you can buy it on Amazon.

Weapons, radios, and intercoms were checked and ready to go.

Charlie gave the *go ahead* hand sign.

Benavides and Cloud crept to each side of the open hole in the large metal enclosure that had been filled with a heating unit. Benavides cautiously extended a tiny video camera on a thin stalk to see inside the warehouse. He rotated the camera for a panoramic view and logged what it saw to a small recorder.

The catwalk looked intact. As expected, a large work table under bright fluorescent lights was in the northeast corner of the building, in the end of the long rectangular building that abutted the Detroit River. On a table in the southeast corner was a stainless-steel tank with a lid, maybe three feet square. There was a man climbing out of a HAZMAT suit next to it. He hung the suit from a peg on a wooden pillar and walked to the other end of the building to join a second man at a table.

After a moment, the men started a loud and energetic card game, filled with invective and the sound of cards being slapped forcefully on the table. Curiously, the video feed showed no presence of guards at the two doors, one a regular man door, the other a sliding vehicle access portal. Benavides and Cloud returned to the team.

"I thought we were going to see more people," Cloud said. "There are only two guys down there."

Benavides played back the video recording he'd made of the reconnaissance for Charlie Bird and General McCandless. The sweep of the warehouse showed no other people in the building, and the floorplan was clear except for regularly spaced beams supporting the roof. No office spaces, no rooms of any kind, no other objects on the floor large enough to hide enemies. The catwalk looked sturdy enough, and it extended left and right to both sides of the warehouse, with ladders down each shadowy wall.

Charlie looked at his watch.

"It's 0934. Maybe the rest of them are gone to breakfast?"

The general said, "I don't know if they're gone to get breakfast burritos or to the can or what, but if we only have two assholes to deal with, let's get 'em dealt with and blow this pop stand."

Everyone looked at McCandless with a concerned face.

"Not literally blow it, of course. Charlie, how do you want to proceed?"

"Smaller folks in first. Benavides, Baker, that's you guys. Step through the hole and onto the catwalk. Baker first, he's probably the lightest. That catwalk has been hanging there since the damned Depression, and we don't know what shape it's in."

Bird spoke directly to Baker.

"Man, listen, be careful on that damned thing. But if it lets go, I expect you to start shooting and keep shooting all the way to the floor, copy?" He smiled. "And land on your feet."

"You got it, skipper." Baker scurried to the metal enclosure.

"Those guys are almost two hundred meters away, the entire other end of the building, playing cards and a loud radio, which helps us a ton. If we can keep the noise down, we might even get in there without them hearing us. I'd rather be on the ground when the shooting starts and not in the air. When Baker gets on the catwalk and assesses it good to go, then Benavides, me, General McCandless, Crosby, and Zave will follow."

Nodding heads all around.

"If the catwalk sucks, we'll rappel in, but that's the noisy and messy option. Each person in turn scoots to opposite ends of the catwalk, then start descending the ladders. We don't want to load up the catwalk with more weight than it can handle."

Charlie pointed at Steve Harris. "You're overwatch. Take a position over there on the far west end of the building and watch the inbound driveway for vehicles. If there are folks coming back from wherever, or maybe it's even a shift change, sing out on the comms. If you see weapons, don't wait, start taking those folks out wholesale. Controlled fire. We aren't here to shoot up the neighborhood."

"Roger that, boss," Harris said. Secretly, he was happy that he didn't have to test the catwalk with his weight today.

Charlie keyed his radio link to the orbiting drone and it relayed the call via satellite back to the CIA office spaces in Greektown.

"Acrobat, this is Dropzone-actual."

The MQ-9L SuperReaper pilot responded. "Dropzone-actual, Acrobat. Go ahead."

"Acrobat, do you have a visual on our position?"

Charlie looked up involuntarily. He knew the powerful laser-equipped drone was loitering up there somewhere, watching. After the drone's autonomous action against Rudy Wolf in the Shelby County forest, Charlie hoped it knew his team was the good guys.

"Dropzone-actual, Acrobat. Got you, sir. Give us a big wave."

Charlie lifted an exaggerated wave at the open sky.

"Good copy, Dropzone, we got you, sir."

"Okay, Acrobat. Our overwatch is on the roof at the west end of the building. The rest of us are going inside. Our DIG emitters are operational at this time."

The assault team members carried experimental self-powered radio emitters that would detect, identify, and geolocate each man to the drone's electronic intelligence sensors as good guys. The ELINT receptions showed up on the Monroe Street control pod's monitor and in the pilot's 3D helmet display as blue triangles, along with a wireframe of the building and surrounding grounds. Other humans not equipped with DIG chips would show up as red circles. If it came to using the drone to attack the building—or to defend the team—the emitters told the drone pilot who *not* to shoot.

Kerry Baker whispered into his intercom.

"I'm in, skipper. This catwalk is solid, hard as Chinese arithmetic. I think even Steve Harris could get down here A-OK."

"That shit ain't funny," Harris said on the intercom.

"No unnecessary traffic, people. Benavides next, then the rest in order," Charlie intercommed. Then, on the radio link, "Acrobat, Dropzone-actual. We're going in. Keep an eye out for vehicles inbound from the street. There are only two tangos here. Others are probably coming back at some point. Keep your eyes open for new arrivals. Out."

On the intercom, Charlie gave the move-out order.

"Okay, let's go. Weapons are free. Stay frosty."

✪

Benavides, Bird, McCandless, and Crosby negotiated the wide hole in turn and scurried to opposite ends of the catwalk. Cloud brought up the rear. The first two men stood overwatch, weapons trained on the two happy card players, while the rest of the assaulters quietly climbed down the access ladders to the floor.

Now the lack of objects in the warehouse worked against the team—there was nothing to hide behind but the support pillars, and they were only about eight inches thick. There was no light to speak of between the card table and the bomb table, opposite ends of the long building, so the assaulters hugged the walls and merged with the darkness as they creeped forward, weapons up.

Then the radio crackled to life.

"Dropzone, Dropzone, this is Acrobat. Vehicles are approaching your position from the Great Lakes Ave side."

Charlie clicked his radio mic twice, acknowledging. The intercom came alive with Steve Harris. "Boss, I got vehicles arriving. Two vehicles, six—seven tangos. No weapons in view."

It was then that McCandless reached forward and tapped Bird, pointing forward to the card table area where many long guns and handguns were left on a picnic table.

"Dropzone, Acrobat. I can see weapons under some shirts on these guys in close-ups."

Charlie clicked his radio mic twice and switched to intercom.

"Listen up. We're going to let the rest of those guys join the party, and then we'll engage and take them all down at once. No run-and-guns here. Let's take these jokers down and be home in time for lunch. A runaway tango in the neighborhood taking hostages is bad COMREL."

Just then, instead of entering through the man door, the new arrivals flung the rusty vehicle door wide open, flooding the west end of the building with the hot light of mid-morning. The third man through the door saw the assault team against the wall on the right side and drew a deep breath to make a wide-eyed shout of alarm.

A suppressed combat carbine shooting on full automatic is not noiseless, despite how Hollywood often portrays it. Rather, it has an almost pleasing, muted mechanical sound as it spits invisible death and destruction at an enemy, roughly like a well-oiled sewing machine operating at an insanely high speed. That's what the team heard when Kerry Baker, across the building on the still dark side, fired his silenced MP4 on full automatic and stitched the third terrorist from knees to eyes in one controlled burst.

From firing positions along both walls, the entire team opened up at once in the same pleasing mechanical harmony. The two card players fell next, pasteboards flying into the air along with hair and brain matter. A few playing cards were hit by rounds and exploded into chaff on their slow-motion flights through the air.

The other two bad guys who entered from the parking lot ducked behind the picnic table, snatching weapons off the top as they went down. But since they were clearly visible behind the table, they became instant bullet sponges before they got off a shot. The last guy ducked back out toward the cars.

On the roof in overwatch, Harris heard the shooting inside the warehouse and saw a man rush back out of the door. The terrorist screamed warnings in Farsi to his companions and herded the other three back to the vehicles. Harris shot two of them, but two made it to the front seat of a Jeep Cherokee.

Just as Harris aimed at the driver through his side window, the entire vehicle was bathed in cherry red light. In less than a second, the men inside were engulfed by their own flaming bodies, writhing and screaming loud enough to be heard by Harris on the roof.

The metal all around the vehicle sagged like hot putty and the paint blistered and peeled. Tires blew out explosively, and the ruby red laser disappeared when the fuel tank erupted with a fiery roar, blowing apart the entire rear section of the Jeep and lifting it briefly into the air. The windows shattered and the interior roiled furiously in cascades of black-tipped orange flame. There was no more screaming from the two men in the Jeep.

Harris was impressed and keyed his radio. "Acrobat, Dropzone-seven.

That's some fancy, ah, shooting, I guess. Over."

"Dropzone-seven, Acrobat. Copy that, sir." The SuperReaper pilot's voice had a little chuckle to it. "It's science, sir, but damn, it works like magic."

Benavides scooted from the warehouse sliding door, alert and weapon up, scanning the west parking lot. He swept the area with a quick glance up to Harris, who covered him. Benavides checked the two dead men on the ground, and then walked around the full perimeter of the Jeep at a respectful distance, his MP4 trained on the interior. But there was no need.

The vehicle burned hotly from the inside out. The two black husks in the front seats no longer presented threats greater than air pollution as they burned.

"Dropzone-actual, Dropzone-six. Sir, we're clear out here."

"Dropzone-six, roger that." Charlie looked up to see through the open doorway the misshapen inferno that used to be a Jeep Cherokee, hot flares of fire still hissing forcefully.

"We're clear inside, too. Break-break. Acrobat, Dropzone-actual. Send the HAZMAT teams and Security One to the warehouse, and send Security Two to the safehouse to grab the other tangos."

He paused for a moment, considering.

"Security Three is clear to hook up those white nationalists in Taylor. And maybe ask for a fire truck and the medical examiner for our warehouse location."

That's when Charlie Bird stepped into the parking lot and viewed the sad shape of the former Jeep Cherokee, now a raging bonfire inside a wilted lump of metal that looked like nothing more than a kindergarten child's sculpture project.

"Dropzone team, Dropzone-actual. Everyone assemble in the west parking lot. You gotta see this."

EPILOGUE

There is no fool like a careless gambler
who starts taking victory for granted.
Hunter S. Thompson (1937-2005), American gonzo journalist

Since the MDZ C-130H was already tarted up with expensively applied Tigers colors and logos anyway, Charlie Bird and General McCandless decided the World Series would get its patriotic opening-ceremony HALO and fly-over after all.

MDZ laid on a dozen more jumpers from among folks they knew back in the day—including Tigers' marketing vice-president Steve Harris, who had already dropped nine pounds in the Tiger workout room—and they executed a perfectly glorious jump into Comerica Park on national television, flags waving and oblivious fans cheering. The television production of the World Series opener would later go on to win an Emmy.

Christmas Kieszek and Candy Clark did a powerful, crowd-stopping low-and-slow fly-over with the Herk, flaps big as barn doors and landing gear extended, precisely at the moment the last strains of *The Star-Spangled Banner* echoed over the stadium and the World Series umpire crew chief screamed *Play ball!* The plane might have been somewhat lower to the stadium than the thousand-foot minimum the FAA demands.

Like Steve Harris had predicted it would, the ballpark demonstration killed.

The Tigers would go on to win the World Series over the Cubbies, four games to three. Steve Harris ensured that everyone who had worked with MDZ—including General McCandless, Major Crosby, the DIA and CID body men, Poppy Benedict, Deb Hemme, Amber, Tracey, and Xavier Cloud—were invited to all the championship parties and celebrations. There were many, and delirious ones, including the joyous victory parade down Woodward Avenue with hundreds of thousands of spectators and live TV coverage on a warm, picture-perfect day.

Just a few months later, team owners the Ilitch family formally presented them all with the same custom-made Major League Baseball championship rings the Tigers players received.

✪

Amber and Tracey were relaxing in the DPD homicide squad bay when Baby Ruth received a visitor dressed in all-black *abaya* kaftan-style Islamic attire. The woman spoke quietly to Ruth, who turned and pointed to Tracey in the bullpen at her desk. Ruth touched a buzzer that unlocked the half gate and the woman walked into the squad and directly for Tracey's desk.

"Miss Lexcellent?"

"Yes, ma'am. How may I help you?"

"*Assalāmu 'alaykumā.* I am Fatima al-Taja. I am Mohammed al-Taja's wife."

Amber stood and vacated the wooden office chair next to the desk. "Please sit down, ma'am," Amber said. The woman nodded appreciatively and took the seat.

"*Wa-alaikum salaam,*" Tracey said, "How may we help you?"

"I am headed to City Airport with my husband. The government has provided one of those helicopter-airplanes. My husband will be buried in Arlington National Cemetery."

General McCandless donated his MV-22 Osprey to transport al-Taja's flag-shrouded coffin, a ceremonial honor guard, and the funeral group to Washington for interment with full military honors.

"I am told that you are the detective who solved his murder."

"No, it was a big team effort, for sure—including my FBI friend and colleague here, Special Agent Amber Watson."

"Thank you as well for what you have done."

"We were just doing our jobs," Amber said.

Fatima held her head high, but her face was awash in pain.

"Yes. People always say that, don't they? Just doing their jobs. It sometimes is more than that. It was more than that to me."

Fatima carried a bag of her husband's effects, just retrieved from the medical examiner. She reached inside and pulled out his golden U.S. Navy ring.

"Perhaps my husband was just another name on a victim list in the city, but I wanted you to know he was much more," Fatima began. "He was a long-time Naval officer, did you know?"

She held the brilliant gold ring with its dark green stone and the golden fouled anchor.

"This was his gift to himself when he joined the Navy. He was so very proud to be American. I am naturalized now, but when I came to this country, long ago, I was alone and frightened. I had not yet met Mohammed. I had distant relatives in Dearborn who took me in, but it was this country who adopted me. Raised me. But my husband was born American, and the importance of that, its responsibility, never left him."

Tracey reached forward and took Fatima's hands in hers. Arabs in some places in America were sometimes as downtrodden as Black Americans had been in the worst days of the civil rights struggle of the 1960s. By the similar comparison, no one could deny that Arabs—Muslim or otherwise—now were challenging the bottom of the racial pecking order in some cities.

"As much as Mohammed loved his Navy, he was always driven to do more. That's why he decided to leave the Navy early and work for the federal government, because he wanted always to do *more* for his nation. Always more."

If Fatima knew her husband had been NSA, and later CIA, she wasn't saying. It was entirely probable that she did not know.

"He was a good man, a patriotic man," Tracey said. "A warrior. We know this. And his grateful nation knows it as well."

"Your words honor him, and honor me," Fatima said. She was breathless and suppressed her sobs, a proud, grief-stricken woman who longed for the sound of her husband's lost voice, longed for the music of their children's and grandchildren's voices she would never hear.

Fatima thrust al-Taja's Navy ring into Tracey's palm, closing Tracey's fingers around the object.

"I want you to keep this," Fatima said, on the teetering edge of tears that flooded her eyes. "He would be proud to know you have it. It will feel like he is still in the fight."

Tracey raised the Navy ring into the light, where the glancing afternoon sun coming through the squad's western windows reflected brightly from the golden surface. She knew she would never succeed in declining the offer, and honestly, she didn't want to. This was a remarkable object, central to everything that had occurred with her and the anti-terror team.

It would be a meaningful talisman for the future.

"You honor me beyond my ability to thank you, madam," Tracey said, now on the verge of tears herself.

Fatima stood and paused for a moment, her water-filled eyes piercing Tracey's. When Tracey extended her handshake, Fatima bowed and kissed her hand, holding it tightly in both of hers until it was covered with tears. Then, without another word, she turned and left the squad.

"Can I see that?" Amber asked. Tracey handed her the ring and then, sniffling, rummaged around in her messy desk drawer for a small packet of Kleenex she was sure was in there somewhere.

"As awesome gifts go, this is pretty damned awesome, lady."

Tracey couldn't answer because she was snorting into a slightly used Kleenex found in the drawer.

"Hey, look at this."

Amber angled the ring into the conical desk light, and both women pressed their heads together to look at the inside band of the ring. Engraved deep into the smooth golden surface were the phrases #ONETEAMONEFIGHT and the slogan SIC SEMPER TYRANNIS.

The latter is a Latin phrase meaning "thus always to tyrants," but it's a shortened version of the longer phrase *Sic semper evello mortem tyrannis,* which means, "Thus always I bring death to tyrants."

It was an entirely fitting epigraph for Mohammed al-Taja.

✪

It was nearly sunset and too chilly to have the Corvette's convertible top down. It was that time of the year when the days pretended to be summer, but the afternoons and evenings were full-on cool fall and people talked about the change of seasons being one of the many good reasons to live in Michigan.

These were some of the best weeks in Detroit. The World Series win invigorated the city and people were becoming optimistic again. Dan Gilbert and his companies were erecting new towers and restoring others all over downtown. The sports complex venues for Tigers, Lions, Red Wings, and Pistons made sports fans delirious, and the city's energetic resurgence was making headlines all over the world.

The thing Amber and Tracey fixated on was a drive down to Hart Plaza and the best hot dog cart in the city. But there was a secondary reason.

There is no public parking in the plaza area. Amber backed into a police-only slot in front of the UAW-Ford Building and flipped down her sun visor with a POLICE placard rubber-banded to it, then she and Tracey walked up to the fountain area and their favorite hot dog cart.

"Corvette *Watson!*" the hot dog man said, arms wide. Amber hugged the man warmly.

"Big Lou, how you been, man?"

"I been good, missy, good. Had a good summer out here this year. Be headed to Tampa for my winter break here d'rectly. You musta been making the world safe for democracy. Ain't seen you since Jesus lost His sandals. Waved at you some weeks ago, 'cross the street."

"Yeah, saw ya. We have been busy. One for each of us, please, and a coupla Diets?"

Big Lou dug into the steamy stainless-steel bin with long metal tongs and pulled out two dogs with one expert grab. In a single smooth move, he gracefully inserted them into fresh buns swaddled in waxed paper.

"Ketchup's on the table," he said, extending the food in one hand and tipping his old newsboy's cap with the other. Amber paid him extra and hugged him and wished him well on his Florida hiatus from street commerce. She grabbed two frigid cans of Diet Pepsi from a tub of ice and she and Tracey sat to eat at a picnic table a few steps away.

"You think she's out here?" Amber took a small bite of her hot dog, thought better of it, and then slathered the top with ketchup.

"Maybe," Tracey said. "She sees a clinic in the GM Building three times a week. Today is one of her therapy days."

And as if on cue, Maggie Prynne strode purposefully up the long sidewalk toward the picnic table.

She stood before Tracey with her hands pushed into a stylish pastel pink North Face parka. She was clean, her blue jeans had no holes in the knees, and matching the jacket, she wore a fun pink knit cap that failed to conceal freshly cut and colored blonde hair. Tracey didn't know how old Maggie was, but she looked a solid fifteen years younger than when Tracey put her in that taxi to Wayne County Hospital weeks before.

"My name is Margaret Havelka," she said, extending a handshake, "and I'm an alcoholic. I've been sober forty-seven days. May I join you?"

Tracey scooted over, eyes wide and incredulous, and Maggie sat down. Amber's mouth hung open in amazement at the utter transformation in the woman.

"I want to thank you both for all your help," she began. "When you sent me up to Wayne County, your friend Amalia put me in the rehab unit again, but it was just going to be overnight. Checking me in, she found my old rehab record in the system and called my sister. Man, I didn't even know I had a sister then, I was so far gone."

Margaret's sheepish smile underscored the obvious. "You may recall that condition I had. Kim came down and got me the next morning and took me directly to Henry Ford Hospital to dry me out. This time, I stayed."

Tracey put her hand on Margaret's arm.

"You look amazing. How did this happen? I mean, no disrespect, but you were nearly catatonic last time I saw you."

"Yes, anxiety disorder, complicated by alcoholism. Some therapy, some Librium for the panic and alcohol withdrawal, sweetened by Diazepam to stabilize. Lots of group therapy. AA. I stay with my sister and her family now. The environment calms me. The doctors say I should fully recover if I can stay away from dat ol' debbil rum."

She laughed, and the sound was pure and happy. "I think I might even try to get my law license back."

Tracey and Amber were genuinely speechless.

"Forty-seven days clean as of today. So, Tracey, and you too, Amber, I want to thank you for giving me my life back. For bringing me back from the dead."

Tracey and Margaret hugged again for several seconds. When they pulled back, both women wiped away tears.

"As it turns out," Tracey said, "I have something else to give you." She reached into her large handbag and pulled out a Michigan vehicle license plate that read 4CE N01.

"Oh, my God!" Margaret said. She reached forward with shaking hands in disbelief. "I thought I'd dreamed it all." She cradled the artifact in her hands. "Believe it or not, I remember this so clearly."

"You do? Can you tell us what it means to you?" Amber asked.

"I actually can. I'd lived on the street a long time, you know. You saw me. Pitiful. I was always drunk, but you know how that works. I was mostly transactional. Ish. Sometimes, not so much."

Tracey nodded, embarrassed to completely understand what Margaret was saying.

"Before my disconnect, as the doctor calls it, I'd been down here surfing the trash cans for returnables. A large man with tan skin and his hair pulled back in a dork knob drove up to the plaza in a black station wagon, and he asked me where the City-County Building was. I gave him the finger with my left hand and pointed across the street with the other. I noticed this odd license plate as he drove away."

Saladin, Amber thought.

Margaret held the plate at arm's length and stared at it, still incredulous at its existence.

"A few hours later, it was starting to get darkish and I was stumbling around over there, and a tall, thin man came out of the building and got in that tan man's car."

Benoit. Casing the building, maybe? Fascinated, Amber rested her chin in her hand and leaned forward to hear the rest of Maggie Prynne's story.

Margaret pulled a clean tissue from her pocket and wiped tears from her eyes as the cascade of memories threatened to over-whelm her and spoil her new makeup.

"A few days later, I was *so* drunk! I was just collapsed against the City-County building, waiting for my head to clear a little so I could, you know, go get more booze. But I dozed off. Then I heard a sound, like a loud pop sound. It woke me up, I guess, and it was getting dark. I was confused, 'cause I didn't know how long I'd been passed out."

Margaret was embarrassed by this behavior. Tracey squeezed her arm as she continued.

Her breath became short and tears again filled her eyes. She choked out her words with sobs.w

"The first thing I saw was that poor man on the concrete behind the *Spirit* statue, his head all crashed in, blood all over. On *me*. I had no concept of time, or how long either of us had been there, and it just freaked me out. When I ran around yelling for help, there was the thin man in the black car, with the tan man. I screamed bloody murder and they drove off. I don't know what happened next. Docs told me all I could say for weeks was 'force no one.'"

She hugged the license plate to her chest.

"I thought I dreamed it all up."

"How do we stay in touch with you?" Amber asked. She gave Margaret one of her FBI business cards. "We might need you to tell that story to some people in a few weeks. Maybe not, but maybe so."

Margaret pocketed the card. "Take down my cell number."

She rattled off a ten-digit number, proud as a new teen with her first cellphone.

"You can text me!"

✪

Xavier Cloud, Poppy Benedict, Deb Hemme, General McCandless, Tommy Crosby, Tracey Lexcellent, and Amber Watson sat at a table in a dark corner of the Sweetwater Tavern having what Poppy referred to as a "hot wash." They went over the highlights of everything that had transpired in the preceding weeks to see if anything could have been done better or differently. The consensus was that, considering the many variables they'd contended with, there probably were always going to be ways they could have done things differently, but no better ones.

"Amber, jungle drums say you are on a countdown calendar to retirement from the FBI?" Poppy asked.

"Yeah, two-digit midget," she said, meaning under ninety-nine days, though she was closer to thirty days. "Hangin' it up."

She stole a look at Cloud that everyone at the table thought was just a click enlightening.

"I've been a badge-toter my entire adult life. I think I'll take some time off and decide what I want to be if I grow up."

"Well, considering all that has transpired among this august group in the recent past, and how well we've all worked together, I was kind of hoping we might keep the band together, you know?" Poppy smiled inscrutably. "Maybe go on tour, so to speak."

Exasperated, Tracey asked, "Have you ever spoken plainly in your whole life?"

Poppy laughed. "It really isn't my style, you know."

He raised his shell of Stroh's in a silent toast and Tracey grinned at him. She was starting to think Poppy was more than just the little government troll she used to think he was. She was also starting to think maybe he was kind of cute, and how sexy she thought smart was. Poppy was very smart. She resolved to investigate that before much longer.

General McCandless turned to Amber. "Did you ever figure out where you know me from?"

It was Amber's turn to be cagey.

"Mmm, not sure, general. Where do *you* think it was?"

"You were in Germany the first time, a fresh Spec-four back before the term changed to just Specialist. You were a traffic accident investigator in Butzbach then, pre-MPI." He stopped and smiled. "Anything yet?"

"General, you probably know the U.S. Army installation at Butzbach Kaserne was closed sometime in the mid 90s—and I was there before that. That's many years and about two careers ago. Can you be more specific?"

"Ha, indeed I can. I remember every moment like it was yesterday. I was a brand-new second lieutenant in the military intelligence detachment, never been out of the U.S. in my life. Never had a beer down my neck until I got to Germany, back when there still was a West and an East. We used to chase those damned Soviet Military Liaison Mission guys all over the countryside when they got spotted out of their authorized zones, and we almost never caught any."

The general looked into his beer like it was a crystal ball as he called up the memories.

"And then one day we did catch one, blocked their Lada in on three sides and wedged 'em tight up against the guardrail. Nothing else for us to do about it, of course, but jump out and take dozens of pictures. They *hated* having their pictures taken. Then we called for MP backup and German Polizei, who just checked the Soviets' papers and escorted them back to their side of the East German border. But that was a huge victory for us, and we went back to town and got some serious drinks."

"I haven't seen you have as much as two beers since I've known you, sir," Crosby said. The general tapped his glass with his West Point ring.

"I know. Been that way a long time now. Because I learned something that day ... from a young MP traffic investigator who pulled me over on the way back to the BOQ."

Amber was struck dumb by the sudden vivid memories now flooding her brain.

"Holy friggin' *shit*, are you *kidding* me right now?" she exclaimed, and laughed out loud. She looked at the general with wide, fresh eyes.

"Shall I take it from here, sir?"

The general smiled. "Please."

"Holy Christ, am I old. So, I'm pretty new in-country myownself and I was patrolling solo traffic in a MP jeep, you know? I mean, one of the prehistoric ones, the M151A1s we used in Germany, way pre-Humvee and all that. The regular patrols had a couple Ford sedans, but mostly we still worked the road in those combat jeeps. Canvas sides, won't heat for crap, and it was *cold*. I was trying to go off shift, and I really had to pee 'cause I'd been swilling coffee to stay warm. Then, coming around the turn in the opposite lane, comes this road-commission orange Volkswagen Squareback wagon and crosses into my lane."

Amber raised both hands and flew them in formation, depicting her jeep and the oncoming Volkswagen trying not to meet nose to nose.

"I had to evade, or we might still have been head-on into a ditch out there in Bad Nauheim somewhere. I whip around and chase it down, all blue lights and Martin horn, and I get it stopped off the road."

"One-Adam-twelve, see the man …" Cloud said.

"Right? So, I'm pissed—and I still have to pee like a Russian race horse. I stomp out of my jeep and up to the car. The driver, this sorry-ass butter-bar second lieutenant, already has his window down and is handing me his documents. He starts talking about being sorry for crossing the center line, he's new here, he wasn't paying attention like he should, and how he had never had German beer in his life until that night, but he only had two and *wow*, was he sorry. I know his whole short career went before his eyes so fast he had to call for a second showing."

Everyone around the table laughed and then looked at McCandless to make sure it was all right. He was grinning, too.

Amber gestured to the general.

"Well, that cat was our esteemed later-to-advance-to-General John Glenn McCandless. He was so pitiful, and I had to pee so bad, I couldn't possibly write him up. I mean, he was only flirting with not-even-tipsy, and I used my discretion to cut him some slack."

She looked into her beer glass as if she expected to find her answers there too, like McCandless had tried to do. There weren't any for her either.

"He was new, didn't know shit from Shinola. None of us did back then, really. I felt he was sober enough to follow me back to the BOQ at Ayers Kaserne, where he promised me faithfully he would stay in the rest of the night, amend his behavior in the future, and be more careful while he got used to driving in Germany. And he let me use his bathroom, so. Win-win."

In a rare gesture of familiarity, McCandless reached forward and clasped his large hand over Amber's small one. Amber appreciated it in the gentle, brotherly way it was offered. She put her other hand over his.

"I thought you were going to be a good officer," Amber said. "We were all so very young then, weren't we? Damn, that was a long time ago. We were feeling our way forward blind in life using the Braille system, trying to find the bumps in the road. Looking out for each other as best we could."

A flicker of a dark memory crossed Amber's face then, but no one recognized it and it passed.

"We made mistakes. We took chances." Some things from those days she still regretted. *Sorry, Jamie.* "They didn't all work out."

Then Amber smiled. "You didn't give me a ration of crap, you weren't *drunk*-drunk, thank God, and I couldn't get off that roadside fast enough. It seems to have been the right decision, all these years later."

"I am and remain grateful for your kindness, staff sergeant," he said. Amber looked surprised. Staff sergeant, the paygrade of E-6, was her last rank before leaving the Army at the seven-year point. She wasn't supposed to have been permitted to accept it, because she either had to extend for a year or reenlist to have minimum time to promote. Neither of those things were going to happen. But then the orders came down from higher and she got promoted anyway, only eight months before getting out of the Army. She figured it was just a classic Green Machine admin error.

It wasn't.

"Yes, I have followed your career from a discreet distance ever since. I'm in the information business, after all. I knew each time you were promoted the rest of that tour—I was even able to jump-start you to E-6 before you got out; my little going-away present to you. I believed such a heads-up woman would continue to contribute all the rest of her life. And looks like I was correct, too."

Tracey started singing softly, "*Kumbaya, my lord, kumbaya …*"

"You never knew how important that singular act of generosity became to me," the general said. "You know how the Army is. A DUI on my record would have gotten me canned even then, when every other soldier was drunk most of the time. At minimum, I would have lost my security clearance and my job just as it was starting. If I wasn't chaptered out with a less than Honorable discharge, the rest of my Army career would have been dull and unpleasant. You saved my actual ass that day, and by extension over the years in my occupation, you have *saved actual lives*. Nothing, and no one, can ever repay the debt I owe to a whip-smart young woman who was in the right place at the right time."

McCandless squeezed Amber's hand gently and sat back.

"Thanks for telling me that, general," she said. She blinked rapidly to diffuse her suddenly watery eyes. Military brotherhood and sisterhood knows no rank structure. Amber had scored numerous awards and accolades over a law-enforcement career spanning three federal departments and as many decades, but when a four-star Army general thanks you for saving his ass, that's big.

McCandless nodded and raised his glass to her.

"Well, this is a helluva team we have here," Poppy said. "Be a damned shame to let it break up."

"Will you *please* spit the sweat socks out of your mouth and tell us what you're talking about?" Tracey blurted. She punched him playfully. "I gotta go solve some crimes and whatnot."

Poppy looked directly at Amber.

"Zave already works with me on staff. When you retire, I'd like you to think about working with us, too."

"Are you nuts, Poppy? I am no kind of spy."

"No, you're better—you're a thinker. You're organized, you have presence, and you can bend into any objective, I believe, such that you'd make a damned fine exec in the new department we're setting up. Broad portfolio, fewer rules of engagement. We're calling it STORM CELL."

"Catchy," Tracey poked. "You make that up yourself, or you got people for that?"

Poppy raised a flat hand as Amber drew breath to object.

"You don't have to decide today." He side-glanced at Cloud and tried not to smile. "Take some time, blow off some steam."

Amber instantly shot back, "Oh, you're a comedian now *too*, huh?" Poppy giggled to himself, and Amber reached out to grab Cloud's hand. He grabbed back.

"You could do a lot worse than to pitch in with this crowd," McCandless chimed in. "And we can use you."

"The best I can say is I'll think about it," Amber said.

She was skeptical, but it was good to be wanted at this late stage of her career. Amber always believed that, as the saying goes, age is just a number. She told Tracey more than once that she must have had brain death at nineteen, because she felt no different today than she did then.

She looked like she was in her early forties, though she was two decades older than that according to her driver's license. "Maybe federal retirements don't go as far as they used to."

Poppy sipped his beer, then said, "This is true. You don't have to stand up to full-time if you don't want to, either. I think once you look at some project-based options I'll provide, you will agree that my freelance rates are, ah, very competitive. But however you decide to participate, we'll put you to good use. And I promise you will never be bored."

Cloud's cellphone vibrated and danced across the wooden table. He picked it up.

"*Now* he checks in?"

"What?" Amber asked.

He showed the phone to Poppy, who smiled, and handed the phone to McCandless.

"Better late than never, I guess," Poppy said. "I mean, he *is* retired ..."

On the screen was a text from Xing Jianjun, inviting Xavier Cloud to meet at the Red Flag.

It ended with the term *9-1-1.*

Everyone at the table got up at once and headed for the door.

✪

As they cross the bar, General McCandless and Poppy Benedict look up to see a large backlit shadow filling the doorway. They are mildly surprised to see the shadow is thrown by their old Mossad friend Shimon Kriegsman. And Kriegsman is a long way out of his usual zone of operations.

"Shimon?" McCandless says, extending his hand and a quizzical look. "Good to see you. *Odd* to see you."

"Yeah, what are you doin' here?" Poppy Benedict asks with obvious suspicion.

"Johnny," Kriegsman says, shaking McCandless's hand and nodding. "Poppy."

He isn't smiling.

"There is a fire."

Following is an excerpt from the next STORM CELL thriller

FORCE MAJEURE

The liberties of a people never were nor ever will be
secure when the transactions of their
rulers may be concealed from them.
PATRICK HENRY

The tree of liberty must be refreshed from time to time
with the blood of patriots and tyrants.
THOMAS JEFFERSON

Let every nation know, whether it wishes us well or ill,
that we shall pay any price, bear any burden, meet any hardship,
support any friend, oppose any foe to assure the survival
and the success of liberty.
JOHN F. KENNEDY

FORCE POSEIDON

The best argument against democracy is a
five-minute conversation with the average voter.
Winston Churchill

YOUR NAME IS AMY IRVINE. You are driving along a two-lane asphalt back road, maybe a little tipsy, maybe just drowsy, your favorite shortcut through the toolies to get to your writing cabin. It's a little two-room thing, hardly more than a shack backed right up to the mountainside, but it has fresh water funneled into a covered reservoir, solar electricity for hot water, refrigeration and internet connectivity, and God's own panorama of the valley below.

With no light pollution out here, the indigo night is perforated with a trillion stars and a giant disk of harvest Moon. You're musing about a sticky angle in your second novel, not paying strict attention to the short tallow cones thrown by low-beam headlights.

You don't use high beams out here because you believe it frightens the desert wildlife.

Then, whipping past—*what* ... are those lights? Reflections? Suddenly, on both sides of the road at irregular intervals, you see streaking past many small flecks of firefly light backed by silhouettes. Your head swivels left and right, seeing dark shapes, random outlines, but comprehending none. After a few seconds, they are gone as fast as they appeared.

When your attention turns back to the road, the man is standing right there doing his impression of a deer in your headlights.

Your brain registers an instant snapshot—he looks military: Kevlar, full camo gear, body armor, heavy boots, assault rifle. Wait, no. You thought it was an assault rifle at first, but this one is different. Much longer, sand colored, with a big scope on top. You've seen those before too.

Your car strikes the man. He flies into the air with the force of a bottle rocket and you recognize two things: His face is hidden by night vision goggles, and he is carrying a Barrett M107 .50-caliber sniper rifle.

Your car crabs a little to the right as you panic-stop, brake sounds chattering across the dusty scrub in full anti-lock. Powerful legs propel you from the vehicle and you run back to the dark shape now like a speed bump in the road, easy to see under the bright night sky. He lies motionless.

The long gun is on the roadside, seemingly intact, but the impact has broken some buckles and shorn the man of his heavy tactical backpack and its contents. Ammo magazines, loose rounds, first aid pouches, and some MRE food packets are blown everywhere across the cracked tarmac.

The man too is largely intact, but his face is not. The skull was fractured by the impact of night vision goggles propelled into his eye sockets at seventy-three miles per hour. A pool of blood has already formed around his head, but blood stops flowing when the heart stops beating. This pool of blood, leaking out from behind the night vision goggles, is small.

Panicked, but angry, too, you look around for help. You are many miles from the nearest cell tower, and there are no other cars coming from either direction.

What the hell do I do now? you think, and look back down to the lump in the roadway. *And what the fuck were you doing in my roadway, dumb ass?*

The stars and the full Moon provide eerie lighting to your indecision.

Then, Jesus—now what? What is that sound?

A strange noise you have also heard before comes from the dead man. You take a knee, thinking he might somehow be alive after all, but no, there is no pulse. And that crackling and hissing sound is not coming from the soldier's crushed lungs, but from a small headset knocked off his head. You pick it up, slowly, and then hold it to your ear like it might hurt you.

You have no idea then how right you are.

"Scorpion-one-six, Scorpion-one-six, Scorpion-six! Ten-sixty-nine, I say again, *say your goddamn status! Over!*"

A running man answers, breathing hard.

"Scorpion-six, Scorpion-four. We think Scorpion-one-six is possibly down hard in a ten-twenty-one, sir, and his telematics are offline. We are ten-forty-three at this time and about two mikes from the scene. Out."

You don't understand the ten-codes from the radio transmission, but you know they are used by cops. And these were definitely soldiers, so that means MPs—military police.

Two mikes—*two minutes.*

Then you hear another sound. Footfalls. Hard, persistent running footfalls and battle rattle, all pretense of stealth abandoned.

And they're coming toward you.

You're sorry their man is dead, and you fervently wish it hadn't happened, but you don't know what this random sketchiness is all about and you don't intend to stay for the out-brief. Clarity returns, just like it always did for you in Afghanistan firefights—and you know it is time to go.

Right now.

You rise to a combat crouch, survey the terrain, and scurry back to your car. Your training always sleeps right beneath the surface.

The bobbing heads of maybe two dozen soldiers can be seen above the brush and in the road as they sprint toward your position.

Christ, the damned car lights are on.

On the way back to the BMW you stoop in a fluid motion and grab the long gun with one hand and a canvas sling bag of ammo with the other. You have a .357-caliber Colt wheel gun up in the cabin, just something to deal with snakes and keep the odd bobcat away, but not much ammo. And the cats converging on you now are not bobcats.

Slide the rifle and ammo bag into the car and jump into the driver's seat, kill the damned lights and curse the darkness when your foot accidentally brushes the brake pedal. The guilty red flash of brake lights can be seen at night for miles out here.

You don't have miles to spare.

Lights out and power-shifting away from the scene on the moonlit road, you are angry at the mystery men whose fault this is and it's pinging your PTSD something awful. You left all that *hooah* military bullshit behind when you got out, one of the first-ever women to graduate from U.S. Army Ranger School, never accorded the respect men gave unbidden to men.

Keep the accelerator down hard to the floor. This is all straightaway out here and you need to put beaucoup time and distance between you and whatever the hell was going on back there in the road when you drove through the middle of it.

You've opened up ten, maybe twelve miles on them already. You don't know how much margin you need, but it won't be enough until you are buttoned up in the writing cabin.

Reach for your cellphone in a cupholder and, holding it low so the light doesn't show, you touch a speed-dial number. In this stretch of desert closer to the mountain, you can sometimes get a bar or two of cell signal, and right on time, there it is. You touch the speakerphone icon and place the phone back into the cupholder. The soft ringing can be heard from the car's stereo speakers.

When a man's voice answers, it sounds like he's in the car.

"I told you never to call me here," Xavier Cloud says, but the man is laughing. Caller ID told him his old battle buddy was on the horn. "What's up out there in God's country, Irving?"

Irving was his playful take on Amy Irvine's last name. Until now, it had always made her smile.

"Zave, man," you say, "I got a situation here."

He hears the anxiety in your voice. It's a little too soon to be scared, but you're thinking about it.

"How soon can you get out to my place in Utah?"

"How soon do you need me, colonel?"

You look in your rearview mirror. No pursuing headlights yet, no flashing blues or reds. Those mysterious soldiers were POGs—people other than grunts—so even elite military police will stand around for a while with their thumbs up their asses before the hive mind collects itself. By then, you'll be long and safely gone.

But if they're hot-shit combat MPs—or better, which is worse—there is no telling what resources they can bring to bear, or how fast. Or how angry.

You steal a glance at the luminous dial of your MTM watch.

"About, ah, about twelve minutes ago. I needed you twelve minutes ago. Can you get out here? I might be in some kind of weird trouble, and I can't risk staying on the pho—" and then the signal is gone again.

Balls. You downshift the BMW *bang-bang-bang* through the gearbox until the roaring car is slowed to a crawl in first gear, then shift into Neutral and handbrake to a stop to avoid triggering the brake lights. With a punch to each side of the roof you smash the bulbs in the left and right interior lights with your academy ring. Open the car door to stand in the roadway and look back down the long ribbon of cracked, gray asphalt.

Nothing yet.

Hold down the cellphone's on-off button until it goes cold. Field-strip out the battery and the SIM card. With a powerful fling that would skip a flat rock across Lake Superior for a hundred feet, you Frisbee the phone into the darkness and ghostly desert scrub as hard as you can.

Wistfully, you wish you were back in your little Michigan hometown of Christmas right now, on the rocky Upper Peninsula shores of Lake Superior.

You throw the battery and the SIM card in different directions. Get back into your car, release the handbrake, and power away in first gear. The writing cabin is less than an hour away.

Why are these people out here in my desert? you wonder.

And what are they going to do next?

✪

A small woman steps off a Manhattan subway at the South Ferry station, closest to the Statue of Liberty. She struggles with a heavy Samsonite suitcase, one of the big ones, with stout wheels and a thick handle. She looks around, evidently a visitor unafraid in a strange place, curious but confident, in a I've-been-here-before kind of way.

Two patrolling New York City transit cops notice the king-size suitcase, the small woman, and the bright blue *hijab* framing her face and possible indecision. One officer is a fresh twenty-three-year-old blue-lint rookie, second day on the job and full of the milk of human kindness. He got into police work to help people, and here was his first chance.

The second officer is a twenty-three-year veteran, the kid's field training officer. He's happy for the rookie's enthusiasm, but he's seen too much of life in almost two and a half decades on the NYPD. No wife, no children, he retires next month to fish and drink a lot of expensive rum in Key West. He thinks the kid too will harden as he grows in experience on the job.

When they approach the woman to render common assistance to a citizen, their new-model body cams and mics record the scene. The high-definition video and audio instantly stream via a heavy-duty police-only WiFi signal out of the subway tunnel and to the headquarters mainframe at One Police Plaza.

When the recording is later reviewed by the President of the United States and his national security team, the last thing they see is the happy, smiling, upraised face of the earnest young woman.

In a clear British accent, she speaks to the officers.

"You know, I have never kissed a man."

Then the screen goes blinding ice-white with a bone-chilling electronic scream.

ACKNOWLEDGMENTS

I've been a writer in one form or another since I was privileged to be the co-editor of my high school newspaper. Since then, I've also been on staff at *Popular Mechanics, Motor Trend,* and *Car and Driver,* and I was an award-winning U.S. Navy journalist. But this is my first novel, and I've been back to school on it as if I'd never before typed a word.

I have reinvented this wheel a bunch of times, including setting out for a Master of Fine Arts (MFA) in creative writing in fiction. That lasted only until my VA education benefits finally ran out. But in that single year in the prestigious Southern New Hampshire University Mountainview MFA program, I got what I was looking for.

I'm grateful to SNHU Mountainview MFA Program Director and novelist **Benjamin Nugent** (*American Nerd: The Story of My People*) for his acceptance and encouragement. Two of my elemental mentors were amazing novelists **Merle Drown** (*Plowing Up A Snake, The Suburbs of Heaven*) and **Richard Adams Carey** (*The Philosopher Fish, In The Evil Day*). I strongly recommend you look up their books and read them. You can thank me by email when you get a minute.

I'm grateful to novelists **Jo Knowles** (*See You at Harry's, Read Between the Lines, Still a Work in Progress*) and **Diane Les Becquets** (*Seasons of Ice, Breaking Wild*), who never once uttered a discouraging word to a genre writer, but offered significant insights.

I'm grateful to great friend and novelist **Ann Wertz Garvin** (*On Maggie's Watch, The Dog Year, I Like You Just Fine When You're Not Around*) for her support, friendship, and wisdom. She can teach you how to do this, by the way: See **thefifthsemester.com** for details on her superlative program. Plus, you will just *love* her, as the rest of us always will.

I learned from **Mark Sundeen** (*The Man Who Quit Money, The Unsettlers: In Search of the Good Life in Today's America*) and the seminal **Craig Child**s (*Apocalyptic Planet, Finders Keepers, The Animal Dialogues*) how and why to lift rocks and look for the unseen. Never take life at face value.

I'm particularly grateful to my friend, novelist (*Fallen*), and Texan **Mike Hancock**. He also pointed me to the online fiction journal *The Left Hand of the Father*, which published a different version of my first chapter as a short story. I'm still grateful to **Mary Ann Escamilla** for taking that on.

Thanks to my brothers, police Sergeants **William Kenneth Ross** (by blood), former Detroit policeman and today in the Warren, Mich., Police Department, and **Jeffrey O'Keefe** (by good fortune), Detroit Police Department. They tried to keep me in the clear on DPD tactics, methods, and equipment. I'm also grateful to Bill for sharing his experience flying an airplane, and pointing me toward good information about that.

Thanks to my long-time stablemate from our *Motor Trend* era, **Mac Demere**, who counseled me on the details of weapons. I'm grateful for encouragement from **John Fenzel**, **John Talbot**, **John Gilstrap**, **Charlie Stella**, and **Walt Gragg**.

I'm particularly grateful to my high school pals and readers **Deborah Hemme Sova** (who plays a CIA character in the book), **Ralph Alter, Mark Groesbeck** (1951-2019) and **Nancy Meyer Saitta**, retired chief justice of the Nevada Supreme Court, for their insightful suggestions and unremitting reinforcement—thanks Shamrocks.

I'm grateful to **Doug Richardson**, screenwriter of *Die Hard 2, Bad Boys, Money Train*, and *Hostage*—and now a rockin' novelist.

Thanks to a group of my writer and reader pals who always generously had time for a read, or suggestion, including **Jeremy Shellenbarger, Shawna Galvin Rand, Ted Flanagan, Nicole Foltin Moschberger, Sarah**

Liniger Eisner, Tanya Maxwell, Tiffany Quint, Laura Sack Brashear, Kayla Collins, April Morehouse, Heather Ouellette-Cygan, Karen Babies, Susan E. Kennedy, Mark "Thor" Freeman, Amanda Junay, Lyndsay Ryor, and Senior Chief Journalist Sonny Auld, USN (Ret).

U.S. Navy Reserve Commander Chris "Christmas" Kieszek is a real, live C-130 driver (I made up her call sign—her real one is "Sparkles") who granted me the use of her name and expertise for a pivotal character in this story. I'm exceeding grateful for her forbearance as I peppered her with email after email about the aircraft and more. All of the C-130 facts are due to her proficiency and are UNCLAS. Any C-130 errors or factual extensions for literary purposes are my sole responsibility.

I'm grateful to Navy Hospital Corpsman 1st Class (FMF) Carlos Benavides, another real warrior pressed into fictional service. He walked me through the ground details of the Al Taqaddum (TQ) airfield in Iraq that escape a guy looking at it via Google Earth. Thanks to my Navy brother Mass Communication Specialist Chief Philip McDaniel, USN (Ret.), who drew upon his previous active Army service in the 82nd Airborne Division to educate me on Airborne training, operations, and methods.

Many thanks to my friend and U.S. Air Force sherpa, Master Sergeant Jeffrey Rosebrock, Ohio Air National Guard. His contacts, and his willingness to ping on them time after time, helped make the Air Force references better than they possibly could have been without him. If I've taken any license with his inputs, the fault for any mistakes is mine alone.

I can neither confirm nor deny any extremely important inputs from assets currently or formerly employed at or by the Central Intelligence Agency or the State Department. But if there are any, you know who you might be, and how much fun it might have been for me to see under the veil with you and your important extended networks.

I spent seven years on active duty in the U.S. Army as a military police investigator (MPI)—since color TV, but before the internet (or cellphones). Lots of that was in long-duration undercover drug suppression operations in Germany. In fact, the early Army career arc of FBI Special Agent Amber "Corvette" Watson has some parallels to my own experience, though I never went on to the ATF and FBI, as she does in the book.

I later was privileged to spend twenty-four years in the Navy Reserve, including a 37-month by-name recall to active duty following 9/11. The truth is I chased them until they caught me. My last reserve post after active duty was to Combat Camera-Atlantic as leading chief petty officer. I retired from the Navy in July 2010 as a chief petty officer.

I'm blessed by the supportive and ever surprising **Andrea DeVoe Ross**, and my constantly amazing and talented children: **Sammie** (13), **Maggie** (15), **Will** (16), and Gunner's Mate 1st Class (DV/SCW) **Daniel Charles Ross II**, USNR (45), who also was a 10-year Recon Marine and today is a hard-charging police officer in Kent, Wash. *Hooyah, Seabee.*

Finally, I'm grateful to you, **the reader**. You take a chance when you spend your money on a new writer. Too many times, you have better odds for a decent return on your investment in Las Vegas. I hope to continue to deserve your readership, because I intend to keep writing these stories.

I wanted to write a story that was as much about the people who do the work as the weapons they use and the explosions that sometimes occur. With more than three decades of military service, Army and Navy, active and reserve, I hope I've done justice to both.

Thank you sincerely for your support. I hope to see you again.

Keep charging.

Daniel Charles Ross
April 2018 • Lima, Ohio

About the author

Daniel Charles Ross is a retired U.S. Navy Reserve chief petty officer, the former chief journalist of the Navy Seabees, and a former active duty U.S. Army military police investigator. His civilian writing career was spent in stints as Detroit editor at *Popular Mechanics* and as national editor at both *Motor Trend* and *Car and Driver*. A Detroit ex-pat, he lives in Lima, Ohio where he is finishing the second STORM CELL novel, *Force Majeure*.

In a world of swords, be a pen

*For more information on this and other exciting
new authors, please see ForcePoseidon.com*
www.genuinedcr.com • reachout@ForcePoseidon.com

Made in the USA
Middletown, DE
01 February 2020